Josey Rose

A Novel

Jane Wood

11/98
For Alicia,
Merry Christmas
Jane Wood

SIMON & SCHUSTER

SIMON & SCHUSTER
Rockefeller Center
1230 Avenue of the Americas
New York, NY 10020

SIMON & SCHUSTER and colophon are registered trademarks
of Simon & Schuster Inc.

Designed by DEIRDRE C. AMTHOR

Manufactured in the United States of America

10 9 8 7 6 5 4 3 2 1

Library of Congress Cataloging-in-Publication Data
Wood, Jane, date.
p.   cm.
I. Title.
PS3573.059448J67   1998
813'.54—dc21   97-49706
CIP
ISBN 0-684-83791-9

Grateful acknowledgment is made for permission to reprint
"Waltzing Matilda." Music by Marie Cowan. Words by
A. B. Paterson. Copyright © 1936 by Allan & Co., Prop.
Ltd., Melbourne. Copyright © 1941 by Carl Fischer, Inc.,
New York. Reprinted by permission of Carl Fischer, Inc.,
New York.

Acknowledgments

WITH MUCH GRATITUDE, I GIVE SPECIAL THANKS TO:

My agent, William Clark, for representing this novel and for making the match with the right publisher.

My editor, Laurie Chittenden, for her insights and talent. She has been a pleasure to work with and has done a superb job bringing this book to press.

My husband, Michael Kowalski, for his enduring love and support.

Denise Silver, for her insights and comments, which have been integral to this project and deeply appreciated.

The Free Library of Philadelphia for its wealth of information and for the willing help of its reference librarians.

Phil Mugler, Robert Clancy, Tim O'Brien, and Bruce Schwartz for their valuable information. And Jean Mugler for her research work at the Marathon Library in the Florida Keys.

Joe Gallatti for his technical assistance. And for their helpful comments, I am grateful to Martha Clancy, Verna Darcy, Patty Gallatti, Michael Hervey, Charlie Mugler, Jean Mugler, Phil Mugler, Ruth Noble, Claire Silver, Chuck Vedova, Pete Vedova, Sarah Wood, and Alan Zemel.

For Marjory Spencer Hoag,
who
saw the moonlight breathe
and heard the earthworms snore

Josey Rose

Prologue

I found Lily in the autumn when all the leaves were falling down and my father's rage had spiraled beyond control. I was eleven years old the night I huddled outside her door in a thunderstorm, scared that a lightning bolt would rip down my spine and fry me for good. Then, with much hesitation and for reasons I'll never fully understand, Lily let me inside.

Now I'm forty-five, and she is with me in Georgia, in the midst of the Savannah marshlands. We live here in secret. Surely we are guilty of what those we left behind suspect, but we did what we had to do. Even on the boxcar—that bizarre train ride heading south out of New Hampshire—we knew it was the only way. We had to get out.

         ❧   ❧

I grew up in the sixties amid NASA's space shots, Kennedy's presidential election, and TV shows like *Leave It to Beaver* and *My Three Sons*. At a time when families were idealized, I lived with an unusual clan: My grandmother hung dead snakes from oak trees to ward off noisy mockingbirds. Our two pet mynah birds sang old Burl Ives tunes and swore up a storm. And my father found rage inside his whiskey bottles, and then, in penance, filled those bottles up again with intricate seafaring vessels that enchanted our home for as long as I can remember.

While some families collect photographs, my family collected secrets.

         ❧

And when those secrets finally unfolded, everything changed. For all these years, I have been silent about what happened, trying to forget. But the memories rush in, some parts giving me joy and others haunting me fiercely.

I figure the only way I'll ever get free of these memories is to tell the story to someone else. So Lily, I hope you forgive me for not leaving anything out and for revealing the most forbidden of all love.

1

September 1960. I was eleven years old. One question tormented me: Where in the world did my father go when he left the house in a fury, angry as wild birds and drunk as a boiled owl?

Last night, I had huddled next to my grandmother as we watched my father hurl the telephone into the fire, toss pickled eggs at the bird-cage, and holler at the walls. Then, at last, he left. Through the front window, we watched him stagger down the driveway to our country road, where he turned right and disappeared like all the times before. Curled in my grandmother's arms, my last thought before drifting off was that the next time my father got drunk, I would follow him and discover exactly where his madness led him.

And, as always, the morning after. "Rise and shine, Josey boy." My father's voice, chipper as a lark. Feeling numb I put on my clothes and made my way downstairs. I had no interest in the Cheerios my father set before me. All I could think of was last night—our two crazed birds fluttering their wings against the inside of the cage while my father pitched eggs at them as if they were targets in a carnival game. I wished Grandma was up, but she always slept late. My father was humming.

For as long as I remembered, he'd been humming that tune as if the events the night before never happened. It bothered me. I wished I had an older brother to exchange glances with or a doting aunt who would cook pancakes for me and cast a sympathetic wink my way.

"Aren't you hungry, Josey? What did you do, smuggle pretzels into your room again?"

I looked at the happy kid on the Cheerios box thinking, He's probably friends with Beaver Cleaver, and I'll bet nobody throws things at his birds. My father went into the living room to put on his work shoes with the steel toes but suddenly stopped in his tracks.

"Goddamn raccoons!" he hollered. "Good-fer-nothing pests. They've raided the kitchen and dragged pickled eggs all over the living room. Look at this mess."

I never figured out if the alcohol was so strong that my father couldn't remember the things he did, or if he simply denied his jags of violence. But he sure had a cunning way of blaming others. Years earlier, after throwing the blender through the back screen door, he had blamed the broken screen on the mockingbirds. To validate his story, he hung dead snakes from the limbs of the oak tree in our backyard because Grandma told him that was a great way to silence noisy mockingbirds. Another time when he'd spent the evening before flinging frozen foods around the house, he said burglars had come in the night and searched the freezer for money they thought might be stashed there. He claimed that when the burglars found no money, they fell into a fit of defeat and tossed the freezer contents against the walls, breaking right through the plaster board.

This morning I walked into the living room, stood on the stairway steps so my eyes were level with his. "You did that, Dad. You drank whiskey last night. Then you threw those eggs at the birds."

"Josey, my son," he said, coming to me and feeling my forehead as if I might have the flu. "All those pretzels are giving you mad, mixed-up dreams."

"You did that, Dad, and then you went someplace. Where did you walk to? Where do you go when you leave here angry?"

"Ain't nobody's business where I go. Especially not yours. You keep your mind on your own doings, kiddo. Your imagination wanders a helluva lot further than my own two feet ever do."

"Last night you threw the telephone in the fire, Dad. And you don't even remember."

He came to me gently, kneeled beside me on the step, and put his arm around my shoulders. "Listen to me, Josey honey. You've got to stop making up these wild stories. I'm your daddy, and I would never do anything to harm you. All this talk of throwing things around. It would never happen. I love you, little guy." Tears welled up in his eyes. "So you run upstairs, get your books, and pedal off to school. I'll see you tonight, and we'll have Spanish rice, your favorite."

Once again, my father's amnesia saved him. If he paid any penance at all, it would be in preparing a skillet of Spanish rice and spending an afternoon trying to fix the charred telephone.

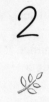

2

Over the years, I had gradually surrendered to the fear and forgiveness that permeated our home. I grew accustomed to my father's unpredictability, but I could never accept his secrets—our family secrets. Try as I might to understand my roots, my father was a master of evasion.

"What was your dad like?" I'd ask him.

"Regular guy."

"Did you have any brothers or sisters?"

"I doubt it."

"What did my mother look like?"

"Eat your Cherrios, Josey. I ain't no family historian."

Such was the litany of our family heritage.

Grandma Ru was my father's mom. She came to live with us the day they found her at the grocery store, pulling baby rabbits from her pockets and setting them free in the produce section. She had somehow taken the animals from the cages of a downtown pet store (without paying for them), transported them to the grocery in the deep pockets of her lavender wool coat, and then set them gently amid the fresh lettuce. When the police arrived, seven bunnies were roaming about, nibbling away in ecstasy on romaine, curly red lettuce, turnip tops, and chicory leaves. And all those plump fresh carrots with their greens still attached. "The little critters just needed a change of pace," said Grandma as the police took her away.

Her name was Ruth Annabelle Rose, but people called her Ru. Ever since she'd moved in with us, the neighbors insisted she'd fallen into an hallucinatory realm from which there was no return, and my friends said she wasn't wrapped too tight. But my father saw it otherwise. "You see," he explained, "things have simply come unhinged in her head so her dream stuff gets mixed up with what's real—that's all."

Hard to say which explanation was right. But one thing for sure, Grandma Ru had revealing eyes. When she talked about what was true, her irises glowed green and sparkling. But when she crossed over to the world of her own imaginings—which was almost always—the black part of her eyes grew so large that I could see my own reflection.

One evening, she told me how Navaho Indians had come into the house during lunch while my father was working and I was at school. She said they set up their rug weaving looms in the living room and pounded corn meal in the kitchen. "They're very polite," said Grandma Ru, with her eyes dark as night, "but sometimes after they wash the dishes, they put things back in the wrong place. Today I found the garlic press in the flour bin."

She described how, on that very afternoon, the Indians dragged in a wooden crate taller than me. They had written "Fragile" on all four sides with war paint. The Indians opened the crate and carefully lifted out twelve live butterflies with seven-foot wings of turquoise. Several other Indians arrived with a small herd of black-and-white cows that smelled of coconuts.

My grandmother explained how the Indians pulled yarn from their rug weaving looms and bound a butterfly to each cow. Then they led the cows out to the lawn. My grandmother stood by the petunias and watched the herd stampede down the stony driveway while the huge butterflies beat their turquoise wings as fast as they could until the cows ascended slowly into the air and flew away.

"Their load was so heavy," said Grandma, "that I could hear the butterflies panting all the way up to the clouds."

"That sounds like a real sight," I said.

"Well, it was downright lovely until just after liftoff, one cow broke wind and dropped a cow pie into the front seat of a powder-blue Cadillac convertible, which happened to be passing by. The driver pulled over, and I spent all afternoon helping him clean up."

So—later that same evening, when Grandma Ru began talking about my mother, I figured it was another tall tale falling through her imagination. My father had told me that my mother died long ago, but lately Grandma talked about her like she might walk in the door any day.

"Your mother is in quite a quandary," she said.

"Grandma, you know my mom died already. Years ago. I was four years old, remember? You were living with us then."

Grandma Ru grabbed my shoulders and put her face close to mine. She smelled of dried roses and her hair gleamed white like a cloud. Suddenly, the huge black pupils of her eyes shrank to normal in a pool of clear green irises. I knew she had come into our world, if only for a moment. "Your mother is still alive," she said.

"Where is she, Grandma?"

Then without answering, the dark part of her eyes grew large again, and she returned to her world of cows and butterflies.

When my grandmother moved in with us in Georgia (where I was born), she brought along two pet mynah birds, Jake and Lulu. Against my father's wishes, the mynahs came with us when we moved up to Willow Junction, New Hampshire. Both birds were lovely. Velvet black with highlights of iridescent green that shimmered in the light of day. Rich purple sheen at their necks. And wise dark eyes ringed in gold. The birds ate orange slices, raisins, dried crickets, and pickled eggs. And they were real yakkers.

While most birds utter phrases here and there, mynah birds have no limits. Lulu recited conversations she'd heard ten years ago. Much of her repertoire came from the records my father played. When Lulu sang "Big Rock Candy Mountain," you'd think Burl Ives was sitting right there in our living room. And, of course, hanging around my father, Lulu learned to swear up a storm. She was definitely an R-rated bird. Jake chatted from time to time, but mostly he mimicked sounds like the vacuum cleaner humming, the telephone ringing, and the doorbell chiming up and down the scale in thirds. Jake could even tweet the theme from *Lassie*, my father's favorite TV show.

Lulu's chatter got out of hand one day when the local preacher came to call in his annual attempt to convince my father to join his church.

Reverend Jasper, the only preacher in all of Willow Junction, stood primly by the birdcage. His constant allergies gave him puffy pink cheeks and watery eyes.

"Good afternoon, Mr. Rose," he wheezed, shaking my father's hand. Reverend Jasper's head was like a giant, overripe peach. Instead of hair, a layer of fuzz hovered just above his tender skull. I had to look carefully to see where the hair was attached.

The reverend waddled over to my grandmother, took her hand gently, and inquired, "How are you, my dear Mrs. Rose?"

"Well," said Grandma Ru, "I feel much more like I do now than when I got here."

"Splendid," said the reverend.

"Although," continued Grandma, "I have deep concerns."

"Tell me, my lamb."

"I fear the world is coming to an end."

"What makes you feel this?" the reverend asked, genuinely concerned.

"They've gone and poked holes in the atmosphere again with their blasted spaceships. And they sent dogs into space against their will. Last week when the Russians launched their capsule, I can tell you first-hand that those two pooches aboard were a wreck. Their anxiety was sent reeling clear around the world. I got word from poodles as far away as Arizona that their chromosomes have begun to migrate. Surely their offspring will be genetically deranged, and then suddenly, decades later, all the dogs of the world will—"

"That's enough, Mom," chided my father. "Reverend Jasper is a man of God, not a veterinarian."

"Dear heart," said the reverend, "I will look into the matter."

Then he approached me and put his pudgy hands upon my cheeks and looked at the ceiling. "Josey, my tender child," he sighed, "may the angels be with you."

When he sat down, I saw the chair teeter on its loose legs and feared the reverend might crash to the floor. His huge fruit of a noggin wobbled on the black and white pedestal of his preacher's collar. And his smooth dark suit covered a ponderous body. He was so large I imagined him naked with the pink folds of his skin pouring down like hot butterscotch. Then I blushed for having such a thought about a man of God.

Jake made vacuuming sounds in the background while Lulu chatted away about beef jerky and strawberry pies.

"Would you like some coffee, Reverend?" asked my father.

"Much obliged, but I'm allergic to coffee. In fact," he said, sneezing heartily into his black sleeve, "I'm allergic to summer, too."

"Josey, get the reverend some tissues," my father said. "On second thought, bring in a roll of paper towels."

"Duck blood," said Grandma Ru. "You need duck blood soup with asparagus. That'll cure your wheezing."

"I'd like to come directly to the point," the reverend began. "Our congregation has grown quite a bit this year, Willie. But I'm disappointed that I haven't seen you there. I often look around and think maybe this week I'll find Willie Rose, his sweet mom, and his young son Josey. But not so."

I returned with a roll of paper towels and handed it to the reverend.

"Extraordinary!" The reverend grabbed my hand. "Come closer, little Josey, let me see your eyes. Is it the light, or are those lavender peepers I see?"

"Yes, sir," I confirmed, "they are lavender. Sometimes they look blue, but mostly they're lavender."

"Yep," said my father, "the kid has the eyes of a snake."

"And," said Grandma Ru, "it will forever protect him from angry Indians."

"Gorgeous . . ." sighed the reverend, at last letting go of my hand, "utterly gorgeous. . . . Now where was I? Oh, yes, don't you think some down-home religion would do your family a world of good?"

"Well, Reverend," answered my father patiently, "we've been sort of takin' care of that ourselves. We have what you might call a homegrown creed, right here within our own humble walls."

"Sad thing is, though," said Reverend Jasper, "as I look around these walls, I don't see one picture of our Lord Jesus."

My father's voice elevated to a notch above moderate. "I reckon we keep Jesus in our hearts," at which point Lulu added, "Son of a bitch."

Turning toward the pacing mynah, Reverend Jasper sneezed hard, disrupting some of the cedar chips at the bottom of the cage. He asked, "Now where do you suppose such a pretty bird learned to talk like that? Seems as if this creature ought to be going to church, too. He needs some real cleansing."

"It's not a he, Reverend," I explained. "That's a she bird."

"Well, that's no language for a lady, even if she is a bird, especially around the young lad. How old are you, Josey?"

"Eleven, sir."

Reverend Jasper rose from his unsteady chair. He came around behind me. I could feel his body heat and the breath of his booming voice that seemed to come straight from the Lord. "Now, Willie," said he, "why not consider some good upright religion if only for the child—this fragile, young impressionable mind here." As he spoke, he laid his hefty stomach on the back of my chair, leaned over, and put his hot hands on my head. As he stroked my hair, he continued, ". . . especially with the boy being motherless and all."

Lulu interrupted with a hearty "You bastard." Jake ruffled his feathers, picked up a slice of fresh orange, and answered Lulu with a perfect impression of a telephone ringing. My father rose and said, "I'm expecting a long-distance call, Reverend, if you'll excuse me."

I turned toward Reverend Jasper. With his fingers still twined in my hair, he sighed. "See what you can do, my child." Then the reverend left. My father walked clear through the kitchen and out the back door while Lulu chanted, "Lassie come home, Lassie come home . . ." in a voice that sounded exactly like June Lockhart's.

3

I don't remember much about my mom, except that she really liked cats. We must have had a dozen of them. After the cats and my mother were gone, the birds often burst forth with feline sounds in the night. Jake began with a couple of long meows while Lulu answered in a purr that sounded more like a jackhammer, quite in contrast to the gentle rumblings of my mother's pets.

I was so young when she passed away that I hardly remember my father telling me how she died—"malignant melanoma," he said. I don't recall her being sick but suddenly she was gone, dead. It seems one day she tucked me into bed for the night, and the next day she wasn't there. And the cats disappeared, too.

The older I got and the more I considered what Grandma Ru said about my mother still being alive, the more it all made sense. The way my father talked of her dying was odd, as if the finality of her death was always in question. He'd say, "She's gone from us, and she's never coming back, no matter what!" which of course led me to think she might return any moment. I imagined her showing up one day saying, "Oh, hello, my darlings, I had a bit of car trouble. It took forever to repair, but it's okay now. Did y'all get something to eat?" And from then on, our family would be complete. We'd go places together, laugh at monkeys in the zoo, have fun birthday parties, go swimming in the river, and drink hot chocolate on cold days. Everything would be warm and cozy, just like the families on TV.

Hard as I tried, though, I could never remember my mother's voice. But I knew how she sounded when she walked. Sometime after she left, Lulu began making an odd clicking noise. When I asked my father about it, he said, "That's the sound of your mother coming home from church, tapping her high heels across the linoleum floor. Click, click, click."

I often lay in bed thinking about that sound, wishing so much to hear her coming into my room. *Click, click, click.* I imagined her walking across my bedroom floor. The scent of lavender would find me when she tucked the blankets around my chin. Then in soft whispers, leaning down to kiss me good night, she'd breathe, "Sweet dreams, my darling," while I'd pretend to be sound asleep.

I imagined this not as a dream, but as something that would really happen. I knew my mother would return one day. And if not, then when I was old enough to ride my bike farther than the other side of town, I would find her and bring her home.

4

Mid-September. School had been in session a mere two weeks. Amid brand-new creased pants, sharpened long pencils, and fresh notebooks, my friends unraveled their summer vacation tales and lamented the long months till June came again. Even though I never had vacation stories to share like the others, I still preferred the safe tiled halls of school to the unrest of our home.

"Josey, you rascal. Get your dawdling duff down here!"

I was lying on the floor next to my bed. The oval braided rug beneath me felt like a magic carpet hovering above the hardwood floor. Hearing my father's voice, I lay back and wriggled my spine into the rug, thinking if I pressed down hard enough, I could disappear into the strips of wool that my grandmother had braided by hand during long winter nights many years ago.

"Hey, you little whippersnapper," my father called again, "where the devil are you?"

Was he angry? I couldn't tell yet. He had a way of hiding anger behind his own mischief. Across the beige terrain of my bedroom wallpaper, brown ponies pranced through pastures, scaled fences, and dashed through shallow rivers, splashing water about. I thought about hopping upon the pony in the river, commanding him to take me full speed ahead to the source of the water, to a different world where fears were like cookies that you could eat up, and they'd be gone forever.

"Josey Rose, I'm coming to get you!"

With the sound of his voice I shifted my gaze to the water stain in the far corner of the wallpaper. I wondered how many beers he'd had and what would get thrown against the walls tonight.

"Hey kiddo," called my father from the bottom of the stairs, "a natural wonder awaits us. Come and see." He wasn't angry yet. The growl in his voice still lay beneath the surface.

"I'm doing my homework, Dad."

His feet pounded up the stairs. "Ha-rumph!" he snarled in jest.

I stood as he rounded the hallway corner. He tottered in the doorway, arms cocked at his sides like a cowboy ready to duel. He had a twinkle in his eye that looked about ready to detonate.

My father picked me up and heaved my small body over his shoulder, joker that he was. As he carried me down the narrow wooden stairway like a sack of potatoes, I caught our reflections in the mirror. My father's angular chin, dimples in his cheeks, and thick dark hair. And me, the younger image of him: My dark hair not yet tangled from the years. A hint of dimples not yet carved. Features still delicate. And lavender eyes—the trait that separated me from him.

I could see from the bottles on the table that he'd had only five beers. He'd been puttering around the house, playing old Burl Ives tunes and eating pickled eggs.

"I got something to show you, squirt," he said as he carried me out the back door and set me in the field grass that went higher than my waist. I felt light-headed from being shanghaied down the stairs. "Lay your eyes upon those stars, Josey. Look how they hang low in the sky tonight." His voice purred like a sleepy tiger.

It was true. The stars had fallen clear out of the sky above New Hampshire and were hovering in our valley like fat cotton balls. Smoke floated from our chimney and curled around the glowing orbs, dusting them with ashes.

We walked back inside. My father chugged a beer, pulled another from the refrigerator, and set it on the buffet next to the two shotguns he'd used the night before to blast apart old bottles in the backyard. Then he prepared a bowl of raisins and egg slices and gave it to the birds.

His mood charmed me. I hung by the stairs, listening to his ram-
blings, yet fearing a change of heart. Grandma rocked in her chair,
softly muttering to the birds.

"Come over here for a minute," he said with a hint of southern ac-
cent—a vestige from his growing up in Georgia. "Help me with this
ship."

My father built ships inside bottles. After my mother's death, my father had become obsessed with his hobby. Sometimes he put other
scenes besides ships in the bottles. Once he made a miniature circus
where elephants jumped over gumdrops and tiny men juggled pearls.
Another time he created an autumn meadow made of shredded wheat,
bird feathers, and locks of my hair.

On this particular night, he was working on an old-time schooner
inside an antique whiskey bottle. He had spent weeks assembling the
ship outside the bottle on his little workstand. He had cut tiny sails out
of bond paper and curved them around a pencil—"to put wind in the
sails," he said. He had built the hull of spruce wood and painted it
dark green. And with the tiniest brush I ever saw, he painted white on
the rails, masts, and dories.

"A dark and foreboding sea," he crooned in a spooky voice as he
laid deep-blue goop in the bottom of the bottle. Then, with a piece of
bent wire dunked in white paint, he dabbed in a surging bow wave and
made the sea boil with whitecaps. All the while, he sang softly, almost
in a whisper,

> Oh! The buzzin' of the bees
> In the cigarette trees
>   Near the soda water fountain
> At the lemonade springs
> Where the blue bird sings
>   In the Big Rock Candy Mountain . . .

The dining room table was strewn with spools of fine black thread,
long tweezers, tiny screwdrivers, clear nail polish, and red sealing wax
for securing the cork.

Now was the critical moment when he would actually put the ship
inside the bottle upon the dark blue sea.

"Stand by, mate," he said. "The fun is about to begin."

First he sucked up glue through a straw and let it ooze inside the bottle, in the gully of the sea where the ship would be set. Next, back to the ship on its little workstand. He undid the lines and gently lowered the masts. The full ship fell into itself, delicately, silently, like a butterfly folding its wings. Then he slipped the entire vessel through the neck of the bottle, stern first. *Easy now.* The ship was only part way in. The topsail might not make it. *Don't move . . . don't breathe . . . don't even think. . . .* When at last the ship was set upon the sea, my father raised the masts, slowly. Majestically, the old schooner opened its billowing wings. Only a little damage to the topsail, but that could be fixed. Now for the hardest part.

"Hold the bottle steady," he said as he reached inside with a piece of wire that had drops of glue clinging to the end. Around and through the tiny masts, rigging, and sails, he dabbed the glue, securing pieces of thread here and there. Then up to the damaged topsail.

"Shhhh," he whispered, "don't talk, or everything will tumble down." Silence. Tension.

Suddenly Lulu burst into song, crooning her favorite commercial:

> *Mr. Clean gets rid of dirt and grime*
> *and grease in just a minute*
> *Mr. Clean will clean your whole house*
> *and everything that's in it*

"Knock it off, over there!" my father hollered. "Can't you see I'm installing a fore gaff topsail here?"

"Knock it off," repeated Jake.

"Dizzy blasted birds," mumbled my father.

"Don't rattle the mynahs," warned Grandma Ru, "or they'll send out bad vibrations. The atmosphere has enough to manage with all these screwball spaceships blasting off into the sky."

My father picked up a pencil and put it in his mouth like a small ear of corn. Then he rolled it between his teeth as he often did when things got tense with his seafaring vessels. Every pencil in the house was ringed with two trenches where his grinding molars had tread.

"Hey, Josey, are you dreaming again? Now hold that bottle."

As I held tightly, I noticed a miniature flock of birds inside the bottle, hovering in the upper regions.

"Dad, where did all those birds come from? They are the tiniest critters I ever did see."

"Those are gulls, kiddo. Get it right."

"Okay, so what are they made of?"

"Your teeth."

"Come on, Dad. Tell me true."

"Well, son," he said hesitantly, "I suppose you have to know some-time—you see, there ain't no tooth fairy."

"Dad, I know that. I'm eleven years old."

Grandma Ru sighed. "Last year, the Indians chopped up the tooth fairy and ate her with their Thanksgiving stew."

"Well, you see," he continued, "I saved all the teeth that you put under your pillow. I kept them in the marble box on the mantel. The other night I cleaned off all the dried blood till they were sparkling white. Then I carved them into little gulls. Pretty good, eh?"

"That's weird, Dad, having my teeth hanging in some bottle."

"Hey, squirt, each one of those teeth cost me a goddamn quarter." He leaned over, grabbed a jug of whiskey off the floor, and took a swig. "Now hush, y'all. This is a delicate maneuver."

As he worked, I looked into my father's eyes. It was hard to believe he was able to construct these delicate ships while only being able to see out of one eye. His other eye was made of glass. He'd lost his real one in an accident.

It happened when my mother was still with us while we lived in Georgia. Grandma Ru explained the event to me several times. She said that my father was always playing tricks on people. One night when he returned home at three in the morning drunk as a skunk, he figured it'd be a dandy idea to climb the hickory tree alongside the house, go to my mother's window, and scare the wits out of her. He didn't rouse my mom right away, but Grandma Ru awoke with a start. She ran to the window just in time to see my father crawling on his belly to the end of a fat limb. He yanked off a branch and scraped it against my mother's windowpane to make an eerie sound. Then he hooted like a drunken screech owl.

"Willie Rose," my grandmother yelled, "what the devil are you do-ing?" My father gave the windowpane one final whack before the main limb cracked, and my father let out a holler and slid down head first.

When he landed, my dad's face struck the next big limb. A dead branch stub drove straight into his left eye. The brittle wood broke off from the tree and protruded from his eyeball.

Whenever Grandma Ru told me this story, she always finished the same way. "I shall never forget," she'd say, "that gruesome sight of your father clinging to the limb with a branch stuck in his eye, howling your mother's name, 'Isabel, Isabel . . .'"

And oh, the nightmares I had about his lost eye! Over and over again, I dreamed about doctors pulling out the branch from my father's face. The long sucking sound of the extraction. Then a loud plop as the victorious doctor held up a dead hickory stub with my father's dark brown eye stuck on the end.

🌿   🌿

"Josey, for Chrissake. Hold still, or the whole blasted ship will fall apart. Quit your daydreaming! What the devil goes on in your head?"

Despite my father's admonition, my thoughts drifted off again, remembering how for a while after the accident, my father wore a black patch, which made him look like a pirate. Then he went to the Wills Eye Clinic in Philadelphia where they fitted him with a glass eye that looked exactly like his real one. But I could tell the difference, especially when he drank whiskey. The whites of his glass eye always remained bright and clear, while the real eye became pink with tiny veins that branched from his tear duct clear across his eyeball.

Scaling trees was nothing new for my father. He had always loved climbing things. Now at his job, he actually got *paid* to climb. He'd drive an hour to Boston to build structural steel frameworks for gigantic buildings. As my father said, they call this "working the high iron." It means climbing around the insides of huge steel skeletons that will become tomorrow's skyscrapers. It means moving steel beams into place, bolting them down, and welding them together. It means doing dangerous things. "'Cause, ya know," he said, "men were born to do dangerous things. It's in the blood."

Grandma Ru snapped me out of my musing when she began singing her favorite waltz: "Hi-Lili, Hi-Lili, Hi-lo . . ."

"I think we got us a full-blown ship," said my father as he dabbed a last bit of glue on the flying jib boom. Then he got up slowly, grabbed two bottles of beer from the refrigerator, and sat down ever so carefully. "Steady as she goes," he growled softly, staring at his delicate masterpiece held together with wet glue. I wondered if my mother had ever seen one of his bottled ships.

"Dad," I whispered, "where is my mother?"

🌿

"Singing arias with the angels," he replied in an uneven voice.

"Grandma says she's alive."

"Grandma sees cows with butterfly wings. She's a nut case."

He looked at Grandma, who had begun to waltz in circles on the other side of the room. "Hey, Mom. Watch yourself there. Don't go stepping in the plants again."

"Hi-Lili, Hi-Lili, Hi-lo . . . ," she sang.

"Watch out for that little fern there. It's a Doodia media, Mom. It's a perfect specimen."

"Hi-Lili, Hi-lo . . ."

"A Doodia *what?*" I asked.

"Shhhhh . . . ," whispered my father, peering into the bottle at his flying jib boom, securing the last part into place.

Suddenly, Lulu called out my mother's name. "Isabel, Isabel . . . ," she squawked.

My father jumped, and his leg hit the table. The flying jib boom crashed to the bottom of the bottle, dragging string and tiny sails with it. Like dominos, the masts tumbled down one by one, and the whole schooner folded into a pile of sticks and curled up chunks of sails. Somewhere in there were my teeth.

My father took another swig of whiskey as if the golden spirits would magically cause all the pieces to rise up and reassemble themselves. Small blood vessels flared in his cheeks and his one live eye. Grandma Ru continued waltzing around the room, still singing and waving her shawl like a feathered boa.

Then my father hollered, "Christ Almighty!" as he grabbed the neck of the ship bottle, hurling it across the living room. It spun by Grandma Ru, who twirled out of the way just in time. The bottle crashed through the front window and ignited into an explosion of glass and tiny ship parts.

"Hi-Lili, Hi-Lili . . . ," sang Grandma.

"Cut the serenade, Mom," grumbled my father as he stomped to the television, flipped the channel to *Leave It to Beaver,* and slumped into his chair.

Jake and Lulu didn't make another peep for the rest of the evening. The whole house seemed to shudder and wait for my father's next move. I hoped he would leave like he usually did on nights like this. Sure enough, after Ward Cleaver had a warm chat with the Beave, en-lightening him on the tough trials of growing up, my father dragged himself out of the chair without a word.

He shuffled over to the liquor cabinet, selected something with an amber color, and took several long swigs. Then he tossed his buckskin jacket over his shoulder and sauntered out the door. Through the broken glass, I watched him make his familiar trek down the driveway and onto the road.

5

Without even thinking, I followed my father quietly, lagging far enough behind where he wouldn't hear me. He was easy to track from a distance, the moonlight reflecting off his tan buckskin jacket like a beacon in the night. I wasn't concerned about him seeing me because, from the looks of his staggering stride, I suspected his world was a blur. But as my father rounded the bend out of sight, I was suddenly sidetracked by a new obstacle. A green pickup truck pulled out of a driveway, slowed down, and stopped beside me. I jumped across the ditch in a flash.

"Hey, Josey, what the devil are you doing out here in the middle of the night?" It was Max Gruner, a neighbor. A wide-brimmed cowboy hat topped his muscular head. With a red scarf tied around his neck, he looked like John Wayne. Country music twanged from the radio, and two rifles hung on the rack behind his head.

"Oh, I'm taking a little stroll, Mr. Gruner."

He leaned across the front seat, opened the door, and commanded, "Hop in, Josey, I'll give you a lift home." A jagged scar lay like a hook across his cheek.

"No thanks, sir, I'm fine."

"I'm sure your daddy wouldn't want you out wandering these dark roads so late at night."

"My daddy doesn't mind."

"Well, then, I'll have to check with old man Willie myself," he said.

"I'm sure I'll find him settin' there at the dining room table shovin' some kind of weird stuff into one of his bottles."

I didn't mention that on this particular night, my father was more interested in emptying bottles than filling them up. "Really, Mr. Gruner, I'll be fine here. You don't have to worry." But I hadn't quelled his concern one bit. He persisted so I had to play along with his demand. "Okay, sir, if you insist. I'll take a ride back to the house."

I hopped in the front seat of his truck. As he drove ahead to find a place to turn, I looked back and saw my father veer right onto Gypsy Lane.

Mr. Gruner turned around in the next driveway and drove me home. I hopped out, walked in the front door, and waited for the truck to disappear down the road. Then I bolted back outside, ran all the way to Gypsy Lane, took a right, and continued on until my father was in sight again.

As I followed him, I thought of all the stories I'd heard about Gypsy Lane and the haunted pine grove. I wasn't ready to tangle with a flock of ghosts, so I hung back, searching the treetops for specters. But the desire to uncover my father's mysteries surpassed the threat of ghosts. Courage, Josey, you can do it, I thought.

Curving along the lane through hills and meadows, I wondered if my father had ever seen the ghosts himself. After another mile, I was astonished to see my dad leap across a ditch and turn directly into the meadow that led to the haunted pine grove. When I reached the point where he had turned, I found no driveway or lane there. Just a raggedy path heading straight for the pines.

An old farm house stood off to the right, but my father wasn't going that way. All I saw was a vast meadow and the grove of tall trees in the midst, like an island rising out of a gently rolling sea.

My father shambled along the path, deeper into the meadow, toward the grove of maple and pine. If he turned around, I could duck within the shroud of grasses. But the autumn meadow was brittle and sparse, and he would surely see me following him. *Please, don't look back,* I pleaded silently. *Keep going.*

I was still following far behind as he neared the grove, but I could see an old dwelling secluded within the tall trees—the remains of some structure of long ago, much like the pictures in my history book of old Roman ruins. Drawing closer, I could see the building had been a small chapel. The steeple stood strong, and most of the walls and stained-glass windows remained, while other parts had crumbled away.

And something peculiar. Hard to describe. The scent of life. Things stirring. A soft glow pulsing through the stained-glass windows. It seemed the light was coming from within. Something definitely moved in there. Shadowy trembling kinds of things. I huddled at the foot of a huge maple tree while my father trudged around the side.

Then I saw the stone tower with the bell. I let my eyes wander slowly up the textured stones, each one a thing in itself. Some shaped like hatchet heads, others like flags in the wind and goblins. And at the very top, yes, something drifting out of the tower. A thin strand—it looked like mist—was twining up through the bell and then out in a curving path amid the treetops. Looking higher, I searched the upper branches for elves, transparent ones, ghosts. But I couldn't quite see.

I felt chilled. I had to keep my mind on other things besides ghosts, or surely I would turn and run all the way home. I told myself, Imagine this as someone's home, as surely it could be. Looking at the chapel windows, I felt oddly comforted by the glowing panes—it was as if someone had been living there for a long time. Signs of home, firelight. No, this wasn't ghosts emerging from the old church tower, but smoke drifting up, getting caught in the brass bell, and billowing out the sides now like a fountain overflowing.

As I crouched at the foot of the maple tree, I noticed that one of the glowing stained-glass window scenes showed a shepherd with several sheep grazing near a river. The shepherd was looking into the sky where angry angels tussled in the air above him, beating their wings in distress as if trying to alert the shepherd of danger. Moments passed. I feared for my father and hoped he was with a friend. To get a better look, I moved in toward this window, where the pieces of glass that made the river were pale enough to see through. Amid the pastel chunks of turquoise, smoky lavender, and milky blue, I pressed my forehead against the stained-glass river and peered inside. The glass was uneven, so everything drifted in and out of focus, but I could see.

The inside of the small chapel no longer contained pews or an altar. Instead it was an enchanted dwelling. Flames dancing in the fireplace. Stone walls with iron sconces holding burning candles. Sculptures taller than me of women loosely draped in fabrics, one carrying a jug on her shoulder, another looking upward with her robe falling away. Marble pillars swirling in rose grain. And rich textures that I could not distinguish. But clearly I saw an old bed with a headboard of dark wood boasting sculpted grape vines and leaves and a quilt of oddly shaped patches in satiny fabrics of maroon, dark blue, and forest green. It was certainly someone's home, but unlike any home I had ever seen.

Then I saw a woman through the glass. Walking across the room, she was willowy, heavenly, dressed in the flowing fabric of an angel—a soft blue gown tied with a golden cord. So lovely, she could have descended from one of the tangled stained-glass scenes. Even now, in the middle of the night, she was bathed in the gilded light of morning. But there was no doubt she was real. Her skin was pale and soft. And she looked very sad.

My father remained out of my view as the woman moved across the room with her head hung low. She sat on the edge of the bed, like a nymph from the sea, staring at the floor. A river of golden hair poured down around her like honey and wine. Over my head, trees rustled above, but I couldn't draw my eyes from this woman full of woe, who sat shuddering now with her face in her hands.

Suddenly a dark shadow moved across the room. Then in the stained-glass window where the river raged strongest, through the pieces of clear glass, I watched my father stagger toward the woman. Even through the thick glass, I heard her crying. My father stood in front of her and threw off his coat. I couldn't tell exactly what he was doing but it looked like he was pulling at his pants. Then he grabbed her shoulders and pushed her back on the bed. He tore away her clothes and threw himself upon her. When she cried out, he raised himself up, shook her hard by the shoulders, and slapped her across the face. With his thundering voice that I had feared so many times, he bellowed out words I could not understand. She went limp as he thrust himself down and rammed his body against her in a way I had never seen before.

My heart grew heavy, my knees gave out, and I fell on the ground. I don't know how long I lay there in a heap before a door slammed, and my father stomped back through the pine grove. I didn't try to hide. I sat in the pine needles, feeling numb, unable to move, waiting for him to discover me, hoping he would find me and know I'd seen him. Then I would run for my life.

I braced myself, and minutes seemed to pass, but he must have been feeling his own kind of numbness because he didn't even notice me. He just staggered down the path in the meadow. I followed him with my eyes, and after he was out of sight, I wanted to dash away from there forever. I wanted to escape everything I had seen that night.

But as I looked at the chapel windows, another part of me yearned to stay. Not wanting to abandon the injured angel inside the chapel, I pressed my face against the window for one last look. The woman lay on the bed, curled up with her arms wrapped around herself, her eyes empty, gazing into the bruised air. At the time I did not fully understand what had occurred, but I knew it wasn't right.

6

"Who is that woman, Dad?" I asked while pouring my morning bowl of Cheerios. Having survived last night's events, I felt bold beyond reason.

"What woman?" he replied, looking around the kitchen. "I don't see any woman."

"The woman in the chapel," I said. "You know, last night."

"There you go babbling again. Eat your Cheerios before your brain gives out."

"Dad, I was there. I followed you through the meadow and into the pine grove. I saw the woman in the stone building with the stained-glass windows."

"Have you lost your only mind, squirt? What the devil are you talking about?"

"You told me ghosts live in that grove, Dad, but there's no ghosts. It's a woman. Come with me. I'll show you."

"We're not going anywhere. You have to get to school," he grumbled. "But I'll tell you this, and you better listen well. Mind your own business, Josey Rose. You'll get yourself in big trouble snoopin' around like that. Now if you're talking about the chapel on Gypsy Lane, I forbid you to go near that place."

"Why, Dad? It's a lady in a stone chapel. What could be the danger?"

"She's trouble, kiddo. Trouble beyond your wildest dreams. You're better off cavorting with the devil than hanging around the likes of that screwball. Stay away from there."

"Who is she, Dad? What's her name?"

"I don't think I'm getting through to you," he roared as he grabbed me by my shirt and dragged me across the kitchen, knocking over three plants. As he pinned me against the back door, his cheeks flushed, and gravel came into his voice. "You will have nothing to do with her, ever."

"Okay," I mumbled, "I hear you."

"If I catch you anywhere near that place, you'll be leaving this valley squawking like a goose. You get my drift? I'll send you to school in the dark hills of North Dakota."

"Well, Dad," I muttered nervously, "I sure wouldn't want to go to North Dakota. I don't even know where it is." I picked up my coat and books for school. "Reckon I'll stay here in good old New Hampshire. Don't worry about a thing, Dad." I hated myself for this incurable habit of babbling when things got tense. "Sure," I driveled on, walking toward the door, "I've never been to North Dakota, Dad, and I wouldn't know anyone there. Everything will be fine now."

I was still mumbling when I walked out the front door and pulled my bike out of the shed. I pedaled and muttered all the way to school. When I sat down at my desk, I pulled out my geography book and looked for North Dakota.

7

Even in my weakest moments, trembling in the wake of my father's harsh words, I knew I would return to the stone dwelling of the mysterious woman. I was drawn to her beauty, her vulnerability, and the way she moved. I wanted to be near her. Surely I would be safe from my father catching me. After all, he only went a few times this month and other months even less. Only four days had passed since his last horrifying trip to the chapel, so tonight I would go. I'd have no problem climbing down the oak tree outside my window in the dark and pedaling off to Gypsy Lane. So pedal I did, and in no time, I was at the edge of the meadow where the path led in. I stashed my bike there and hiked through the tall grasses.

I nestled in the pine grove watching the stained-glass windows flicker in all their colors. I was trying to figure out the stories in the windows filled with angels and doves, shepherds and moonlight, women playing harps, and wild horses running through water, when suddenly a pine cone slid through the quiet air and crashed to the ground. I jumped to my feet. Feeling a little creepy, I walked slowly around the building, which settled my heart somewhat or at least made me less aware of its pounding. At the back part of the chapel near the bell tower, someone had built a second chimney. Around the other side, I found an old stone wishing well with a wooden bucket hanging from a thick rope. A couple of jugs leaned against the side.

On the far side of the building, more stained-glass windows glowed

in colors beyond the range of any rainbow. Finally coming around to
the front of the chapel, I stood before two huge, richly carved wooden
doors held by gigantic wrought-iron hinges. Gargoyles with drowsy
faces guarded the entrance. Off to the side of the doorway a clear glass
window revealed the warm glow of the chapel inside.

Feeling uneasy about being so close to the lighted window, I drew
back and slid under a pine tree, out of sight in case my father came.
The clear glass window revealed only a little from this distance. I
glimpsed three huge candles, several feet high and set in large holders
that rose up from the floor. They were covered with years of multicol-
ored wax drippings. And in the upper regions of the high ceilings,
something twinkled like stars.

Suddenly, footsteps crunched through the pine needles. I backed
farther under the tree. If it was my dad, I'd either be dead or attending school in North Dakota. As his footsteps grew closer, I heard a
dragging sound, too. By the time he lumbered only a few feet from my
hiding place, my heart beat madly. When I looked at the ground off to
my side, preparing to greet the black boots of my father, I beheld instead the pale bare feet of a woman and a large canvas bag trailing behind her.

The pine needles rustled a bit too loudly as I moved farther back
against the tree trunk. The woman dropped the bag and pressed into
the lower branches of the pine tree. Then in a soft, smoky voice, she
crooned, "Yoohoo, who scampers there? Who is this animal lost in the
grove?"

As she wove in and out of the branches, I moved behind the tree
trunk and back into the thick layers of pine, getting poked in the eye
with needles and bopped on the head by big pine cones.

"No need to be afraid," she said, "it's only Lily here. I won't hurt
you. I'll find you a tasty treat. But, yoohoo, how will I know what to
bring unless you show me what you are?"

Perhaps she realized that any normal critter, including myself, would
hide or quickly scamper away rather than approach a stranger bearing
a canvas bag, crawling on all fours through the pine. So she stopped
calling to me and rested beneath the tree, only a few feet from where I
lay. All the motion among the branches had set free the scent of pine.

Then peering through the pine needles, I saw her. Lily with honey
hair pouring all around her, radiating her own light even in the darkness. She was clothed in gossamer—layers of blue, green, and lavender,
the fabric in some places sheer enough to reveal her fair skin. My imag-

ination ran wild as I pictured her at any moment sprouting wings and swooping into the air to alight on a branch with a swarm of forest elves.

We both remained huddled there in silence for several moments. Then at last she slipped away from under the tree, picked up her canvas bag, and dragged it inside. When Lily disappeared into an alcove within the chapel, I began crawling from under the tree. But she quickly returned, carrying something. Moving quietly like a fawn, she slid a bowl of milk under the tree, three feet from my knee, and went back inside.

Through the window, I watched Lily open the canvas bag. I remained long enough to see the contents. Nothing would have surprised me. Perhaps she had a collection of dead possums in there. Or tree roots for concocting magic potions. But instead, she drew out a hodge-podge of fungus specimens shaped like the ears of panda bears—big ones and small. I had seen this kind of fungus growing around the base of tree trunks. My friends and I had found many—we called them "ballerina trees" because the fungus around the trunks looked like scalloped tutus with brown and beige on top and smooth white crinolines underneath.

I thought it was weird to collect fungus in the dark. I wondered if she had a job during the day. I couldn't imagine this woman dressed in layers of chiffon standing behind the counter of a doughnut shop or selling shower curtains in a department store. Lily lined up the fungus on a table by the fire, then ambled to the other side of the room, filled a glass with something green, and drank it.

A creepy feeling passed through me—maybe my father was right, maybe she was crazy. I crawled from under the pine tree, walked slowly back to my bike, and rode home. The moon had already reached the top of the sky, and I had school the next day.

8

Early evening. Still September. I combed Grandma Ru's long white hair with her favorite silver comb while she paged through the *Ladies' Home Journal,* cutting out pictures of thermostats. Having gone through six years of magazines, she had clipped several advertisements of round Honeywell thermostats shown in various colors to match the decor of any modern living room. She was gluing them into a scrapbook she had entitled "Round Things."

I looked around the room cluttered with my father's endless projects. Somewhere underneath all his stuff was a hint of what the place had looked like when we moved in seven years ago. The wallpaper swirled in curling patterns of silver, cream, and butterscotch. Near the ceiling, an ornate wall border danced along in fleurs-de-lis and golden garland. And the curtains were a tangle of vines and rambling flowers.

On top of this original decor lay piles of debris that looked like they might have drifted in during a flood. One table provided a pedestal for my father's fishing lures, broken reels, and sinkers of all sizes. Another held the ingredients for tying fly lures—feathers from chickens and pheasants, hair from deer tails for his buck-tail flies, thread on spindles, red yarn, and a small silver vice for holding his hooks. He used the same vice to secure live mosquitoes when he cut off their stingers.

One side of the living room harbored fifteen terrariums where over the years my father had cultivated entire plant worlds inside huge bottles, some almost two feet high. The south side of the room flourished with pots of crawling vines and ferns. Pans of moss lay all over the floor.

You never knew what you might find in his terrariums: Tiny pagodas on mountainsides. Mirrors creating the illusion of water. Curling driftwood draped with Spanish moss. And plants winding all over—orchids, ferns, and Venus's-flytraps. Some terrariums housed small amphibians, which delighted me no end. Tiny toads snuggled beneath the ferns. And lizards took siestas under the soft purple petals of African violets.

Next to the stairway, a long buffet table held the things he used for creating his miniature ships. Fancy china bowls overflowed with tiny masts, rigging, sails, and twinkling gems for stars. On the floor lay his collection of bottles, which he had personally emptied one by one and which he used to house his ships. Strewn about the mantel and tables were ships in bottles that he had completed over the years. Beautiful ships—an old brigantine, a three-masted coastal schooner, a sixteenth-century carrack, and a topsail schooner called the *Nellie Bywater,* which he had modeled after another he'd seen.

Other tables had become permanent resting spots for unopened mail, books, and so many magazines—*Life, Look,* and the *Saturday Evening Post.* On top of a pile of old *National Geographic*s was my report card from two years ago that he had meant to sign but never got around to it. On the mantelpiece rested the rose marble box where he had stored my teeth. Since my father kept the box locked, I didn't know what else it contained, but I imagined it harbored secret things and a bit of order.

So on this evening while I combed Grandma's hair, my father filled a small bowl with dried crickets and orange slices for the birds. Then he returned to the dining room table and the captain's chair, where he was cleaning his guns. His collection of pistols and shotguns covered the table. He held a long narrow rod with a cloth stuck in the end, poured a stream of gun-cleaning oil onto it, and jammed the rod into the barrel. There was something about gun-cleaning oil: I loved the aroma, like boat marinas and fresh paint on summer cottages.

"Josey," he called, "lay down that comb and come over here for a spell. Sit at the table here."

This evening his breath smelled of tequila.

"Dad, maybe you shouldn't drink any more tonight. You know how you feel bad in the morning."

"It's okay, son," he said like a smooth politician. "I'm cleaning the cabinet. There's too many liquor bottles in there, and we need some extra space for all them oranges I'm bringing home tomorrow. You know how Lulu loves oranges."

"Dad, I was wondering something."

"What's that, squirt?"

"Where is my mother buried?"

"Why all these questions about your mother? She's gone, kiddo. Gone for good."

"Gone, but not dead, right?"

My father pumped the rod in and out of the gun barrel. "We've got to take a trip somewhere, Josey, so you get your mind on other things. Life's too damned easy for you around here. I want to show you some real adventure—the inner pit of the world."

I wasn't sure I wanted to see the inner pit of the world.

"Moderation is for monks," he continued. "There's a lot to experience out there. The sizzling heat of the desert. The foamy rapids of rushing rivers. And the sound of lightning whizzing through the air three feet from your head."

I was horrified of lightning. The thought of being anywhere near that kind of electricity made my skin creep. I hated to show my fear, especially around my father. But he must have known because whenever the storms came, I curled at the foot of the couch and hid under Grandma's afghan.

"Hey squirt, hand me that clean rag over there."

"Why do you call me squirt, Dad? Sounds like a piece of water."

"Now listen to me," he said as he jammed the clean rag into the barrel. "You'll grow up to be nothing but a big squirt if you keep pussy-footin' your bones around here, combing your grandmother's hair, and asking a bunch of questions about a mother who's gone."

He pulled out the rod and cloth, placed his good eye at the upper end of both barrels, turned toward the light, and carefully inspected the inside of each long metal cylinder. Then with a slam, crunch, and click, he closed the gun, now cleaned to his satisfaction.

"You got to go to the edge, Josey boy. You got to see your own death before you ever shake hands with life. Hey, you want to know what I was doing at your age?" This called for a sip of tequila. "Let me tell you about the time I climbed so high I fell down a smokestack. It all started when—"

"Look at all these thermostats," said Grandma Ru. "Two pages full.

There's a thermostat in every color of the rainbow except indigo. Or is this indigo? Josey, is this purple or indigo?"

"Looks like indigo to me, Grandma."

"They don't make indigo thermostats," said my father.

"Then I'll have to paint one," she said.

"Okay, but don't run out of glue." The last time Grandma Ru had run out of glue, she'd collapsed in a heap on the floor, sobbing until we woke the neighbors to borrow some Elmer's.

"Doesn't anybody want to hear my story?" grumbled my father.

"Yes, dear," said Grandma, "we adore your stories."

"Well, it happened like this," he began. "Me and my friend Horace made plans to climb the tallest smokestack in all of Georgia—the one down at the old dye factory . . ."

My father described how the factory had been around for a hundred years. Decades of rain had dissolved much of the mortar between the bricks, leaving sections of walls crumbled away. On the highest smokestack—the one my father intended to climb—several metal prongs jutted out from the bricks that he would use as footholds in his ascent.

For rope, my father found some old parachute line he bought from an army surplus store. He attached one end of the line to his belt. On the other end, he tied a small rock, which he threw up and around the prongs above him. In this way, he inched up the old smokestack, clinging to the prongs and the uneven bricks. The rope saved him a few times on that climb. Like when he pulled up with all his weight, and the rusty metal came loose along with several bricks around it. Down he went, but the trusty rope caught him. Even after he stopped swinging from the fall, he still had the rusty prong clutched in his hand. Meanwhile, Horace scrambled back down the stack, offering to keep watch on the ground for intruders.

After securing the rope on the top rung, my father climbed the smokestack to its pinnacle. Horace took a picture of my father standing there with his hands outstretched in victory for having reached the top of the world. I still have the photograph.

As my father leaned down to wind up his ropes, a bird suddenly flew out of the chimney. Its wings beat furiously against my father's ankle. His heart jumped, and his foot slipped. Down he went into the throat of the old stack. He crashed past a bird nest and some wire mesh, falling into the darkness along with an entire family of baby birds. The rope was still attached to the upper prong on the outside of the stack. It caught him with a snap. He remained dangling from his lifeline, suspended inside a dark, echoing abyss while the frantic fledglings descended all around him, then fluttered up and past him, learning very quickly how to fly. Wings beat against his face as he hung between the curved brick interior walls covered with fifty years of soot.

"Now that's living on the edge, son," my father said. "That's lookin' life straight in the bare-assed eyeballs. Yep, suspended there in the darkness inside that old chimney, I saw the whole enchilada—my past, my present, and maybe the future, too. That ain't whistlin' Dixie."

"Yeah," I agreed, "that ain't whistlin' Dixie no way, no how." And I was thinking how I'd rather whistle Dixie than have any part of that adventure.

Then my father went on to describe how Horace ran home, his mom called the fire department, and they rescued my father with ladders and rope. He showed me the article from the local newspaper. The headline read, "LOCAL BOY TAKES DANGEROUS PLUNGE."

"It's those kinds of trials that build character, son." He slammed the tequila on the table. "And I ain't lettin' the years soften me up none either. Working the high iron, you can't get no higher. Yep, the only things higher than me are the angels in heaven."

Lulu warbled a lovely melody while Jake meowed.

"You got to be tough, Josey boy. You don't want to be no bundustin' buttercup. Remember, you ain't no milksop, and you don't take shit from nobody. You hear what I'm saying?"

"Yeah," said Grandma Ru, "and you don't ever buy a beige thermostat from Honeywell."

My father chugged a large amount of tequila and went in the kitchen. I curled up on the couch to watch *My Three Sons* with Grandma, who murmured to the birds, clutching her bottle of glue.

As we watched TV, I thought about these three sons and their cozy family. Even without a mother, they seemed to live a wonderland existence.

"Oh, those Douglas boys," sighed Grandma. "What a nice family. Isn't it a shame all this will end."

"How's that, Grandma?"

"The earth is wounded, you see. Too many space shots punching holes in the atmosphere. All that's good is beginning to bleed out the holes. It's oozing, Josey, like puss from a boil. All the stuff that keeps families together is being lost to space. You watch, Josey, you wait and see."

"What will happen?"

"Everything will go kerflooey. Parents will ignore their children. Children will roam the streets. Common folks will carry guns. And stores will run out of glue."

That's when my father sauntered into the living room. He leaned down and put his face close to mine. A slight bit of moisture had accumulated in the dimple of his chin. He held up his almost-empty bottle of tequila and said, "Now for the best part, Josey boy. At the bottom of this bottle is my treasure—my Cracker Jack surprise."

I searched his live eye to gauge how far gone he was. The red rivers were rising.

"Do you see it, Josey?"

"See what?"

"My prize."

I looked closer at the one inch of remaining tequila. "No Dad, don't drink that. There's a dead worm in there. Look closely. See, there it is."

"Yes, my son. That is my prize. I have duly earned this tasty treat for having struggled through the entire bottle of tequila. Now I can drink the little vermin raw."

"Dad, you wouldn't. You don't know where he's been."

"He's right where he should be. Ah, yes, my sweet little agave worm. Somebody pulled him out of a cactus and put him in this bottle just for me. And the tequila has preserved him well. He's a real cutie, don't you think?"

"He's disgusting."

My father swirled the clear booze around, worm and all, then put the bottle to his lips. *He's teasing me, I know it.* I looked back to the TV where the middle son, Robbie, was chasing his little brother, Chip, around the living room. But when I saw the bottle go bottoms up, I turned back just in time to see the worm slither into my father's mouth in a rushing stream of tequila.

"Oh, gross!" I hollered as I jumped up from the couch. "Spit it out this minute before you get sick and die."

My father gulped down the tequila, then clenched the pale larva between his teeth. Liquid dribbled from the corner of his mouth as he slowly bit into the worm, rupturing him and tearing him in two. "You want half?" he asked.

"You shouldn't share your food," cautioned Grandma Ru. "You might catch a cold."

Then my father tilted back his head and swallowed both halves of the worm. My stomach turned over.

"Virility," he gasped as he flexed the muscles in his arms. "That little critter is chock full of virility."

"What's virility?" I asked as I backed up to the other side of the room.

"It's the stuff that makes you a man."

"Dad, you were born that way. You don't have to eat worms to be a man."

"You're too young to understand all this, but you'll grow into it."

"You can bet I'll never grow into anything that means eating worms."

"Well, let's just say these juicy little morsels give me all the vigor I need when it comes to dealing with the female species."

"What are you talking about?"

"Josey, let me tell you a thing or three about women. You got to understand that dames are the weaker sex. They were born that way. That's why they like a strong, forceful kind of man. You always gotta let them know who's boss. And man, oh, man, they love to be dominated. Every goddamn one of them."

"Dad, they're not all like that."

"Hey, kiddo. When you grow up, you'll see how they are—the way they whine and carry on. Now it's nothin' against them, mind you. Just like bats fly in the dark, women can cry up a storm. But that's why they need a man to set them straight. A man to give them some good ol' down-home, hurly-burly *virility.*"

I wondered if my father was right about women.

"So you see," my father said, "men are the superior race. You can thank your lucky stars you were born male."

Well, at least I had something going for me. Then my father jabbered on about how men age better than women. "Look at Maurice Chevalier," he said. "He becomes more distinguished with the years, while Helen Hayes is simply crumbling into a sad-faced old hag with skin that wags when she walks."

As he rambled on, I tried to think of other old people. Grandma Ru was the only one I knew, and she wasn't a "sad-faced old hag." I wished I had other grandparents to compare. But I couldn't think of any other relatives I'd ever known in my whole life.

"Dad," I said, "don't you have any brothers or sisters?"

"Not a one."

"What about your father? Where is he?"

"Six feet under next to my mother."

"What do you mean? Grandma Ru is your mom."

"She's my stepmom. She married my father after my first mom died."

"Well, how did your mom die?" I knew he wasn't completely soused—he was only *one* sheet to the wind. He was in that limbo state where he might tell me things he normally wouldn't. I was curious about my father's family. It was as if he had no history, like he had arrived unattended from another world.

He sank into his chair and gazed with melancholy at the closing credits of *My Three Sons* with the picture of three pairs of feet tapping to the music. Lulu sang the closing theme song straight through the next three commercials.

"You ask too many questions," he mumbled.

"But I'm curious, Dad. What happened to my grandparents? What about your mom? What was she like? How come I never see any pictures of her?"

"You want to know what happened to my mom?" he asked with a voice that spooked me out.

"Sure."

"I killed her," he said.

I couldn't tell if he was kidding. "Oh," I mumbled, considering that maybe I didn't want to hear about it, after all. If he killed his mother, then he sure as heck could kill anybody, maybe even me. I vowed never to do another thing to upset him for the rest of my life.

"Well," he pressed, "don't you want to know more?"

"Ahhh, not really, Dad. You don't have to talk about it. I better go feed the birds now. I can hear their stomachs growling. You know what they ate today? Well, let's see, this morning—"

"I killed her the day I was born," he said.

"Mm-hmmm?" I murmured as the walls crept in, and the air grew strange.

"I waited too long to be born," he explained. "You see, I was a procrastinator even then. I hung around inside the womb longer than I should have. I grew too big. And I took my mother's life trying to be born."

"Well, Dad," I sighed with relief, "that's not your fault. You weren't old enough to know any better. Right? I mean you weren't any age at all."

He seemed to be falling into a dark and solitary place. "Well, gosh," I stammered, "so you grew up like me without a mom?"

"Only for a while," he said.

Jake broke the tentative air with his impression of a telephone ringing. Lulu answered, "Hello, hello." And Jake replied, "I want my Maypo."

"So what happened to your father?" I asked hesitantly.

"Well, the man was a fierce ol' bugger, if you can imagine—"

Yes, I could imagine.

"After my mother died, he took out his misfortune on the world. Figured Jesus and everybody else owed him something for snatching up his wife like that. Maybe he was right. But when Jesus didn't respond one iota, he reckoned he'd get payback from me. So he hounded me endlessly. Whenever I didn't move quick enough for him, he'd throttle me. 'You little bastard,' he'd yell, 'if ya weren't so bloody slow, your mama'd be alive today.' No matter what I did, I could never make up for the sin I committed before I was born."

I dared not speak. As hard as his words fell upon my heart, I knew he was telling the truth—things I'd never heard. Family secrets.

"So it goes," he continued, talking more to himself than to me, "one autumn night about a year after my father married Grandma Ru, he went down in the basement to light the pilot on the furnace. There was a gas leak, I reckon, and the whole thing blew up. Singed bolts sailed across the room. Warped sheet metal crashed against the ceiling and embedded in the walls."

"What a terrible way to die!" I gasped.

"That's not how he died. He was quite alive after the explosion, but his skin was badly cut from the debris. Burns all over his arms and face. Did you ever smell burning flesh? It's not an aroma you want to savor."

"Worse than skunk in a rainstorm," agreed Grandma Ru.

"Anyway," continued my father, "the ambulance took him away. Your grandma went, too. They wheeled out the driveway and left me alone. On the way to the hospital on the main highway, my father threw a fit, yelled at the driver, insisting he was heading the wrong way. My father dragged himself from the stretcher, all bloody and crazed, and grabbed the steering wheel. The ambulance crashed through a construction barricade and sideswiped a semi truck. Grandma Ru got shaken up pretty good. My dad and the driver were killed."

How strange, I thought. We sat in silence. Perhaps I should have asked him where he and Grandma Ru lived after his father was killed, and where he met my mom, and a hundred other things. But I'd had enough family history for the night. Anyway, this conversation made my father slump into a murky place where I didn't want him to go any deeper. So we sat together for a while. The birds kept the conversation going, their chatter drifting into the air.

I considered what he'd said. With all that had happened to my father, it's no wonder he drank and carried on. When he threw things through the window and hollered at the walls, was I supposed to forgive him because his mom died early? It didn't matter, though, did it. He was my father, and I had already forgiven him.

But how quickly his mood changed that night—like hot lava gushing from a cool calm lake. "Holy Jumpin' Mother of Jesus!" he suddenly shouted.

"Jumpin' Jesus! Jumpin' Jesus," echoed Lulu.

"Shut the hell up!" he yelled back. "You feathered fools don't know your feathers from the grass in the ground."

"She's just a little bird, Dad. Don't yell at her," I pleaded.

"Knock it off," squawked Jake.

My father picked up a leather boot, tossed it at Jake and Lulu's cage, and growled, "Knock it off yourself, you bastard!"

"Dad, stop," I cried, "you'll hurt them!"

The birds screeched on. Then my father grabbed his other boot and hurled it even harder. Orange slices and dried crickets flew out the sides. Then the whole cage crashed to the floor.

"Now, Willie," cautioned Grandma in a soothing, motherly tone, "you mustn't throw things in the house. Go outside for that sort of thing." Then she went back to her scrapbook.

My father slumped back into the chair. Jake was in a tizzy, walking in circles on the floor, making new sounds I never heard before—something like a tweeting whimper. Lulu was trapped inside the mangled remains of her cage, her wings fluttering limply like the fins of a dying fish. I lifted her from her fallen world and held her in my lap. Her wing was hurt, but she wasn't bleeding. Tomorrow I would take her to the vet, but for now, I didn't know what to do.

Meanwhile, my father lit a cigar and sat in a stupor while a cloud of smoke formed above his head. "Goddamn foul-mouthed birds," he muttered, "they got the language of a lumberjack. We shoulda got rid of them feathered fools a long time ago." But he didn't leave the house. I stayed in the living room with Lulu until my father sauntered off to bed.

9

After the first night when I saw Lily under the pine tree offering milk to whatever lost animal might be there, I vowed never to return. The thought of peeking in on her like that seemed wrong, but I didn't know how to approach her.

Despite my vow, I visited the pine grove several times, observing bits and pieces of Lily's puzzling world, trying to come up with a plan to meet her. I went at night with the darkness to protect me. Each time I arrived, a bowl of milk awaited me under the pine tree. On the third visit, a piece of dark bread sat beside the milk.

My obsession with Lily confused me, and I couldn't figure out how my father might be involved in her life. And even though the threat of being exiled to North Dakota gave me the creeps, part of me wanted to continue these jaunts to the pine grove just so my father would catch me there and expose himself as well.

Another part of me was deeply enchanted by this uncommon creature with long honey hair. In those rare moments when I saw her through the window, ambling around the chapel, she seemed to drift in a fine mist as if she had descended from another world. She was a woman, and that alone was a mystery.

My obsession compelled me to lie in bed at night, listening for the sounds of my father's footsteps. Sometimes I heard noises outside and ran to the window to see if it was him again, shuffling down the driveway. But most often it was only the wind blowing leaves in fitful circles.

One night I lay in bed thinking about Lily until I could stand it no longer. "Just one more time," I said, shimmying down the tree. And I was off. Pedaling along Gypsy Lane, I noticed the sky swelling up with clouds. The meadow passed into shadow as the moon sank behind a bank of darkness. It'll pass over, I thought. But when I took my place under the pine tree, the tree tops quivered in the wind.

I found a fresh bowl of milk. And this time, beside the bowl, lay a soup bone as big as a grapefruit. Maybe Lily thought she had attracted something large like a Saint Bernard or a stray bear that had wandered in from the deep woods of New Hampshire.

Then through the clear chapel window, I saw Lily sitting at a table with several candles around her. I wished I could be there beside her, nestling at the edge of her long tangled skirts. The candlelight wavered, but I could see. She was moving slowly, contentedly, working on something. She was holding a knife with a long silver blade . . . lifting something from the table, too small for me to know for sure . . . and slicing it in two. When the severed parts fell, a faint smile showed upon her lips.

She moved her hands around the tabletop, as if shifting bits and pieces of all the things she had been slicing up. Then, without the forewarning of most storms, lightning scorched the air somewhere in the meadow nearby. Thunder rattled my bones and probably shook the bedrock to the inner core of the earth. I curled in a ball and burrowed into the pine needles as far as I could. I wished I was a worm so I could crawl into the ground, out of danger from the deadly lightning. This pine grove had the only high trees in the vast meadow. Electricity would surely seek out the tree I was lying under, spiral down the trunk leaving a giant wooden corkscrew in its path, and burn me worse than any fire. In the morning, Lily would come out and find her empty milk bowl, along with a serving of charbroiled human with fried soup bone nuggets on the side.

Then, as if to justify all my fears, the lightning and thunder merged into one violent beast and lit the pine grove brighter than if the sun had fallen from the sky and set itself upon Lily's doorstep. The chapel doors flung open, and Lily stood on the upper step, under the shelter of hanging eaves. The breeze enveloped her and carried her long hair off to the side. Layers of fabrics swirled around her. She looked as if she had actually become the wind, transparent and powerful, spinning at the chapel entrance.

Then Lily kneeled down and saw me under the tree. If there had been a family of wild tigers there, perhaps she would have opened her arms to welcome them. But when she saw my lavender eyes, she jumped back and shut the door.

I couldn't bear the horror of the storm anymore. I ran up the steps and banged on the door with all my might. "Please let me in!" I cried. "I'm afraid of the lightning!"

Another flash of excruciating light and then thunder. "I won't hurt you," I sobbed. My knees gave out, and I fell down and huddled against the door, shivering like the weakling my father said I was. I wished I had never followed my father and found this place. Because then I'd be home, safe in bed instead of crying on the front steps of a chapel whose only inhabitant was a woman who dragged fungus home in a canvas bag, drank green beverages, and sliced things up with a long silver blade.

The door creaked open suddenly and I fell partway through the slit. I looked up into her wary eyes so far above me and wept, "Won't you let me in, I'm so scared."

"Why are you here?" she asked with hesitation.

"Because . . . because . . . I like this stone chapel . . . and the pine trees all around . . . and the angels in the stained-glass windows, and—"

She left the door ajar and backed away. I slithered in and went to a place in the center of the room so no matter which window the lightning came in, the electricity wouldn't get me. I sat on some large floor pillows next to a marble column that went clear to the ceiling. A fire blazed in a stone fireplace large enough for a grown-up to walk inside without bending down. "I'm sorry I frightened you," I murmured.

She walked away.

"Are you going to call the police?" I asked. "I promise I'll leave as soon as the thunder stops."

"No, no, that's impossible," she said, turning toward me again with a restless pace.

"What's impossible—my leaving? You mean you're never going to let me go?"

"No," she said. "Calling the police is impossible. I don't have a phone, you see."

"Yes, of course," I said. "Well, I won't be a problem. I'm scared of the lightning, that's all."

⚘

"And I'm scared of visitors," she whispered.

Lily paced in front of the arched entranceway where she had let me in. Her bare feet fell silent on the stone. The sheer blues and greens of her dress partially veiled the curves of her body, like seaweed draping from a mermaid.

Thunder and lightning tortured all sides of the chapel. The wind blasted against the far wall, making the stained-glass pieces in the window chatter like frightened teeth. The rain pressed so hard against the glass that it found its way through the spaces where the old leading had come loose. Lily gazed up to one window where water drained down the faces of three hovering angels, then flowed into tiny rivers across the stone floor.

"The angels are crying," Lily said.

She walked silently to the main entrance of the chapel and flung open the huge doors. She stood in the archway facing out while wind blew her hair. The chapel came alive with a hundred tinkling chimes suspended from the rafters. Bells echoed around the ceiling even higher than that. Strips of fabric, the same colors as her dress, lifted off a table near the door and spun in circles across the floor.

A gust of wind carried in rain while lightning lit up the whole inside. I buried my head in my arms. After the thunder had its say, Lily closed the doors and walked in front of the fireplace. Her cheeks were flushed from the wind. I feared for her life, knowing that a bolt of lightning could soar down the chimney at any moment and arc over to where she paced, set her aflame, and burn her to ashes. She paused beside a milky white statue of a nude woman almost as tall as Lily herself. The woman in marble held a piece of fruit near her lips while her other hand clutched some fabric that appeared to be falling to the ground. A couple of birds fluttered about the chapel rafters.

Lily's hair glowed from the fire behind her as she eyed me still with suspicion, perhaps trying to decide what to do with me, this loathesome intruder. Then she turned decisively and trudged back to the table with the silver knife. My imagination got the better of me, and I thought she might chase me around the chapel and cut me into pieces with her long blade. But I feared the lightning more. So I remained by the marble column, staying as quiet as possible.

Lily sat at the table and lowered her head in concentration. From where I sat in the middle of the room, I could only see her from behind. Her elbows moved as she shifted small pieces around on the table. Then she began slicing things again with her knife. I thought if

I asked her gently, she might tell me what she was doing.

"Lily—"

She turned abruptly with startled eyes, the knife blade reflecting the flame of her candle. "How do you know my name?" she asked.

I had to think. She'd been Lily to me for so many days now that it had slipped my mind how I knew her name. "Well, yes," I recalled, "it was under the tree. When you heard me that night, you came in through the pine branches, and . . . you said your name."

"That was you?"

"Yes."

"Lurking beneath the pine?"

"I wanted to meet you, Lily."

"You have a strange way of making acquaintances." She returned to her work in silence.

"Lily," I finally asked, "what are you doing?"

"Thinking."

"No, what are you doing on the table there?"

"It's a puzzle."

"You mean you want me to guess?"

"No, I mean it's a puzzle. Would you like to see?" she asked shyly.

Since she wasn't too close to a window, I walked over. Coming around her, I saw stretched out across the table a partly assembled jigsaw puzzle. But it had no straight borders like normal puzzles, and the picture was, well, it was a landscape scene but things were not in their proper places.

"What's the knife for?" I asked.

"It's for when the pieces don't fit. I cut them into the proper shapes." She showed me the piece she was working on—a bit of sky, which she sliced to fit into an empty space in the river below of similar blue. She had carved a small indent to fit around the bulge in another puzzle piece of the river.

The resulting scene looked nothing like what the puzzle company originally intended, or any land I'd ever seen.

"Why do you do that?" I asked.

"To pass the time on rainy nights."

"No, I mean why do you cut up the puzzle pieces."

"To make them fit, of course," she said, looking at me closely. "Have you never done a puzzle before?"

"Sure."

"Well, how can you get all the pieces together if you don't cut them to fit?"

"Do you have the box lid?" I asked. "You know, the cover."

"No, I use this for a cover," she said as she pulled out a black velvet cloth and laid it over the puzzle pieces. "That way the birds don't fly off with the shavings to build nests."

"Lily, I mean the box cover with the picture on it. The one that came with the puzzle."

She reached under the table and pulled out the box cover filled with more puzzle pieces. She dumped them out and turned over the lid, revealing a landscape with mountains, wild flowers, and a river running through.

"See, that's how it's supposed to look," I explained.

She gazed off, perplexed and disappointed. "Oh," she said sadly as her eyes searched the rafters. Then she let her head droop in silence.

I went back to my place by the marble column. The storm had subsided to a distant rumbling of what was now someone else's thunder. A glimmer of light from above the rafters caught my eye. Looking up I saw hundreds of crystals hanging from the ceiling, collecting the candlelight and sending it off in twinkling rays.

I walked back to Lily. Her head still hung low. She held a strand of chiffon from her clothes and twined it around her wrist.

"I have school tomorrow," I said. "I better go."

She nodded her head as if to say yes, but I sensed she'd rather I stayed. After the storm I felt close to her somehow.

"Can I come here again?" I asked.

She gazed at me. A log fell loose in the fireplace. Her mouth trembled, but she didn't answer. In her eyes all filled with candlelight and shadows I saw the reflection of my own, and I felt safe.

To make sure the rain had stopped, I looked up at the stained glass where the water had poured in earlier.

"The angels stopped crying," she said.

"Yes. Good night, Lily."

When I walked through the meadow on the way home, I knew I had found someone who would never treat me badly. No matter what, I would let nothing get in the way of going to see her in the chapel. Not even my father would stop me now.

Lily was like magic, and she didn't even know my name.

10

On the wings of my bike, I raced home through the darkness. Gypsy Lane was the same old road, but it felt like a different world. Hard to explain, maybe like being inside a song with whirling music and so many voices.

Long past midnight. Everyone would be asleep. But pedaling in the driveway, I was surprised to see lights still on in the house. And through the front window, I glimpsed my father pacing in the living room and Grandma Ru sitting by the birds. What I did not realize is that they had been looking for me all night.

I quietly slid my bike into the shed, slowly enough so the fender wouldn't rattle. I climbed up the oak tree and slipped through the window.

I slithered into bed, and in that drowsy beguiling place just before dreams, I wallowed in the warmth of my new friend, beautiful Lily, imagining when I would visit her again. And for the first time in a long while, I felt happy.

Just as I was falling asleep, two cars wheeled into the driveway. I heard people talking and footsteps shuffling across the living room, then heavier steps like men in big boots pounding up the stairway to my room. Strange voices babbled about the lightning storm. My bedroom door burst open, and a bright light blinded me—perhaps a lost lightning bolt had found me at last, forcing itself into my room, pressing against my face.

"Dad!" I yelled, quaking in fear as I flew out of bed to run for help. I ran directly into a wall made of two legs wearing dark pants and shiny black boots. My hand fell upon the cool metal of a gun. As my eyes began to focus through my screams, I was relieved to discover that the gun was packed into the leather holster of a policeman. When he turned on the bedroom light, however, I trembled at the sight of the long lanky cop with red hair. His head hovered close to the ceiling, and his ashen skin gave him the look of a vampire. Another cop stood beside him, a roly-poly dumpling of a man.

More footsteps bolted up the stairs, and my father flew in the room. "Josey!" he hollered. "Where the hell have you been?"

"We found him in his bed," said the tall cop in a deep, eerie voice.

"Yeah," said the other, "sleeping like a possum."

"But he's been gone all night," said my father.

"All right, Mr. Rose," said the dumpling cop, "reckon you're all set now."

"Next time you lose your son," suggested the other, "check his room before calling us."

"I tell you, the kid wasn't here."

"Look under the blankets. Sometimes these young tykes curl up in balls at the bottom of their covers."

"He wasn't anywhere in this house," insisted my father. "But I thank you gentlemen for stopping by. His grandmother and I were very worried."

"Willie, honey, come quick!" called Grandma Ru. "I've run out of glue."

"Oh, cripes," said my father as he dashed back down the stairs. By the time the policemen came down, Grandma was on the floor, weeping desperately.

My father asked, "You fellows wouldn't happen to have any glue, would you?"

"No, Mr. Rose, we're plumb out of glue," said the vampire cop. He leaned down to comfort Grandma, who lay moaning on the floor.

While the two men attended Grandma, my father stomped up to where I was sitting on the top step. "All right, what's the story?" He sat down, his eyes level with mine. "You wouldn't happen to be out visiting any strange chapels now, would you?"

I wasn't ready for a trip to North Dakota, not yet. "I was scared of the lightning," I said, "so I slept in the closet."

"I checked the closet, kiddo, and there weren't no sleeping children there."

"Did you look under the pile of clothes?"

"Listen," he growled, grabbing my collar, "you tell me exactly where you were."

I was glad the policemen were still downstairs in case my father started throwing things.

"Okay, okay," I said, rummaging my brain for another lie. "It was the stars . . . all the stars in the sky you showed me." I hoped the mention of heavenly orbs might soften his mood.

"I suppose you rode off in a chariot with Orion."

"No, just watching how the stars hang low in our sky. Like you showed me . . ."

"Yeah," he said, "and your Grandma Ru is the ambassador to Madagascar."

I was running out of excuses. I had to get out of this. "Grandma," I called, "I have some glue for you." I pulled a small bottle of Elmer's from my desk and, leaving my father, ran down to her. When I placed the glue on the scrapbook in her lap, she clasped my hands tightly. Looking up at me with green eyes that had become milky in her anguish, she droned like a priest, "Thank you, my child. You shall live a long and prosperous life."

When at last I fell asleep, it was nearly dawn. The next morning both my father and I overslept. When the angle of the sun finally roused me, I ran into his room to wake him. I had already missed an hour of school, and my father's high-iron project was progressing without him. We both rushed through our Cheerios and grabbed our coats. As we flew out the door, I plucked some change from the china shoe on the mantel so I could buy more glue for Grandma.

11

Ralph Bentley and Casey Lark were my trusty buddies. Ralph was eleven, like me. With all his extra weight, you'd expect him to waddle and stumble around. But Ralph had the grace of a gazelle. When he moved, he appeared to drift as if gravity did not affect him. Ralph's smooth porcelain skin gave him the look of a round china doll. He had butter-colored hair, turquoise marble eyes, and puffy pink lips that always puckered in a smile. He even grinned in his sleep. I know this because once when I stayed overnight at his house, I waited until he fell asleep. Then I turned on the night light and beheld his smiling face.

Ralph collected stamps and dead bugs. Sometimes he found the insects already dead. But mostly he captured them alive, stuck straight pins through their bodies, and, with an eye dropper, doused them with alcohol. Ralph enjoyed watching the droplets plunge upon their tiny heads. He sorted the bugs by species into jars, which he lined up on a shelf in his room. He had one mayonnaise jar filled to the brim with dead flies. For the more exotic species—like June bugs and dragon-flies—he glued them to his shelves and furniture. Above his bed, a swarm of dead butterflies drifted in the air, suspended from transparent fishing line. His mother, being an immaculate housekeeper, insisted that Ralph dust his butterflies every other month.

Casey Lark was thirteen years old, a whole two years older than Ralph and me, and he often reminded us that being older meant he knew things we could not yet understand. He reveled in making Ralph mad by finding rare butterflies and cutting off their wings with his Swiss army knife.

I had known Casey for as long as I lived in Willow Junction because his father, Eddie Lark, worked with my dad on the high iron. Casey was an only child like me. Sometimes my father, Grandma Ru, and I went to Casey's house for dinner.

Ralph, Casey, and I were a trio. Not a weekend went by that we weren't up to our shenanigans.

᪣   ᪣

And so it was that Saturday in October, I rode my bike to Ralph's big yellow house, where I found the family in a bustling frenzy. Ralph's family was like the ones on TV—always in a tizzy about something.

On this day, everyone was preparing for a formal gala to be held the next evening. "Autumn Equinox Revival," they called it, even though the equinox had passed nearly two weeks ago. Ralph's meticulous mother demanded that everything be just so. She proficiently managed all the tasks of party preparation. Scrubbing the thimble collection with a toothbrush. Running dust mops along the ceiling to whisk away any cobwebs that might have settled there. And cleaning the antique wine glasses, which never got dusty anyway because they were hermetically sealed in a china cabinet. And, of course, Ralph had to dust his butterflies.

Fortunately Ralph's mother had four equally meticulous daughters whom she could count on to assist in the preparations for the big event. All four daughters were delightfully lovely in a skinny, awkward, teenage sort of way. None of them had Ralph's gracefulness, but they all had long blond hair and eyes like the blue light of flame. Acquaintances could tell them apart only by their variations in height. When they lined up next to each other, as they had done for the family portrait hanging next to the china cabinet, the four daughters, with their long hair and gawking gazes, looked like a family of afghan hounds, arranged in ascending size.

The daughters had been destined for consistency since birth. Their mother gave them all names that began with "C" and ended optimistically with an "i"—Christi, Carri, Cathi, and Connie. Connie was the one exception since her name ended in "ie." She claimed this distinction as the signature of her individuality. They all signed their names by dotting the "i"—not with a plain poke of a pencil, but with a cute little open circle.

When I entered the open front door, Ralph's mother greeted me promptly with instructions about walking *around* the carpet, stepping *only* on the floor since the carpet had been professionally cleaned that very morning. "And don't sit on any furniture," she warned, "especially with those clothes you're wearing. Connie spent all morning cleaning the furniture with special upholstery solution."

"But Mrs. Bentley, aren't you having your party out back on the terrace like always?" I asked.

"Well," she explained, "you never know. Someone might wander in."

Carri rolled her eyes while she continued dusting the picture frames.

"Okay, all boys outta this house, now!" I was the only boy around, so I left.

"Ralphie's in the cellar," Carri called out the door.

At the Bentleys', women ruled the house. On this day, Ralph's father had been relegated to the backyard where he balanced on a ladder, silently stringing colored lantern lights amid the treetops. Like a spider, he wove his web of lights from branch to branch, moving around in circles with no one to help him. And worse than his father, Ralph had been banished to the basement with no tasks at all during this crucial time of preparation. Because, as his mother said, "Ralph is too pleasantly plump to balance on ladders."

I found the back entrance to the basement. Ralph was huddled over his father's workbench immersed in a project. The sun poured in the window, bathing Ralph's round body and blond hair in a patina of yellow light.

He was surrounded with blue china bowls—one filled with walnuts and another with open walnut shells. I figured he was lunching on these goodies, until I looked further. A third bowl brimmed with kidney beans. A large bottle of Elmer's glue sat off to the side of a humming jigsaw where Ralph carefully pressed the nuts against the whizzing blade, sliced them open, extracted the meat, and set the empty shells aside.

"Hey, Ralph," I greeted him, "the squirrels will appreciate your opening all their walnuts for them."

"No way," replied Ralph, "I'm not in the nutcracking business here. This is a secret operation. I'm here on official party business. They're all upstairs cleaning a house that nobody will see anyway, and I'm down here preparing high-priority food."

Seems I often found Ralph in the basement working on something or another. Overwhelmed by his sisters, ignored by his father, and frequently exiled to the basement by his mother, Ralph survived boredom by making his own projects. So today, Ralph described his self-assigned task for the afternoon. "See, Josey, I slice all these walnuts here, exactly on the seam. It's got to be precise or the mission flops." Ralph demonstrated as he talked. "Then I extract the meat of the nut very carefully so as not to crack the shell. And finally I insert three kidney beans and glue the shell back together again."

"Why are you doing this, Ralph?"

"Hey, don't you get it? Tomorrow I put all these nuts in the silver serving bowl along with the nut cracker. Then we get to watch people open walnuts and find kidney beans inside. Isn't that a gas?"

"Ralph, you got weird growing up with all those sisters."

"Then," continued Ralph, "I stuff another batch with flour so that when people open those nuts, white dust explodes all over their clothes. And in the third batch I add honey. Won't that be cool when the goop dribbles all over some lady's evening gown?"

"Sounds like cheap thrills to me, Ralph."

"It's not *all* cheap thrills. Over here are the winning nuggets. Inside these shells, I put the best specimens from my sisters' jewelry collections. This one has Christi's silver poodle pin with the rhinestone eyes. This one has Cathi's necklace with the gold nugget. And this one—"

"What's the rotten banana for?"

"I'll chop up some nuts and mix them with squished banana. Whoever opens that one will think it's completely rancid."

"Uh-huh, looks like serious stuff."

"Here's the best part. For this bunch, I'm going to leave the nuts in and add some of these ugly little bugs." Ralph pulled down three jars from the shelf containing various live insects including five fat spiders, an earthworm, and dozens of black ants.

"What if the bugs die before anybody opens them?"

"All the grosser," said Ralph. "Anyway, I'm in this for the long haul. Next time I plan to take up Casey's suggestion. He said he'll show me how to mix food with large doses of Ex-Lax and give everybody diarrhea."

"Say, Ralph, how about if I help you finish this nut job, then you can come with me to Casey's."

Ralph unscrewed the top of the Elmer's and instructed me on the fine art of gluing walnut shells together. We opened and closed every nut in the lot, carefully inserting various configurations of food, jewelry, and insects. Then we ate the leftover walnuts.

      ☙ ☙

Ralph and I departed the big yellow house, leaving the party preparations to the women. We pedaled our bikes down the highway, clouds gathering along one side of the sky, our clothes flapping like sails in the wind, and our stomachs stuffed with walnuts.

The road to Casey's house was like the road to home. I had practically lived there over the past few years. The Larks were the closest thing to family I had. Ralph and I wheeled full blast along the country road dividing two counties, then turned off onto a dirt lane, which curved through the woods and descended into the moist coolness of a small glen. Rounding the last curve, leaning into the wind, we hit the grumbling gravel of Casey's driveway.

Unlike Ralph's sunny residence, Casey Lark's log cabin was nestled in the shade of stately pine trees so huge they dwarfed all else, making his home look more like a rustic playhouse. Thirteen years ago, Eddie Lark had built the log house himself while his wife, Abigail, remained in town with their infant son, Casey.

For years now, I had romped the grounds of Casey's pine forest. In the fall, pine cones crashed upon the rooftop, thundered down the incline, and accumulated in layers so deep that Casey and I often pushed pathways through the endless sea of pine cones, exposing the soft brown pine needles on the ground underneath where we ran for hours along our winding trails.

Even at the height of noon on sunny days, only the most willful light pierced through the thick layers of pine branches that swept above Casey's house. Twilight prevailed all day long as old lamps burned inside to illuminate the rooms.

Just like the outside, everything inside the house was naturally colored. The walls were built of logs. Tables, chairs, and odd-shaped footstools were hand-hewn from exotic wood that came all the way from Africa with swirling grains of rose, green, and indigo. Brass and wooden lamp bases twisted their way through the musty air as if they had grown right out of the tabletops during the rainy season.

The light from these lamps fell like soft rainbows around the room. On rainy days when Casey and I played Monopoly on the Oriental carpet in the living room, we had to move close to the hearth by the firelight to read the rents for the properties around the board.

Then there were the family pets—two lethargic bulldogs, Homer and Hector, who perpetually wandered through the house drooling from their jowls. Homer was the worst. Seems his head was simply too heavy to lug around. Sometimes he'd pause next to a table, put his head on top of a pile of magazines, and leave it there for a while. Abigail kept a box of Kleenex in the living room in a wooden tissue box, so people could wipe away the saliva when Homer deposited his heavy head on the lap of an unsuspecting guest. When the two bulldogs were not drooling and pacing about, they lay next to each other in the middle of the living room rug, exchanging long exasperating sighs.

Over the years, Abigail had become so attached to the family's previous pets that when they died, she had several stuffed by a taxidermist so she could place the animals in their favorite places around the house. Lying beside the fireplace was a cocoa-brown standard poodle and, next to her, an old Irish setter, graying through the ears. Nailed to the window sills, staring at the bird feeder, were two Siamese cats, one with a short tail that had been severed by a lawn mower when it was young. New guests often did not realize these pets were stuffed until they wandered over and gave them a pat on their cold hard noggins.

Whenever our family came to Casey's house for dinner, Grandma Ru wandered around the living room with a box of dog cookies. She'd place them gently in the live bulldogs' mouths and pat their soggy noses. Then she'd mosey over to the other stuffed pets and place cookies in their mouths, too, patting their dry dusty noses, waiting for them to swallow. Homer and Hector never snatched up the uneaten cookies, as if they respected the spirits of these long dead pets.

And there was Casey's Aunt Kitty. Actually, she was Casey's father's aunt, so that made her Casey's great-aunt. In her later years she lived in silence, sitting by the fire, but it wasn't always so. When I first began visiting Casey, Aunt Kitty was a spry character. She tottered around the house, dusting the knickknacks. In the spring, she chased dandelion seeds through the field across the road, capturing them and stuffing them in her pockets to prevent the fluffy white puffs from taking seed near the house.

Aunt Kitty's real passion was betting on the horses. Every chance she got, she'd drag the whole family to the racetrack. She'd bet on every race. She won plenty of money, but lost even more. And she knew how to bet in the rain. She had learned which horses could run in the mud. "Bet on number seven," she'd say. "That one's a real mudder." On the last race, she always bet the trifecta. She picked long shots to win, place, and show. She said someday, when at last she won the trifecta, Eddie could retire, Abigail could have a maid, and Casey could go to college. Then she wouldn't have to bet on horses anymore.

When Aunt Kitty couldn't attend the races, she'd sweet-talk Abigail into driving her into town to visit the Irish bookie who worked out of the back room at Kelly's Happy Tap. When Eddie Lark found a bunch of Aunt Kitty's losing tickets around the house, he'd holler, "Whoa, Aunt Kitty, what in thunderation are you doing here? Half your Social Security goes to them goddamn horses."

"Don't you complain, buster," she'd say. "One of these days I'm gonna win the big one."

Aunt Kitty read books and traveled whenever she could. But more than anything, she was a chatterbox. She'd wag her tongue about any darned thing. She'd start jabbering about peat moss, for instance, and she wouldn't quit until she told us everything there was to know about the stuff. She'd prattle on about the different textures of peat moss, the various ways you can apply it, and all the people she knew who had used peat moss as well as the tragedies that befell them around the time of their peat moss applications. Maybe that was Aunt Kitty's burden— to remember everything anyone ever told her and to carry it around in her head.

But one night, things changed. Sometime after dinner, Aunt Kitty wrapped a blanket around her shoulders and headed for the door.

"Aunt Kitty," called Eddie, "where the devil are you going this time of night?"

"I'm off to see the moon."

Casey and I followed her out. Eddie suspected she might be heading for the racetrack. "Casey, don't let her out of your sight," warned Eddie. "And if she heads for the road, get your tail back here and let me know."

But Aunt Kitty wandered around back of the house, through the forest of pine trees, all the way to the meadow on the far ridge. As Casey and I trekked along behind her, she babbled on about all the things in the world that are influenced by the moon. She said the moon lifts ocean water up so far that it overflows upon the beaches, carries in turtles filled with eggs, and displaces low-lying clouds. She talked about how the full moon affects the heartbeats in babies, stirs the blood of lovers, and determines the way bread rises.

When the three of us arrived at the edge of the pine forest, we found the meadow ablaze in the light of the full moon. Near the ridge, Aunt Kitty spread her blanket, and we lay there in the meadow grass and looked at the sky. Stars foamed along the horizon. High above, the moon flared like a huge spotlight coming toward us, so bright that it overpowered most all the higher constellations. We watched for a while, talking above the crickets and the lone call of a whippoorwill. Then, in the magic of midnight, we were stilled to silence as we gazed in wonder at what Casey and I had never seen before.

Something began slowly to eat away at the perfect full circle of the moon. It began in the corner, first as a slight curve of deep shade. Then a darker predator slowly munched its way into the milky orb, devouring it before our eyes. In time, the moon was gone, entirely chomped away, leaving only a dark copper plate, barely visible as a faint hint of where the full moon had been.

"What happened, Aunt Kitty?" Casey asked. "Where did the moon go?"

"Do you want it back?" she asked, telling us nothing of lunar eclipses and the alignment of heavenly bodies that had made all this happen.

Looking around at the dark lonely meadow, Casey and I agreed. "Yes, yes, we want the moon back!"

"Then watch closely," she whispered.

We gazed at the copper plate until a faint glow emerged along the edge and spread like the dawn. We beheld the moon until hours past midnight as it magically swelled, renewing itself before our eyes. When the moon was completely full again in all its glory, Aunt Kitty looked up, put her hands on her hips, and said, "Now ain't that the berries."

That was the last thing Aunt Kitty said for the rest of her life. After that, she spent the days sitting in her chair staring earnestly into the air. I knew she saw something there because her eyes shifted and focused, as if she were following the trails of some kind of shapes—maybe round balls of vapor, visible only to her as they bobbed, drifted, and crashed into each other in the enchanting arena surrounding her.

She even lost interest in the horses. But Abigail, respecting tradition, drove into town once a week to see the bookie. She put five dollars on the trifecta, always selecting three long shots to win, place, and show. She tried using the same logic Aunt Kitty did when she had made her choices.

The year before Aunt Kitty stopped talking, Eddie Lark brought home a pet boa constrictor for the family. He was nine feet long, and they named him Benny. He had a strong triangular head and velvet skin with beautiful patterns of reddish brown and gold, deepening to maroon toward the tail. And his belly was the color of caramel. Abigail said he was handsome.

Since everyone in the family adored the snake, especially Abigail, Benny was allowed to roam the house, slither upon the furniture, and drape himself wherever he pleased. He was not content to seek the solitude of lonely corners, but instead he lounged about with the family, sometimes sprawling himself upon three laps at a time, or simply hanging from the tree limbs that Eddie had nailed to the walls and ceilings around the house. At night, Benny festooned the upper crosspieces of Eddie and Abigail's canopy bed with his body. Then when the alarm clock rang in the morning, he wound down the bed post, slithered across the bedroom floor, crawled up a tree limb in the bathroom, and draped himself along the reinforced shower curtain rod while Abigail bathed. Nothing pleased Benny more than to wallow in the steam that ascended from Abigail's hot bubble baths.

When Aunt Kitty could still speak, she and Benny shared a mutual understanding. Aunt Kitty was often chilly. The air could be ninety degrees with drenching humidity, and Aunt Kitty would say, "I feel like ice cubes are rattling down my spine." Yet her skin, when you touched it, felt in fever. To fight her perpetual chill, she wrapped layers of crocheted shawls around her shoulders and sat near the fire. Benny likewise wallowed in warmth and sought places with as much heat as possible. So Benny enjoyed draping himself around Aunt Kitty's warm shoulders during the evening news. She often patted Benny on the head during commercials.

Now with Aunt Kitty having sought refuge in silence, the family was unsure if she still felt the same about Benny's company.

"Maybe Aunt Kitty has had a change of heart. What if she fears Benny now?" guests would ask with genuine concern as they watched the snake curl around her shoulders.

"People don't change," Eddie would say, "they only drift a little."

"And who could be afraid of Benny," sighed Abigail. "He's such a dear sweet soul."

On that afternoon when Ralph and I arrived, Casey was playing cards on the floor of his bedroom while Benny lay sprawled on

Casey's desk, his scaly head snuggling with the debris of the open desk drawer. Ralph and I entered and stood beneath Casey's ceiling of tiny stars that he had painted upon a field of midnight blue. The stars glowed in the dark. Casey knew all the constellations and could point them out on his ceiling.

"Hey," said Ralph, "what are you doing, playing strip poker with your snake again?"

"Greetings, comrades," said Casey, his voice beginning to change. He still spoke in soprano, but sometimes his voice cracked into a deeper timbre.

Outside, the clouds that had been gathering earlier as we rode to Casey's house suddenly opened into a thunder shower. But at Casey's house, we never felt hard rain. By the time the downpour fell through the layers of tree branches, the water lost its vigor and simply dribbled off the pine needles onto the rooftop of Casey's log home. I told myself again and again that the lightning could not find its way through all those trees.

Ralph's sisters had taught us two techniques for getting through rainy afternoons. One was Monopoly and the other was a game called triple solitaire (or quadruple or quintuple solitaire, depending on how many people played the game).

Casey pulled two more decks of cards from the drawer where Benny's head lay for his afternoon snooze. He also grabbed some corn chips and Snickers bars from a food stash on the top shelf of his closet. We each took a deck, sat in a circle, and laid out our hands. When Casey said "Go!," we shifted cards around and raced to stack them in the center of our circle upon piles beginning with aces and rising all the way to kings. The first person to get rid of all his cards won.

Distracted by the distant thunder, I couldn't move as quickly as Casey. And Ralph was playing with only one hand because he used the other to stuff corn chips in his mouth. As we grabbed and tossed cards about, Benny awoke from his siesta to find he wasn't getting enough attention. So he slithered down from Casey's desk, onto the bed, and along the floor where his probing head entered the circle of our game.

"Let him be," said Casey, "he won't bother anything."

Casey was right. Benny could cut trails around filled wine glasses on a white table cloth without disrupting a thing. In his delicate way, he wound his long body through our cards, respectfully confining his trail to the space between the piles.

"Yessiree," said Ralph, stuffing more food into his mouth as we continued playing, "there ain't nothing weirder than watching Benny the Boa eat lunch—swallowing baby chickens, feathers and all."

"Oh, yeah?" gruffed Casey. "There's definitely something weirder than Benny."

"What's weirder than your creepy-crawling nine-foot snake?" I asked, tossing in the six, seven, and eight of hearts.

"The Ghost of Gypsy Lane."

My heart winced. "Casey," I sighed, hoping to divert him from the subject. "You've been talking about ghosts for years now. I live near Gypsy Lane, and I never saw any ghost. Something just spooked you out there."

"Nope," said Casey with authority, "it's as real as you and me. And it's a girl ghost, you know. She's never been seen in the light of day."

"How do you know it's a girl?" asked Ralph.

"Hey, I know a girl when I see one, and this one's a full-grown, full-blooded, female ghost."

"Ghosts don't have blood," said Ralph.

"Reckon you're right about that. You can see straight through this ghost. She walks around in a mist."

"You're goofy, Casey," I said. "Next thing you know, you'll be seeing Indians like my Grandma Ru."

"When the rain stops," said Ralph, "we'll go there and check it out."

"Naw, not now," said Casey. "She only roams at night. We'll go after dark."

"No!" I demanded. "Leave her alone."

"Who are you to protect a spook?" asked Casey.

"He's scared," taunted Ralph. "Josey Rose, scared of a little ghost—a girl ghost, no less."

I wanted to keep the secret from my friends, but how far could I go? Admitting false fear was a steep fare. They already called me scaredy-cat.

"Yeah, Josey," pressed Ralph, "are you chicken? Let's go tonight."

I figured if I didn't go, Casey wouldn't either, so I tried another angle. "I'm not messing with any ghost," I said with all the conviction I could muster. "Least of all the ones in my neck of the woods. I never saw one, but I hear there's no end to their torments. They string you by your toes, drill holes in your head, and suck out your brain."

"Eww," gasped Ralph, "what do they do with the brains?"

"They eat your memories when they get tired of their own."

After five more games of triple solitaire, three bags of corn chips, several candy bars, and some cherry Pez that I had in my pocket, Ralph suggested we play Crazy Eights.

"That's a kid's game," said Casey as his voice cracked again.

"Oh, yeah?" Ralph shot back. "You think you're such a grown-up hot shot, just because you're thirteen years old. If you keep aging the way you think you are, by the time you're twenty, you'll be bald as a grapefruit, sitting in a rocker with Benny wrapped around your shriveled-up body."

"Hey, you want to play cards?" asked Casey. "I've got some *real* cards for you." Casey reached under his bed to a place I never saw him keep cards before. He jumped up, shut his bedroom door, and returned with a full deck. He spread out the cards across the circle in front of us. The numbered sides were up, and they looked like regular cards to me.

Then he said, "Check this out, guys," as he slipped two fingers under the cards at one end and lifted them up, causing the whole lot to turn over like dominoes and revealing the other side of the entire deck.

There before our eyes lay a long line of black-and-white photographs on the backs of the cards. They were all photos of women without any clothes on. Some of the women were touching their breasts, while others leaned back in odd poses. And all their faces were filled with strange looks as if they really enjoyed themselves, but their mouths hung agape, and they seemed to be gasping for air.

"What are they doing?" I asked, totally astonished.

"Having sex," said Casey.

"What kind of sex is that?"

"Hey, chowder head," said Casey, "this is fucking sex, you know like making babies."

"I know how that happens," said Ralph, "and it's got nothing to do with these pictures."

"Okay, numskull, how does it happen?" asked Casey, as if he knew something we didn't.

Ralph explained, "Jerry Sander's older brother—he's fourteen—told me that when a man kisses a woman, sometimes sparks fly out of the man's head and arc across to the woman, and that makes her pregnant."

"Oh, yeah?" rebutted Casey. "Well, Jerry Sander's brother is a fart blossom."

"Well, then, if you're so smart, Casey Lark, why don't you tell us how it happens," I suggested.

❧

"Like this," he said, spreading out the cards even farther. "It happens like this . . ." He lifted one card from the line and threw it on top of the pile. It was a picture of not only a woman with no clothes on, but also a guy, and he was crawling on top of her.

I looked through the cards with all the naked bodies. My eyes devoured the extraordinary pictures. Then it hit me: Was this what my father had done to Lily that night in the chapel? My hands ached as if someone was dragging my fingernails along an endless chalkboard.

"Hah!" said Casey. "Got ya speechless, huh?"

Suddenly we heard footsteps coming up the stairs. It was Abigail. Casey grabbed the cards and threw them under the bed. He sat on a couple cards that didn't make it. Ralph and I scrambled to lay out another deck like we were in the middle of a game of Crazy Eights.

The bedroom door flew open, and Abigail sauntered in, wrapped in a light blue bath towel, her sun-streaked hair piled loosely on her head. She cooed lazily, "Benny, darling, it's time to take a bath. Come along, and let's soak up some steam."

Benny slithered off to take his place on the shower curtain rod. Abigail probably wouldn't have noticed anything at all if Casey hadn't slammed his hand on another card that hadn't quite made it under his rump.

"What was that?" inquired Abigail, who was no dodo when it came to childhood shenanigans.

"Pinochle," said Casey. "I'm teaching the boys the proper rules of pinochle."

"Pinochle, my foot," said Abigail. "Let me see that card."

Casey was a tough fellow, until it came to his mother. Abigail had total command over him. In one swoop, she grabbed Casey by the right arm, pulled him forward until he came clear off the floor, and picked up the card with her other hand. Then she examined the picture of a man descending with vigor upon a woman who had her legs spread-eagled.

"Pinochle, eh?" muttered Abigail. "I suppose this is a meld between the queen of spades and the jack of diamonds."

Casey's face turned beet red.

"Where is the rest of this fine art collection?" she addressed us all.

"Oh, that's it, Mom. That's all we got for now," said Casey, his voice wavering.

"Don't lie to me, Casey Lark—I'm your mother, remember?" She yanked his mattress clear off the bed, revealing three *Playboy* magazines, which Casey told us later had similar pictures of women and which he had found under his father's mattress earlier that week. Then, through the bedsprings, Abigail saw the other cards strewn across the floor.

"Pick up each and every card right now," she commanded. Then turning her head toward the doorway, she called to the snake, who lay coiled in a mound at the entrance to the bathroom, "Benny babe, I'll be there in a minute. Yes, my sweet serpent, the steam is rising . . ."

As Casey gathered the cards into a neat pile, Abigail admonished him in a low composed voice. "Casey, your friends are only eleven years old. How dare you expose their tender, innocent minds to such disgusting smut."

"But Mom," protested Casey, "see those magazines there? I found them under Dad's side of the bed. Do you yell at him for reading smut, too?"

Patiently, she explained, "When you're thirteen years old, this is smut. When you're thirty, it's entertainment.

"And Josey," she continued, "what do you think your papa Willie would say about this?"

"Oh, he'd be mad as birds, Mrs. Lark. Please don't tell him."

Abigail Lark talked hard, but she was really a soft touch. I could tell by the way she deepened her voice on purpose. She probably felt what had occurred here was nothing to be overly concerned about. It was just one of those "boys will be boys" things.

12

Weeks had gone by, and I hadn't seen Lily, although I thought about her all the time. Today I would go to see her. It was a gloomy Saturday with thick clouds trudging in columns across the sky, but the forecast promised clearing. I hoped the afternoon would be warm and that Lily and I could walk in the forest—or maybe Casey was right about her only roaming at night.

"I'm off to see Ralph!" I yelled to my father as I pulled my bike from the shed.

"What about your grandmother's lunch?" my father called back.

"We ate. Grandma wants to clean the refrigerator before the Indians come."

As I pedaled down our road, the fender on my bike made such a racket that all the birds flew away long before I reached their part of the road. Furthermore, I had grown so much my knees clunked against the handlebars.

So far, I hadn't told a soul about my visits to the chapel. Casey thought Lily was a ghost. So no one knew, and I intended to keep it that way. Lily was my secret, as I was her protector.

I wheeled onto Lily's lane, and farther along I hid my bike well off the road in the grass. I kept my head low as I ran through the meadow. It was well after lunch, and I hoped she was not out wandering. Butterflies flocked in my stomach as I knocked on the huge chapel door.

All was silent so I knocked again, a bit louder. No answer. I retreated back down the steps, and then I heard the door creak.

"Oh," she breathed as if she had just seen a mouse.

I turned around and looked up. Even through the narrow crack in the door, I could see she looked different than before. She wore a white robe and perhaps nothing else. Her hair fell tangled, and her voice crooned deep and drowsy.

"Lil-ly," I stammered, "did I scare you?"

"A little," she whispered.

"Like when someone says 'Boo'?"

She held the door open only a crack.

"Lily, I came to visit. I was wondering if . . . I was wondering . . ."

"Come in, it's okay . . . Boo," she said as she walked away. The door was still ajar so I opened it wider and slid in.

"Please close the door," she called nervously. "It's so bright out there."

"Yes, yes." I shut the door and hooked the huge iron latch. "But Lily, actually it's quite a dreary day. It's not at all bright, you know."

"Far too dazzling for me," she said, rubbing her eyes.

"Did I wake you?"

"Indeed, but I'm glad you did."

"Do you always sleep this late? I mean it's afternoon by now."

"Yes, well . . . ," she said, lifting a bucket of water onto the old wood stove, "I suppose I have a different sort of schedule."

She opened a small door in front of the stove and filled it with kindling. Coals already burned within. Then she picked up two more buckets and slid them on the stove as well. I wondered if she was preparing her breakfast—perhaps a very large amount of oatmeal. When she lifted the fourth bucket, it did not quite make it. She let go of the handle and it tumbled to the floor, spilling water across the kitchen.

"Oh, well," she sighed. "I'll have to take a short bath today."

"Where's the water, Lily? I'll get some."

"Nooo, maybe later."

"I remember—the well, right? I saw a wishing well out back. Is that where your water comes from?"

"Mm-hmmm."

"Be right back."

As I scooted out the back way, Lily called, "Don't open the door too wide."

The rigging on the well looked complicated, but I was determined to figure it out. To let the bucket down, I simply wound the arm backwards until it hit the water and sank. The problem was getting the bucket back up. The handle would not turn the other way. I tugged as hard as I could, but nothing budged. I needed some help after all.

"Lily," I called through the door, "I think the bucket is stuck. Can you show me how to wind it up?"

"Not now, Boo."

When I opened the door to come in, she jumped back and turned away from the light.

"Are you okay?" I asked.

"Close the door!" she gasped with her hands over her face.

"I'm sorry," I said humbly, latching the door, confused by her reaction.

"Here," she said trembling, "we can use some cooking water." She emptied a huge pitcher into another bucket.

I lifted the water on the stove while she put more kindling in the already roaring blaze. Then I sat down on a wooden stool by the stove so I wouldn't botch up anything more. Lily came toward me slowly, tentatively. She kneeled down and looked at me with her sleepy eyes. She reached for me, putting her hand on my cheek. Her touch riled up the butterflies in my stomach again and stole away my voice. She gazed at me for a while, and I felt a little scared.

"Who are you?" she finally asked.

"I'm from down the road."

"What's your name?"

If I told her, she'd realize I was the son of Willie Rose—the man who hurt her, the man whose footsteps I would never follow. "Call me Boo," I said, "like you did before. I like that name."

"Well," she whispered, "would you like some orange juice, Boo?"

I nodded. She stood up, sliding her hand from my cheek. I felt a tingling ache where her warm fingers had been. Such a strange sensation that I leaned over near the silver part of the stove and checked my reflection.

Lily cut three oranges and turned them back and forth upon a pale green glass dish with a knob in the center. She poured the squeezed juice into a heavy glass and put it in my hands. Then she carried the buckets of steaming water to the window and set them next to a small, old-fashioned bathtub with lion-claw feet. She opened several bottles of powders and potions and poured them into the tub. When she dumped in the buckets of water, a hazy mist swirled in the air. The aroma of lilac and jasmine filled the room, making me pleasantly dizzy.

Lily stirred her bath with a wooden paddle. Then she untied her robe and let it fall to the floor. As she prepared to step in, her curving body melded with the mist. That's when the heavy glass of orange juice fell from my hands and crashed to the floor.

"Oops, are you okay?" she asked as she tested the water with her hand.

"Oh, f-fine," I stammered. "It's only that I never saw . . . I mean people usually don't . . . you know, take off their clothes like that in front of people. I mean we're almost strangers, you know."

"Oh, sorry," she said, without a hint of shame. "I'm not used to these things."

"What things?" I asked.

"You know, having visitors. Next time I'll warn you so you can avert your eyes."

As I watched her slip into the mass of blue bubbles, I was sorry I ever mentioned it. Looking at her, I could feel tiny rivers forming all around inside my body. My only other view of a nude woman had been from Casey's cards. Lily was different, more pale and delicate. But despite her slender frame, her breasts were full mounds of soft pink. When she eased into the water, I said, "It's okay, Lily. You don't have to warn me. I can get used to it."

"Okay, Boo . . . ," she hummed as she lay back her head and drifted off to a place that did not include me.

While Lily bathed and dreamed, I indulged in what surely must have been forbidden territory for my eyes, although I wanted to give her the privacy that she deserved but didn't seem to desire. She squeezed a fat sponge and let water drain down her luscious terrain. I was mesmerized until, suddenly, shame overwhelmed me. I tore my eyes aside, sought the far end of the room, and watched the stained-glass windows come alive as the clouds dissolved and let the sun pour through. From the flowing, pale golden skirts of an angel, a beam of light cut through the glass, sliced through the air as a gilded ray, and fell as an oval upon a table illuminating the puzzle that Lily had been working on before.

After a while, Lily rose from the bath like a moist nymph, her skin flushed from the heat. She dried herself without telling me to avert my eyes. She went into an alcove and put on a smock made of layers of chiffon, this one in shades of sea blue and pale green, tied again with a golden cord. She emerged, still in bare feet and wet hair.

"Do you want to go into the sky?" she asked.

Without asking what she was talking about, I followed her. On the far side of the chapel, she led me past alcoves bordered by walls rising only partway, like ancient ruins in foreign lands. I followed her up a narrow spiral stairway made of wrought iron, which ended at a wooden platform high above the rafters.

This perch in the sky was enclosed in a dome made of clear glass panels, mostly of large triangular shapes. The glass dome extended above the chapel roof, alongside the steeple. When we sat on the pillows there, I felt as if we had alighted in a huge nest upon the roof—a cozy world protected by glass where sun poured in on us both.

"Lily, how can you feel comfortable here in this light when you don't like the doors open?"

"We're safe, Boo. The glass protects us."

From a small wooden box, she drew out a bottle of deep purple liquid, which she poured into her hand and massaged through her hair. It smelled of roses. Then she lifted out a tortoiseshell comb and an old silver brush with beige bristles. She began drawing the comb through her wet hair. As I watched, I thought about Grandma's hair. I wondered how it would feel to run a comb through Lily's river of gold.

"Can I comb your hair?" I asked.

She continued combing, looking up into the light. She was quiet for a while, then lay the comb in my hand.

As the sun bathed us in our nest inside the sky, I combed Lily's long hair. Sudden bursts of wind sent leaves of orange and yellow spinning all around us on the other side of the dome. Sometimes a shadow drifted across, but always gave way to sunlight again. Neither of us spoke. I combed her hair for a long time—until the strands were dry and smooth as silk. Then I set down the comb and used the brush. I had to move around, across her back, and to her other side so as not to leave any areas undone. Then I moved in front and crawled upon her outstretched legs. Facing her, I said, "Now lean forward, Lily. Farther than that. I need to part your hair from the top all the way to your forehead."

"Ah," she said, "you'll never get it straight. Parting hair is too hard when you can't feel your own skin."

"Shhh, be still . . ." I whispered, with my hands on her shoulders. "When you talk, you wiggle. I can't part your hair when you wiggle."

Just like with Grandma Ru's hair, I drew the comb from the back all the way to the tip of her nose. Though I'd done these same motions a hundred times before, this felt different. Somehow Lily's golden mane evoked enchantment beyond the gentle wave-wanderings of Grandma's white cloud.

I let the comb fall away and drove my fingers into the opening of Lily's hair. Pulling the strands aside, I found her there, eyes closed like when she was in the bath. She was haunting.

"Lily, open your eyes," I whispered.

Then I waited quietly. She could take all the time she wanted to open her eyes. I felt content, sitting on her lap, watching her there with the sun bleeding through the thin chiffon, illuminating her fair skin with all its shapes and textures. Lily had her own pace. When she was ready, her eyes would open. I smoothed the side of her hair against her ears, and suddenly her eyes flashed open in a gush of lavender.

❧   ❧

After we walked downstairs, I ran to the door, flung it open, and called, "Lily, let's go into the meadow. Show me where the fungus is!"

What an idiot I was for not remembering to keep the doors closed. Light burst in, leaves spun along the floor, and chimes tingled across the ceiling.

Lily screamed and fell to the floor. I threw the door closed and latched it tight, finally realizing that open doors were most unfavorable to her. "Lily, Lily," I said, kneeling beside her. "It's okay, I'll never do it again. I promise."

She surprised me. Lily was so strange. One minute she was like some mystical angel, and the next minute she was a lost and helpless child.

"Why are you afraid of the outside?" I asked.

"Because it's too big."

"What's too big?"

"The world," she said.

Then she told me she only went out in the night because she feared the daytime. When I asked her why, she said the light overwhelmed her and made her afraid, and that she much preferred the softer glow of night where the light came only from the moon and stars.

"That sounds weird, Lily."

"Well, there are other reasons."

"What? Tell me."

She was quiet for moments, then said, "I was locked in a basement for a while."

"How long? Like for a whole day?"

❧

"No, three years."

"Who—"

"That's enough, Boo. All you need to know is that I was in the darkness so long that now I can't go into the open light."

I was stunned to silence. Finally I asked, "So you only leave here at night?"

"Yes, that's why I sleep in the day."

"How do you get your food?"

"My friend, Leon, lives nearby, in the farmhouse by the road. He brings me food and is very good to me. He's the only person besides you who is good to me."

I wondered why she didn't mention my father, and what possible connection he could have to Lily. Especially if she never went out in the open light. Despite my curiosity, I vowed never to mention my dad to her.

"Lily," I asked, trembling from my own thoughts. "Do other people come to see you?"

"No, just Leon and you and . . . that's all that matter."

Wishing I hadn't asked, I let her voice trail off to a restless silence. I looked around her place. Shells and stones lay all over the shelves, tables, and floor, while in one small alcove a marble statue of a woman carrying a jug rose up from a floor of river stones. And a small skylight of odd-shaped glass let in sun that drenched the area. Plants nestled in nooks on different levels. Vines twisted around each other and climbed the walls clear to the glass sky above.

"Lily," I said, trying to change the subject away from her fear of light and whatever darkness I had provoked, "what about these clothes you wear? Where do they come from?"

She stood and took my hand, leading me to another alcove. A side window let in golden light in a late-afternoon angle. A metal rod spanned the back wall from which hung dresses of varying lengths and shawls of veil-like fabrics. Piles of material lay next to a sewing machine.

"Curtains," she said. "I make the clothes from old curtains and other soft fabrics that I ask my friend to find for me. There's chiffon, tulle, and this one is called faille. I like the colors."

"They're mermaid colors," I said.

"Do you want to see my crystal garden?"

"Can I come back sometime? The sun is getting low, and my father . . . I mean, you know, I should go home for dinner."

She walked away quietly, lit a candle by the fireplace, sat in an over-stuffed chair by the hearth, and stared at the stone floor.

I went to her. "Can I come next Saturday?" I asked.

"Not unless you tell me your name."

"Boo. Remember?"

"Your real name." She refused to look at me.

I sat on the arm of her chair for a while. If I told her my name, she would make me leave—I'd probably never see her again. "Can I sit in your lap," I asked, "like before when I combed your hair?"

"Okay," she said, still staring at the floor.

I crawled into her lap and curled in a bed of chiffon and softness. Sitting there was like being in heaven, knowing I would get kicked out any minute. I felt her curves as I lay my head on the cushion of her breast. The fabric was thin enough there that I could feel her warm skin. She folded me into a scented embrace and entwined one hand in my hair. While she stroked my head with her fingers, I yearned to linger in her chapel forever, with her never knowing my name, and me staying with her always, perhaps not ever again seeing the light of day. But I knew I had to tell her my name, and she might ban me from there forever. Or maybe she'd understand I came to her because both of us were victims of my father's rage. With this small hope, I turned toward her. Our eyes locked, and my heart burned with sadness. "My name is Josey Rose," I said.

"My God!" she gasped, tossing me off her lap. Clenching my shoulders, her fingers trembling, she brought her eyes level with mine. "Your father doesn't know you're here, does he?"

"He doesn't know."

"Listen to me, little Josey—"

"Boo. I like that name better."

"Okay, Boo, you can never come here again. Do you understand what I'm saying?"

"I know my father doesn't want me here, but why, Lily?"

"No! I will not tell you—just listen. You cannot be here, that's all. It's for your own good."

Regrets swamped my heart, and I tried not to blink so my sadness wouldn't show.

"Good-bye, Josey Boo. Thank you for combing my hair. You made me happy today."

"Lily—"

"Go home now, quickly, or your father will come here looking for you."

She held my hand and walked me to the entranceway. Since it was dark outside, she unlatched the door and opened it wide. Air whirled around us.

"Run fast with wings on your feet. It's long past dark!"

"Lily, no—"

"Good-bye, Josey . . . good-bye." She closed the door.

I ran through the field, tears streaming down my cheeks. When far enough away, I let myself sob out loud. If I hadn't feared my father coming there to find me, I would have thrown myself into the meadow grass and stayed all night. I absolutely hated who I was. Why couldn't my name be Casey Lark, or Ralph, or anyone else? Then everything would be better. Instead I was the son of Willie Rose, nurtured on lies and raised in fear. I was living with two chattering mynah birds, a grandmother who can't live without glue, and my father—the man who abused the one person I truly adored.

And where was my mother—how could she have left me unless she had really died? I wondered if her hair was dark like mine, and her eyes lavender, too. Where were all the old photographs that other families display like trophies on gleaming shelves? Instead my family collected secrets and stowed them away in locked rose marble boxes, dusty drawers, and the hidden chambers of my father's guarded memory. The other night, he had talked about his mother and father. But I knew there was more. Endless family secrets—the mainspring of my father's rage. As for Grandma Ru, my father's madness had driven her to seek solace in the company of Indians who dwelled in her head, wove rugs in her living room, and set free huge butterflies into an atmosphere plagued with spaceships.

I wanted to see a picture of my mother. The only albums in our house were filled with magazine cuttings of thermostats and other round things. I wondered why we had no family pictures. I wanted some proof of my past, to know where I'd come from and who I was. Most of all I wanted a normal family—with a mother. I wondered what she looked like and if she was as beautiful as Lily.

13

"Now where the hell have you been?" My father was pacing across the living room with three sticks of beef jerky in his hand.

"At Ralph's," I said angrily.

"Don't lie to me, kid. I called Mrs. Bentley, and she hasn't seen hide or hair of you all day."

"Well, Ralph wasn't there so I went off on my own."

"Till nine o'clock at night?"

"There's no school tomorrow."

"Hey, squirt, I think I see a future for you in North Dakota."

"Dad, I want to see a picture of my mother."

"Don't change the subject."

"But Dad, I need to know what she looked like."

My father stopped in his tracks, then walked to his captain's chair. He sat down slowly. Lulu sang a melody I didn't recognize.

"What's gone is gone," my father said. "Why would you want to see a picture of someone who no longer exists?"

"I'm curious. Does she look like me at all?"

"No," said my father, "not a bit. Everybody says you're a spittin' image of me. Except for them spooky eyes."

"I like my eyes."

"They're beautiful eyes," he said, "but sometimes they give me the creeps, that's all."

He pulled out his wallet and opened the part with pictures and cards. He stared at the ceiling for a moment, then drew out an old photo and handed it to me.

"There she is, my Isabel Rose. But you see, it's not a picture to know her by."

"Why not?"

"There aren't any cats in it. The woman was perpetually surrounded by her friggin' cats. Everywhere you looked—silent, stuck-up, neurotic cats. Cats on the table, cats in the bed, and cats in the sinks sticking their little tongues up the spigots. That dizzy calico spread out in the silver bowl on the mantel like a bunch of wild grapes. And the Angora—that fat oaf whining on the shelf for hours until somebody opened the door to the china closet so she could sit in there and dangle her tail in the demitasse cups."

The photograph of my mother was thin and frayed. It had taken on the curve of my father's wallet. Even in the faded brown-and-white picture, I could see her thick dark hair pulled back loosely. She had rich eyebrows, high cheekbones, and a strong chin. Her eyes were steady and serious, but I could not distinguish the color. Looking at her image, I remembered my mother like a lost dream found, but only for a moment. Her memory faded, then slipped away just as she had done years ago.

"Thanks, Dad," I said, handing him back the picture.

"It's okay, kid."

"You know," I said, walking toward the stairs, "she looks different than I thought."

"Yes, she was . . . very different."

I said good night to Grandma and ambled up the stairs.

"Hey, whippersnapper," called my father, "you better sleep fast. I'm waking you early in the morning."

"For what?"

"We're going to church."

14

Church. Whispers and wiggles and coughs suppressed. Mothers pressing hankies to their little babies' noses. And a man on a cross with nails stuck through his hands. That Sunday was my first experience with church—the place that housed the mysterious rituals that Reverend Jasper had talked about on his annual visits to convince us to join his parish. Until this day, church had been a secret conclave that seemed accessible only to those who attended the gatherings. From what my friends described about the sermons, I imagined the reverend cloaked in flowing black robes, leaning from a tower high above the congregation, calling out holy phrases that his faithful followers locked away to use later in unravelling the riddles of life.

But it was all quite different. The pulpit was like a tower, yes, but closer to the people than I had imagined. As the reverend recited psalms and scriptures, I stared with curiosity at the sculpture above the altar—the man on the cross. I knew this was Jesus, but why was he hanging there? And the look on his face—even with nails piercing his hands, he seemed peaceful as if gazing upon a calm sea, but other times he looked stunned, as if he had seen a ghost. No doubt that sculpture told a solemn story, quite in contrast to the images carved across the front of the altar—a frolicking feast of twelve men with long hair and one with light radiating from his head. They were gathered at a huge table overflowing with food and wine. I knew my father would like that part.

Scrunched between my dad and Grandma Ru, I listened to Reverend Jasper speaking from a podium off to the left, reading from a thick book with gold edges, lit faintly by a small brass reading light. He read and sneezed and rambled for a long time. I was relieved when everyone suddenly stood up at once and began singing. Then came snack time. Four boys about Casey's age passed out tiny glasses of grape juice and the kind of bread cubes Abigail used to make stuffing on Thanksgiving. I would have preferred a jelly doughnut, but for the moment, the juice hit the spot. At first I thought the snacks were free, but then the same boys passed around baskets where we had to pay for the food.

Then came the scary part. Reverend Jasper walked past the altar and dragged his enormous body into the high pulpit. Leaning out toward the people, he ranted on in a loud voice, waving his arms about, and showering the first two rows with the fruits of his sneezes.

"Come hither to your hearts," he bellowed as his jowls shook like laundry in the wind. "Set aside the yearnings of your daily life—all the greed, the avarice, the envy. Turn your eyes to your own empty souls because, alas, your souls are destitute and famished as much as the stomachs of starving children. And how do you rise above this impoverished condition? There is only one way, *yes!* Your souls need . . . need . . . ah . . . ahhhh-CHOOO!"

A fountain sprayed from the reverend's mouth into the pews. A beam of morning light illuminated the tiny golden globs as they descended on a curved trajectory to the front pews, which were empty due to the congregation's years of experience.

"Your souls need . . . *appraisal,*" he continued. "They need total, objective, and honest appraisal. And the only way to truly appraise your souls is to lay before you all the sins of your daily life, every breach of contract you have made with the Lord. Reach into your hearts and tear out your misdeeds—your vices, petty crimes, and most secret offenses . . ."

Out in the pews, all squirming ceased. No one in the entire congregation moved, as if their stirrings would reveal the sum total of their own private sins and expose them in the light of day before the whole congregation.

" . . . and lay your misdeeds out like fruit upon the table. Now, my friends, remember, this is an appraisal of the self. Do not look upon others in the same light. The Bible says, 'Judge not, that ye be not judged.'"

From the base of the reverend's nose, a bead of liquid began to hover and flap about as he wagged his puffy head.

"Heed Jesus' words," he roared. "When at last you lay your sins before the Lord, you shall be free. Yes, my friends, when Jesus casts his eyes upon the sum total of your misdeeds, he will reach down from the sky in tender descent, take each and every sin in his holy hands, and wash your wrongdoings in the flowing currents of his love. He will drink your shame and quell your straying desires. Yes! Your sins are his sins. My sins are your sins . . . I mean . . ." He stumbled and corrected himself. "*Your* sins are *mine.*"

"Yes, *yes!*" Beads of sweat began to accumulate on his brow. "Embrace thy trespasses, and for the rest of time, in the hallowed halls of eternity, you shall . . . you shall . . . ahhhhh . . ."

What followed was a bodily function that resembled the stirring rumble of an outboard engine. The reverend's lips flapped together as he failed in an attempt to keep his mouth shut. Another spray of golden mist showered out in a fanned arc. From internal pressure, the liquid must have oozed up through his brain, too, because he became speechless. He tilted his head sideways and rammed it against the palm of his hand like someone trying to get water out of his ear.

We never did find out what would happen to us in "the hallowed halls of eternity." Reverend Jasper became distracted with his wheezing. In a touching finale, he gently dabbed his moist eyes with his sleeve. Then he wrapped his pink nose in a wad of tissues, raised his other wavering arm high above his head, and gasped the benediction the best he could.

After the service, we lingered on the lawn in front of the church. Autumn leaves rained down as wind danced through the trees. The white steeple gleamed like an arrow pointing straight to heaven.

In the distance, I saw Ralph floating across the lawn with his four blond sisters. Then the Larks came by to talk, but Casey wasn't there. Abigail sauntered along in a dress remarkably revealing for church. As she walked, her long legs emerged through the slits of fabric that cut clear above her knees. Her wide-brimmed bonnet threw a shadow across the cleavage she proudly displayed.

"Hello, hello," sighed Abigail. "Shall we all get together tonight and tally our sins?"

"Hah!" laughed Eddie. "I don't reckon ol' Willie can count that high."

"Abigail," said Grandma, "how are you, my dear? And how is that handsome snake of yours?"

"Well, you know . . ." Abigail breathed deeply. "He gets so restless in the autumn. If he were a woman, I'd swear he was going through the change."

"Abigail," grumbled Eddie, "if that snake were a woman, he'd have strangled the livin' daylights out of you long ago."

"Honestly, darling," she sighed, turning away, "you can be so irrational."

"Now if that ain't the pot calling the kettle—Oh, good morning, Reverend."

As Reverend Jasper greeted us, Eddie and Abigail wandered off. "So glad to see the Rose family in church today."

"Fine sermon, Reverend," said my father, politely.

"Reverend," said Grandma Ru, "I noticed you did not address the problem with the Russians."

"What problem is that?"

"About their spaceships breaking through the atmosphere carrying live dogs, innocent creatures. And now they're planning to send *people* into space, which will surely affect their genetics, and before you know it, reverse evolution will kick in, and we'll all start looking like monkeys again."

"Mom—" My father groaned as the wind caught the brim of Grandma's hat, knocking it off balance. As my father helped her fix it, the reverend leaned down to talk with me. He placed his hand gently on my cheek, making tiny circles on my skin with his pudgy finger. On the edge of a whisper, he said, "Good to see you too, little Josey. Oh, those eyes, as lovely as ever."

"Good morning to you, sir," I stammered as his fingers wandered across my cheek.

"Why don't you come by the parish sometime, and we can talk about anything you like. I always keep cookies around. You never know when—"

"Good day to you, Reverend," said my father abruptly as we turned to go.

I saw other kids from school with their families rambling about as well. Church seemed to be a regular town attraction. I wondered if all the people there planned on counting up their sins as the reverend had commanded. And my father—I was most curious about him. Why had we come here today? Perhaps he really wanted to change. Maybe he would let the Lord snatch up his terrible misdeeds. I hoped so much it was true.

On the way home, my father asked, "So what do you think, Josey boy—should we go to church again?"

"Sure, Dad."

"Well, we'll see how it goes," he said. I wondered what that meant.

"Dad," I asked, "how many times do you have to go to church to get into heaven?"

"You got me, squirt," he replied. "Reckon we'd have to hear the 'Admission to Heaven' sermon for that information."

Then my father turned to Grandma Ru. "How about you, Mother? How'd you like church?"

"I think the guy on the cross should get a haircut," she said. "He looks like a bloomin' beatnik."

15

Ah, nothing like time to dilute good intentions. And so it took only two seasons—autumn and winter—for the reverend's words to disappear from my father's heart.

Maybe I should have anticipated the madness that would happen that April night when even the brazen harvest moon had timidly surrendered its glow to a bank of incoming clouds. But unlike the moon, I was not a diviner of things to come. My father's behavior had been fairly mild all winter, perhaps having heeded Reverend Jasper's words. Not until the peril of that night shook me by the shoulders did I realize that the mending of his ways was not meant to be.

Early that evening, I was sprawled on the living room floor doing homework. All the while, Grandma Ru absorbed herself in a new scrapbook called "Rectangular Things," which contained nothing but the word "LIFE" taken from the titles of *Life* magazines she had collected from our subscription and from other people we knew. She had glued in ninety-seven pages of red rectangles with "LIFE" in white block letters. She made various designs with them—spirals, star bursts, and stairways.

My father sat at the mahogany dining room table with a new project strewn about him. A big round glass of Drambuie sat off to the side. Scented vapors rose from the dark caramel liqueur and thickened the air above it. And an aroma like honey and herbs wafted around the room, intoxicating the birds who prattled on in lazy gibberish.

Spring's warmth was whispering its way back into the air as if winter had fallen through gravity and was now chugging its way up the long ramp of springtime. As Grandma Ru once said in a rare state of coherency, "As you grow older, the seasons go faster and faster like a spinning top moving toward the edge of a table where it will fall off one day into an enchanting abyss."

My dad's project at the dining room table involved building his own rendition of the solar system inside a clear sherry bottle with a large bulbous bottom. My father, Willie Rose, creator of fine ships, was now constructing an entire region of the universe. I had watched his solar system progress for hours now, all the while Burl Ives songs played in the background.

For the sun, he used a small Christmas ornament made of translucent gold glass, less than an inch in diameter. He painted a couple of small dark swirls upon the golden sphere, which he said were raging storms on the solar surface. Sun spots, he called them. As he worked, he sang along with Burl Ives,

> Once a jolly swagman
> Sat beside the billabong
>> Under the shade of a coulibah tree
> And he sang as he sat
> And waited by the billabong
>> "You'll come a-waltzing, Matilda, with me."

When he worked closely like this, he turned his good eye toward the details of his project, while his glass eye remained off to the side, reflecting light as faithfully as the live one.

For the planets, he used various glass beads except for one he created by drawing out strands from a cotton ball and rolling them into a sphere. He said this one was Venus, the planet of love, which was covered in such thick vapors that no one had ever seen her surface. A planet of secrets, he said.

> . . . And his ghost may be heard
> as you ride beside the billabong
>> "You'll come a-waltzing, Matilda, with me."

While he painted the red spot on the bead of Jupiter, he explained how this gigantic banded planet spins so fast its day lasts less than ten hours, and that Jupiter is so buoyant that if we could ever find an ocean large enough to hold the humongous planet, it would float. For Jupiter's many moons he used tiny glass beads of purple and gray that came all the way from Germany. For Saturn's rings, my father stopped drinking for ten minutes straight while he sucked on a lime-green Life Saver. Then he removed the delicate circle from his mouth just before the breaking point and placed it around the glass bead of Saturn.

The asteroid belt was simply a band of tiny chunks of stone he had dug up from the backyard and smashed with a hammer. For all the planets and moons, he sprinkled golden glitter on the sides facing the sun. This was to show the light.

With his long silver tweezers and slender, almost invisible, wire, he assembled all these parts together, yielding a complete solar system suspended inside the galactic bulb of the glass bottle. To me, this was sheer magic.

The last thing he added was a comet made of silver and violet fibers, which he installed with its tail flaring away from the sun. As he set the comet into the bottle, I listened to the weather brewing outside. Darkness had fallen completely, and the winds swept through our valley breathing promises of rains to come.

As my father completed his creation, he chatted on about all the planets and moons. When he talked about Jupiter, I felt cold thinking of venturing into a landscape of ammonia and methane gas. Mars was more warming to my imagination, with its blue-green regions sweeping across the red rock terrain. I imagined sailing a boat along the web of canals, lying on my back, and watching the restless moon Phobos rise and fall three times a day.

But the planet that most captured my fancy was Venus. It wasn't so much the physical geography of this cloud-covered orb as it was the mythology that attended her.

"Dad, tell me more about Venus, the one with all the vapors."

"Venus is the goddess of love," said my father. "She has big bazooms, ivory skin, and she walks in the mist."

"Why does she walk in mist?"

"Because she's filled with mystery."

From his description, I formed the details of my own Venus—vague, lovely, and lusciously rounded like the women on Casey's cards. I imagined Venus taking me in her ivory arms where I would curl in her lap and lay my weary head on the clouds that shrouded her soft mysterious breasts. I blushed and wondered if my father could tell what I'd been thinking.

As my father delicately placed the wisp of a planet into its orbit among the other glass spheres, he had no idea of the delicious images he caused to bloom in me that night by simply discussing Venus, the goddess of love. Had he known, he may have chosen instead to dwell more on the details of Saturn, the Roman god of agriculture, or Mercury, who ran around delivering messages to all the other gods. Instead, he talked about Venus and gave me the touchstone for an image that I blended with Casey's stirring photographs to build a vision of my ideal woman that would haunt me and compel me for the rest of my life.

Suddenly Grandma Ru let out a whooping scream.

"Grandma, what is it?" I ran to her.

"A hundred pages!" she exclaimed. "I reached a hundred pages of rectangles! Look, Josey . . ."

She showed me the ninety-ninth page, filled with red LIFE rectangles carefully spelling out the word "IS." Then she proudly turned the page where she had glued one more LIFE title upside down in the middle of the page.

"That's great, Grandma," I said.

"That's not all. Look, I still have three more."

"Okay, but don't run out of glue."

"Oh, I know," she said, holding the bottle of Elmer's close to her heart. "I hate it when that happens."

꧁   ꧂

What is it in alcohol that can turn a gentle soul into a crazed madman? While drinking Drambuie that night, my father migrated from discussing gods and planets to a rage that would have stilled Jupiter in his tracks. I knew things were about to change when he added beer chasers to his Drambuie and began scraping through the beer bottle labels with his fingernail. I watched his thumb as it drove downward, cutting a mean trench straight through the label.

Distant lightning softened the darkness, and it began to rain. I hoped the storm would keep far away so my father wouldn't see me scared.

"Hah!" he suddenly bellowed out of the blue, "I don't take jack shit from nobody." Then he lifted up the Drambuie and guzzled it straight.

꧁

He slammed the bottle on the table, accidentally knocking over his entire collection of little glass moons. Jake and Lulu quit their yapping.

"Dad," I said, attempting to divert his gloom, "what about Neptune? Why don't you tell me about Neptune's gods? Are they Roman, too? And the moons, do they have mythology like the planets?"

"Hey, kiddo! You want to see a heavenly orb? Close your eyes and hold out your hands. I'll give you an orb like you never saw before."

Trying to keep him on this hopeful track, I shut my eyes and held out my open hands. I waited a moment as I imagined him searching the table for a special round object—the makings of another planet perhaps. I felt his heavy, moist breath upon my forehead. The honey and herbs I had enjoyed earlier now smelled like they were rotting in a bin of turpentine.

My father leaned forward and dropped something in my palm. It was a curious sensation, warm and wet, almost alive. As I folded my hand completely around the thing, afraid to open my eyes, the warm juices squished into the spaces between my fingers. The thunder caught up with the lightning in a crashing flash of brightness just as my eyelids lifted. Peering down at my trembling hands, I slid my fingers apart. To my horror, I was staring directly into the twinkling iris of my father's dark brown eye.

Trying to comprehend the warm glass object in my hand, I sat in silence looking down. When at last I faced him directly, he smirked back at me with a gaping hole where the eye in my hand used to be. The skin of his upper eyelid hung limply over the moist cavity above his cheek. His lower eyelid drooped down sadly as if death were nestled inside the hollow chamber of his eye socket. Normally the eyeball must have provided some support because without it, the left side of his face hung down slightly, creating sagging lines in his skin in places you would not expect.

"Willie, honey," said Grandma Ru, "you really should put your eye back in. Without it, you have a slightly unbalanced look. You know, like when you used to wear stripes with plaids."

Slowly, I opened my hand farther and let the eyeball fall away. The slimy goop that had covered it still oozed on my palm and between my fingers. Long filaments of wetness stretched out from my hand as the eye fell away and plunked on the floor. It rolled across the wood planks, leaving a narrow, uneven ribbon of secretion in its path. Grandma jumped up and ran after it.

Grandma, no. Not wanting her to touch the thing, I bolted across the room and retrieved it myself. It was still wet and now covered with hair and dust. I placed the eyeball on the table in front of my intoxicated father and asked with tears streaming down my checks, "Why are you doing this?"

"To make you strong, son. I'm bringing you sweet tidings from the real world, so you'll grow up tough like me. Life is full of thorns, you know." He burped Drambuie and grumbled, "You want to know how tough I really am? You ain't seen nothin' yet."

"No. I don't want to see anymore!"

"Come here," he demanded.

"I'm going to wash this stuff off my hands," I said, running toward the stairs. The wetness from the eyeball had begun to cool into a clammy goo between my fingers. My father darted across the floor and snatched my collar. He yanked me off the stairway so hard that buttons popped from my shirt and rattled across the floor. Then he threw me in the chair at the same table where we had sat happily together such a short time ago.

I stared at the gaping hole in my father's face. The air pressed in around me, making it hard to breathe. My father reached across the table with a delicate, gruesome gesture and wrapped his fingers around the stem of a brass candlestick. Then he slowly slid it along the table until it rested directly between us. When he lit the candle, the burst of flame brought life to all the debris left over from his solar system project. Beads, spiraling wire, and silver fibers twinkled in the flickering light. My legs quivered as the thunder rumbled around our home.

"I'll show you what it means to be strong," hissed my father as he pulled the candlestick closer to him.

"Stop this madness," I pleaded. "All winter you didn't get crazy like this. I thought you made some kind of bargain with the Lord. Now here you go again."

"Bargain with the Lord—hah! Jesus is short on experience. He ain't seen half of what I've been through. And his daddy, Sir God—what a yellow-belly milksop. He's got the manners of a spoiled child."

"Dad, you don't know what you're saying."

"Who ya gonna listen to, Josey boy—your wise old man, or some spook hangin' out in the clouds who ain't got the guts to show his face when the goin' gets tough? After my mother died, I didn't hear from the bastard once. How do you like them apples? Not one 'how-de-do'!"

Then my father placed his hand over the flame and held it there. "Now I'll show you endurance that demands respect."

"Grandma, make him stop," I yelled. But Grandma had sought refuge in the birds, showing them pages from her scrapbook. I was scared of my father, scared of the storm outside. I wanted to curl up in somebody's arms and keep my eyes shut tight until my father's rage passed, but that didn't seem likely to happen tonight.

I begged my father to stop as lightning flashed again and revealed the full horror of what hung in the dark recesses where his eye used to be. Maybe some kind of infection lived in there the way yellow-streaked fluids dripped down like stalactites in a cave. Fears filled my heart that maybe the gray folds of his brain were beginning to drip through the rotting skin and, if left to drain like this, would soon fill up the empty chamber of his eye and dribble down his face.

The skin on my father's hand sizzled and the aroma of burning flesh sickened the air. I felt at any moment I would either throw up or pass out.

"Stop!" I cried.

Grandma Ru sighed deep. "You know what really frustrates me," she said. "On these magazine covers, they make the photographs go over the red part of the LIFE title. Then it's not really a true rectangle—is it, Josey?"

"Don't worry about it, Grandma, it's okay," I said, shivering.

"You think so, honey? Do you think I can still put it in my rectangular collection?"

"Yes, it's okay."

"Pay attention, Josey!" my father persisted as he continued holding his hand above the candle. "I want you to see the depths of endurance. Then maybe you can try it, too. Or how about if we barbecue Lulu's little feet. Sure, we'll toast her toes and make her tough as nails. Hah! or soft as ashes if she turns out to be a sissy like you."

Blood from my father's burning flesh began to drip into the candle flame.

"No!" I screamed as I flung my hand across the table and knocked over the candlestick. It smashed into a pile of would-be planets and rolled across the mahogany table, gouging the grain on the way. The flame blinked out, and the candlestick crashed to the floor. I jumped up and ran for the stairs. My father grabbed my arm and jerked me around the room as he snapped off the lights one by one, yelling, "You little bastard, taking away my light. You like the dark, kid? I'll show you darkness!" He dragged me in the crook of his arm, shattering light-bulbs with his bare hand.

My father continued on his rampage as I screamed for him to stop. In a grand finale he swiped his already scorched palm across the last burning bulb in the living room. With every light snuffed out, he made one last-ditch effort to toughen me up. He opened the front door and threw me into the pouring rain. I landed in a puddle on the wet stones of the walkway and wondered if any bones were broken.

I was certain a bolt of lightning would come screeching from the sky and fry me to bits. I imagined hot electricity searing down my throat, leaving a trail of ashes. Veins of fire gathering in my stomach. And heat blowing into my lungs until my whole chest exploded.

I lay in the puddle, wishing I could dissolve like a sugar cube and get washed away in the rain. I was too weak to do anything but sob. Somehow, between the lightning bolts, I ran to the shed.

A last flash of lightning lit my way as I opened the shed door and found the corner where some old blankets lay next to my bike. I curled my soggy body there and listened for his footsteps, but he didn't leave the house.

16

"Have you lost your ever-lovin' mind, squirt?" a voice hollered. "Why the devil are you sleeping out here?"

My father was standing in the doorway of the shed. His body loomed as a dark silhouette against the blaze of morning light behind him. Even across the room, he towered over me as I lay huddled in the corner. "Rise and shine, little whippersnapper. You're already late for school."

Remembering last night, I wanted to hop on my bike and ride away from there forever. Maybe I could live at Casey's house, or in Lily's chapel, or somewhere even farther, at least until I found my mother. I wished I had an aunt and uncle in another state where I could go. I went inside and put on clean clothes, but I felt like a sack of straw. I sat down for breakfast. Another bowl of Cheerios.

"You're letting these thunderstorms get the best of you," said my father.

"What do you mean?"

"I mean, are you really so scared of a little lightning that you have to sleep in the shed?"

"That's not why I slept in the shed, Dad."

"Why else would you go romping through the rain to camp out all night in a roomful of hammers and pitchforks?"

"You, Dad. It's because of you."

"You're beginning to sound like a lost loon. Eat your Cheerios, Josey."

I mushed the cereal around with my spoon, then began slicing a chocolate doughnut for Jake and Lulu.

"If you keep feeding that junk to the birds, you're going to have a couple of sick pets," he said as he jammed three pieces of beef jerky into his mouth and sat down to a plate of fried Spam and hot peppers. "And no keeping the windows open after dark. Last night the squirrels got in, crawled on the dining room table, and dumped over my entire collection of planetary moons."

My face grew hot. I was mad at the world. I wanted to throw myself against my father and pound him senseless. I wanted to run upstairs and shake Grandma Ru from her sleep and yell, "Why didn't you help me last night? Were you so busy talking to the dizzy birds you couldn't stop your son from tormenting me?" And I wanted to find my mother and cry in her arms until all the tears in the world were used up.

Disgust rose up my spine and surpassed my worst anger. I realized how much my thoughts sounded like my father's actions. Calling our pets "dizzy birds" and wanting to "pound my father senseless." These were his words, his ways. The last thing I wanted was to be like my father.

But why confront him? I could tell him he drank Drambuie, dumped his moons, pulled out his glass eye, and threw me out in the storm. All that would come out of it would be another serving of Spanish rice or worse. Nothing ever changed.

I dawdled over my Cheerios in silence. Riding my bike to school, I planned what I would take with me when I ran away from home.

❧   ❧

"Casey, can I live at your house?" I asked after school at the bike rack.

"You already do—practically."

"No, I mean for good. I'm leaving home."

"You're not supposed to leave home till you're eighteen."

"And my father's not supposed to throw me out in lightning storms."

"He did that?"

"Last night. So how 'bout it? I'll pack some clothes, sneak out in the middle of the night, and bike over to your house. Then I'll throw pebbles at your window, and you can let me in."

❧

"Okay, but if you live with me, you have to help me do all the chores my mother gives me."

"Like what?"

"Like dip cotton swabs in Windex and clean the eyeballs of our stuffed pets."

"Deal," I agreed.

"Deal," he replied, and I shook hands with my new brother.

*   *

My plan was to wait until everyone fell asleep before leaving. So upon returning home I acted like everything was normal. I did my home-work, combed Grandma Ru's hair, and went upstairs. No one sus-pected a thing. Only one problem—I fell asleep before my father came to bed. But that didn't stifle my mission. At four in the morning, the mockingbirds woke me. I tossed three sets of clothes into a canvas bag—I would come back for the rest of my belongings someday when my father was at work.

Then I wrote a note and left it on the bed. When my father came to wake me in the morning, he would read,

> Dear Dad,
>
>   I really don't like getting thrown out in the lightning and all the other mean things you do. I'm going to live with a real family. Then when I'm old enough, I'll find my mother. Grandma, I'm sorry I won't be able to comb your hair. I left you all my glue.
>   Josey

In the shelter of darkness, I departed my room. The stairs creaked loudly as if protesting my untimely footsteps. I had to sneak past my snoring father, who had spent the night before drinking beer with Eddie Lark and teaching Lulu to say, "I'm a high-iron hussy." Later my father had fallen asleep on the couch, snuggling with a bottle of Johnny Walker Red. The afghan draped over his stomach, while his bare feet dangled off the end of the couch.

I walked across the living room, almost stepping in a pan of moss from my father's latest terrarium project. When I opened the refrig-erator, light shot out and lit up the back kitchen wall. I quickly un-screwed the bulb, and the world went dark again. I grabbed some leftover pizza and chugged orange juice straight from the carton.

When I turned around to slip out the back door, I knocked into a small round table holding a bunch of empty beer bottles. One bottle fell over and landed like a cherry bomb. My father's afghan flew into the air, and he chanted, "Wha—, wha—, what's that? Who's there?" I ducked under the table with all the beer bottles until I heard him lie back on the couch and grumble, "Them goddamn squirrels better not be messing with my moons again."

After some restless tossing and turning, he grew calm. Then I heard him say my mother's name. "Isabel, Isabel," he sighed. Why did he call her like that . . . as if she hung just out of reach . . . as if he could summon her in a whisper to come to his side, serve him warm tea and toast, tend to his loneliness, and heal his wretched ways? I stayed under the table, awaiting more mumbles and maybe a clue to her whereabouts. But he drifted off until the living room once again rumbled with his snoring. I rose slowly, set the fallen beer bottle back with the others, and slithered out the kitchen door. My adventure was about to begin.

The stars winked at me as I hopped on my bike and pedaled down the country road. In the quiet of the night where even the roosters still snoozed, the crooked spoke on my back wheel hammered against the fender.

I rode to Casey's house and tossed pebbles against his window. He dropped his trusty rope—our preplanned approach route—which I tied to my bag. Up went my three changes of clothes, down went the rope again, then up went me.

Aside from Abigail's cool surprise—"We don't usually see you 'round so early"—the morning went smooth as silk. Friday flew by as fast as possible for enduring school all day. I figured any moment the principal would call me from class and hand me over to my ranting father, at which point I would tear from the building, hop on my bike, and bolt down the road. But no one summoned me all day.

At last school was out, and home we rode. That night after dinner Abigail caught me alone as I passed through the living room. "Josey," she crooned, stroking Benny's velvet skin, "why don't you sit with me for a moment."

I moved Benny's tail aside and sank into the end of the couch.

"So, sweetheart," she sighed, "you've run away from home and plan to live here the rest of your life?"

"Only till I graduate, Mrs. Lark. Then I'll get my own place. That is, if it's okay with you."

"You know I love to have you around, Josey. But how do you think your Grandma Ru feels about your plan? Who's going to comb her hair, listen to her stories, and keep her in glue?"

"My father?"

"She needs you, Josey, and you might not believe this, but your daddy needs you, too. He told me. He's worried sick about you. Feels real bad."

"He sure has a funny way of showing it."

"Stay for the weekend, Josey, then it'll be time to go back home. They'll be missing you plenty by then."

Abigail's voice soothed me some—it sounded like Dad actually cared and maybe even needed me. But she also made me feel sad because, well, I had to run away from home to hear such words of affection. And even then, my own father couldn't tell me he cared—he had to get Abigail to do it. Part of me felt like sitting close beside her and lamenting just a little for having missed a mother's tenderness all those years. But Benny had already claimed her lap, and anyway Casey might come in and catch me doing a sissy thing. Her words were soft, but they did not change my plan.

"So what do you think, honey?" she asked.

"I'll never go back to my father—ever."

17

Over the years, Casey, Ralph, and I had thoroughly scouted the back woods of southern New Hampshire. The rock caves served as our forts. The stone walls of last century's property lines provided makeshift defense embankments where we huddled to reload ammunition during our ruthless imaginary wars. The sky—when we could find it through the thick canopy of trees—was our reminder that there were no limits.

We were a brave trio—Casey, Ralph, and I. Together, we faced endless peril and impromptu battles with dangerous enemies of all shapes and sizes—black bears as big as buildings, snakes that roamed in packs, and killer ants that could chew a person up, right down to his bare bones.

So you see, unlike my father's weak image of me, I really was brave. I could slaughter bears and confront the mightiest monsters.

For my first Saturday in my new home, we planned another journey into the woods. Casey, Ralph, and I pedaled down Route 11, stashed our bikes in the trees, and slid down the riverbank by the old stone bridge. The shallow river under the bridge flowed into Willow Junction at the old railroad yard, wound lazily through woods and backyards, meandered out the other side of town by Henderson's dairy, then emptied into the Merrimack River.

As we stomped through the water, we searched for amphibians and talked about fish guts. Then we hiked out past the train yard and along the tracks. We were getting hungry. That's when we saw something in the grass.

"It's an alien creature," said Ralph.

A ball of golden fluff with two button eyes and a wet black nose tottered along on a crooked trail. Tipping from side to side, it waddled over to Casey and Ralph, gave them a sniff and then hobbled my way. As I sat in the grass, it jumped on my lap and quivered nonstop while its tail wagged in delight.

"Looks like a lost pup to me," said Casey. "Whatdya say we tie him to the tracks and see if he pops back into shape after the train runs over him."

"You're a sicko, Casey Lark," I said, "and by the way, it's not a he, it's a she." I turned her upside down to prove my point. "I'm going to keep her," I said. "If she stays here, she'll get hit by a train."

"Forget it, Josey," said Casey. "Put down the pretty pup, and let's go get some grub."

"At least let's find out where she lives," said Ralph.

"Well, fuck me pink," said Casey, "we got us some real sentimentalists here."

"Eat dirt," said Ralph. That was the meanest thing Ralph knew how to say. He often told Casey to eat dirt.

We continued to trek through the woods, looking for civilization. Then we broke into a spirited trot, moving easily down the sloping grade. The puppy bobbed in my arms, her ears bouncing with my gait.

"Her name is Maggie," I said.

"She's probably already got a name," said Ralph.

"Well, then, now she has two names."

Even before reaching the bottom of the hill, we saw a small settlement of houses off to the right. We followed a creek that flowed out from the woods and wound through an open meadow. The bottom of the creek was covered with river stones that looked like gray, blue, and speckled brown bird eggs. We splashed along in the water until we reached the settlement.

When we knocked on the door of the first home, a pale man with blond hair greeted us.

"Hello, sir," I began. "We have found this puppy and are in search of her owner."

"Oh, yeah," replied the man, "them puppies come from the Mc-Nallys' house down the lane."

"Harvey!" called his wife. "Don't you go sending these sweet young boys to the McNally house. You know that woman is crazy as worms in honey. That's no place for any living soul, least of all defenseless children!"

"I reckon we can handle it, ma'am. Now where do the McNallys live?"

"Six houses down," said Harvey.

"Don't go there, kiddos," his wife cautioned. "Take the pup to the SPCA. Or leave it in the middle of the highway—it'll have a better chance of surviving. That woman is a maniac."

"Mind your own affairs, dearie," Harvey purred back.

We departed and walked in the direction the man had pointed. We decided that nobody could be as nutty as the two crackers we just talked to.

Six houses down, we opened the wobbly front gate, walked up the stone path to what appeared as a place of residence, although we weren't quite sure—it was hard to tell with all the junk lying around. What was once a front porch now held two old washing machines, a refrigerator painted pink, a rowboat, and an overstuffed couch with matching pillows. Stacked on the couch was a pile of dusty afghans. And on top of that lay a basset hound who let out a lethargic yowl that ended in a yawn. On the rickety frame of the front door hung a piece of wood with hand-painted letters in turquoise that said "Peaches and Edwin—Welcome to our Home."

A skinny man, maybe in his fifties, answered the door. He wore baggy jeans with suspenders and no shirt. A small crop of hair grew in the middle of his chest. His face was lopsided with a piece of Kleenex stuck in one nostril. "Yeahhh?" he muttered.

"Is this your puppy?" I asked.

The man made a snorting noise that caused the basset hound to roll off his pinnacle of afghans and land on the couch, launching a cloud of dust and down feathers into the air. Then the dog fell on the floor and hobbled away.

The old man sniffled and wiped his bare arm across his dripping nose. "I'm allergic to dogs," he said.

✿

"Oh, sorry, sir," I replied, backing away so the puppy wouldn't upset his sinuses any more than necessary.

"No, sonny, it ain't that dog that gets to me. It's the fourteen mutts we have inside."

Then a hefty woman, apparently Peaches, arrived at the door. "Shut up, Edwin!" she yelled as she whacked him on the head with a *Saturday Evening Post*. "Come in, sweetie pies," she said to us in exactly the mellifluous voice you would expect from a woman named Peaches.

"Oh, ma'am," I said, "we can't do that. Our feet are wet from running in the river."

"Not to worry, kids. A few squishy sneakers never hurt anybody."

Reluctantly we stepped inside, but hung close to the door in case we had to make a quick getaway.

"Are you boys hungry?" sang Peaches. "How about a little snack?"

Well, the truth was, without as much as a Necco Wafer to tide us over, we probably would have swallowed rabbit turds if someone told us they were raisins.

"No thanks, ma'am," I said.

"Oh, yes, we're famished," said Ralph.

"Indeed," said Casey, "we're as hungry as three bears from the wild yonder."

"Well, okay," I agreed.

Peaches was a plump specimen with curly red hair and a healthy mole on her cheek. She wore an old-fashioned house dress and a full apron with cooked noodles hanging from one of her pockets.

"Well, I happened to have a fresh batch of chocolate-covered noodle balls," she said. "Come on in and sit down."

"Peaches," whined Edwin. "Would you please not stand in front of the TV."

"Shut up!" blustered Peaches as she belted Edwin with the magazine again like she was swatting flies. "Don't mind him kids, he just lives here."

"Peaches, babe, I'm watching my man, Kennedy. He *is* our president, even if you deny it."

"The man was weaned on a pickle, Edwin. Nixon should have wiped him out."

"But Kennedy's a man for the people."

"He's a blasted Catholic," squawked Peaches. "He'll make us go to

confession to file our income tax returns. Before you know it, we'll
have to cross ourselves before takin' a pee."

"He's a good leader, dear. Believe me."

"Believe you? Edwin, you have the brain of a retarded clam. Come
on, kids. Chow time."

With Maggie in my arms, I understood why Peaches didn't jump for
joy upon seeing the puppy when almost a dozen dogs of various breeds
scampered in and sniffed our clothes. All the dogs were odd and fear-
ful. When we entered the kitchen, an animal with long legs was lying
by the oven. The old mutt had stringy brown hair with a gray head. He
looked thin in an unhealthy way. When I scratched him behind the
ears, his tail thumped on the floor, and he whimpered softly as if to say,
"Take me with you, *please*."

"Good dog," I said.

"Ah, that's George. He's old as dirt. He lays around by that oven all
day just trying to keep warm."

"Well, I like you, George," I said.

The three of us took our places around the kitchen table. The enam-
eled surface was covered with the makings of Peaches' cooking endeavor. I had expected to see the finished products rather than merely
the raw ingredients. But apparently the chocolate-covered noodle balls
were still in the making. As we sat there, an Afghan hound walked
under the table and methodically licked the mud off our sneakers. The
strange-smelling air grew warmer and began closing in around us.

"Now watch this, me lads," crooned Peaches in an excellent imita-
tion of Julia Child. "You shall see for yourself the makings of my fa-
mous, most delici-oh-so, mouth-watering specialty. Homemade by
Peaches McNally herself. It's an old southern recipe my grandmother
gave me before she died of food poisoning. Yer gonna love it."

I looked at Ralph and Casey, who were staring at each other.

"Now hear this," Peaches began. "You take a handful of noodles
and dump them in a bowl. Like this. Then you blend one cup of goop
and mix it with the noodles. The goop is important. . . . It's made of
molasses, raw eggs, a touch of buttermilk, and my secret ingredient—
aged bacon grease. Yessiree, it's the old grease that holds everything together."

She mushed these ingredients around with her bare hands. Noodles wound through her pink fingers like pale seaweed. Goop oozed
everywhere.

"Oh, I almost forgot! Oregano," said Peaches as she spun around

and fetched a jar of green leaves. Then the basset hound came in carrying a small slab of beef.

"Hey, gimme that!" blustered Peaches as she pulled her hands from
the clinging noodles, pinned the dog against the counter with her fat
knee, and yanked the meat from the dog's mouth. The beef was frothy
with basset hound saliva, but she put the hunk back in its marinade on
a low stool off to the side. Then returning to her project, she plunged
her fingers, still dripping with saliva, into the noodle concoction and
sloshed it around.

"Here comes the fun part," she said as she grabbed handfuls of
gushy noodles, rolled them into three-inch balls, and plopped them on
a cookie sheet. "All we have to do now is cook these suckers, dip them
in chocolate, and coat them with fresh coconut."

All I could think was, *We've got to get out of this zoo.* As I clutched
the puppy in my arms, Edwin walked in, picked up the pan of mari-
nating beef, and perched himself on the stool.

"Peaches, babe," he sniffled, "you wanna make me a sandwich?"

Ignoring her husband, Peaches snatched up the cookie sheet with all
the uncooked noodle balls and walked toward the stove. Old George
lay sound asleep in front of the oven. Peaches tripped on his front
paws. "Move your duff, old hag," she grumbled. Then Peaches lost her
balance, and all the noodle balls began sliding off the cookie sheet,
plunking on the floor one by one, and rolling across the linoleum.
Hearing the thud of food, several hungry dogs tore into the kitchen
vying for the rolling specimens. Peaches sparred with the mutts, grabbing whatever balls she could. Sometimes she yanked the noodles right
out of the dogs' mouths, quickly reformed them into balls, and put
them back on the cookie sheet.

One of the noodle balls rolled toward George. Without getting up,
he feebly reached out with his heavy head and gently took the ball in
his mouth. That sphere of sticky noodles might have been the first thing
he'd sunk his teeth into for quite a while. As he indulged in the savory
taste, Peaches flew across the room and kicked him in the ribs so hard
he sailed halfway through the kitchen, expelled the noodle ball, and
yelped in pain.

"Peaches, you crazed maniac!" yelled Edwin. "Lay off that old
dog."

"Shut up, dolt!" Peaches shot back.

Edwin shut up, and Peaches carried on, "Don't mind him, kids, he
only comes here to feed. And he can't even do that right. Look at that

pathetic body—you can see his ribs, for pity's sake." With her hands slimed with noodle goop and dog saliva, she took a big pinch on the side of Edwin's torso. "Yeah, feed and breed, that's all he does!"

"Now hold your tongue, Peaches pet," Edwin muttered.

"Hold my tongue? Hah! Edwin, you have the personality of a dial tone!" With that she picked up a bowl of flour and dumped it on his head.

That was enough for me. "We gotta go, ma'am," I said.

"Yeah," concurred Casey, "we told our parents we'd be home by three."

"But you haven't tasted my delicious noodle balls yet."

"Maybe another time," Ralph said as we all bounded toward the door.

"Hey, not so fast, kid," Peaches called to me. "You got my puppy there, so you better leave him where he belongs."

"He's a she," corrected Ralph.

"It's okay, ma'am," I said. "I can take care of her. I'll call her Maggie." I can't leave a helpless puppy in this den of madness, I thought. No wonder she tried to run away.

Peaches grabbed the puppy from my arms. She kicked open the back door and tossed her through the air into the yard. I heard the puppy cry out when she landed. I wasn't brave enough to intervene as Maggie's savior, so I followed Casey and Ralph straight out the front door. Peaches chased behind us with two noodle balls yelling, "They'll be done in ten minutes. Then it's *mangia, mangia, mangia . . .*"

"Let's get outta this loony bin," said Casey as we hit the stone path at the front of the house.

"Wait," I insisted and ran around back to where Peaches had thrown the puppy. There was Maggie scratching at her empty water bowl. Next to that was another bowl with a few nuggets of dried dog food with ants crawling on them.

Then the back door flung open, and Peaches staggered out in all her fury. I jumped behind a bush while she marched over to Maggie like an angry soldier. She picked up a huge rock. I thought she was going to flatten the puppy. But she paraded past the quivering ball of fluff and slammed the rock into a dirt hole where Maggie had probably escaped earlier that day.

"You ain't going nowhere, no how, ever again," Peaches growled. "You hear me, mutt?" The puppy quaked in fear. "You're gonna grow up here where you were born. If this dump is good enough for me, then it's good enough for you." She stomped back in the house.

I reached quickly under the fence and tried to push aside the big rock that Peaches had dropped there. Too heavy. I might as well try to move the Rock of Gibraltar. So I jumped the low fence into Peaches' backyard. That's when Casey and Ralph came around the corner.

"Are you nuts?" yelled Ralph. "Get back here, Josey. That woman will kill you."

Then Peaches crashed through the back door again with an empty colander in her hand. Casey and Ralph took off. I grabbed Maggie and ran to the far end of the yard while Peaches clamored along behind, yelling, "Thief! Thief! Dog thief on the run!"

I leaped over the fence and turned around as Peaches yelled, "Dirty, rotten, dog-stealin' scoundrel!"

"But Mrs. Peaches," I protested, "you torture this puppy. You throw her around, and you don't give her enough food."

"Hey, kid," she ranted, bashing her metal colander on the fence, "I'll treat that puffball anyway I want. She belongs to *me!* So if I want to chop off her ears for hors d'oeuvres, I'll do it. If I want to fry her blood and make earrings with her eyeballs, I'll do that, too. I own her so you get your hiney back here right now!"

No more time for talk. I turned and bolted toward the creek. Mission accomplished, or so I thought until I heard the clunk of the back gate opening. I looked back and saw Peaches grab a hatchet next to the wood pile, then dash after me in plump pursuit.

As I ran through the creek, Peaches followed, treading through the meadow grass along the edge of the water. All the while, she lambasted me with language that made my father seem like a patron saint.

"You bandicoot!" she yelped. "I'll have every cop in the county after your wretched bones. First they'll string you up by your toes, then they'll cut a hole in your stomach, grab the end of your small intestines, and pull them out very slowly in one long strand. Yeah, all those intestines crammed into your stomach like spaghetti—when the cops stretch 'em out, they'll be twelve feet long. You'll make one dandy clothesline—hah!"

Peaches ran along with the hatchet in one hand and her colander in the other. "Never mind the cops," she persisted, "I'll get you myself. I'll drag you to the basement and chop off your hands so you won't steal nothin' again. Then I'll make noodle balls with your brains and cook your innards in chicken broth. Your fresh heart will still be beating when the brew comes to a boil. Then I'll feed it to Edwin and tell him it's liver soup. That ought to fix his runny nose!"

Don't listen to her, I muttered. *Just keep running.* I raced on as fast as I could, with Maggie in my arms. In all the excitement, the puppy didn't try to get free. She bobbed along, perhaps relieved not to be riding in the empty colander of the hatchet lady. Casey and Ralph were long gone.

By now Peaches had gained speed and was running along the opposite riverbank even with me. I bolted through the creek while she stormed alongside on the bank. Maybe she was afraid to get her feet wet. As she ran, she picked up large jagged stones and hurled them at me. "I'll bomb the living daylights out of you till you're dead as a doornail. You . . . you . . ." she stammered and tripped. ". . . You grasshopper turd. You little piece of inconvenience!"

At last the creek turned into the woods. Now the advantage shifted my way since she had to dodge trees along the edge of the creek. But my stamina was waning. I felt breathless and weak in the knees. Looking back, I saw Peaches thrashing her way through the woods, whisking away branches with her hatchet and throwing small logs in my direction.

I knew if I ran much longer, my legs would give out. Any moment I would collapse in the middle of the stream and get stoned to death. Or maybe have my head chopped off with her hatchet. So I chose another escape route. After the creek made a sharp bend so she couldn't see me for a moment, I jumped onto the side bank and dashed into the woods about thirty feet. Then knowing I could run no farther, I crawled into the protective center of three bushes and sat cross-legged on the ground with Maggie in my lap. I was panting so heavily the bushes shook with my every gasp. I suppressed my breathing the best I could.

This tactic worked. Peaches continued through the woods up the creek as if in the midst of a marathon run. My body rested, but my mind ran wild. Maybe Peaches would never stop running. Perhaps years from now, rumors would abound about the old demon lady who wandered the woods with her bloody hatchet, slaughtering unsuspecting wildlife and lost children, tearing out their hearts and carrying them around in her colander.

Still recuperating, I scratched Maggie behind the ears. I wondered how this little pup would grow up having lived under the rancor of

Peaches McNally. Would she develop a mean streak, or become a sniveling wimp like Edwin?

"We made it, pup," I whispered. Maggie's tail wagged, and she licked my cheek—probably less from gratitude and more for the taste of salty sweat all over my face.

Then we heard a dreaded sound—Peaches on the rebound. Her heavy footsteps came stomping down the middle of the creek. Apparently she wasn't afraid to get her feet wet after all. Her approach had a strange rhythm: slosh, slosh, pause and clunk . . . slosh, slosh, pause and clunk . . . When she rounded the bend, I could see that the sloshing part was her footsteps, the pause was her leaning down to scoop up a stone, and the clunk was when she threw it into her colander. As she tramped along collecting stones, she hummed a cheerful tune.

When she reached the part of the creek that was closest to our hide-out, Peaches leaned her head back and let out a roar—a loud and brutal sound. I feared the trees would shake loose and tumble down. Maggie whimpered, and I clasped my hand gently around her snout.

Then Peaches held out her rock-filled colander and tipped it upside down so all the stones fell into the water. She put the colander on her head like a soldier's helmet and continued down the creek, swinging the hatchet at anything that resembled life. Suddenly, she broke into song—not a hounding rendition from her demonic soul, but a familiar lullaby, delicately chiming in a Tinkerbell voice:

> *When you wish upon a star*
> *Makes no difference who you are*

As she sang sweetly, she sliced young saplings at their base, wiped out full-grown bushes, and dismantled entire groves of reeds along the edge of the creek. When there wasn't anything to kill, she swung the hatchet in circles like a discus thrower, slicing the air around her.

Maggie and I watched Peaches mosey down the creek. All the while, her voice became more fragile, almost angelic, as she continued her song until she was clear out of sight.

Maggie looked up at me with dark puppy eyes as if to ask, What now?

"Let's go home," I said. Tired and relieved, we walked up the hill, along the tracks, and down the river to the old stone bridge. No need to run anymore.

18

When I introduced Maggie to my new family, everyone loved her but Homer and Hector. The puppy's bouncing spirit was contrary to the bulldogs' mellow air. The two older dogs glowered at her with disgust as she scampered across the floor, slid around corners, and ricocheted off walls. And when Maggie rammed her fluffy body into the bulldogs, trying to rouse them from their lethargy, Homer growled and Hector bared his teeth, exposing a font of saliva. I was constantly wiping away bubbly strands of wetness that had drained onto Maggie's head.

"Would Hector bite?" I asked Abigail.

"He could," she said.

I picked up Maggie and set her on my lap.

"Josey," she said, "how do you think Grandma Ru would like Maggie?"

"Oh, she loves animals. She'd spoil her rotten and tell her stories about the Indians."

"Why don't you take her home then. Let your grandma meet Maggie."

"But my father—"

"Honey, sometimes you have to do things for the sake of other people—to make things better for them."

"Better for who?"

"In this case, for your Grandma Ru, Maggie, and even your father."

"I don't know, Mrs. Lark. My father . . . he's so hard."

"Think about it, Josey. Think about it real good."

By late Sunday afternoon I was overcome with worry, imagining my little pup embedded in the eyeteeth of Hector's drooling mouth. With school the next day, I couldn't leave her alone in such danger. I figured for the sake of Maggie's life, I would consider returning home. Furthermore, I'd used up my three outfits, and Grandma's hair must be in tangles by now.

So with some reluctance, home I went—my bag tied to the back of my bike and Maggie in the crook of my arm. I had failed in my attempt to run away from my father, but I had faced danger, and now I had something to call my own.

*   *

"Just what we need is another goddamn critter around here!" My father and Grandma Ru were sitting at the kitchen table as if I never left. They had pushed aside the beer bottles to make enough room for their dinner of beef jerky, pretzels, Velveeta cheese with hot mustard, and jalapeño peppers on the side.

"But she'll be a good critter, Dad."

"It ain't the goodness of the critter," he argued, "it's the quantity. We already got too many critters. We have birds yappin' day and night, squirrels invading our home, and hoot owls keepin' me awake till dawn. We don't need another life form around here."

"I like hoot owls," Grandma Ru said. "They make good stew."

"Look," I said, setting Maggie down, "watch how she walks."

Maggie waddled across the floor, squatted on top of my father's slippers, and peed all over them.

My father's voice began low, then crescendoed to a roar. "Get that lame-brained fluff ball out of here! He ain't stayin' here."

I snatched up the culprit. "It's a she, Dad. Her name is Maggie."

"I don't care if her name is King Tut, *Queen* Tut, or the Prince of Shamoo—he *or* she is not staying in this house."

"Why not?"

"She'll pee on my moss."

As it turned out, Maggie stayed. Actually, we settled on a compromise. My father would buy the dog food, and Maggie could come in the kitchen to eat it. Sometimes she could even go in the living room during the day, but she had to sleep outside. As my father said, "I don't want no knuckle-headed foo-foo traipsing around the house at night drinking water from my plant specimens and romping around my moss beds. And if that puny little runt takes as much as a nibble out of one flying jib boom or mizzen-royal staysail, we'll be using her hide for a doormat."

That was okay by me. I knew I could train her. I built her a cozy bed in the corner of the shed with a red-plaid flannel blanket and a fluffy blue pillow. I added some dirty socks from all three of us so she could rest easy amid familiar aromas. Under the blanket, I put an old windup clock because Grandma Ru said puppies are comforted by ticking, which sounds like the heartbeats of their mother and their puppy siblings.

But the best part about Maggie's bed was that she never slept in it. Every night I walked Maggie out to the shed and set her in her bed. Then I went upstairs to my room, crawled out the window, climbed down the old oak tree, and brought her back up to my room, where she curled at the end of the bed and slept on my feet.

The whole situation did wonders for my bad habit of sleeping late in the morning. I had to rise early enough to get Maggie back to the shed before my father looked out the window and discovered me descending the oak tree with puppy in hand.

Grandma Ru took a liking to Maggie. My father hid the dog cookies, but Grandma always found them. She'd sneak them to Maggie, silently slipping them into her mouth. When my father caught her red-handed, he'd lecture her on the worthlessness of fat puppies.

After saving Maggie from the wrath of Peaches McNally, some kind of strength germinated in me. I actually felt proud, having confronted something real. My friends and I had fought giant bears and fire-breathing dragons, but our adventures were mere trifles compared to defying a live woman wielding a hatchet. I felt brave enough that maybe now I could even confront my father when he got into one of his rampages. If I made it through the rage of Peaches, I could certainly stand up to Willie Rose and tell him to stop throwing things at the walls and to quit being mean to the birds. I vowed that the next time my father got angry, I would stop him.

19

Once home, I understood what Abigail said about my grandmother needing me, but I still felt trapped. I busied myself with Maggie. And when sadness lurked, I escaped on the rails of Lily's memory. Even though she'd said I could never see her again, I dreamed of going to her, knocking on her chapel door where I'd find her cutting curves in puzzle pieces or sitting on the platform under the sky, combing her golden hair. I hadn't seen her for months—ever since the day she banned me from her company because I was the son of Willie Rose.

But her memory had filled my mind so much that I kept to myself. Recently I'd been avoiding Casey and Ralph. I spent most of the time in my room until one day I decided at last to go back to Lily's. As soon as school let out, I would ride my bike to Gypsy Lane.

All day long in the classroom my daydreams ran wild. I sat at my desk thinking of things she and I could do together. The day dragged on—the minutes plodded by and the hours were endless. When at last the teacher bid us adieu, I grabbed my jacket and ran to the bike rack. I was leaning down, trying to straighten the fender, which had chattered ceaselessly on my ride to school.

"Hey, where've you been, Josey Rose?" It was Casey. I hadn't seen him for a few weeks—since I left his house that Sunday afternoon. And I was still a little mad at him for abandoning me at Peaches' house.

"Yeah, what's up?"

"You're the one with something up. You been running off every day like you really got someplace to go. First you want to live with me, then I never see you. So what's the story, morning glory?"

"Not much, really. I gotta go buy glue for Grandma. You know how it is when she runs out of glue."

"You wouldn't be hiding something hot from your best friend now, would ya?"

"No, really, it's just glue."

"I get it," said Casey. "You're mad at me 'cause I didn't convince my mom to let you stay longer."

"No, Casey. It's okay, really."

Suddenly Casey turned toward Norman Johnson, who was walking by the bike rack. "Oh, Christ!" said Casey. "Here comes a load of coal."

"Casey, give the guy a break," I grumbled, tired of Casey's ongoing pestering of Norman just because he was the only black kid in our school. Norman Johnson was thirteen, in the same grade as Casey. I knew he lived near me—after school sometimes I'd see him walking along the same road home as I soared by on my bike. But Casey had a grudge against him because he was so dark. Maybe he picked it up from his father. Sometimes when Eddie Lark drank beer with my dad, they'd talk like that.

"Glory be!" said Casey loud enough for Norman to hear. "Methinks nighttime has fallen early. Suddenly the darkness is overwhelming."

Norman walked past us without the slightest twinge. Casey hopped on his bike, wheeled it around, and came to a skidding halt directly in front of Norman, who was forced to stop dead in his tracks.

"So tell me, Norman, how did a spear-chucker like you get from the jungle to the hills of New Hampshire?"

"I was born here, Casey Lark, just like you."

"Hey, you ain't nothing like me," said Casey. "In fact you're even darker than most colored folks. You're so dark you look purple. Yeah, when the sun hangs at a certain angle, I'd swear you was deep purple."

"You got the fever, Casey Lark. Reckon your mind's brewin' up hallucinations again. Next thing you know, you'll be seeing green elephants."

"If I see a green elephant, Norm, it'll be 'cause he's settin' here next to me. And when that happens, I'll make him walk over there and plop his rump smack dab on top of you until you turn into black bean soup."

"Casey," I pleaded, "cut it out."

"Don't worry," said Norman. "I can handle this creep."

"Go on, burrhead," Casey jeered, pulling back his bike, "get yourself on home before your mother thinks they used you for alligator bait."

"I don't have a mother," Norman said as he walked past Casey and went on his way.

"Yeah," muttered Casey under his breath, "you probably just formed out of the muck somewhere."

"Casey," I said, "why do you have to be so mean?"

"Who are you, the patron saint of niggerdom? I suppose you're gonna protect every last one of them friggin' jiggaboos? How you gonna do that, Josey boy—shoot cosmic rays from your violet eyes?"

I thought about Lily. "I gotta go, Casey."

"Go on home to your dingbat grandmother."

"Casey, I don't think I want to talk to you anymore."

"Hah!" he laughed. "That's going to be pretty tough since your whole family is coming over for dinner tonight."

"We are not."

"See you there, squirt."

If Casey was right about dinner tonight, then going to Lily's would be bad timing. My father would have the cops after me again.

I went to the store instead, bought a large bottle of glue for Grandma, and pedaled home. On the way, I saw Norman on the main road farther along than usual because of my errand. As I passed him, I swooped out to the middle of the road but didn't wave or say anything. Despite my attempts to stop Casey's taunts, I still felt that Norman was different from me, and I'd never had the courage to get close to him— no one else at school was his friend either. I didn't know what Norman thought of me, but I'd been raised to be wary of people with skin so black it really did look purple in the setting sun.

❧   ❧

When I got home, my father wasn't back from work yet. Grandma Ru was sitting on the floor, feeding dog cookies to Maggie, one by one.

"Grandma," I scolded, "take it easy with those snacks. She'll be fat before she's grown."

❧

"Oh," she sighed to Maggie, "that Josey sounds more like his father every day. He'll grow up just like his daddy."

"I'll never grow up like him. You can bet I won't eat raw worms and throw kids out in lightning storms."

"Life works in strange ways," she said.

"What do you mean by that?"

"I mean you never know how you'll grow up, Josey. When you carry hate in your heart, it slips into your soul. That's why so many people grow up to be the very thing they despise."

"I don't understand."

"You have to take care where you throw your passions, Josey. Whether you love your father or hate him, he's a part of you."

My heart sank clear to the basement. I feared my father's blood more than his rage. Grandma fed Maggie another cookie, and I thought of Casey's house and what he had said earlier about dinner. "Are we going to the Larks' house tonight?"

"We have been invited to a special Navaho ceremony so that we may give gratitude to the clouds, which will in return deliver us much needed rain. We shall arrive before nightfall."

"Did the Indians visit again, Grandma?"

"Yes," she said, "and we must depart soon because Tucson, Arizona, is a long drive."

When my father returned from work, he changed his clothes while Grandma filled a paper bag with empty bottles. She said if it showered during the rain dance, she wanted to collect as much water as possible to bring home. She would keep it on hand in case anyone got tapeworms.

"What are tapeworms?" I asked as we piled into the car.

All the way to Casey's house, Grandma Ru described how these flat white worms grow in your bowels. If left untreated, they grow longer and longer. Then, looking for a bigger place to live, they crawl up from the bowels into the stomach where they feed all day on chewed up food and grow as long as six feet, although they remain quite slender.

"That's disgusting," I said.

"Everybody has some kind of worms," said my father.

"Not me."

"Sure you do. Maybe not as big as tapeworms—some are microscopic. They live in your gut and feed on bacteria."

Grandma said there's only one way to get rid of tapeworms: After starving yourself for three days, you make bean and okra soup from Navaho rainwater. Then you hold a bowl of the steaming brew against your chin. Being famished from days of starvation, the tapeworm slithers up your esophagus and crawls out to drink the soup. Then you grab him by the head and keep pulling until he is entirely out of your stomach. But you have to pull fast before the tapeworm lodges its tail into the lining of your stomach. If that happens, when you pull up the last part of the worm your stomach comes up through your esophagus, inside-out, causing an obstruction to the lungs, which leads to suffocation.

This conversation worried me, and I wanted to know how to keep from getting one of these worms in the first place. "How do you get tapeworms, Dad? Is it from eating some kind of food?"

"No," he said, glancing at me, "it's from roaming in places where you don't belong." Then I heard the familiar crunch of stones from Casey's driveway as we pulled up to the Larks' log cabin in the pine forest.

Dinner at Casey's house was usually fun—there was someone for everyone to talk with. Eddie Lark and my father hung out together. Grandma Ru sat with Aunt Kitty. Casey and I went to his room. And Abigail cooked dinner while she puttered around with Benny. All this was great—just like being part of a real family.

But after my tiff with Casey, tonight felt different. I didn't feel like running up to his room and pulling out the Monopoly board, so I sat in the living room where Grandma Ru described various Navaho rain dances, and Aunt Kitty showed us a drawerful of stubs from the horse races she had bet on over the years. Then Aunt Kitty reached out with her hands, caressing invisible things in the air, catching some of them, and putting them in her pocket. Whatever they were, she had caught plenty of them.

In the middle of her description about a rain dance for bean crops, Grandma Ru leaned down and reached for something on the floor near Aunt Kitty's left toe. "Here," she said handing nothing to Aunt Kitty, "you dropped one." Aunt Kitty put it in her pocket.

Feeling a little bored, I focused on the glowing Tiffany lamps around the room and stared for a long time at the one of dragonflies and grapes, with bronze vines crawling up the base. The tiny pieces of cut glass made me think of the stained-glass windows in Lily's chapel.

The two bulldogs lay half asleep, drooling tiny rivers in front of the fireplace next to the stuffed standard poodle and the Irish setter. Benny lay curled on the window sill next to the stuffed Siamese cats. He was sunning himself in the late afternoon light, all golden upon his back. While Abigail was setting the table, Casey came downstairs, walked through the living room, and sauntered into the dining room, paying no attention to me.

"Casey," said Abigail, "where have you been? Why don't you show Josey your new hula hoop."

"Nah," said Casey.

"Now that's no way to treat a guest. What kind of host are you?"

"Well, I guess I'm a host of a different color," Casey said sarcastically. "But at least I'm not purple."

"Your hormones are making you moody, Casey Lark," remarked his mother.

I knew Casey would never back down, so it was up to me to make peace. I got up and followed Casey to the far side of the dining room, where I asked him to play Monopoly.

"Why?" he asked.

"Because it'd be fun, like always."

I could tell Casey thought about ignoring me more, but I think he was getting tired of sitting in his room by himself, so he agreed.

We laid out the board in front of the fire and began rolling dice and collecting properties. But we had barely gotten around to Marvin Gardens when Abigail called us to dinner. A truce had been made, and we decided to finish the game later.

Eddie lit the candles on the table, while Abigail brought out bowls of steaming broccoli, baked potatoes with butter and chives, sliced tomatoes wallowing in marinade, hot buns tucked in red checkered towels, and fish with their heads still attached—wet lemons lying across their broiled bodies. The dogs sat on the far side of the living room while Benny crawled up his tree limb and wove himself amid the curling wrought iron of the chandelier above the dinner table. He let his head droop down into the steamy vapors rising from the meal.

My father and Eddie were feeling good and loose from all the drinks they had before dinner. They told high-iron stories, each one trying to top the other.

"Hey," said my father, "how about old Knuckles."

"Yeah, he's a piece of work," said Eddie.

"Tell us about old Knuckles, dear," suggested Abigail, trying to corral the family into one conversation.

"Well," said Eddie, "he's a tag-line man on the Boston job. He's supposed to hook rope around the ends of the beams. But he's got some kind of condition called narcolepsy—falls into a deep sleep any old time of the day."

"He isn't getting a proper night's rest," said Grandma Ru. "Tell him to try hot milk and dill pickles before he goes to bed."

"The man can't help it," said Eddie. "He'll be hookin' rope one minute and sleeping like a baby the next."

"You ain't whistlin' Dixie," said my father. "The foreman calls for Knuckles to do some job, and he's nowhere around."

"Glory be," sighed Abigail.

"But the guy snores like a chainsaw, so he's easy to find."

"Last week," said Eddie, "I found him curled up in the groove of a corner brace."

"Oh, yeah?" topped my father, "Yesterday I found him sprawled out on that big beam hanging off the crane. The only way I could rouse him was to throw four-inch bolts at him."

"Hah," said Eddie, "it's a damned good thing ol' Knuckles don't walk in his sleep."

"And lucky for him he's the foreman's brother, or he'd be out of a job, sure as shootin'."

"You know," continued Eddie, slurring his words, "Knuckles is from that same damn town you and Isabel used to live in."

"Put a lid on it, Eddie," commanded my father in a suddenly serious tone.

"Who's Isabel?" asked Casey.

"She was my mom," I said, and the table grew quiet.

"Well, now," sighed Abigail, changing the subject. "We sure did enjoy Josey's visit a couple weeks ago. He's welcome to come anytime he likes."

My father set down his fork and rolled his eyes. No more was said of my mom or of my running away. Then as always near the end of dinner, Benny crawled down from the chandelier and slithered along the Oriental carpet over to Aunt Kitty's chair. He used her lap as an access route to the dining room table. While everyone continued talking,

Benny slithered between the two candlesticks, around the bowl of broccoli, and curled up next to the remains of the fish. His tail curved halfway around the base of my father's beer bottle.

"Honey," whined Eddie, "we've got to teach Benny not to crawl on the table when we're eating."

"But Eddie," said Abigail, "he's not hurting anyone. And he's never spilled a drop in his life." This was a never-ending conversation at the Larks' house.

"Oh, you're always defending Benny," complained Eddie. "Someday I expect to come home and find you in bed with that reptile."

"I never let him on the sheets. You know that, dear. He only hangs from the canopy," said Abigail, winking at the rest of us.

As if Benny sensed Eddie's disapproval, he cut a curved route around the dinner rolls toward Abigail. When Benny's head reached Grandma Ru, she selected her biggest piece of buttered broccoli and put it in front of Benny's mouth. He kept his lips sealed, so she curled up her other hand and gently knocked on the top of Benny's head. "Are you in there?" she asked. Then she bopped the broccoli upon his scaly nose and sang, "Open your mouth, close your eyes, here comes a big juicy surprise . . ."

"No, Mother!" yelled my father. "Benny doesn't eat broccoli."

"Why not?" she asked.

"He eats baby chickens and guinea pigs."

"And small rabbits," added Casey. "But he only eats once a week."

"Hmmm," sighed Grandma, pulling away the broccoli. She shook her finger at the snake and said, "You should eat more shrubbery, Benny, or you'll get scurvy." She petted him on the nose and went back to her own dinner.

❧   ❧

At last, Abigail served her special dessert of chocolate pudding with homemade whipped cream—my favorite. Then Casey and I returned to our Monopoly game. After two trips around the board, already landing in jail once, I asked, "Do you still have those cards, Casey?"

"My mom confiscated the whole bunch, but I got some more pictures. You want to see them?"

"No, no, that's okay."

❧

"Why, you seen any naked girls lately?"

"Sort of," I said.

"Well that sounds promising. What did ya see?"

"I heard about one."

"Okay, 'fess up. Who is she?"

"Venus."

"Who the heck is Venus?"

"A planet."

"Don't get weird on me, Josey."

"No, really. There's this goddess from the planet Venus. My father told me about her."

"Your father talks to you about naked girls?"

"No, Casey, she's not really naked—she's partially dressed. She has long hair, and she walks around in the mist."

"You're in the mist, Josey. A real fog. This Venus thing is lame, so why'd you ask about my cards?"

"Just curious."

"Hmmm, I'll bet you are."

"Casey, I'll tell you what I'm really curious about."

"Large breasts?"

"No, wacko, my mother."

For a minute, Casey got serious. "I thought she died," he said.

"Casey, I'm sure she's still alive."

"You mean 'cause of what my father said? He doesn't know what he's talking about. He's really lit. They've been sippin' all night. Next thing you know he'll be swinging from the chandelier with Benny."

"It's the way my father talks about her—like he's trying to convince himself she's really gone."

"Reckon so," mused Casey. "Hey, I'm buyin' Park Place."

"Go ahead, spendthrift. Nobody ever lands on it."

"You'll be calling me 'Sir Landlord' by the time this game's done."

"Anyway," I said, "Grandma told me my mother is still alive."

"Your grandmother's bonkers."

"She has her dreams mixed up with her life, that's all. She's probably smarter than the whole lot of us."

"Who takes care of her anyway?"

"What do you mean?"

"You know, like my mom bathes Aunt Kitty and helps her get dressed."

"Grandma takes care of herself. Most of the time she knows what she's doing. She's okay as long as she has enough glue. I'll buy Mediterranean Avenue."

"Hah! Hangin' out in the low-rent district."

While Casey and I played Monopoly, Aunt Kitty resumed pawing the air for stray vapor balls. Grandma Ru meandered into the pantry and found a box of dog cookies shaped like little bones. She wandered around the living room, placing them gently into the drooling mouths of the bulldogs. As the dogs chewed, they worked up a vigorous froth, and I could hear them sloshing clear across the room. Then Grandma tried feeding the stuffed Irish setter and the cats on the windowsill. Casey and I let her carry on since this was her normal routine. Then she went back and sat down on the couch, where Benny had curled with his head on a pillow.

What we did *not* know is that after a while, Grandma Ru returned to the pantry and retrieved a kitchen knife. She must have been trying to feed cookies to Benny, who refused to open his clenched mouth. Maybe Benny had draped himself around Grandma's neck before she tried using the knife. Or maybe not. We weren't sure how it began. All we knew for sure was that Grandma Ru inserted the kitchen knife between Benny's thin lips and twisted it, trying to pry open his jaw. She had accidentally pierced his skin and frightened him enough to rouse his only instinct to protect himself. By the time we heard Grandma's choking cries, Benny had wound himself around her neck and constricted his body to twice its thickness. Grandma had turned blue, and her green eyes were protruding out of their sockets.

"Dad!" I screamed, "Benny's got Grandma." I ran to the couch. Too scared to grab Benny's head, I pawed at his tail, trying to unwrap the huge muscle. My father and Eddie stumbled into the room, knocking over two end tables. Eddie clutched Benny's head, and my father handled the other end. Blood from Benny's wounds dripped down Eddie's hands and trickled around Grandma's neck. The bloody knife and uneaten cookies lay at her side.

Abigail ambled in, tossing her dish towel aside. She sat softly on the couch and gazed sympathetically at the snake. "Now, Benny," she reasoned, "don't lower yourself to revenge. An eye for an eye doesn't apply here."

Benny looked up at Abigail with an adoring gaze.

"Grandma Ru didn't mean you any harm," Abigail gently continued.

"She was simply offering you some treats. She's the nurturing type, you know. She wasn't aware that you are not fond of dog cookies."

The men struggled but Benny wouldn't let up. Grandma's hair bun had come undone. She could no longer make choking sounds, and her blue skin was deepening to purple.

"Let's let bygones be bygones, now," Abigail said soothingly. "Let Grandma loose, and she won't bother you anymore."

"Shut up, Abigail," yelled Eddie. "You're distracting us."

"Honey," Abigail replied, "Benny needs some understanding. He's a little confused right now." She dabbed his bleeding lips with a tissue.

The bulldogs added to the commotion by putting their heads on Grandma's lap, begging for more cookies.

"Casey," hollered Eddie, "help me with his head. Here, grab him below the neck and pull like hell."

They were getting nowhere. All we heard were grunts and groans, the bulldogs' snorting breath, and the soft rhythm of Aunt Kitty's rocker as she continued pulling things from the air. Suddenly Eddie slipped, fell backwards, and landed on the floor. He lay there stunned as if he had accepted Grandma's demise.

"Benny," sighed Abigail seductively, "I'm going upstairs to take a long hot bath. Do you want to come along?"

Abigail strolled toward the steps. She turned and called softly, "Come on, Benny, *the steam is rising . . .*"

Benny loosened his grip and slid off Grandma, enthusiastically crawling along the floor and up the stairs with Abigail. That's the last I saw of Benny or Abigail that night. When she didn't return after a while, Eddie seemed annoyed. Meanwhile, Grandma's head slumped over. My father picked it up by her hair and held it there until her purple skin gradually melted to pale gray.

"Mother, Mother, are you okay?"

"Call Chief Sitting Bird this instant," she demanded in a quavering voice. "He has a remedy."

"We'll get you to a doctor, Mom. Where does it hurt?"

"No," said Grandma Ru, "not for me, you imbecile. I'm talking about the snake. Chief Sitting Bird has a concoction guaranteed to open the mouths of the most obstinate reptiles. He mixes up some kind of roots, cooks them over an open fire, and puts the snake head smack dab in the vapors. The potion is so good, snakes yawn for days."

"Grandma," I said, "you're going to be okay. Did I tell you I bought you some glue today?"

"Really, Josey?" She perked up. A rosy glow returned to her cheeks. "Can we go home now? I'd like to try some of that glue."

"One more drink," said my father, "then we'll be off."

By the time we left Casey's house, Eddie was completely drunk. When he walked us to the car, he looked into the sky and said, "By golly, there are two moons out tonight." As we pulled out of the driveway, I noticed Abigail's bathroom window veiled in drenching steam. I never found out why Abigail didn't come down that night, but years later, I realized that Casey's family was not the perfect family I thought it was.

That night when we got home, Grandma Ru wrote a letter to Chief Sitting Bird and glued pictures of tiny flowers all around the edges of the paper.

20

The third of September—my birthday. After lunch, I pedaled over to Ralph's with Maggie. Even though almost half-grown, she still looked like a ball of fluff. The day before, I had built a bike basket for her to ride in. I lined an old wooden box with part of the same red-plaid flannel blanket that served as her bed in the shed—the one she never slept in. Then I put in her blue pillow to give her a smooth ride. I attached the entire box to the back fender behind the seat. It worked perfectly. The box was big enough for her to grow a little more, but low enough around the sides that she could see out in all directions.

Our trip to Ralph's was Maggie's first bike ride. To encourage her to stay in the bike basket, I gave her some beef jerky, which she began chomping on as soon as we took off. We arrived okay, but Maggie looked a bit woozy after three beef jerkys and four miles of bumps, shaking up the contents of her stomach.

I walked into the living room carrying Maggie. Carri rounded the corner. "Oh, what a cutie! Ralph told us about your puppy. Mom, why can't we have a dog?" she whined. "We never have any pets."

"Pets are dirty, darling."

"Oh," cooed Carri, "let me see him."

I was about to advise her of Maggie's proper gender when Carri grabbed the dog from my arms and whirled her around. All I could see was the blond fountain of Carri's hair, spiraling above her long bony legs.

Suddenly, Maggie burped loudly. Carri stopped in surprise, giggled, and set her on the floor. Before I could grab her, Maggie stumbled in a crooked path to the middle of the white carpet, fell on her nose, and threw up three half-digested beef jerkys. Ralph's mother screamed, and I ran out the front door in search of water for my nauseated pet.

Figuring I'd better stay out of the house, I took Maggie and walked around back, where I found Ralph relegated to the basement again.

"Hey," Ralph said, "how'd you get that dog here?"

"We traveled by bike all the way. But Maggie got sick in your house."

"Maggie . . . I always thought that was a kooky name," said Ralph.

"I suppose you'd call her Candi or Catrina or something that begins with a 'C,' like all your sisters."

"Heck, no, that's all we need is another one of them. Call her 'Quat.' Yeah, then when you want her to come, you can say 'Kum Quat . . . Kum Quat . . .'"

Ralph was preparing high-priority food again—this time for an anniversary party the following night. So for hours, the two of us sat secluded in the basement, mixing large amounts of Ex-Lax with the vegetable dip that Mrs. Bentley had specially prepared.

"Josey," said Ralph, "where've you been lately? I haven't seen you all week."

"Oh, you know. Buying glue for Grandma Ru and lugging out boxes of my father's empty beer bottles."

"But you always had to do that stuff."

"I don't know then. Maybe I'm getting distracted in my old age."

"Oh, yeah? You sound like big-shot Casey, now that you're turning twelve years old today!"

By now Casey was fourteen—a full-fledged teenager. Even though he was still only two years older, it seemed the distance between us had grown. Over the summer, he'd been spending more time with kids his own age, leaving Ralph and me to our own adventures.

"So what are you doing for your birthday?"

"Eating Spanish rice and cake."

"How come you never have a party for your birthday like other kids?"

"My dad thinks birthday parties are for sissies."

Then Ralph grew serious and asked if he could come over to my house during his parents' party the next night.

"Sure, Ralph, but why would you want to miss the big feast?"

"Because when the guests scarf down this vegetable dip, there won't be a bathroom open for the rest of the night."

I wondered if Ralph would ever stop his pranks. After completing the Ex-Lax project, Maggie and I rode home.

Maggie was a natural-born retriever. She waddled around the living room, picking up objects and proudly dropping them in my lap like she was giving me a present. I was the lucky recipient of soggy terrarium specimens, my father's dirty socks, and objects from behind the couch that had been given up for lost years ago. As my father anticipated, we could not stop her from drinking water from his exotic plant specimens. "Get your blasted tongue out of my asparagus fern," he'd yell. But contrary to his predictions, Maggie never peed on his moss.

Jake and Lulu referred to Maggie as "the pudding-headed dingbat," which my father taught them to say in less than a week. Every night after dinner, he held up Maggie by the cage, pointed to her, and said "Pudding-headed dingbat" over and over again.

When we returned home from Ralph's, my father and Eddie Lark were drinking Ballantine ale in the kitchen.

"Hey, birthday boy, where you been?" greeted my father.

"Oh, preparing vegetable dip over at Ralph's."

"Well, I whipped up some Spanish rice for you. It's all ready for eating."

Dad scooped out our servings from the skillet and brought a plate to Grandma Ru, who preferred dining in her chair in the living room. Finally he prepared a bowl of orange slices for the birds. As my father, Eddie, and I enjoyed our helpings at the kitchen table, I spooned out another plateful and gave it to Maggie.

"Hey, what are you doing, kid?" asked my father.

"It's a special occasion, Dad. Let her eat Spanish rice on my birthday . . . please?"

"I've been slaving all day in the kitchen cooking this grub."

"Hah!" laughed Eddie.

"Okay, squirt," said my dad. "Let her lap up the main course. I tell you, Eddie, that mutt eats better than most people."

"Yeah," said Eddie, "you can see she's growing good."

"She ought to," said my father. "She eats beef jerky for breakfast and steak and chicken for dinner. Lord knows what the kid gives her for lunch. The dog will have the gout by Christmas."

With dinner done, my father said, "Well, since it's your birthday, I suppose you figure you deserve some kind of present."

"Well . . ."

My father went out back and brought in a red bow the size of a bowling ball, with a long ribbon attached.

"What in the world is this?" I asked.

"Don't know," said my dad. "Reckon you'll have to follow the red ribbon road until you find the rainbow at the other end."

That I did. I followed the ribbon out the back door and across the yard. It wound in a spiral up the old oak tree. I followed it through the branches, wondering if it led to some kind of bird house high in the tree. But farther along, the ribbon went into my bedroom. I climbed through the window and followed the red trail under my bed and into my desk and several drawers until it led under the rug and out my bedroom door. Then it streamed into my father's room and out his window. I darted downstairs and dashed around the side of the house where the ribbon poured from my father's window like a skinny waterfall. I followed it around the side of the house and to the shed. I scampered around the back of the small building. There before my eyes, gleaming in the late afternoon sun, was a glorious, sparkling, brand-new red bike! A Schwinn, no less.

"Holy mackerel," I whooped. My dad and Eddie came out the back door and watched me hop on the bike, sail down the driveway, turn around by the road, and holler in delight. "Hey," I called out, "the fenders don't squeak!"

My dad ran back in the house, grabbed his camera, and popped a picture of me standing proudly next to the gleaming Schwinn.

"Go ahead," he said. "Take her for a spin. But get your hide back here before sundown."

I pedaled down the road, not toward Gypsy Lane but in the other direction. I sailed straight into the sunset, happy as could be.

By the time I returned to the house, the sun had slipped away without my noticing. It was dark, but my father didn't seem to mind. He and Eddie had completely filled the table with Ballantine bottles, and they were feeling pretty jovial about it.

"Hey, kiddo," mumbled my father, holding a bottle toward me, "how about an ale on your birthday? Yeah, what's the drinking age in

New Hampshire? Twelve years old, isn't it? Give or take a decade."

"Say Willie," said Eddie, "don't you have some dessert for the kid?"

"Well, ain't that the truth. I forgot. Okay everybody, get your ass-teriors in the other room. The apple dumplings are about to be served."

Eddie and I went in the living room, where Grandma Ru was humming lullabies to the birds. After the sound of numerous beer bottles falling on the kitchen floor, my father stumbled into the room carrying a birthday cake with twelve full-sized dinner candles stuck clear through both layers and blazing above.

Everyone sang. *Happy birthday to you . . . Happy birthday to you . . .* My father tripped on a pan of moss and, in an extraordinary feat, regained himself. *Happy birthday, dear Josey . . .* He dropped the cake, and it crashed fully intact on the dining room table in the midst of all his debris. *Happy birthday to you.*

"Hey, Willie Rose," said Eddie, "you're a real piece of work." I hadn't seen my father that soused since the night he threw me outside in the lightning storm.

"Okay . . ." said my father as pieces from his latest shipbuilding project tumbled to the floor. "Now, Josey, blow out them candles."

"Yo, sport," chuckled Eddie, "they look more like torpedoes to me. Where'd you get them big mamoos?"

As I drew in my breath with all eyes upon me, Eddie said, "Hey, Willie, the kid looks more like you every day."

"Yeah," said my father, "spittin' image, eh? All except for them bloody eyes."

"Righto," said Eddie, "just like you know who."

"Hey, shut the fuck up already," said my father as my breath quavered, and I backed away from the cake.

"Say, Willie," stammered Eddie, "do ya ever hear from old Izzy?"

"Eddie!" shouted my father. "Wake up over there. Isabel died of pneumonia."

"She did?" I gasped. "I thought she died of malignant melanoma."

"Well, whatever," said my father, "she's dead. That's the point . . . Hey, birthday boy, ya want to let that cake burn to ashes, or you gonna lay a little gust on them candles?" My father was great at changing the subject.

I sucked in another giant breath, then let out all the wind I could muster. I blew out every candle but one.

"Now get it right," said my father, three sheets to the wind. "You gotta go for the whole enchilada. None of this halfway stuff."

As I gathered up another inhale, my father reached over to the china closet, opened the top drawer, and grabbed a pistol. I jumped back as he aimed straight for the burning candle and pulled the trigger. The bullet blasted the cake all over the dining room table. Blue and yellow roses flew through the air in all directions. The bullet ricocheted off a steel bucket and smashed through his largest terrarium bottle, shattering it to pieces.

"Hah!" yelped my father, "Reckon we nailed that sucker!"

"Willie, honey," said Grandma Ru, sighing, "that's no way to cut a cake. We have knives for that sort of thing."

"Hey," said Eddie, grabbing the gun from my father. "Cool it, man."

I ran for the stairs. "Dad," I blubbered, holding back tears, "I gotta go upstairs now. Thanks for the bike. Really . . . I mean it . . . I like it a lot."

I jumped into bed with all my clothes on. Even with my fingers stuck in my ears, I heard my father and Eddie yelling and objects crashing against the walls. A little while later, the front door closed and Eddie's car wheeled out of the driveway.

I unplugged my ears and listened intently. More objects hit the walls while the birds sang. Then the most dreaded of all—a sound I hadn't heard all summer—my father's uneven footsteps across the floor and the front door slamming. I jumped out of bed and tied up my sneakers. As I stuck my leg out the window reaching for the tree, I looked down the driveway in time to see him slip something in his pocket and turn for the road.

21

Once he was out of sight, I followed the red ribbon back down the tree and pulled out my new bike from the shed. I waited anxiously at the end of the driveway, trying to gauge how long he would take to reach the turn to Gypsy Lane. When at last he was out of sight, I soared full speed to the turn. Then I followed a good distance behind him, zigzagging along the lane.

I arrived at the meadow path and laid my bike extra carefully in the tall grass. When my father reached the chapel, I hid in the pine. Smoke poured from the chimney. He rapped on the door and tried to force it open. When Lily didn't answer, my eyes scanned the landscape. In the dark, she could be anywhere—gathering fungus or chasing the moon for all I knew. When my father stomped around back, I circled the other way and surveyed the meadow. Finally in the distance, I saw something moving—a light, a lantern, I wasn't sure. I prayed it was her. Then, in a moment, I saw it was Lily's candle in the darkness.

Like an animal on the run, I bounded through a narrow path in the grass, staying low so my father wouldn't see me. Bent over, I could hear the sound of my own breath as I ran along, tall dried grasses slapping my face. I sprang up only now and again to make sure my bearings stayed straight for the light. One look back, and I saw my father beginning to head my way. He must have noticed the light, too. As I approached closer to Lily, I could see her candle glowing like the one left burning on my cake before my father had shot it apart with his pistol.

When I came upon her, Lily's greeting was far from welcoming. "No, Josey, go home!" she reproached. "You cannot be here—not even for an instant!"

"Lily . . . Lily . . ." I could barely speak out of distress.

"Turn around now, Josey," she said sadly, "and go on home."

I tugged at her shawl, pulling it from her shoulders. "Get down, Lily! He's coming."

"Who?"

"My father," I gasped.

"Oh, blazing glory!" she fell to her knees, still holding the candle.

"No, Lily," I said, pulling her sideways, "get off the path. Come into the grass where he won't find you."

I took the candle from her trembling hands and blew it out in a whisper. Lily tumbled to the ground beside me, and my birthday wish came true—she let me stay as we huddled in the tall grass, well off the trail.

I stood up slowly and peered down the path. My father was still heading our way, with determination even in his wobbly gait. I shot back to the ground.

She lay her head against me, quivering like a captured animal. "I'm so scared," she murmured.

"Shhh, he'll hear you."

When his footsteps came in range, she put her arm partway around me and moved her head against mine. My father tramped through the grass, calling gruffly, "Where are you, wench? Hey, hey, oh, wicked wench of the North. Show your face, I know you want me like you want the dark."

His muttering waned as he moved along toward the river, and in the moonlight I could see he'd brought the gun. But then he circled back. Coming past us again, only two feet away, his voice towered above us as he babbled on. "Hey, wench, have I got a treat for you. How would you like the feel of cool metal against your hot body? How would you like a pistol barrel to soothe your aching bones?"

"What's he talking about?" I whispered too loudly.

"Hush!" she shot back and pulled my head so close against her I couldn't speak if I tried. She held me there, and I let myself loosen within the heat of her fear. As my father's voice finally drifted into the distance, my body melded into her warm curves, and I held her, too. Nestling there, I turned my head slightly toward the sky, where stars foamed across the inky night. Still breathing hard from the run, I lay panting against her, frightened but wanting it to last.

Then came that feeling again, like when I watched her step into the bath—tiny rivers within me, the aroma of green apples, and now a hint of almonds. The stars fell down, and the air began to whirl. I think I saw a swarm of vapor bubbles like the ones Aunt Kitty chased with her hands.

In the midst of my reverie, Lily gasped, "I hope he doesn't find us."

Pulling away to look into her eyes, I asked, "Why does he come here like this, Lily? Why does my father hate you so much?"

"It's a long story—hard to explain."

"I want to know. Tell me everything."

For a while she was quiet. Then she sighed. "Well, let's just say we're related."

"Who's related?"

"You and me, Josey. We're cousins. Your father is my Uncle Willie, and he has legal guardianship over me."

I was stunned. "Do we have the same last names?"

"No, I'm Lily Milan."

I hadn't even considered that she had a last name or a family nearby—much less mine.

Lily went on to tell me that her mother and my father were brother and sister. When her parents were killed in a fire, Lily had come to live with my mom and dad before I was born, and somehow she ended up in this chapel.

"Josey, we can't talk about this anymore."

I wanted to ask more questions, but I could tell she was serious about ending the conversation. Knowing we were related, the last thing I wanted to do was lose the only person in my family who understood. I knew she'd tell me more someday soon.

Together we raised our heads cautiously above the meadow grass and saw my father walking along the path to the road. He had given up on Lily for the night, and what joy I felt.

"Gone," she breathed with relief.

I sat back in the grass with my head in my hands. "Lily," I asked, "what were you doing out here wandering around with a candle?"

"Hunting for fossils. I was looking for a break in the river. Do you want me to show you?"

"No. We should go back inside and keep a lookout for my father."

"He won't return. When he doesn't find me on the first pass through, he leaves for good. At least for the night. Anyway, he'll never find us where the fossils are."

We rose warily from the grass. "I'll watch for him anyway," I said, determined to protect her.

We walked along in silence. I thought about her fossils, and finally I asked how she would ever find them in the dark. She held my hand as I followed behind, but she didn't answer. She led me into the woods and along the river until she found a spot to her liking. She marked it by laying a branch in the path. I trailed her back to the edge of the meadow where I had first found her. She picked up a large canvas bag and dragged it to the riverside.

"Lily," I said skeptically, "you'll never find enough fossils to fill that big bag." I had been on a fossil expedition at school. At the end of an entire day, I had only enough of the tiny specimens to fill the bottom of one pocket.

"No, the bag is for our tools," she said as she dumped out the contents on the bank of the river. A pile of very long white candles rolled silently across the moss. "You see," she said, "that's how we find fossils in the dark."

Lily stepped into the water with her bare feet. It was cool for September. She had chosen a portion of the river where shale ledges extended out from the riverbank in layers like so many shelves all around us. She lit a candle and tilted it to let the wet wax plunk onto a shale shelf. Then she lifted the candle upright again, inserted it into the pool of clear wax, and held it there until the wax hardened to white. She continued this as though she had done it a thousand times. By the third candle, I had joined her by holding each candle in the wax while she prepared the next one. In the end, more than twenty candles, two feet high, flickered all around us—our lanterns in the night.

The blaze of flame illuminated the area like late-afternoon sun. Lily went back to the bag and unrolled a blue cloth. Within were tools for fossil hunting—silver hammers, chisels, tiny probes with pointed ends, and small velvet bags of deep purple.

"Tie this pouch to your belt," she said as she threw off her shawl and attached her velvet bag to a strip of chiffon that was part of her dress. We migrated along the river edge, chipping away at the layers of shale. Candles quivered in the night with a warm glow. Our earlier fear dissolved in silence as the work of our chisels tinkled and echoed down the river. The sounds floated up into the canopy of trees, which blanketed us so thickly that not even the stars could find us now.

Knowing what to look for, I discovered small fossils embedded in the rock. I had learned in school that the small round ones were stems from plants that lived 350 million years ago. The ones that looked like weird bugs were trilobites, and the ones like closed-up clam shells were brachiopods.

In our endeavors, we got a bit wet, working along the edge of the river. Lily waded in the water up past her ankles, and my sneakers were soaked.

"Aren't you cold in your bare feet, Lily?"

"A little," she said. "It'll get chilly now as the season moves on. Next time I'll wear my boots for sure."

"You'd better, or you'll be walking in ice."

"But I'll miss feeling all those pebbles on the river bottom. They're like Chiclets under my toes."

I stood up to slip a brachiopod into my velvet pouch. Lily was chipping away—her golden hair shimmering in the candlelight, her dress trailing in the water and the thin fabric clinging to her skin.

"You look like a mermaid," I said.

"Oh, yes," she called, arms outstretched, "mermaid of the sea, here among all the glowing suns!" She swept her hand playfully along the candle flames, making them wild in the breeze of her dancing. She sang to the stars. Then she twirled around three times, and I fell in love. I was twelve years old and had found the woman of my dreams.

"Lily," I exclaimed, "guess what!"

"Ah, let's see," she sang, "the sky is falling down?"

"No."

"They figured out a way to grow blue broccoli?"

"No. It's my birthday today!"

"Really?" she said with melancholy surprise. "How old are you?"

"Twelve."

"Yes," she said almost in a whisper. "Hmmm . . ."

"What?"

"My son was born in August. He'd be a little older than you—about a month older."

I was shocked. "You have a son?"

"I lost him," she sighed.

"Did he die?"

"No, I had to give him up."

"Why?"

She thought for a moment, then said, "Same reason butterflies die when they come out of their cocoons too soon."

"Why is that?"

"Bad timing." She looked down into the water.

"Oh, Lily, I didn't mean to make you sad."

"Hey, Boo," she said, touching my chin and turning my head toward hers. "Happy birthday. And may all your wishes come true."

I smiled back, knowing that my wish had indeed come true, at least for tonight. But I didn't tell her, not yet.

"Hey," she said, suddenly concerned, "you're shaking like a leaf. Let's get back to the house before you turn blue!"

We ran through the water, blowing out the candles and pulling them from their shale pedestals. We tossed everything in the canvas bag and trotted back to the chapel.

Once inside, Lily lit oil lamps and candles. I sat on the arm of the chair by the fire but couldn't stop shivering from the cold.

"Josey Boo," she said, "you'll never get warm with those soggy clothes." She handed me an afghan. "Hang your wet things by the fire, and wrap yourself in this until I warm a robe for you."

She laid three logs on the simmering fire and disappeared into one of her alcoves. When she returned she was wearing a long smock of pearlescent fabric and soft lace on top of that. As she walked across the room, the fabric flowed behind her. She carried the white robe she had worn when I woke her on my last visit. She hung it by the fire and walked back to the old wood stove.

Still shivering, I looked around the room. Old oil paintings hung high on the stone walls. Marble columns ascended from the floor, reaching into the lost ceiling above. The place was bewitching, soothing, and oddly familiar. This was Lily's home and her prison, too. But she had made a heaven of her captivity. It touched that place deep within me, maybe the place Reverend Jasper called the soul. My teeth chattered with my shivers.

Lily drifted over, carrying a small pot of steaming herbs. It smelled of wild flowers. She set it on the back of the couch and went to the fireplace to retrieve the white robe. I stood up and let the afghan fall away. When she wrapped the hot robe around me, it felt like the summer sun had come to earth and embraced me. My shivers were now from delight.

"Lily, what's in that pot?"

"It's essence of meadowsweet blended with crushed red pepper. It will take away your chills."

"Do I have to drink it?"

"Sit down here and face the fire."

Lily slid onto the arm of the couch behind me. She pulled back the loose white robe, uncovering my neck and upper back. She dipped her hands in the pot and rubbed the salve across my shoulders and down my spine. It felt warm at first, but then cooled as any cream would.

"Stay still for a moment. It takes a little time for the mixture to work. When I return, you will be warm." Then she ambled back to the stove. I didn't want to disappoint her by admitting that her magic potion felt like cold mud on my skin. I would probably have felt warmer pulling the robe up around my shoulders and huddling closer to the fire. I heard her puttering around by the stove, throwing in more wood, and stirring up another concoction. I looked at the marble statue by the hearth of the nude woman holding an apple close to her lips, hesitating as if it were poison.

Shivering again from a deepening chill, I turned back toward Lily. If she wasn't looking, I would go to the fire. My hands reached back to pull up the robe when suddenly the potion took hold. A resounding heat penetrated my skin, migrating across my shoulders, descending in the path where Lily's fingers had traveled down my spine. My entire body flushed with warmth until sweat formed on my brow, and I wanted to throw off the robe and run outside into the cool air. The warmth traveled beyond my spine to places she hadn't touched. It plunged past my waist, coursed through my blood, and drove clear down to my toes.

"Lily," I called, "I'm on fire." She was already walking toward me with another cup of steaming brew. She knelt beside me, handed me the cup, and said, "Drink this. It's for your inside parts."

"What is it? More red peppers?"

"Hot chocolate," she said, as she plunked in a fat marshmallow.

She returned to the arm of the couch. "All right now," she said, "we'll take care of this goop." She rubbed it into my shoulders and spine until the cream absorbed completely. Her hands ran along my skin, smooth and slippery. Her fingers felt as if they were melting into me like hot syrup draining through mounds of ice cream, slow and sensual. I was light-headed and lost again in some kind of delirium.

"Lily, were there apples in your potion?"

"No apples. Why?"

"I smell them."

"Can you feel the warmth rising?" she asked. The truth is, I could feel heat soaring clear past my scalp, draining out my toes, and totally enveloping the room. But I didn't want her to stop rubbing my shoulders.

"Oh, I still feel a bit of a chill. I think I need more."

When she was done, she sat beside me.

"Are you cold?" I asked. "Can I put some on you?"

"No, Josey, I'm not chilled. You must use those herbs only when you're chilled. Otherwise your cells drift apart from each other, and strange things can slip in and nibble at your heart."

Disappointed, I leaned against the pillow by the arm of the couch with my toes tucked next to Lily. When my breathing mellowed to a deep, dreamy place, she hummed, "No, don't fall asleep. There is so much heat in you now that your dreams will be restless and filled with demons and fire."

I wondered what the demons would look like.

"Let me show you my crystal garden," she said, rising and walking across the room. We moved silently, she in her white gown and me in white as well, the long robe trailing behind me. She led me to an alcove with smoky mirrored walls and sparkling crystals hanging above. Pillows made of Oriental fabrics lay all over the floor, and streams of chiffon hung from the ceiling like clouds and sheets of rain. Lily wandered through, her willowy body becoming lost amid the maze of fabrics, while the chiffon veils glazed the top of my head as I followed her in.

"Close your eyes," she said as she held my hand and led me to the edge of the room. "Now kneel down and keep those eyes shut tight."

"Lily, the last time somebody told me to close my eyes, I ended up with my father's soggy eyeball in the palm of my hand."

"Well, not this time. You will see magic tonight."

She walked to the far side of the room and picked up something. I heard a match strike loudly and explode into fire. When she returned and kneeled beside me, I smelled smoke and warm wax. With her arm around my shoulders, she put her lips near my ear and whispered, "Open your eyes."

In the space before me, a dazzling garden of crystals rose up from a ground of sand and tiny stones. Lily wedged her candle into the sand. So much wonder lay before me. Hunks of amethyst that looked like lavender ice. Spires of clear quartz. And geodes with sparkling cores.

Clusters of long clear crystals were arranged like a bouquet in the front while several huge shells lay opened, exposing their opalescent interiors and revealing tiny pearls within.

"What are these things?" I asked.

"These are the important things in life," she said.

We sat in silence, kneeling in front of the crystal garden with her arm still around my shoulders. Candle wax dripped and made pools across the sand. Flame licked the air while the crystals grabbed the light and cast it out in slender rainbows, which sliced through the dusty rose smoke swirling up from the candle. Lily reached into the center of the garden and pulled the longest faceted crystal from the sand. She handed it to me.

"Happy birthday," she whispered.

She left the room, and I watched the flickering crystals for a long while. Then I went to the fireplace and changed back into my clothes, which were now warm and dry from the fire. When I said good night to Lily, I didn't talk about coming to see her again, remembering what happened the last time I asked. When I left, she kissed me on the forehead.

A little confused, I walked slowly along the path. There was something haunting about Lily, but I couldn't quite grasp it.

Then a new feeling began to swell in my chest, and I broke into a run. Suddenly, I clearly understood why Lily felt familiar to me and why she stirred me so. My father had given her image to me last spring, but it seemed like a long time ago. It was the night he built the solar system inside a bottle, and he had talked about the planets. As I raced through the meadow even faster, my confusion melted into delight because I knew who Lily was. She was the woman I had imagined walking through the mist. She was Venus.

I returned home after midnight when everyone was asleep. Apparently nobody missed me. The next morning, I wandered around the house picking up little blue and yellow roses that had flown off the birthday cake when my father shot it apart. Maggie had gobbled up all the ones that landed on the floor. As I collected sugared roses from the fireplace mantel, the glass doors of the china closet, and the rolling terrain of my father's moss, daydreams of Lily danced though my heart.

22

"By golly, if it ain't the living flesh of darkness!" Casey's voice came from around the turn in the road by the old school bridge. "Yessiree," he continued, "it's the bleedin' nighttime descended on us in one fell swoop. By Jove, it's Norman!"

As I pedaled around the bend on my way home from school, I found Casey standing head to head with Norman Johnson. Casey's new friend, Frank Rapper, stood firm on the other side of Norman so he couldn't escape. Frank had a crooked nose, dragon eyes, and a neck wider than his head. And he weighed more than two hundred pounds.

Casey looked into the sky and called, "It's a bird . . . it's a plane . . . it's a big black balloon. . . . No, it's Sambo, the double-dip coon."

"Casey, you creep," I hollered, "stop it!"

"Better get out of here, kid," cautioned Casey.

"No," I yelled back, "*you* get out of here before you hurt somebody."

"Niggers don't feel pain," said Frank.

"Anyway," Casey said, "we have us a real opportunity here. We are standing in the very midst of an astronomical wonder. Did you know that Norman here is a walking, talking total eclipse?"

"Nah," said Frank, "eclipses ain't purple."

"Lay off," said Norman rather boldly, considering his situation. "Don't you fellows have anything better to do?"

"What could be more fun than dancing in the darkness of a total eclipse?" said Casey.

"Hey, bootlips," taunted Frank, "what are you gonna do with all them books? They don't read in the jungle, do they?"

"Of course not," said Norman. "We're too busy grinding the points of our spears so we can ram them through big game like you."

"Oooh, dish the dirt, black boy," sneered Frank as he lunged toward Norman and yanked his elbows from behind while Casey tore Norman's pile of books apart. In the struggle, I jumped off my bike and ran behind Casey, trying to pry him loose from Norman—but I was like a fly on his back. Casey grunted as he continued tearing pages from Norman's books. Despite my efforts, Casey won out. While Frank easily held Norman from behind, Casey snatched away all Norman's books and threw them off the bridge, one by one. Three large textbooks soared toward the water. Then several black-and-white composition notebooks flared open on their trip through the air, revealing pages filled with meticulous notes written in peacock-blue ink. The ruffled notebooks hit the water, spun in the current, and drifted downstream.

"Now ain't that a pretty sight," sighed Frank.

"Just think," snickered Casey, "how all that lovely ink on them pages will blend in with the water. I reckon by spring, that stream will be bluer than the South Seas."

Norman broke from Frank's grip and ran down the bank to the river. He hit the water at full stride, chasing his books through the current.

Then Frank grabbed me by the collar. "What are we going to do with this little twerp," he grumbled. "We can't throw him in—he'll contaminate the water."

"Lay off him, Frank. He's harmless," said Casey.

"Yeah, like dirt," said Frank, "a little piece of nothing."

"Casey," I cried, "you got to stop doing this mean stuff. It isn't like you."

"Hey, you don't know who I am anymore."

"And I suppose you know everything."

"I'm saving your hide here, and this is the gratitude I get?"

"Hey, twerp," said Frank, grabbing my coat, "go play with the little kids where you belong. Don't be gettin' in our way again, or next time it's downriver for you. Yeah, you can go rafting on Norman's history books."

"Go on, Josey," said Casey, with a hint of sadness in his voice. "Get on home now."

As I left, I saw Norman disappear around the curve in the river. The books had gained on him. I figured the only way he would ever see them again was if they hit a beaver dam or got caught in a back eddy. I hopped on my bike and pedaled home. I wondered if Casey had noticed my new bike. If so, he probably didn't want to say anything in front of his new friend, the creep.

⚜   ⚜

Toasted cheese sandwiches—my second favorite next to Spanish rice. My father covered four slices of Wonder Bread with thick hunks of Velveeta cheese. Then he put sliced tomatoes and rings of purple onion on top. He broiled them in the oven until they bubbled and fizzed. Fantastic. And if that wasn't enough to top off the day, my father was in a good mood.

"Dad, what do you think about Negroes?" I asked.

My father left the room with a toasted cheese sandwich and gave it to Grandma in her chair by the birds. He set a little bowl of crickets and raisins in Jake and Lulu's cage. Then he sauntered back into the kitchen, sat down, and leaned back in his chair across the table.

"Well, Josey, it's like this . . ." He assumed the deep authoritative voice he used whenever he prepared to reveal his truths about life. He sounded sincere so I knew I could believe what he was about to say. "You see," he explained, "colored folks got bad blood. They can't help it—they were born that way. Like you have dark hair and lavender eyes, they have bad blood."

"All of them?" I asked.

"Kid, I grew up in the South where the place is lousy with coloreds. I never met a good one yet."

"Well, how are they bad?"

"It's something about the way they think. The blood gets into their brains, and they can't reckon as deep. That's why you can't trust 'em. If they got the chance, they'll rob you blind."

"Somehow it doesn't sound right."

"Well," he continued, "don't be thinking they're all bad. They have some good qualities, too. You know, son, there's good and bad to everything. The colored folks got some dandy traits to be downright proud of."

⚜

"Like what, Dad?"

"They've got strong bones, and they can run fast."

I had seen Norman run after his books, and he was pretty fast. But the rest of the stuff sounded wrong to me. I dropped the subject and strolled into the living room. Grandma Ru was sitting on the floor, carefully removing all the onion rings from her toasted cheese sandwich while Maggie licked off the cheese. Then Grandma stood up, opened Lulu's cage, and hung the purple onion rings from the wooden trapeze.

"There you go," she murmured. "Now, Lulu, you can fly through the rings like tigers jump through hoops. Yeahhh, we'll turn you into a trick bird, and then we can both run away with the circus."

"Grandma," I said, "would you like me to comb your hair?"

"I would adore it."

I found her silver comb and set her in the chair. I undid her bun and let the white silky strands fall down her back. While I combed out the tangles—slowly, so they wouldn't pull—she wavered back and forth between awake and asleep. When she drifted back toward wakefulness, she'd say, "Yes, divine . . ." and then nod out again.

While her head hung calm in slumber, I brushed her hair forward. Then with the silver comb I sliced a perfect part from the crown of her head to the top of her forehead where her widow's peak grew. When I pulled aside the hair, she lifted her head, looked at me with clear green eyes, and said in a lucid voice, "So how is your mother, darling?"

"Grandma, I hope she's all right wherever she is."

As I combed her hair toward the back and began braiding it, I asked, "Do you know where she lives, Grandma? I'd like to write her a letter."

"Close," she said as she drifted off again.

When I went back toward the kitchen, I saw a bottle of whiskey and five beer bottles lined up on the table in front of my father. At first he didn't see me standing in the doorway while I watched him scraping a trench down the middle of the label with his thumbnail.

The fear of him leaving for Lily like the last time pressed against my chest. "Stop drinking!" I yelled as I grabbed the bottles from the table.

My father threw his head back and cackled, "Hah! Are you afraid I'm going to go get the wench again?"

"Why would you call her a wench, Dad? What did she ever do that was wrong?"

"You want to know what she did wrong? I'll tell you," he said as he finished off his beer. "She was born—that was her sin."

I left the kitchen, went upstairs, and huddled by the railing at the top of the stairway with Maggie. I watched my father punch the air and mutter, "Isabel, Isabel . . ." Then he sat quietly, his head hung low. A fat furry spider crawled along the edge of the table, then strolled boldly toward my father's empty dinner plate. My father became mesmerized with the insect. He watched it creep past his beer and around the plate. He set another beer bottle in its path, but the spider rerouted around the obstacle. Then he set another and another until the only hope for escape was to crawl up the bottle.

When the insect got to the top, my father tipped the bottle upside down and shook it until the spider fell onto the table. He pressed a kitchen knife against one of the spider's legs. Then, with a tiny pair of scissors from his Swiss army knife, he cut off its legs, one by one. When he was done, the round furry body rolled helplessly from side to side. My father placed his finger gently upon the spider and squished down slowly until green fluid oozed out around his finger. He put the eight spider legs on his empty plate and went to the refrigerator for another beer.

I waited patiently at the top of the stairs, determined to stay awake all night if I had to. As the evening wore on, my father became more restless. I lay on the rug by the top step, but kept my head propped up with one hand. But sometime after midnight, I fell asleep. Grandma Ru must have stepped over my sleeping body when she went to bed, because I awoke to the sound of the front door opening—my father returning. Before he saw me, I ran into my room. Angry with myself, I looked out the window. The sun was just rising.

23

The day after my father squished the spider, I skipped school and went to Lily's. It was a short visit because she didn't let me linger, insisting that I go back to school. But I stayed long enough to see the results of my father's visit the night before.

I had pedaled off in the morning, like normal. But I went only as far as the school bridge, waiting there until my father had left for work. I hid in the woods so no one would see me. When Norman walked by on his normal route to school, I saw him carrying some fat warped textbooks with wrinkled pages and several brand-new composition notebooks. Well, at least he had retrieved the textbooks and didn't have to pay for new ones, I thought. After about an hour, I returned to the house, saw my father's car gone, and went in to get Maggie. Lily hadn't seen my puppy yet.

I knocked on the chapel door, and butterflies filled my stomach. Surely I would wake her. A few minutes passed before the door opened, but only a crack. Lily was there in her white robe. She looked at me sadly, left the door ajar, and walked away so she wouldn't be too close to the light. I slid in and bolted the door.

"I woke you, didn't I?"

"No . . . ," she said as if to herself. "Actually I was thinking of sleeping soon."

"You were up all night?"

Without answering, Lily sat on the edge of the couch. She had arranged a circle of round river stones on the floor with a pillow in the middle. Maybe she was sitting there when I knocked. Cups of aromatic herbs were placed nearby with stubby candles burning underneath to keep the brew steaming.

"What's in the cups?" I asked.

"Wild cherry and chamomile mixed with valerian roots. They're very tranquil herbs, which you're supposed to drink. But the valerian gives me illusions so I make a potpourri instead. The vapors help me feel peaceful. Sometimes it works. Sometimes . . . ," she trailed off.

Looking around, I saw the place was a mess—things strewn all over. Chiffon had been pulled from the alcove and lay like clouds across the floor. A new puzzle she had been working on was in pieces all over the stone floor. And shells from her crystal garden were shattered across the hearth.

"I'm sorry," I said on the verge of tears. "I wanted to warn you, but I fell asleep. I'm so sorry."

"Josey, don't get yourself in the middle of this. He'll hurt you worse than me."

"Lily, how does he get in with all the locks? Look at those huge bolts on the door."

"Anyway he can. He's broken through the windows and . . ."

"What?"

"He threatens me."

"How?"

"Oh, things . . . let's see. He says he will come back the next day and drag me into the light. Or he says he'll put me in a mental hospital."

"How can he do that? You're not crazy. You can tell them you don't want to go."

"Well, it's a bit more complicated than that."

"Why?"

"Listen, Boo. You need to go back to school."

Then I thought about my grandmother saying last night how she and Lulu would run away with the circus. "Lily, let's you and I go somewhere together—forever and so far away that no one will find us. We'll take care of each other. I'll do all the daytime things so you don't have to go into the light. At night we'll do puzzles and go fossil hunting together and—"

"Hey," she said swiftly, "what's this bundle of fur you have here?"

"That's Maggie. She can come with us when we run away."

Lily held out her hands, and I passed Maggie to her. When Lily looked down, her honey hair fell all around the half-grown pup like a waterfall of gold. "Come on over here," she said. "Oh, such a little ball of fluff. Let me get you some milk."

"She was much smaller when I got her. She's actually growing fast."

"Well, I think I'll call her 'Smidgen' because she's absolutely the littlest dog I ever did see."

Maggie lapped up the milk with delight, and Lily laughed and poured another bowlful. Then she became serious and said, "Time to go to school now." She stepped back farther from the door so she wouldn't be too close when I opened it.

"When can we leave?" I persisted. "We'll go far away."

"It will never happen."

"Then at least can I live with you?"

"No. You need someone who can take care of you. And your Grandma Ru will miss you."

"How do you know about Grandma Ru?"

"Remember, we're cousins. I know about your relatives."

"So I can't live with you?"

"No, Boo."

"Then, will you marry me when I grow up?"

"No," she laughed.

"Why?"

"We're cousins. And cousins don't marry each other."

24

I didn't get to ask Lily about my mother. I wanted to know where she was and why she didn't come for me. Perhaps she thought I was dead, just like my father made me believe about her.

Lily's kindness and the terror of my father's rage strengthened my resolve to find her. Before my mother married, her name had been Isabel Bouvier. Apparently she was a distant relative of Jackie Bouvier, who later became Jackie Kennedy. But the relationship was too distant for my mom to be invited to family gatherings. Grandma Ru said that when my mother spoke her maiden name it was soft and lingered like the southern air of her birthplace. Then my father married her and turned her from Jackie Bouvier's distant relative into Isabel Rose.

There was one particular project my father had built that often made me think of her. It was a castle inside an old bottle made of pale-blue glass. The slender castle within had spires that reached toward the neck of the bottle as if they embraced the heavens. The uneven grain of the old glass made the castle waver when I moved the bottle.

Throughout the stony castle walls, my father had attached gems and tiny crystals, which he had plucked from the jewelry that had come down to him from my great-grandmother. Several opals were imbedded in the tower walls. My father said those were magic stones whose sole purpose was to hypnotize enemies into a stupor if they dared to look upon the castle walls. Twinkling diamonds were attached to the pinnacles, which, when struck by the late afternoon sun, split the light into colors, as if the castle were made from the stuff in rainbows.

When I missed my mother, I gazed into the bottle with the castle inside. When my father and Grandma Ru were busy elsewhere, I carefully carried the bottle over to the window by the light and hoped that maybe this beautiful world inside pale blue glass might be the kind of place where my mother lived in heaven, if she were really gone.

But beyond offering a bit of comfort, something else captivated me about this castle that my father had built before I was born. There was a spirit to it, and I often wondered: How could the hands of a man who worked high iron and threw pickled eggs at the birds create such delicate beauty as the castle inside this bottle?

25

As autumn passed, I became more and more obsessed with my father's drinking. When I opened the refrigerator for some milk and saw beer on the shelf, I was angry at him. When he drank even a little, I went up in my room and wouldn't talk to him. I became withdrawn and planned on biding my time until I could convince Lily to run away with me, and together we could find my mother.

It was the first of November, and on the afternoon before, the first big snow had come to New Hampshire like angora blankets laid down by angels. Grandma Ru and I had pressed our noses against the window and watched snowflakes as big as cotton puffs drift from the sky in layers across our valley. By the next morning, the weather had cleared. Even before the sun rose, I knew the skies would turn azure blue.

My father woke me very early. "A perfect day for fishing," he said as he set out his rods and reels all over the dining room table and chose the best specimens from his lure collection. "Hey, kiddo," he commanded, "get your gear together. The excursion party leaves in fifteen minutes."

"But Dad, how can you fish in the snow?"

"As long as the temperature is above freezing, the lines won't ice up. We'll give it a go."

"So early in the morning?"

"I have to get back in time to help ol' Eddie move a grand piano.

Anyway, there's nothin' like fishing at sunrise. We can catch the critters off guard before they've had their breakfast. They'll be biting like deer flies in the heat."

I put on my red long underwear and gray wool coat and leggings. With my leather mitts and Davy Crockett hat, I was ready to roll. Although I didn't admit it to my dad, I was really looking forward to this adventure—a chance to talk and maybe improve things between us.

"Hey, what the devil are you doing with that mutt?" asked my father. "If she can't carry a fishing pole, then she can't come."

"But she loves the river," I said, stuffing six beef jerkys in my pocket.

"Your coat's gonna smell like jerky for the rest of the winter," he said, changing the subject. I knew that meant Maggie could come.

As we crossed the valley to the river, I followed behind my father, trying to walk in his deep footprints. For every one step he made, I made two. The snow came up almost over my knees. Maybe I should have listened to him about leaving Maggie home. When she tried to follow, she jumped out of one footprint, but couldn't leap far enough to the next. The fluffy snow did not support her weight, so she fell straight through, and I had to keep stopping to feel around in the drifts to pull her out. To keep from losing her in the maze of powder, I carried her the rest of the way to the river.

Lugging a fishing pole, small tackle box, and Maggie, too, would have been somewhat manageable if it weren't for my wool leggings—they attracted snow like a magnet. By the time we were halfway to the river, small balls of the white stuff began matting to the wool. I looked like an alien creature made of marshmallows. Only thing is, they weren't light airy marshmallows—they were dense nuggets getting bigger and heavier with every step. But a deal's a deal. If you can't carry your own fishing pole, then you can't go fishing. So I accepted my burden and made it to the river.

When we arrived, I dropped Maggie and all my gear and flopped on the ground. My snow nuggets clicked together like a mariachi band. My father thought it was so funny that he pulled out his camera and snapped a shot. My clumsy condition would be forever etched on film. While my father cut away the white nuggets with a hunting knife, I fed Maggie all six strips of beef jerky. Then my dad opened his thermos while I lay back, watching him with envy as warm steam drifted up and swirled around his head.

"Want some?" my father asked, holding out a cup.

"I thought kids don't drink coffee."

"It's hot chocolate," he mumbled. "I made it for you and me."

I sat up with a start, took the cup in my fat leather mitts, and savored every warm luscious sip, thinking this is what family is all about. Early-morning fishing expeditions. Hot chocolate and marshmallows. Father and son. I wished the scary parts never happened.

"Hey," he said, "we should have saved one of those marshmallows from your leggings. You could have floated it on top of your hot chocolate."

"Yeah," I replied, "there were enough marshmallows for an army."

"Okay, enough of this lollygagging," commanded my father. "Time to reel in some dinner." He rigged up my line with a tiny silver spinner for casting. Then he put one of his homemade fly lures on his line, slipped on his black hip boots, and waded into the river. He instructed me to cast downstream from him, since my line would run out farther than his.

"Watch those maples behind you, squirt. Don't snag any branches. You ain't gonna find fish hanging from the trees."

I walked downstream a ways, found an open spot on the riverbank, and cast into the middle of the water. I watched the lure grab the morning sun and toss it back out in a twinkle. As I reeled in the line, the silver spinner looked like a tiny star that had fallen from the sky and was swimming upstream. And it was cold. My line was freezing up in places, causing slender strings of ice to wind up in the reel. I spent most of my time untangling the line.

How could fish live in water this cold? I wondered. When the river freezes completely, I imagined them caught in the ice, unable to do anything but hover there and wink at each other.

I looked upstream at my father. He scanned the water, evaluated currents, and flicked his wrist just right to get his fly lure to look enticing. The man was serious about the task. I wished his enthusiasm for fishing and tiny bottled worlds would spread to our relationship.

"Hey, Dad," I called, "what happens to the fish when the river ices up?"

"Somebody puts the critters in freezer bags and attaches little labels."

"Oh, sure."

"Get back to your business, Josey. The fish know who's serious and who's just fooling around."

As much as I enjoyed fishing, I had a hard time keeping my mind on it. My attention drifted to the icicles along the river edge that hung like glass ornaments from the shale ledges along the bank, and my cheeks flushed with thoughts of Lily. We were fishing in the same river where she and I had gathered fossils by candlelight only weeks ago. I imagined her walking through here now like a winter princess with snow in her hair. I drifted out on the strand of that daydream, and suddenly a fish hit my line. I was so startled I dropped the pole in the water.

"Idiot!" my father yelled as he splashed downstream straight for me.

"It slipped, Dad," I said quickly. "It slipped right out of my hand."

"You're a hopeless case, Josey Rose. A dreamer. God forbid you should keep your mind on something for five minutes straight—even if it's smack dab in front of your face. Christ Almighty. It comes with the eyes."

With his fly line dangling behind him, my father ran past me, cursing up a storm, chasing my rod downstream. All the while, the current took his own fly line downstream as well. When he was two feet from my rod, he tripped on his own line and fell flat on his face in the middle of the freezing water.

"Jesus, Mary and Joseph!" he hollered. Maggie scampered back and forth along the river edge, whining and fretting.

"Let me help," I called, preparing to step in the water.

"Stay on the bank before you get us in more trouble."

When my father managed to stand up, he was wrapped in his own line with a fly lure stuck to his coat like a red boutonniere. I ran back to his bag and grabbed the camera.

"Smile," I called as I clicked the shutter.

"Hey, put that blasted thing away before you drop it into the river, too. You can bet I'll tear up that shot. I don't want anybody seeing this friggin' fiasco."

"Hah!" I yelled, "you're a real sight."

"Cripes," exclaimed my father as he trudged out of the water with the two rods, "there's only one problem with the pictures on this roll of film."

"What's that?" I asked.

"There ain't no fish in them."

"Should we give it another go?"

"Listen, kid," he said as he took off his wading boots and poured out several gallons of water, "you try drenching your bones in a frigid stream and then stand around for an hour."

I saw his point. We left fishless.

"Well," I said, trying to console him, "what kind of fish would we have caught, if . . . you know . . . if we had caught any?"

"Trout, son. Plump, luscious rainbow trout."

We didn't talk for the rest of the way home. What's worse, it began snowing again—as thick as the day before. My father's soaking-wet clothes became stiff from the cold, and I still had to carry Maggie and my pole. As difficult as our trek became, there was, somehow, beauty in the slowly falling snow. In the expanse of the valley, I imagined us as tiny ants trying to walk across a bowl of flour while the cook sifted more from above.

At last we arrived home. With ice and snow and marshmallows all over us, we were a sight. Even my Davy Crockett hat had turned from raccoon to white rabbit. My father was freezing cold in his wet clothes. After he put on dry long johns, he was still shivering. I thought about Lily's remedy.

"Rub red peppers on your body," I said.

"Where in the blazing hell do you come up with these cockeyed ideas?"

"Well . . . this was on TV. Yeah, they said to get rid of chills, you mix red pepper with meadowsweet and rub it on your shoulders and down your spine."

"Quackery, son. Pure unadulterated quackery. You want to know how to get warm? I'll show you." He opened the china closet and carefully brought down one of his grandmother's antique champagne glasses. Then he filled it to the brim with golden whiskey. Somehow, with the glow of the morning still strong, the whiskey didn't bother me.

"First," he said, "you bless the potion . . ." He closed his eyes and waved his hands above the glass.

"Reverend Jasper would like that part," I said.

"Yes, yes, then you consecrate the drink with the magic words . . . *Abracadabra, warm thy body with the heat of this brew* . . . " He lifted his glass and swirled it around in the air in front of him, tilted his head back, and let the whiskey drain down his throat in one long gulp.

"Ahhh," he growled contentedly, "blessed be the brew that binds." His cheeks flushed like roses, and he poured another glass. So much for a grand day with my father—the booze was his only companion now.

"I thought you'd let up on your drinking, Dad," I challenged. "I thought things had changed."

"Nothing changes, kid. Just seems that way."

"Why can't they change? Why can't you stop drinking?"

"Sure, no problem. But first do something for me, will ya? Stop the memories, Josey, and change the past. Then I'll do whatever you want."

I wished I knew what to say or do, but I couldn't contend with my father's memories. He grew more agitated, staring at the ceiling with the bottle in his hand. I thought I'd be helping him move the piano, but decided to get out before the anger came. So I took off for Casey's house. I didn't want to be around when his "blessed brew" took hold.

✺   ✺

"Casey," I complained, "why did you do that the other day?"

"Do what?" he replied. "I've accomplished so many feats this week, you're going to have to remind me which of my triumphs you're talking about."

"You know darned well what I'm talking about—tossing Norman's books in the river."

"Ah, well, you could have been referring to the time I dragged him to the old railroad viaduct, strung him from his toes, and shoved grapefruits down his throat."

"You didn't!"

"Better check it out. You might find grapefruit seeds still scattered across the tracks."

"Casey, you're—"

"Josey, I'm just kidding!"

"But what you did at the school bridge was lousy."

"Listen, here's the best thing for everybody," explained Casey. "You leave me alone at school, and I'll leave you alone, too. We get along fine at our houses, but not at school—not when I'm around my friends."

"Yeah, 'cause you're trying to play the big shot."

"Doesn't matter what I'm doing. It's none of your business. So you stay out of it, you hear?"

"You're going to get into trouble—acting all wild like that."

"Wait till you get older, Josey Rose, you'll be wild, too. It comes with the territory."

While I was hanging out with Casey, my father arrived to pick up

Eddie so they could move the grand piano. Before sunset, I left Casey's house so I wouldn't have to ride my new bike along the snowy road after dark. My father was still out when I returned. I made liverwurst sandwiches for Grandma, Maggie, and me. Then I built a blazing fire and did my homework while Grandma nodded off.

%   %

That's when my father arrived home in a rage. No gradual rise to this spree. Just a grand entrance through the door, and then things started flying. The first thing I noticed was the blood. My father's hand was wounded along the knuckles.

"What happened, Dad? Be careful, you're bleeding all over the floor."

"You wanta know what happened? I'll tell you what happened." He took a slug of whiskey that was still opened from his "blessed brew" earlier in the day. Then he fell into his chair. "It went down like this: Eddie and me are minding our own business, you see, down at Hank's Bar. This fellow saunters over and gets in my face, asking me all sorts of nosy questions like don't he know me from somewhere, and don't I work high iron on the State Street job, and don't I live in the valley in that old stone house. So I says to him, 'Hey, Bucko, who the fuck are you—my personal historian?'"

"Willie, darling," sighed Grandma Ru, waking up from the ruckus, "he was just trying to be friendly, that's all. Maybe he's lonely."

"Blasted you!" he hollered. "I don't care how lonely the bugger is, I'm trying to tell a story here. So then the fellow says, 'Hey, Jack, what's your problem? You got a tie rod up your ass?' Can you imagine such idiocy—talking to me like that?"

"Dad, let me get a bandage for your hand—you'll lose all your blood."

"Screw it," he said. "I heal fast, like a bear in the woods. See, it's co-agulating already." He held out a disgusting display of torn skin, ripped tissues, and exposed tendons.

"Oh, honey," sighed Grandma. "you're hurt bad. Josey, get the Bactine."

"Grandma," I said, "I think he needs more than Bactine."

"So then the dummy comments on my drinking. He says something about 'excessive.' I tell him, 'I'll show you excessive,' and I let him have it right in his ugly puss."

%

"What happened to the guy?" I asked.

"Last I saw that numskull, he was lyin' on the floor picking teeth out of his mouth."

I ran in the kitchen and fetched some rags and a pan of warm soapy water. The only thing I knew about cleaning wounds was what I saw on television. I set the pan on the table next to my father.

"Put your hand in this, Dad. You don't want it to get infected."

"Hey, don't treat me like an invalid. I'm tough, and I can take it. Always remember one thing, Josey boy."

"What's that, Dad?"

"Don't take no shit from nobody. Anybody gives you trouble, you give 'em the four-knuckle salute. You give . . ." He leaned back, curled his bloody fist, and slammed it through the living room wall. The flowered wallpaper split apart, and his hand grazed a two-by-four and embedded itself in the inside panel. Blood dripped down the broken wall. When he pulled out his hand, pink insulation stuck to the loose tissue around his knuckles.

"Temper, temper," sang Grandma Ru.

The birds chirped and fluttered in their cage, trying to escape. My father stared at the blood draining from his hand.

"Isabel, Isabel . . . ," sang Lulu.

"Knock it off, you little tweet!" yelled my father as he stood up and staggered toward the cage. "I'll bop your beak so hard you'll never peep again."

"No!" I screamed.

Maggie tried to scamper out of his path. My father tripped over her and stumbled on the rug.

"There's too many goddamn critters in this house! Get outta my friggin' way." He pulled back his foot and kicked Maggie so hard she flew clear across the living room and landed in the fire.

"Hah!" laughed my father. "Ten points for a winning goal!"

Maggie yelped all the way through the air, but that sound was like a gentle songbird compared to the howls when she hit the flames. I ran to the fireplace and tried to pull her out, but the fire was too hot. I saw her wild, frightened eyes roll in her head as she screeched in pain. I grabbed the poker and pulled her onto the hearth. Then I snatched up Grandma's shawl that was lying by her chair and wrapped it around Maggie. When the flames went out, she lay limp in my arms. She wasn't breathing.

"You idiot!" I yelled. "Look what you've done. You mean, miser- able jerk. How could you—"

"Josey, take it easy."

"Don't tell me to take it easy. And don't tell me you did this because of your father. No matter how mean he was to you—it doesn't give you the right to hurt Maggie. What did she ever do to you?"

I was frightened and angry. I didn't know what to do so I wrapped her further in the shawl and ran upstairs. I lay her on the bed and put my head down next to her quiet body and cried. Then the worst sound of all—my father's footsteps. Surely he was coming up to do me in as well, maybe toss me out the window or lug me downstairs and throw me out the door. I was really scared this time.

When his footsteps stopped, I waited, trembling with my head buried in the bedspread beside Maggie. When nothing happened, I looked up and saw my father standing above me, dazed and white as a ghost. We stared at each other for a moment, then the doorbell rang, and my father left to answer it. Peeking out from the top of the stairs, I saw the same two cops who came the night my father couldn't find me.

"Mr. Willie Rose, how are you doing tonight?" asked the one who looked like a vampire.

"Well, I'm fine and dandy," my father said sarcastically. "And why might you boys be so interested in my welfare?"

"Mr. Rose, we have a gentleman back at the station who says he wants to press charges against you. Claims you knocked out his teeth down at Hank's Bar. Does that ring any bells for you?"

"There does seem to be a hint of familiarity in what you're saying, officer."

The one with the red hair scanned the mess around the room. "What's going on here, Willie? Looks like things are a bit riled up."

"Oh, the kid and I were having a little pillow fight. You know, boys will be boys. He's a real whippersnapper when he gets going."

"Where is the little whippersnapper? Perhaps we could have a word with him."

"Reckon he's sound asleep by now, sir. You know he has school to- morrow."

"Tomorrow's Sunday, Willie."

"Well, you know . . . one of these days he has school, and I want him to be rested when the time comes."

"If you don't mind, sir, we'd like to wake him up and have a chat— you know, standard procedure."

"What kind of procedure is that?" argued my father. "Some guy says I rang his chimes in a bar, and you want to talk to my son?"

"Things look a bit strange around here, Willie. We want to check it out. And what is that odor? Smells like burning hair."

"Oh, that. Grandma's shawl ended up in the fire. She's been a little off in her later years—throws things into the flames and prays to the Indians. The other day, she tried to burn the blender."

"Would you like to get your son, Willie, or shall we go up and rouse him?"

"Be right back," said my father. When he walked into the bedroom, my face was still buried in the bedspread. I couldn't look at him. He pulled me up and held my head so I was forced to see his eyes.

"The cops are going to ask you some questions, son," my father breathed in a roaring whisper. "If you say one word about what happened here, they'll take me away to jail, and they'll put you in a foster home. And let me tell you this, kid—living in a foster home is pure hell. It makes North Dakota look like a South Sea island. So you keep your yapper shut, or it's the blazin' foster pits for you. Remember, the only thing on fire around here was Grandma's shawl when she threw it in the fire. Got that?"

When I walked down the stairs, I held onto the railing because my knees were shaking. The short dumpling cop took me aside. "You want to tell me what's going on here tonight?" he asked.

I looked at the floor, not saying a word.

"Josey, how did that hole in the wall get there?" he tried again.

Silence.

"It's okay," he said, "you can talk to me. Nothing bad will happen to you."

I looked over his shoulder at my father, who swiped his finger across his neck.

"Tell me about the smell, Josey," the cop said gently. "Why does the house smell like burning hair?"

"Well," I said, trembling through to my bones, "my grandma pulled her shawl from her shoulders . . . and she rolled it up with her hands . . . and she put it in the f-fire."

"Oh, that must have been scary for you, was it?"

"Yes, it was."

The dumpling cop let me go and went back to the vampire with red hair. "He won't talk," he said.

"Okay," said the tall one, "get your coat, Mr. Rose. We're taking you down to the station to ask you a few questions. Then we'll run you to the hospital and take care of that hand. You, too, Josey—you come along with us."

"Please," begged my father, "keep my son out of this."

"We don't want to leave him alone with his grandmother," said the cop. "The last time we were here, she threw a fit."

"She only does that when she runs out of glue," assured my father. "She stays with Josey all the time. He's twelve years old."

"Yes," I agreed. "I'll be fine."

"All right," said the cop, guiding my father out the door.

"Is he ever coming back?" I asked, afraid I might have to go to a foster home.

"Now what would make you think he wasn't coming back?" asked the dumpling cop.

I leaned against my grandma's chair as they closed the door and walked to the car. I despised my father. He had returned to drinking with a vengeance. He had killed Maggie—the only thing I could call my own. And he had reduced me to a quivering coward. I felt like a prisoner. Nowhere to turn. Imagine trying to explain this to Casey or Ralph without crying and looking like a fool. Mrs. Lark would only try to soothe away the sorrow with her soft voice. No one could possibly understand my dilemma. No one in the whole world except Lily.

26

With my bike out of the shed, I prepared to tuck Maggie into the basket behind the seat where she always rode. But I was too broken-hearted to let her out of my arms. She was still warm. So I left the bike and walked along the winter road to the chapel.

When I arrived at Lily's door, my arms were full with Maggie so I couldn't knock. "Lily," I called, "it's me, Josey. My father, he—the police, Lily, they took him away, and—"

The door opened, and Lily found me huddled against the archway with a bundle in my arms. When I looked up, her soft eyes caused me to burst into tears again.

"Hey, little Boo, why are you weeping? What could be so sad?"

I stood up and came in slowly. Lily guided me to the couch by the fire, but I couldn't sit. The sputtering flames made me tremble.

"Take your time," she said. "You can cry as long as you want to, it's okay."

"M-M-Maggie," I stammered.

"What about Maggie?"

"This is her," I said, looking at the bundle. I was too upset to do anything but stare and babble.

"Is she hurt, darling?"

"No, she's . . . m-my father kicked her into the fire."

Lily took Maggie, walked across the room, and laid her on the table.

"No, don't look at her," I cried. "It'll make you feel bad. She's not fluffy anymore."

"Boo, if it's okay, I want to make sure. Maybe she's still alive."

I knew she was dead, but Lily seemed magical—perhaps she could bring her back to life somehow. She unwrapped the shawl, slowly. When she tried to open the last fold, she could barely pull away the fabric as it had adhered to Maggie's charred body. She managed to move away a small area by Maggie's head. Lily gazed down with a shudder, then carefully lay the fabric back over Maggie and wrapped her up as before.

"And the police," I stammered. "They took my father away."

"How did the police know to come? Did you call them?"

"No, my father got in a fight at Hank's Bar and hurt his hand and knocked out some guy's teeth and punched a hole through the living room wall, and then this," I said, looking hopelessly at Maggie.

"I see. Are you dressed warmly?" she asked.

"Yes."

"Then we'll bury her now."

Lily went into her alcove of fabrics and put on several layers of long skirts, a woolen shawl, and furry boots that went up to her knees. She put some things in a bag, grabbed a shovel, and we were off.

"Would you like me to carry her?" Lily asked.

"No, I've got her," I said, wiping my tears on Grandma's shawl.

Only a slender wisp of moon shone in the sky, so the night was dark and very still. Lily lit a candle and led the way through the snowy meadow. The flickering flame gave light to a small area around us, making it feel like we were high above the ground. Lily's long skirts trailed behind her, and the warm glow from the candle enflamed her hair. The folds of her shawl were like soft wings upon her back.

"Lily," I whispered.

She turned around and kneeled down with the candle.

"Do dogs go to heaven?" I asked.

"I don't know," she said. "I haven't been there, so I can't say for sure."

"Oh," I said, disappointed.

"It would make sense to me," she said, "that if people go to heaven, then dogs should go, too, don't you think?"

"Yes."

"And probably squirrels as well," she continued, "and butterflies and bumblebees. I imagine it's a real zoo up there."

We walked on through the snowy clouds until she paused and asked, "Where do you think we should bury her?"

"Gosh, I don't know."

"There's a lot of ground out here, Josey. We can put her wherever you like. If you're not sure, we'll keep walking until it feels like a good spot. You'll know when we've come to the place because it will feel right."

"Okay," I said skeptically.

We walked clear across the meadow to the edge of the forest, but I didn't get the feeling anything was "right."

"Would you like to go into the woods?" Lily asked.

I looked into the dark tangle of trees and then back at the meadow with its open rolling terrain. "Let's walk along the edge of the meadow," I said. "It's more like heaven should be."

As we moved along I heard the river deep in the woods—the same river where I had been fishing with my father that morning. The same river that had swept away Norman's composition books. And the same river that I had run downstream the day I rescued Maggie from the fury of Peaches McNally. But I had let my Maggie down. She would have been better off with Peaches than at my house after what happened tonight. My heart sagged low in my chest as the cool air stole warmth from my bundle.

After we walked on awhile, the heaviness suddenly lifted. A wave of peacefulness enveloped me, if only for a moment.

"Lily," I said, "this is the place."

It was a part of the meadow that dipped into the woods like a small bay. It was open, yet cozy.

"It's a meadow nook," said Lily.

Whatever it was, this would be Maggie's spot. I held the candle while Lily shoveled away the snow.

"Wait," I said, "how can we dig if the ground is frozen?"

"It's still early in the season yet. The snow is like a blanket keeping the earth warm for a while. Digging will be no problem." Lily knew all the important things in life, I thought.

I helped her dig, and when the hole was made, we kneeled in the snow, which formed a low wall around us. She held out her arms, and I gave Maggie to her. I clutched the candle while Lily laid Maggie in the ground, tucking Grandma's shawl around her little body. Then Lily lit two more candles and set them in the snow.

"You picked a nice place here, Josey."

"How is it good?"

"Well, in the summertime, chamomile and Queen Anne's lace grow here. Maggie will make the ground rich, and she'll nourish the plants. She'll become part of the white blossoms in the summer, and she'll give nectar to the butterflies who will fly all over the meadow filled with Maggie's spirit."

"Then the butterflies will take her to heaven," I said.

Lily leaned over Maggie. "Good-bye, little Smidgen, I'm glad I had a chance to meet you."

I tried to say something to Maggie, too, but I could only be sad. Lily came beside me, took my candle, and pressed it into the snow. I lay my head in her lap and watched the wax from all the candles pour like clear honey, cutting canyons in the snow and making tiny rivers that all ran to Maggie. When I sat up, Lily opened her bag and handed me some sweet-smelling leaves.

"Dried rose petals," she said. She took some, too, and we sprinkled them over Maggie—handfuls of them—until all we could see was a pile of rich red petals deep within the snow. The night air was filled with the scent of roses. I closed my eyes so I could see more clearly. In my mind I imagined Lily and me kneeling in a summer garden. Flowers drooping, heavy with dew. Swarms of butterflies all around, fluttering in slow motion through the perfumed air. As my thoughts drifted, some of the butterflies grew very large with wings of turquoise and silver. They were Grandma Ru's butterflies. I remembered how they had been bound to the backs of cows who stampeded down the driveway and lifted off into the sky. I chuckled lightly, still with tears in my eyes.

"I'm sorry," I said. "I didn't mean to laugh."

"Josey Boo. You can do anything you want to." So I wrapped my arms around her shoulders and lay my head in the folds of her scarf. I watched the vapors from my breath crawl up her neck and swirl around the curve of her ear. Then we covered Maggie with dirt and snow and followed our path back to the house, carrying our candles away from Maggie's meadow nook.

Upon our return, I snuggled amid the pillows on the couch and held the afghan close. Lily stoked the fire to keep it burning low. Then she laid a mohair blanket over me and made some hot chocolate. There wasn't much to say.

Shortly after, Lily was brewing up some herbal concoctions on the wood stove when a soft knock sounded at the door. She unbolted the door and opened it to a tall man with skin as black as Norman Johnson's. The man walked into the kitchen and set three bags on the table. Then Lily gave him a gentle hug, and they sat down to talk. They murmured quietly as steam spewed from the pot on the stove.

My curiosity roused me as I heard them whispering and glancing my way. They talked like old friends. When they finished their private chat, Lily called, "Josey, come on over. I'd like you to meet my friend Leon. He lives in the farmhouse across the meadow. And Leon, this is Josey."

"Hello," said Leon in a deep easy voice. "I'm sorry to hear about your pup. Lily was telling me."

I stared at the floor. Lily talked about Leon's flourishing vegetable gardens. She explained how the chapel was on Leon's land, and that many years ago, a church had leased the property from Leon. But before their lease ran out, they had abandoned the chapel, and it fell into disarray until Lily came.

"Want a muffin?" asked Leon as he sorted through one of the bags. He pulled out a white bakery box with six fat blueberry muffins. Their tops blossomed out like giant mushrooms.

"Okay."

Lily gave me a china plate with the muffin, and I wandered back to the couch. Halfway back, I turned and said, "Thanks, Mr. Leon."

Lily and Leon talked while I ate the muffin slowly, feeling downhearted like the last dead leaf hanging from a stark tree. My Maggie was gone. My father might be in jail. And Lily had other friends. Leon was probably her best friend. When the muffin was done, I put the plate on the floor and thought of how Maggie used to come lick up the crumbs from my plates. I stared at the fire, the flickering tongues of flame.

Then I heard their footsteps—Lily and Leon. They wandered over and sat near me. We talked about the evening's events, and while we found no particular answers, I felt better. I needed the comfort. The patter of voices. Leon asking, "Why did he slam his fist through the wall?" And Lily gasping, "How utterly frightening!"

It felt good to find people who understood—people whom I could talk with instead of listening to my father's harsh demands telling me, "Don't take no shit from nobody" and how I "gotta look life straight in the bare-assed eyeballs." I'd found people who cared.

As far as what to do next, there wasn't much Lily and Leon could offer. Going to the cops was unrealistic—I'd end up in a foster home for sure. Running away hadn't worked. At first I'd hoped they might have some ideas, but if Lily knew what to do, she surely would have done it for herself by now. After all, we were both victims of my father's torment.

In that way I felt trapped, and I mumbled more to myself, "The only way out is through."

"What did you say?" asked Lily.

When I told her she said, "Perhaps so." Then after a moment, she sighed. "But the other side seems so far away."

That's the first time I really considered how much Lily needed comfort, too. We both needed to find a way through.

By the time Leon had left, the fire hummed lazily. The room was filled with the scent of lilac potpourri steaming up from the small pots around the room. Lily wandered off to work by candlelight at the same table she used for her puzzles. This time, she was surrounded with pieces of fungus that she had gathered from tree trunks in the forest— maybe the same ones she had dragged home in the canvas bag the night I watched her from under the pine tree. They were nice specimens, shaped like open fans with bands of beige, gray, and shades of brown. The other side was like white velvet. Some of the fungus pieces were almost a foot wide, while others were small as clam shells.

Lily was leaning over one piece. With a slender silver tool, she etched detailed lines into the velvety side of the fungus. With the afghan wrapped around me, I wandered over to take a look.

"Boo," she whispered, "how you doing?"

"Okay," I said. She kissed me on the forehead, then continued working. I watched the metal point cut tiny trails in the soft white surface, leaving dark lines, forming shapes of exotic fish and underwater plants.

"What happens if you make a mistake?" I asked.

"I turn the mistake into something else. See this angel fish over here? It was supposed to be seaweed, but I made the leaves too fat so it turned out to be the tail of an angel fish. How do you like the colors?" she asked, turning over the fungus to show the other side.

"How come there are different colors if it's always growing on the same tree?"

"Different moods, I suppose. Like this one here, the fungus was feeling rather gray, but over here he was having an almost purple day."

Then Lily and I named all the colors in the fungus based on what they looked like. We found rings that resembled toast, olives, suntan, maple sugar, figs, spring leaves, and almonds.

"Here's a ring like pearl," she said.

"This one's made of colors all mixed together," I noticed.

"It's the color of a sparrow."

"And this one," I said, pointing to a dark band, "looks like Leon."

"Yes," she chuckled, "it really does."

"Is Leon your best friend?"

"Oh, as if I have so many friends! You and Leon are my two friends. But if I were to figure out who was my best friend, I suppose I'd have to compare the two, and I see no use in that, do you?"

"Well, I have two friends, Casey and Ralph. Casey is my best friend, and Ralph is next."

"Hmmm, how odd," she said. Some things Lily couldn't understand.

"So what's Leon like?"

"Well," she mused, "he's very kind. I'm lucky to have Leon as my friend. And he lives so near, just across the meadow."

Lily went on to tell me how Leon bought things at the store for her and helped around the chapel, like reaching the high places with his ladder to hang her crystals from the ceiling. Lily confided to me that she marveled at the way Leon could work in his gardens all day in the bright sun.

Lily and Leon were opposites. She was like pale light, living in the darkness of the night. And he, black as midnight, worked all day in the blazing sun.

"Lily, you know, you really should be careful around Leon. He has a different kind of blood, you know, being colored and all—and you never know when he might hurt you."

Lily laid down her etching tool. "Who told you this?" she asked.

"That's what my father thinks. And everyone else, too."

She stayed quiet for a while and seemed sad. But it was enough for me to realize that other people's ideas about black people might not be entirely accurate.

"Come on, sugar Boo. Let's do something together."

She held my hand and walked me into the alcove with the crystal garden. Candles flickered all around us as the chiffon hanging from the ceiling touched softly upon my hair. From behind a pile of shells, she drew out a glass jar filled with polished stones. We lay on the floor amid all the pillows and fabrics. She poured out the stones onto a pile of rainbow chiffon and laid a round mirror in the middle. We rolled the smooth spheres around on the mirror, looking at their colors. Brilliant, speckled, and milky pebbles. Stones as big as robins' eggs and others tiny as peas, but all so beautiful.

Lily told me what they were made of. "Pink quartz and amethyst," she chanted, "topaz and jade." Her smoky voice mingled with clinking sounds of glass and gems. Her eyes reflected candlelight with colors I had never seen.

"Do you want to make a wish?" she asked.

"Yes."

"Then pick your favorite stone and come out into the night where wishes are made." I drew out a green stone with thin veins of pale pink. She led me to the water well behind the chapel. She set the wooden bucket aside, and we leaned over the wall and saw the water below reflecting stars and planets and a slender crescent moon.

In a voice softer than mist, she said, "Josey, I wish for you to forever see things as they truly are." I was feeling too weary to ask what she meant.

I whispered into the well, "I wish for Maggie to go to heaven." My whisper echoed back like angels breathing.

We dropped our stones into the well, listened to them plunk below, and watched the stars spin circles upon the water. We went back inside, and I slept until just before dawn. When I awoke, Lily was walking around the chapel blowing out the candles.

"Time for you to go home and for me to sleep," she said.

I wrapped up in my coat, put my arms around her shoulders, held her, and left.

27

I returned home with the morning. The sky smoldered in orange and violet. The sun was low but gaining height. Soon the light would burn through Lily's windows while she hid safely inside her dreams.

My father was home. The cops hadn't put him in jail after all. He was still sleeping so I crawled into my own bed for a morning nap. As I drifted off, I imagined living with Lily, being awake through the night, and sleeping all day long . . .

"Josey, Josey! Are you sick?" My father's hand upon my shoulders shook me from slumber. "Wake up, whippersnapper. Why are you still snoozing at eleven o'clock in the morning?"

I curled into a ball.

"Rise and shine. Time for breakfast."

I dragged myself from bed and plodded into the kitchen, where my father was frying hot peppers, scrambling eggs, and trying to make toast without burning it. He accomplished all of this with one hand—his other one was wrapped in bandages that wound past his wrist.

"Don't forget the Worcestershire sauce," said Grandma Ru.

I sat at the table with Grandma and stared at the grain in the wood. I thought about the spider my father had tortured here on this same table.

My father laid down a plate of eggs and toast with the burnt part carefully scraped off. I wasn't hungry.

"Are we a little moody this morning?" he asked. "What's the matter, you pissed off at your old man for having a little fun down at Hank's Bar last night? Hey, the creep deserved a good belt in the puss for asking me all those questions. And don't worry about my hand, I heal fast."

Dad and Grandma finished their plates. The butterflies in my stomach trembled and pressed upward, trying to get out. Nobody said anything except Grandma, who talked about the medicinal effects of Worcestershire sauce each time she doused her eggs in it. I considered throwing my whole plate at him and screaming out every mean thing he ever did.

"Hey, kid," said my father, "you're not saving all that home-cooked food for that mutt of yours. Maggie ain't gettin' any of this specialty—no sirree."

I looked straight at my father. "You're right about that, Dad. Maggie won't be eating my breakfast anymore."

"Glad to hear you're finally getting some sense in you, kid. Where is the critter, anyway?"

"Don't you remember? How could you possibly forget what happened last night? Maggie's . . . gone."

"Cripes, now I know your mind's gone kerflooey—sleeping till eleven, you don't eat your breakfast, and now you're talking that way about your sweet pup."

"Dad, you got drunk last night, and you don't even remember what happened."

"Please pass the Worcestershire," said Grandma. She made a puddle of it on her plate and drenched a corn muffin for dessert.

My father had heard about as much as he could take. He pushed away his plate and leaned toward me with a smirk. "Well, since you think my memory is so bad," he chided, "why don't *you* tell me exactly what happened last night. And while you're at it, maybe you can explain where in the hell you went. I didn't see you leave, but your sleeping this late tells me you didn't hit the hay at sundown."

"I'll tell you what happened," I said, still looking him in the eyes. "You kicked Maggie into the fire. She was burning so hard I couldn't pull her out except with a poker. You made me lie to the cops, and then they took you away."

※

My father stared at the table, then tilted his head as if trying to re-arrange the words I had spoken.

"You want to know where I went? To Lily's place. And you know what—when I called to her, she didn't answer the door at first. What do you think she was afraid of, Dad? She thought I was *you* coming to hurt her. How could you—"

"I told you to stay away from there. I told you never to set foot in that place . . . Christ—I don't believe this." He slammed back his chair and bolted into the living room. He looked at the fireplace, where the poker still lay on the hearth with ashes strewn about.

"No!" he called out as he buried his face in his hands. "Mother, tell me this didn't happen."

"Well, honey, you did get a little rambunctious last night."

"Where is she now?" asked my father.

"Who?" I shot back. "Maggie or Lily? Which of your victims are you referring to?"

"Maggie," he barely whispered.

"Buried in the ground. Her body will feed the flowers, and the but-terflies will take her to heaven."

"You're going to need some big butterflies," said Grandma, "and I know just the place to get some."

My father collapsed into Grandma's chair by the birds. He put his hands over his face and cried. "Josey," he sobbed, "how can you be sure? Maybe if we take her to the vet—"

"She was in the middle of the flames, burning up. Her heart stopped beating, Dad. She's buried in the ground."

He put his face in his hands again. Then he babbled unconnected words about anger and his father and the past. I think he said my mother's name. Then his mutterings coalesced. "I'm good at fixing things," he choked. "Nothing I can't put back together. Lord knows I've had to repair a few things around here . . . with all my rampages. But this—I loved Maggie. And you—to think of the sadness I've brought you."

I never saw him so lost.

"Josey," he sobbed, "come here."

I didn't want to, but I walked slowly across the room and stood in front of him, several feet away.

"I'm so sorry," he whimpered, holding out his hand toward me. He looked around the room, everywhere except the fireplace. "I can't ask you to forgive me, but I promise you this: You'll never see me drunk again. I won't hurt you like that ever again. I love you, kiddo."

❧ ❧

I told him I forgave him, and I treated him respectfully, but things changed after that. A distance crept between us. For more than a year, my father avoided getting rip-roaring drunk. Sure, he had a few beers now and then, but he always remembered what he did the night before, and he rarely threw things at the walls. I was glad for that.

Throughout that time, my father's life swung between his work and his projects. During the day, he balanced on high-iron beams, building skyscrapers. At night, he sat at the dining room table, creating delicate ships inside glass bottles. When we spoke it was tentative. If we laughed at all, it was hollow.

During that time, I fell into daydreaming so deeply that sometimes moments went by where I was barely aware of my father saying my name and talking to me. When at last he roused me back to this world, I'd look at him but my eyes focused somewhere far beyond him. "Hey, Josey Rose," he'd say, "come back here. Where is your mind?" And when his voice finally registered again, I'd hear lectures about me being a dreamer and that dreamers get themselves in muddles, botch things up, stumble off curbs, and fall into open manholes.

All in all, there was a sadness between my father and me. And the only way we got along was to be apart.

So for a while, Lily was entirely mine. She was my cousin and my friend. My fear that my father would hurt her waned for a while because he was drinking less and so never worked up enough fury to go to her. Whenever I left the house he didn't ask where I was going—I guess he assumed I was off with my friends.

Although I would have wanted to see her every day, Lily insisted we keep our visits only to the weekends so I wouldn't be sleepy during school and, even then, not every weekend. For me, it felt like an eternity between our times together.

Lily was like a butterfly—a rare specimen trapped inside a glass bottle, another jewel in my father's secret collections. She fluttered about, enveloped in layers of chiffon and long golden hair. If Lily were a time of day, she would be the dawn, even though she had slept through almost every sunrise for the last ten years. Lily was light coming out of the darkness. And the glow always followed her around.

My feelings for Lily mellowed to a deep adoration. I had never met anyone like her. For one thing, she could cure whatever ailed me. One afternoon, I got stung by three bumblebees while drawing water from her wishing well. She made a poultice of mud and herbs to draw out the poison. And when mosquito bites drove me mad with their wandering itches, she pounded frankincense to a powder, blended it with oil of bay, and rubbed it on my arms and legs.

One day, I piled six books on a chair trying to reach a crystal suspended from the ceiling. Just as I touched it, spinning it with my fingertips, rainbows whirled around the room, and I crashed to the stone floor and hurt my knee. Lily gave me a drink made from the roots of an orchid called lady's slipper. "It's an anodyne," she said. I lay on the couch while the air fizzed with hallucinations that kept me in awe for hours. And when I couldn't sleep, she brewed a blend of honey and herbs that sent me off to sleep right away.

Lily grew most of her own herbs inside her alcove of plants. If she hadn't been afraid of the light, she would have nurtured a garden outside the chapel like Leon. But as it was, she made her gardens inside. Sometimes I helped her water the plants. I'd fill the bucket from the well and carry it into the alcove. Then we'd pour water into sprinkling cans with long slender spouts and water all her herbs, crawling vines, and peculiar flowers.

Like a mother, Lily knew the idiosyncrasies of every plant. Some preferred a total drenching, while others lived happily on a scant sprinkling now and again. Others, called air plants, rarely took water at all—they simply clung to the stone of the alcove wall waiting for Lily to squirt mist at them. On that alone they lived. Some plants enjoyed a touch of salt in their water, some lived in sand, while one thrived with its roots set in coffee grounds.

Lily talked to the plants while she watered them. For the tropical ones, she told lush stories of the jungle. For the herbs, she described open meadows with gentle breezes and bees with pollen stuck to their hairy legs. For the cacti, she dwelled on the desert and the blazing sun, as if her descriptions could quell her own fear of the light. "Imagine a place," she said to the cacti, shuddering, "where the sky is as wide as the world, where the beach has no ocean, and where the only things that move are scaly reptiles and the hot sun, scorching its way across the sky." Lily recoiled at her own words, but the cacti responded happily by producing spiny skin and purple flowers, while one grew white hair from head to toe.

Lily showed me one plant that looked young and ordinary. "In ten years," she said, "this plant will blossom."

"Why does it take so long?"

"She's resting now, gathering energy. But when at last she shows her flowers, she'll capture the heart of anyone who sees her during that one short season."

"In ten years, I'll be twenty-two."

"Yes, and you'll be done with school."

"Will you still be my friend?" I asked.

"Maybe, but you'll have other interests then. Trekking though this meadow to visit me and all my plants will be the last thing on your mind."

Even then, I knew she was wrong.

28

Over time I became used to Leon, although I liked it best with only Lily and me. Each time Leon came by, he brought groceries, a big chunk of ice for Lily's icebox, and sometimes piles of beautiful fabrics.

The second time I saw Leon, he had come to help fix a leak in the stained-glass. I couldn't understand why Lily wanted him to repair that particular leak, when other leaks were more of a problem. Across the room, for instance, rain drained through the cracks in the leading, trickled down the stone wall, and ran in tiny rivers through the kitchen. But Lily said this one needed tending because the water flowed from the faces of angels and made them look like they were crying. "Who wants to live with a flock of sad angels?" she said.

Leon spent hours taking apart the pieces of glass near the wings of the upper angel and around the faces of the others where the water trickled in. Needing some extra help with the leading and the grout, he went back to the house to get his son. Meanwhile, Lily and I began arranging the pieces of colored glass on a large piece of violet satin. That way Leon would know how to put the pieces back together.

A short while later, Leon returned with his helper. "Josey," said Leon, "I'd like you to meet my son." There in Lily's chapel, where I thought we were isolated from all the world, stood Norman Johnson with skin so dark it looked purple.

Norman was quiet while he worked, and I was too stunned to speak. As I watched Leon and Norman reassemble some of the pieces in the huge glass puzzle, carefully laying the leading between the glass, I thought about how Norman and Leon had come from two different parts of my life, but were now closely linked as father and son. I made hot chocolate for us all in Lily's fat mugs and floated marshmallows on top.

Lily and I had sorted only some of the pieces. Piles of glass chunks remained to be organized and fitted together.

"Norman," said his father, "why don't you sort out the pieces over there. Lay them out like the picture so I know how to put them back in."

"Okay," he said, wandering over to the table, unsure of where to begin.

Well, now, that's just dandy, I thought. I'm here working with Lily, and Norman comes in and completely takes over my job.

"Dad," said Norman, "how do you expect me to put these pieces back together when I have no idea what the picture's supposed to look like—what is this anyway? Looks like sheep or some kind of fuzzy snow."

"It's angel wings," I said, ambling over to show him. "The wings are made of feathers, sort of like swans. See up there where your Dad's working—the bottom of the wings are still in the window. The part on the table here is where the wings curve above her shoulders. There's sky behind with lots of swirling colors—mostly blue, green, and lilac. And some doves, you see, over here." I showed him the different piles of glass chips Lily and I had arranged.

"Okay," said Norman, "which way do the wings curve?"

"In an arc, like this." I showed him, and Norman and I worked together, assembling our puzzle of glass chips.

"Now," I said, "we need to find all the feathered wings in lavender shadow. They go behind her head."

"What goes in this space?"

"Her hair—the golden pieces, over there. Yes, that's it."

Norman had an extraordinary sense of how things fit together—he assembled the angel's golden river of hair almost as quickly as he had run through the much darker river under the school bridge a few years ago.

"Hey, Norman," I said hesitantly. "Did you find all your books that day in the river?"

"Yep, sure did. Found them around the bend. All soggy—couldn't even read the ink in the notebooks. Why do you want to know?"

"That was mean what Casey and Frank did."

"Sure was," he said, rounding the curve of a feathered wing in sunlight.

"I bet you get used to it though, huh? I mean lots of people are mean to you, and you're always cool."

"Nope," said Norman, "you never get used to it. You expect it, but you never get used to it."

I knew exactly what he meant.

When Norman and I finished the puzzle of angel wings and doves, we handed the pieces up to Leon one at a time while Lily held the leading and grout. We all arched our necks watching Leon, his dark hands pressing gently upon the pale faces of angels and the lily-white feathers of their wings. He worked slowly, steadily, carefully adjusting the glass pieces, twining the leading around the curved edges, and applying the grout just right.

But mostly I watched Lily, where the shimmering colored light poured through the sky and spilled upon her. Blue, sea green, and violet light drained along her smooth skin, down her bare arms, as if she were another stained-glass figure who briefly slipped away from the window to help reassemble her broken world. I watched bits of clear sunlight burst in through the transparent glass of the doves and sparkle like stars along the soft terrain of her curves. She was lovely.

When the project was done, the four of us rejoiced in the perfection of the job. We decided that the next time it rained, we would come together and see if there were any leaks. Sure enough, the following week—I happened to be at Lily's that night—the clouds broke open in a downpour. Moments later, Leon and Norman burst in with their rain gear, having just sailed across the meadow in the storm. We stood together upon the stone floor, looking up, hailing the perfectly dry area all around the glass chips. No more angel tears to sadden Lily's home.

※   ※

There was no phone where Lily lived. In fact, no wires of any sort went in or out of the chapel. Somehow that made the stars and the moon all the more important, as if they were, for Lily, some kind of link to other places. She'd wander up the spiral stairway to the platform under the glass dome in the ceiling, and she'd sit there for hours, watching the stars as if she were reading important telegrams from afar. Sometimes I'd come with her and comb her hair.

※

We talked about all sorts of things—our favorite fossils, why ice doesn't sink, what the chapel looked like before Lily and Leon fixed it up, and what kinds of creatures might live on Mars. I told her about Ralph's dead butterflies, the stars on Casey's ceiling, and Benny's love of steam. And I talked about the invisible things Aunt Kitty pulled from thin air.

"Spirits," suggested Lily.

"What kinds of spirits could she possibly carry around in her pockets?" I asked.

"Spirits of the dust," she explained.

For hours I watched Lily tending her plants, sorting through her seashells, mixing various blends of potpourri, and etching unusual shapes into the velvet undersides of fresh fungus. I felt closer to Lily than anyone in the whole world, but occasionally she drifted off to a place that did not include me. She'd gaze into the air and focus somewhere beyond the room or maybe even beyond all of New Hampshire. I never intruded on this quietness, never tried to reel her back in. Watching her there deep in thought, I considered myself her protector. She looked vulnerable, transparent, and so utterly still that I thought she might float up amid the rafters and join the other angels in the stained-glass windows above. But she always came back on her own. Softly, she'd turn to me, put her hand on my cheek, and say as if I were the one who had drifted, "Hey, Boo, where've you been?"

One day when she said that to me, I asked, "Where do you go, Lily, when you are so quiet?"

"Far away," she said.

"Is it farther than New York City?"

"Yes."

"Is it on the other side of the world?"

"I think," she said, "it's on the other side of the sky."

"What is it like?"

"It's a tranquil place. And it's dark—there's not a drop of light because it's farther away even than all the stars."

"It sounds scary."

"Not really. It's simply darkness. Nothing to do, nothing to say, nothing to run away from. Sometimes it's hard coming back, though. The darkness wants me to stay."

When she told me that, I felt sad that the joy of our being together wasn't enough to keep her from the dark place. All I could do was let her go there when she wanted and be here when she came back. So I waited beside her, listening for the sound of her voice, softer than rain, when she turned to me again to say, "Hey, Boo, where've you been?"

In the wintertime, it was chilly near the glass windows of the chapel. I wrapped myself in the afghan and often nestled near the fire or up on the platform where the rising heat stayed caught inside the dome. But Lily was impervious to the cold. She'd sit near the windows with bare shoulders as if in the middle of August. Sometimes she'd crank open the windows to let snow pour in on the breeze. Candles flickered around the chapel, and small drifts formed on the floor beneath the windows. When she went out for water at the well, always in the darkness, of course, she never wore a coat. Walking across the snow, she looked like an enchanted princess born of the northern lights with her pale skin and flowing chiffon all around her.

As time went by, I wanted so much to ask her about her past, about the son she lost, my mother, and her fear of the light. Several times I was on the verge of asking, but the fragile look in her eyes made me hesitate, as if reminding her of such terrors would make me lose her somehow.

29

Nights with Lily drifted into seasons. Before long, something in me was changing—like grumblings in the earth, hot lava creeping slowly beneath the surface, searching inner crevices for a place to burst out and find release in the air.

Lily's awareness of my changes put a distance between us. The tender affection that once poured freely soon came tentatively, as if somewhere in her mind Lily was unsure. I thought she was abandoning me.

One night in early April, Lily and I were working on her crystal garden in the alcove where the fabric strips hung like clouds from the ceiling. "I've grown," I said. "Remember how the clouds used to touch my head? Now they come clear to my shoulders."

We had added some fossils, arranging a trail of brachiopods spiraling out from the abalone shells. Several hours before the dawn, a dull ache crept along my bones and made me warm. It seemed the only way to resolve the feeling was to be close to Lily, to touch her somehow. While she kneeled on the floor sorting through some cockleshells, I came behind her and wove my fingers in her hair. Gliding my hands through her river of gold, I said, "Lily, when we're done with the crystals, I'll comb your hair."

She pulled away so my hands could no longer reach her. "That's not a good idea, Boo."

"Why not?"

"Too many tangles," she stammered, standing up, backing away.

"But it's been so long since I combed your hair."

As if confused, she changed the subject. "How about if we make a line of cockleshells around these crystals like a path through the garden?"

Feeling rejected, I told her I should go and put on my coat.

"Can I kiss you good night?" I asked.

"Sure, Boo."

She came beside me. Instead of kissing her on the cheek as usual, I put my fingers there instead, softly on her skin. Then I pressed my lips lightly on hers. A delicious warmth rose from within and flushed my every pore. She pulled away suddenly and said, "All right, that's enough, sweetheart."

"Doesn't that feel good to you?"

"Come here, Josey." She took my hand and led me to the couch near the fireplace and explained, "We cannot be close like this anymore. You have grown. It's not like before when our affection was innocent."

"I can stay innocent," I pleaded.

"Not when your heart races and your cheeks burn like this."

"I can't help it, Lily—it just happens."

"Of course, it's natural. Someday you'll find a girlfriend whom you can kiss as long as you like. But not me."

"How about when I'm older? You can be my girlfriend then."

"No, Boo, I can never be your girlfriend."

"Why not?"

"Because it isn't right."

"I don't understand."

Lily pulled the afghan from the back of the couch and wrapped it around me. "I'll make you a blend of chamomile and mint to drink. Then we'll talk some more."

While she added kindling to the stove to make tea, I gazed gloomily at the marble statue by the fireplace—the nude woman holding an apple tentatively to her lips, the fabric falling from her hand to the ground. How much different the woman in marble looked to me now, compared to that first night when I huddled by the fire and shivered in fear of the lightning while Lily sliced puzzle pieces with her long silver knife.

I watched her return with the tea, walking carefully across the floor. I held the cup, too hot to drink, and let the vapors crawl up my neck.

She gazed at me, penetrating through my longing, her eyes looking sad. "Josey, we cannot be together like this," she said. "You need to spend more time with your friends at school."

"But Lily, I'm thirteen years old. I'm growing up."

"Yes, and you need your friends to grow up with. And you need to be with your Grandma Ru more."

"Grandma Ru doesn't know if I'm there or not."

"That's not true, Josey Rose. Just because she doesn't always answer you directly doesn't mean she can't hear and feel what you say."

"How can you say that? You don't even know her."

"Josey, remember, she's my grandmother, too."

My hands wavered, and Lily took my tea. "If we have the same grandmother," I stammered, "then why don't you ever see her?"

"Your father forbids her to come here, and she is too old to fight him. My fear of open space and light prevent me from traveling so far where you live. And besides, your father would be there."

"Lily, it's three miles. You could come in the dark, some night when my father is gone. Then I could take you back here the same night, all while the sun is on the other side of the world."

"It's still too far. I'd be afraid."

"Oh, Lily! Does she know you are here?"

"I suspect she knows I'm nearby. She always had a sense about her. She often knew things without being told. And you know what else?"

"What?"

"She used to sing to me. She'd hold my hands, and we'd spin in circles while she sang, 'Hi-Lili, Hi-Lili, Hi-lo . . .' It's a lovely waltz."

Lily danced lightly across the room when suddenly we heard a crash. My father had burst through a stained-glass window and leaped inside the opening, tearing his clothes on the shards of glass and shattering our peace. He was running straight for Lily and me.

Lily wrapped her arms around me. My father grabbed her by the shoulders and hurled her to the floor. For the first time in more than a year, he was lit to the gills with booze.

"You wacko broad," he snarled, "you can play the wench with the nigger, but not with my son!"

"You have it all wrong, Willie. Just like you've always had it wrong!"

"Well, it goes like this," growled my father. "You see, I happened to be out with my pal, Eddie Lark. I come home—a bit late, so figured I'd go upstairs to bed. Then, thought I'd check on the kid. Funny thing—

no Josey to be found. So where do you think is the first place I come? By golly, here I am!"

Lily lay shuddering on the floor. I tried to reach her, but my father grabbed me by the collar and roared, "Say good-bye to the wench, kid. Your visits here are over. Now check out of this joint, pronto."

"No, I won't let you hurt her!"

"Oh, really," he jeered, "feeling your oats, eh? And who are you— the skinny white knight saving the damsel in distress? Well, in this case, the damsel is a cuckoo bird."

"Josey, leave!" cried Lily. "Go now, I beg you."

My father yanked me away from Lily, dragged me across the room, unbolted the door, and heaved me out in the cold. I ran around the chapel to the broken window and crawled up through the glass. With one leg slung over the sharp edges, I leaned forward to jump into the room. My father grabbed me again and pushed me back so hard I fell on the ground.

"See this?" he yelled as he held out a pistol, shaking it at me. "If you don't turn around and run full speed back to the house where you be-long, then you're gonna hear a gunshot in here, echoing through the empty head of Miss Lily, not that it would affect her in any way—she's already lost her marbles." My father stared at me.

My blood chilled, and I froze. There was nothing I could do. Lily needed me now more than ever, and I couldn't even protect her. As much as I had grown, I was still no match for a drunken high-iron worker with a loaded pistol.

"Yeah," he sneered, turning briefly to Lily, "it's been a while, hasn't it, my dear? Don't you miss your Uncle Willie?"

If I provoked him, he was mad enough to use his gun, and Lily would surely be the one hurt. So when my father turned, I ran straight for Leon's. I heard my father laughing in the distance. I sailed through the meadow with my father's words screeching in my head. When at last I reached the house, I pounded on the door.

"Josey," said Leon. "You look like you've seen a ghost."

"My father," I panted, "he broke through Lily's window. He's there now. He has a gun."

Leon threw on his coat, bolted out the door, and ran toward the road.

"No," I called, "this way, toward Lily's."

"Josey, we got to get the police. We'll catch a ride into town, my car's broke again. Someone will stop for us on the road."

"Leon, we have to go to her now. He's with her, tormenting her."

✿

"We can't mess with your father and a gun. Someone will get hurt bad for sure. Trust me, this is the only way."

"Please," I hollered, pulling his arm. "No police. Lily would be more afraid than she is now. She's petrified of strangers. You know that."

"Josey," he said, jogging along the road, "I can't explain all this now. I just got to stay out of jail, that's all."

"But you wouldn't go to jail—my father would."

"Hah! You get a colored guy scrappin' with a white guy—if somebody gets shot, you can figure almost certain who ends up in jail. I was in trouble with the law once before, Josey, for something I didn't do. Can't let it happen again. I got to be here for Norman."

Leon was halfway down Gypsy Lane—me running behind. When a car drove by, Leon held out his hand. The vehicle slowed, then sped up and passed by. After ten minutes, two more cars passed, but no one wanted to stop for us in the middle of the night. All the while I begged him to turn around and go to the chapel. When I could stand it no longer, I turned from Leon and ran back toward Lily's on my own.

"I'll go there myself!" I yelled back.

"Not alone you won't," said Leon, turning. Now he was chasing me all the way back down the lane and through the meadow, yelling for me to stop, or he'd wrestle me there in the field. But he wasn't much of a runner, and I stayed a bit ahead. By the time we got to Lily's my father had left. She lay curled on the couch, wrapped in the afghan, shivering.

"There now, there . . ." murmured Leon, sitting beside her, arm around her shoulders, Lily shuddering against his body, he breathless from the run. There was nothing to say. I could tell he had comforted her like this before. I understood the feeling. In my own way, I'd been there many times.

Confusion churned in my heart. I was relieved that we did not find Lily in a pool of blood. She had survived, but I brimmed with bad feelings. Anger for what my father had done. And jealousy that I was not the one she embraced for comfort.

When Leon and I left, I knew from her adieu that this was good-bye for a very long time. She said it was best for both of us if I spent time with people my own age now. I could no longer seek refuge in Lily's chapel. I had to grow up and try to face my own problems at home. She told me not to worry about her—she had Leon to look after her, and after tonight, I knew that was true. Nothing made sense anymore.

30

When I arrived home, I was beside myself. I couldn't think straight, and I felt I would burst from whatever fluttered in my stomach, clamoring to get out. I wanted to pull my father from bed and pound him. All I could think of was hurting him like he had hurt all of us for so long—make him realize how he made others feel. These thoughts scared me, and I lay in bed trembling. When at last the sun came up, I paced the floor downstairs, ready to confront him with everything. My father was still sleeping.

An hour passed. While he slept I kept pacing and thinking. Why I made my next move, I'm not sure. How could I have thought that bringing my frail Grandma Ru to Lily's could solve anything? I certainly didn't expect Lily could be saved by a woman who talks to Indians and chases giant butterflies. Perhaps I wanted to confront the whole tangled mess. Maybe I figured that by corralling the entire family, all our secrets would be revealed somehow and the truth would fix everything. At the very least, I wanted Lily to have a chance to be with her own grandmother.

"Grandma," I said when she finally awoke, "we're going somewhere together—just you and me."

"When shall we be departing?" she asked.

"Right now."

"Is it farther than Arizona?"

"No, it's close."

Even though the air was fairly mild, I put a shawl around her shoulders and found her fuzzy boots and lavender coat. I guided her out to the old Radio Flyer wagon that my father pulled me in when I was a little boy. I slid the red railings around all four sides so Grandma wouldn't fall out. She sat happily in the wagon while I pulled her all the way to Lily's meadow. She sang of pomegranates and kumquats as we rolled along with the sound of the wagon wheels humming down the road.

We left the wagon at the meadow's edge and walked along the path to Lily's chapel.

"Is this Indian territory?" she asked.

"No, Grandma, this is where the butterflies live."

The air was filled with blossoms of early spring—fragrant white petals floating in the breeze.

"Josey," whispered Grandma Ru, as if someone else might hear, "the weather is getting strange. Ever since they've been poking holes in the atmosphere with their space ships, the climate has become peculiar. Maybe you can't notice, but the caterpillars in this meadow are beside themselves."

Suddenly a flock of yellow butterflies swarmed around us and fluttered along as we walked. I wondered if they had been to Maggie's meadow nook and if her spirit was within them. When we neared the pine grove, I said, "Grandma, we're going to visit Lily."

"My Lily?"

"Yes."

As we entered the grove, I noticed some boards covering the hole where my father had broken through the window—maybe Leon had fixed it for her. As we walked up the steps to the chapel entrance, Grandma's eyes shone wide like a child's. I knocked on the gigantic door, and Grandma stood off to the side examining the grain of the old stone wall.

Lily opened the door a crack. She saw me and scolded, "Josey, you cannot come here."

"But Lily—"

"You only make it more difficult for us both."

"Lily, please, I have someone who would love to see you."

"No company!" she exclaimed as she closed the door on the threatening light.

I knocked again. After some minutes, Lily returned. Before she could protest further, I drew Grandma next to me. Lily brought her hands to her face in surprise. Then overwhelmed with the afternoon light, she walked back into the chapel leaving the door ajar.

"We've startled the poor child," said Grandma.

When we walked into the room, Lily was standing by the fireplace, flames glowing softly behind her. A circle of stones lay on the floor by the couch where she had no doubt been sitting quietly, trying to rise above the terror of last night. Grandma walked over to Lily and stood quietly before her. She put her hand on Lily's cheek. "Your eyes tell of joy and sorrow, my dear, and how beautiful you are."

"Grandma," Lily wept.

When they embraced, I slipped out the door. The last thing I heard as I walked past the boarded window was Grandma Ru singing like she would never stop, "Hi-Lili, Hi- Lili, Hi-lo . . ."

※　　※

When I returned home, my father was trudging down the driveway. "Where is Grandma?" he demanded.

"She went out for a Sunday jaunt," I said.

"Tell me where she is, or I'll have the cops after her."

"I don't think the cops will have much trouble with Grandma stopping by for a visit with her granddaughter, do you?"

"Blasted sweet Jesus!" he cursed as he pulled me in the house. I sat in the living room and watched him stomp around the house collecting various things. He grabbed a pillow, some blankets, and a bucket. He filled three bags full of food.

"Are you going away, Dad?"

He didn't answer. He clomped upstairs and returned with a pile of my clothes. Apparently I was the one taking a trip.

"Yes," I said, "send me away. I'll be glad to be away from here!"

I figured he'd really gone off the deep end when he opened the basement door and threw everything down the stairs. The bucket bounced along the wooden steps, the food tumbled out of the bags, and the blanket and my clothes landed in a heap. He pulled a can of soup from the cupboard and threw it at the basement ceiling. The only lightbulb down there exploded into smoke and shattered to the floor. Then he grabbed me like a pile of garbage and tossed me down, too. Thank goodness for the pile of blankets at the bottom of the stairs because that's where I landed without a scratch.

I heard the door lock but had little concern. I would wait until he was away from there and open the lock myself. I'd done it more than once before when I had accidentally gotten stuck down there. Once I escaped, I would leave home for good. If Lily wouldn't let me live with her, I'd stay with Casey, even though we had grown more distant, and he still carried a grudge for seeing me talk with Norman.

But several minutes later, I heard my father's footsteps return. He opened the door, threw down a roll of toilet paper, and shut me in again. Then I heard pounding as he nailed what sounded like boards across the door. Judging from the time it took him to pound in each nail, the boards were very thick.

Too stunned to move, I pulled one of the blankets up to my chin. I realized I was not getting out of there anytime soon. Although it was late afternoon, only a cloud of hazy light made its way past a crack in the foundation and into the depths on the far side of the basement. Lying there in the darkness, recounting the certainty of how my father had put me there, it came to me how Lily had been locked in a basement for three years.

❧ ❧

When the front door slammed, I expected soon to hear my father's footsteps again once he had gone to the chapel to retrieve Grandma Ru. But nighttime fell, and all was quiet. I groped about in the dark, and I was scared. It took me awhile to figure out what to do. First I realized what the bucket was for—I kept it in the farthest corner along with the toilet paper. That night, I slept at the bottom of the stairs, but the next morning I gathered the blankets and made my bed where the pale cloud of light hovered during the day. I measured time by the progress of that light as it rose to a timid glow during the afternoon, then waned to hours of darkness. After a couple days, a sick feeling overwhelmed me, not knowing how long I would be there. To track the days, at every sunrise I etched a line in an old plank next to my bed.

Sounds were few—only the wind rustling and rare peeps from the birds. Apparently Jake and Lulu saved their voices for when people were around. During my time in the basement, they remained quiet except during the fifth day, when they burst into an extraordinary explosion of song. They were getting hungry, no doubt.

For food, I scrounged through the goodies my father had thrown down the basement stairs. I began with the perishables like bread and cheese. Then I consumed the rest—sardines, dried cereal, and lots of beef jerky. He'd packed enough food for two weeks, but on the tenth day I slowed down, conserving what was left, in case I was doomed to this dungeon for a long time.

After the first week, I began feeling confused. It seemed I needed light to think. In the darkness, my thoughts became disoriented. I tried to piece things together, but my conclusions fell like dust in the dark. Sometimes I called out, but the sound of my voice gave me the creeps. In the quiet, everything sounded louder, and I felt like easy prey with no one anywhere near to protect me.

I wondered what was happening at school. Why didn't anyone come searching for me? I heard no knocks at the door, not even the sound of the mailman. For the first time in my life, I understood what it meant to be a little nuts. I was migrating to another realm, perhaps the world where Indians come visiting and butterflies grow seven-foot wings. I would have welcomed any kind of visitor, even one inside my head.

When at last my father returned, I had etched eleven lines in the plank beside my bed. I heard him grunt as he yanked the boards away from the basement door. He opened the door and trudged into the living room. When I came out, the light assaulted my eyes. I sat in the kitchen with my hands over my face for quite a while, opening my eyes gradually to adjust to the hideous brightness.

When I walked into the living room, I felt like a drunk stumbling across the floor. My father was sitting in his chair by the TV. Dizzy and sick to my stomach, I collapsed on the couch.

"We're going to start over, Josey," my father informed me. "You and me are going to get a few things straight."

"Dad, where is Grandma?"

"Are you listening to me? You've been getting away with too much around here. Now it's time to straighten up and fly right. You'll go to school. You'll do your homework. And you can visit your friends, Casey and Ralph. But the rest of your shenanigans are over. The goings on with the nut case in the chapel is history. So forget it ever happened."

"Dad, you locked me in the basement for eleven days. You want me to forget that, too? And how about Lily—was it you who locked her away for three years?"

He stood up and shuffled across the room. He yanked me from the couch. It's a good thing he kept hold of my shirt because otherwise I would have fallen down. With a slow, threatening voice, he said, "Let me put it this way, kid. You either make tracks in the right direction or take a trip to someplace else. This is your last warning. I'm the father here, and you do what I say. That means you don't go anywhere or see anybody unless I say it's okay."

"Well," I said, with tears of frustration welling up, "at least tell me where Grandma is."

"Grandma's getting old, son. It's time she stayed in a place where she can be cared for properly. She's in a nursing home."

"Where?"

"Far away, in Arizona. That's what took me so long. You know how she always wanted to go to Arizona."

"Dad," I cried, "you locked me in the basement, and you took away my grandmother!"

"Hey, kiddo, she's where she should be."

"And I suppose the basement is where I should be."

"Well, let me say this. If you tell *anyone* about your trip to the basement, that'll get you a first-class ticket to—"

"Yeah, I know, North Dakota. Seems I have to keep a lot of secrets around here. First how Maggie died and now getting locked in the basement."

"You're catchin' on, son. And while you're on a learnin' streak, here's another one for you. For the last eleven days you've had a terrible bout with the flu. That explains why you've been away from school. Now do you think you can keep all that straight?" He let go of my shirt, and I fell on the floor. I felt like throwing up.

"I'll never treat my children like this, never! No matter what."

"You have to learn to forgive, kiddo. I'm your father, and I love you. I'm doing this for your own good. You'll understand that some day."

I dragged myself up the stairs and crawled into bed with my clothes on. It was afternoon, and the light was too bright. I closed the curtains to bring back the darkness.

31

I had been sleeping for twelve hours when my father woke me for school. I showered for the first time in eleven days and ate breakfast without talking. As I walked out the door, my father handed me a note. "Give this to the school nurse," he said. After I pulled my bike out of the shed, I unfolded the note and read,

> Please excuse Josey's absence from school. As we discussed on the phone, he's been sick with the flu.
>
> Willie Rose

I rode my bike to the school bridge and hid in the woods. After enough time for my father to leave for work, I returned home. I gathered up as many clothes as I could fit in two bags, tied them to the back of my bike, and rode to Lily's. All winter I had passed through there cautiously, usually in the dark. Now I was in the wide-open meadow filled with the slender grass of spring. It was broad daylight, but I wasn't afraid. I was going home.

The day was young yet, so I knew Lily would be asleep. When I arrived at the chapel entrance, I was shocked to find the door boarded up with huge planks. Did my father really think he could keep her prisoner in her own house? I pounded on the door so we could talk through the thick wood. When she didn't answer, I went to the window near her bed and tapped softly so as not to frighten her from sleep. But after ten minutes, she hadn't responded, so I rapped hard against the wooden window frame. No response.

I walked around to the window that Leon had boarded up. I found a strong branch and pried away the wood. The silence within the chapel didn't seem right. I crawled in the window and rushed to Lily's bed. She was gone. I ran to every alcove and up the spiral stairs to the platform in the glass dome. I called her name, again and again. Searching every nook and cranny, I could not find her. The sun was blazing, so there was no way she'd be outside.

I went back out the window and flew across the meadow to Leon's. I knocked on his door. No answer. Then I went out back and found him in the field, pushing his hand tiller through the dark soil.

"Leon," I called, "where is Lily?"

He walked over to the edge of his garden. "Your father didn't tell you?"

"What?"

"He took her to the hospital, Josey. Sometime after he broke through the window. I wasn't around when it happened, but sure as heck she didn't go on her own will."

"What hospital, Leon? Is she hurt?"

"A mental hospital. Your father said she went crazy somehow. But I'm sure the whole thing is his doing. When he told me, I wanted to see her right away. But your father said she's at some special institution far away and that Lily didn't want anyone to know where she is."

"That's impossible."

"Josey, she never wanted to go to no hospital. She called it the loony bin."

"She was afraid to go," I said. "You've got to help me find her. We'll search every hospital there is!"

"Josey, my friend, I care the world for Lily, you know that. But I can't go messing around behind your father's back."

"Why not? I'll help."

"Norman and me are the only colored folk in this whole part of town. There are people around here who would jump at the chance to put me in the slammer. You have to understand, I can't take the chance. You know, I have to be here for my son."

"My father says he'll send me away, too, if I step out of line. Leon, I don't know what to do."

☙

Leon put his hands in his pockets and looked out on his garden. Then he scanned the horizon as if to find an answer there. "Lily will be back," he said. "We can only wait."

"No, Leon . . ."

"I know a bit about your father's ways. Don't get the man angry, Josey. He'll never tell you where Lily is, and I fear for what he would do. For now, wait for Lily—she'll come back. And when she does, you will know. Meanwhile, you'd do best to stay away from the whole business."

Leon took me inside and brewed some tea. With each sip of the warm drink, sorrow bled down my throat and penetrated my whole insides. I had lost my only love.

Leon broke the silence. "What is it," he asked, "that makes a man hurt someone the way your father does?"

"His own niece, no less."

"And his own son, too," added Leon.

"Maybe," I pondered, "he's driven by the same thing that makes people hound Norman the way they do. Maybe that's just the way people are. Maybe we have to get used to it."

Leon clenched his fist and looked at me earnestly. Then in a voice more deep and passionate than I'd ever heard him speak before, he said, "Josey, don't ever get used to it. Never! The day you accept that kind of violence is the day you give it all up."

"Give what up?" I asked.

"Your dignity."

I didn't say much for a while, but I let my eyes wander through the kitchen door into the living room. "Leon," I said gloomily, "you sure do read a lot of books. Look at that, a whole wall full of them."

"Oh, not me," he explained, "I'm a gardener. I get all my learnin' from the dirt and the sky. Those are Norman's books. He's only fifteen years old, but he reads all the time—like his mom before she passed on, God rest her soul. I reckon Norman will become a doctor someday. He's plenty smart, and he likes learnin'."

"A doctor, really?"

"Oh, my," Leon said, his voice drifting, "sometimes he gets to talkin' about things like livers and spleens and weird goings on inside the body. Half the time I don't know what he's yackin' about."

"Well," I said, "he's lucky to have you for a dad."

We sat for a while, looking out the kitchen window. Leon talked about how the clouds were shifting—probably meant rain.

"I'm worried," I said. "At the hospital, will they keep Lily safe from the light?"

"I sure hope so."

"Well, at least she won't have me coming around all the time."

"What do you mean?"

"She told me she didn't want to see me anymore. She wanted me to hang around my friends instead."

"You think she did that because she doesn't want to see you?"

"Who knows."

"Josey, how do you think Lily feels about you?"

"I thought she cared, but since she told me not to come anymore, I'm confused."

"She adores you, Josey. Like no one else in her life. Don't you see? She didn't want to steal these years from you. Wants you to get on with your friends. Lead a normal life."

"Lily is my life, Leon."

"And you were hers, Josey. That was the problem."

My mind spun with confusion. Time to get going before the rains came. I needed to figure all this out. I thanked Leon and pedaled back to school. It seems I had lost everything I cared for—first Maggie, then Grandma, and now Lily. My father had taken these things away from me. I had no idea what to do next.

❧   ❧

Following Leon's advice, I did not confront my father about anything relating to Lily—I didn't even tell him I knew she was gone. But I continued going to the chapel to take care of things. I didn't want Lily returning to a dusty, abandoned place filled with broken glass and dead plants. And in the chapel, I could be at peace with my thoughts.

I cleaned up the glass and sorted out other things that had been left in disarray after my father's rampage. Then I devised a concealed entrance for me to enter the place easily. With Leon's help, I nailed several large boards together with crosspieces. Then we hung the structure from hinges over the window my father had broken through. It worked like a boat hatch, hinged along the top edge and free along the other three edges. The hatch looked like a boarded-up window. But for me, it was the doorway to Lily's world. All I had to do was carry over an old wooden crate, pull open the hatch, and slide inside.

❧

32

I decided to make one last attempt to talk with someone about my dilemma. Although it had been years, I remembered Reverend Jasper's offer to visit him at the parish. When he had mentioned it that Sunday after church on the lawn, it was as if he knew I was troubled, even back then. When I knocked on the parish door, he was wearing his long black robe.

"Oh, my dearest Josey, come in." We walked past his office to a waiting room with magazines on the table and pictures of Jesus on the wall. I sat in a chair while the reverend disappeared around the corner and returned with a plate of chocolate chip cookies. He sat on the couch near my chair.

With hope, I unraveled my story to him, pouring out all my woes about how my father killed Maggie, sent away my grandmother, and put Lily in the hospital. "And please," I begged, "my father must never know that I came here to see you."

"Of course not, my sweet," he said tenderly. "Sad Josey, come over here on the couch with me, and I shall talk to you about your sorrow."

I sat next to him as he put one hand around my shoulder. With his other hand, he stroked my cheek like he did in the churchyard that Sunday. "You must learn to understand your father's grief," he purred as his fingers caressed my neck and pressed playfully on the buttons of my shirt. "Your daddy has had much sorrow with losing his wife as he did. The only greater ordeal would be to lose a child.

If you retreat from him now, that's how he will feel."

He undid the top button on my shirt so he could reach more deeply into the area around my neck. The affection made me feel warm, as if he truly cared.

"You see, sweet Josey," he continued with a voice that soothed my heart, "you know that Jesus preached of love, and it is that love that your father feels for you, even though sometimes it seems otherwise. And it's that same love and adoration that I feel for you now."

Then his hand moved down. His fingers slid along my thigh, reaching up inside my shorts. In a way, his affection did not seem right. No one had ever touched me like that. I was confused.

His fingers tickled under my shorts. "Does that feel good, my fair one?"

"I think I should go home now," I said, my voice trembling.

"No, not yet. I have a message for you about love."

"Please don't do that, Reverend Jasper."

"Hush, my child, you must learn of God's caring. If you leave me now, you shall not have learned your lesson. Then I'll have to speak with your father about it."

"No," I cried, pulling away, "please don't tell my father, or he'll send me away."

"Then, come here my lamb, and I will soothe your weary soul."

I came timidly and stood before him. My heart pounded as he lifted my shirt and laid his pudgy hand upon my stomach. His trembling fingers crept under my belt, and I quivered as they moved. His jowls flushed, and his hot breath swept over my neck.

"There now," he wheezed, "this is the magic of love. You are a beautiful, luscious child with your soft skin and lavender eyes. Feel your beauty down deep, my dear. Yes, there . . . do you feel it in your tummy? Let me—"

I felt a rush of astonishing warmth. It felt good . . . it felt wrong . . . I was ashamed. I pulled away and dashed to the door.

He lunged forward, kneeled down, and embraced me in his arms so I couldn't move, couldn't breathe. As he drew his hand behind me and pressed me against him, he panted in my ear, "One last word, Josey Rose. If you don't tell your daddy about our meeting today, then I won't tell him either." He kissed me gently on the lips. "And sweet child, do come again."

He let me go, and I ran out the door. I had the sinking feeling I was really on my own now. There was no one left to turn to.

33

My hope for Lily's return never waned. Years went by, and I continued taking care of her place. During that time, a most extraordinary situation developed with her indoor gardens. When Lily was in the chapel, I had helped her care for her plants for almost two years. Now that she was gone, I treated them the same way—repotting them when they grew, trimming their leaves, and even talking to them the best I could.

I drew their water from the well like before and poured it using the same long-spouted watering can. But the plants grew as never before. The vines became furry with tender pale shoots. Some lengthened and deepened to green, crawling along the alcove walls, clinging to whatever they could find until they had nowhere to go but hang down from the ceiling like vines in a jungle.

When the plants blossomed, flowers grew so heavy that the branches could barely hold them. The air was always perfumed from their blossoms. And roots escaped through the pots, reaching out, creeping into the dirt of other plants, in search of deeper soil.

It seemed I was making a career of repotting plants to keep up with their demanding needs for space. Since the alcove was overrun with foliage, I moved half the plants up to the platform by the glass dome and set them loose there. In a matter of months, vines and flowers draped over the platform like garlands. One pathetic specimen, which Lily had spent years trying to bring back to health, sent out curly stems laden with violet blossoms.

Leon came by one day to help fix a small leak. Weeks had passed
since he'd been inside. When he walked in, he was dumbstruck by the
vegetation. "What the devil are you feeding this jungle?" he asked.

"Water from the well," I said.

"Then there's something in the well, Josey. Something . . . almost
magical."

❧   ❧

As the seasons passed, Lily's absence became part of my life. I missed
her dreadfully, but I had accepted her disappearance as my fate, at least
for the time being. The obsession to find her had melted into a life of
waiting for Lily to come home. I knew she would return.

I avoided my father as much as possible. He was drinking again, and
he seemed like a coiled snake ready to strike. When circumstance re-
quired me to go in the same room with him, I stayed silent. For a while
I wrote letters to Grandma Ru. I asked her, What did she think about
all the space shots? Did she suppose that the blackout in New York
City had anything to do with the astronauts flying to the moon? And
were there butterflies where she lived? But she never wrote back. One
day I dropped off her birthday card in the mailbox by the school. It
came back with words scribbled across the envelope: "No Such Person." I asked my father about it.

"She died, son."

"When?"

"In the winter."

"Why didn't you tell me?"

"You don't tell me nothin'," he said, "so why should I talk to you?"

And so it remained that way for many years.

❧   ❧

I rekindled my friendship with Casey and Ralph. I wonder what Casey
would have said if he knew I was pounding nails and watering plants
with Norman and his father. As it was, I never talked about Lily's
place. By the time I was fifteen, Casey had immersed himself in adventures with his buddies, drinking beer and going to wild parties. Nothing pleased him more than to discover that somebody's mom and dad
were going away for the weekend, so he and his friends could congre-
gate and drink beer all night long. I knew if he ever got wind of the

empty chapel, Lily's home would be invaded and destroyed in their frolicking. Instead, I let it remain for Casey as an old house where the long-lost ghosts of his childhood dwelled. I kept it to myself. The only ones who knew about Lily's place were Leon, Norman, and me. And my father, of course.

Ralph's interests migrated from stuffing walnuts to hanging out at the soda shop. He still loved to eat. He could consume two ice cream sundaes and three jelly doughnuts in one sitting. But wouldn't you know, among the three of us, Ralph was the only one with a girlfriend. Her name was Tina, and she was slender like a vine and awkward as could be. She'd blunder along, trip on curbs, and walk into lampposts. Sitting at the soda shop, she'd knock over her soda glass—her whipped cream and cherry often landing in someone else's lap. Ralph, on the other hand, remained as graceful as ever. Tina and Ralph were worlds apart but always together.

Casey went out with girls, but never kept one steady. Sometimes he'd ask me why I didn't have a girlfriend. "With your looks," he'd say, "you could get any babe you want."

"I'm waiting for the right one to come along," I replied. But I didn't tell him that I had been watering her plants for years.

✀   ✀

During the year when my voice went low, I thought of Lily constantly. I dreamed of being with her in the river with candles all around on a hot summer night. Like the evening we had collected fossils, Lily danced in the water with wet chiffon clinging to her skin. She twirled around, and we laughed so hard we fell into the water, the river rushing around us, and she held me close. I dreamed that the river was steaming in warmth. Running in its course were the curling tendrils of water lilies that wound around us, weaving themselves in our embrace, and somehow finding their way inside my body where the spiraling strands wrapped around places deep in my groin and grabbed me there in a luscious ache until I awoke in a panic with the hot river now draining into a warm pool on my stomach.

My dreams came only from my memories, and I imagined all the things we had done when I was a child, like walking through the meadow, sitting by her crystal garden, and drinking her steamy herbs by the fire. I thought of combing her hair, braiding it with ribbons and flowers. "Lilies for my Lily," I would say. I imagined lifting her golden

✀

mane and resting my head on her pale shoulder. Then I would come around to the front and brush all her hair forward, part it slowly, and move my fingers across her cheeks flushed with tenderness. And in my daydreams, I imagined our conversations.

"Does this feel good?" I would ask.

"No one has ever touched me this way," she'd whisper, "so gentle and slow."

All the while, I knew that in reality, Lily would have thrown me out long before we reached that point. I was certain no one else in the whole world had ever felt this compelled. I rationalized and said I would punish myself later for all that I dreamed. But for now, I let my thoughts wander along the small of her back, the curve of her hip, my lips drinking from the wells of her neck. Even in daydreams, Lily drove me into a frenzy.

I suppose I had been a child to her, maybe a reminder of what she had lost. But to me she was everything.

As time progressed, my daydreams of Lily became more lush and abstract, like floating with her above steaming pools of lavender where I kissed her deep without touching our lips so she could not say that what we had done was forbidden. Always when I thought of her, scents filled the air of my imagination—aromas of green apples, jasmine, and almonds.

How wonderful if these inner thoughts could have continued undaunted during those years. But the pure stream of pleasure I found in dreams of Lily soon became infected with the memory of Reverend Jasper's amorous advances years before. This tormented me.

I wished I had never gone to him that one day, pouring out my woes. For years I was cursed with the memory of his pudgy hands trembling against my skin. After all, he was the only physical experience I'd had. Though I never went to him again, his invitation haunted me. For every lustful urge that crossed my mind, Reverend Jasper's memory was there by my side with a tender offering of sweet release. I knew his advances were wrong, so I felt guilty and confused by my urges as I grew up.

I kept that day a secret in the back of my mind, afraid that somehow I was to blame. Perhaps my lavender eyes had drawn him in. Or maybe by not resisting his words and his touch in earlier years, he thought I wanted his peculiar affections.

Although Ralph, Tina, and I spent time going to the soda shop, sneaking into the movies, and standing on the corner, Casey never joined us in public. It wouldn't have been cool for him to be seen with kids two years younger than him. But we often got together on the weekends at Casey's house, so he wouldn't be caught in our presence.

Sometimes I stayed the whole weekend at Casey's—knowing my father preferred my not being around. On one of those stays, a near tragedy occurred that threw the Lark family into turmoil. Casey's father tried to commit suicide by jumping off a Ferris wheel at the Firemen's Carnival. When it happened, Casey and I were in the seat in front of him. Suddenly, we heard Abigail scream as if hundreds of rats had fallen from the sky and landed in her lap. Casey and I turned around just in time to see Eddie stand up in the swinging seat at its highest point on the ride and bail out head first. Being on a run of bad luck, Eddie landed in another seat farther down—instead of crashing to the pavement below as he had intended. He survived the calamity with a few minor cuts and bruises, while the people he landed on broke twenty-three bones between the two of them.

Casey's father isn't the kind of person you'd imagine being down enough to commit suicide, but something drove him to try: One afternoon, a few weeks before Eddie jumped off the Ferris wheel, Casey and I were sitting in the living room listening to records. As usual, Aunt Kitty was pawing the air with her fingers, trying to find whatever it was she had been searching for all those years. In the middle of "Love Me Do," Aunt Kitty stood up and cupped her hands above her head. Then speaking for the first time in ten years, she exclaimed, "At last, I've caught a good one!" Then she fell on the floor and died.

Knowing how to plan an affair, Abigail took over. She commissioned a printing company to do a special design for those little cards handed out to people attending the viewing: The front of the card had a lovely picture in pastel colors of a shepherd with a lamb gazing into the starry sky. The back had gold scripted letters that said, "Love makes time pass. Time makes love pass." Aunt Kitty lay in the casket in her pink velvet dress, opal earrings, and her favorite pearl necklace.

Abigail even thought to place Aunt Kitty's weekly trifecta bet, one last time. But she didn't go to the bookie down at Kelly's Happy Tap as usual because he never gave her any ticket to show for the bet. No paper trails with the bookie. So Abigail went to the track and put twenty-five dollars on the trifecta in the last race. She picked three long shots to win, place, and show. Then on the back of the trifecta ticket, she wrote "Forever in our hearts" and slipped it in the casket under Aunt Kitty's pillow, along with several photos of the family.

Later that afternoon at the church service, Reverend Jasper read psalms from the Bible and stormed on about how Aunt Kitty was now in the hands of the saints, our Lord Jesus, and all the guardian angels in heaven. We drove to the cemetery, where they put Aunt Kitty's mahogany casket in a deep hole. They covered her with dirt, and the next day Eddie found out Aunt Kitty won the trifecta. The long shot bet paid off an eye-popping $410,000. The winning ticket was six feet under.

Abigail was delighted. "Now she can truly afford her ticket to heaven. Don't you think that's nice, darling?"

"Oh, Christ," griped Eddie, "she can't spend her winnings where she's going. There ain't no bills in heaven! And there's no racetrack up there to redeem the goddamn ticket."

"Darling," said Abigail, "it's the thought that counts."

Eddie went into a tizzy. In an attempt to retrieve the ticket, he called the church, visited the cemetery office, and argued with government officials for weeks. He filled out forms to have the body exhumed, but the request was denied.

"Ah, well," sighed Abigail, "she'll redeem her winnings with the Lord." That's when Eddie jumped off the Ferris wheel. And I realized not everything was as perfect about the Lark family as I'd once imagined.

34

By the time I was a sophomore in high school, Norman and I had become good friends. He stopped by Lily's while I worked with her plants. As I watered, repotted, and snipped away dead blossoms, Norman babbled on about medical stuff. Having decided he wanted to be a surgeon, he had developed a strong interest in internal organs. He rambled on about kidneys, gall bladders, stomachs, optic nerves, heart valves, sweat glands, and the cerebellum. He even knew the name of that thing that hangs down in the back of your throat. "It's called a uvula," he said.

One day he asked, "Did you know your body has sixty thousand miles of blood vessels? Yep, if you string them out in one long line, they'll go around the earth more than twice."

"Who would want to do that, Norman?"

"Nobody, really. It's just an interesting fact—at least I think it's interesting. Sure as heck no one at school wants to talk about the length of blood vessels."

"Hah! Did you ever try discussing tuberous begonias? People don't want to hear about plants either. Reckon our interests aren't entertaining enough for our school."

"Do you ever see girls, Josey?"

"Oh, just haven't met the right one, I guess. How about you?"

"Are you kidding?" said Norman. "In this town?"

"Did you ever try?"

"I asked Sandy Millhouse if she wanted to go to a basketball game. You know what she said?"

"What?"

"She told me to back off, or she'd have her daddy after me for attempted cross breeding."

"Man, I don't know how you put up with that stuff."

"When I go away to college, it'll be different."

"How do you know?"

"It can't be this way everywhere."

Norman once told me, "I'll understand if you avoid me at school. People will rail you for hanging around the black kid." But I talked with him whenever I wanted. And Norman was right—several people took up badgering me at school. Casey's friend Frank Rapper was the worst. Walking past me in the school halls, he'd jab me in the ribs and mutter things like, "Had any good dark meat lately?" One day he cornered me near the school bridge when no one else was around.

"Hey, coon-lover," he said, "where's your boy Sambo?"

"Bug off, Frank."

"No, I think we should chew the rag a bit—you know, talk man to man. Or is it man to fag in your case?"

"Go play with the big boys," I said as I walked into the road to go around him. He lunged at me, grabbed my collar, and slammed me against the stone railing of the bridge.

"Lay off, Frank, or you'll be sorry," I said.

"So what are you gonna do," he taunted, "send your drunk daddy after me? Hey, I hear your father's a real Romeo, carrying on with that crazy whore."

"What are you talking about?"

"You know, Lily the loon lady."

"Shut up, Frank!" I yelled, twisting under his grip.

"Yeah, that Lily's a regular harlot. She even does niggers. Yessiree, I hear tell that people seen Norman's daddy trottin' in from the farm next door, bringin' her groceries and all. I wonder what he gets paid for all the bologna in them bags."

I struggled to get loose, but he had my arms pinned against the bridge.

"Sure thing, Bucko, your daddy's a real cowboy. You could pick up some tips from him. Maybe he'll even share the babe with you."

For one moment, I felt confused. I could hear my father yelling, "Don't take no shit from nobody!" And I could imagine Leon in the same situation, with quiet dignity, turning the other cheek. But my father's influence won out. As Frank ranted on, something surged within me. I pried my hands loose and punched away at Frank. My reaction disgusted me. Maybe all my father's lectures had taken seed and were coming to fruition. Is this what he felt like when he threw things at the walls? But the rage seemed deeper than that. Whatever it was, it had hold of me, and I was throwing myself at Frank Rapper as if doing him in were my only purpose in life.

"Well, look at that. Josey Rose all pissed off, just like his daddy when he gets drunk down at Hank's Bar."

"Hey, creep, you don't know what you're talking about!"

"Aw, isn't that touching, defending your daddy's honor."

I punched away until my arms gave out, and all that remained was anger. Then Frank threw me down on the concrete and laughed. So I pulled myself up again, rushed at him, and punched fiercely some more. And it wasn't for anyone's honor but Lily's.

❦   ❦

By the time I was seventeen, Lily had been gone for four years. I could no longer accept the fate of her departure. My father refused to give me any information. So I began my own search. As soon as I got my driver's license, I spent all the money I'd saved over the years on a used car—a light blue Chevy Impala with a convertible top. I drove to every psychiatric institution in the state. I called or wrote to places all across the country. For two years I searched. No one had ever heard of Lily Milan.

While trying to find Lily, I often thought of my mother. Perhaps my father had taken me from her and never told her where we had gone— just as he had stolen Lily from her chapel. I imagined my mother inquiring at schools around the state. "Is Josey Rose enrolled here?" she'd ask again and again. She'd scan endless schoolyards for a four-year-old boy with dark hair and lavender eyes, then depart, having failed again. If all this were true, I wondered how long she had looked for me before giving up. I knew I would never stop searching for Lily.

What I didn't know at the time was that with all my attempts to find Lily in far and distant places, she was actually less than sixty miles

❦

away. My father had admitted her to a psychiatric hospital near Boston. He had registered her in my mother's name, Isabel Rose. Lily had no identification to prove otherwise. He had taken her there in the light of day, the same afternoon he had locked me in the basement. The fierce sun had frightened her so terribly that she fell into a catatonic state.

My father explained to the doctors that she had delusions about being a woman called Lily who lived in a chapel. He told them nothing of her fears of the light, so she was constantly subjected to the brightness of the sun, which kept her frozen in fear. In the few times she came out of her catatonia, her delusions were confirmed.

One day while preparing Lily for bed, the nurse said, "Now, Isabel, see if you can help me with this nightgown. Lift your hands above your head."

Speaking for the first time since her arrival, Lily said, "My name is not Isabel, it's Lily Milan, and I want to go home."

"Now, dear, settle down, this is your home for now."

"Call Josey Rose," she insisted.

"Isabel, your husband explained how your Josey died in childbirth. In fact, I often hear you mumble about your lost son in your sleep. So you see, on some level you have already begun to accept reality."

"No, that's not how it is!"

"Work with us, Isabel. Talk with me—we can help each other. I'm going to fetch the doctor now. He'll be so glad you are able to speak."

By the time the doctor arrived, Lily had drifted back into her prison of silence. So her life continued like this for six years. She had a bed by herself, around-the-clock care, prescribed drugs, shock treatments, and daily walks in the blazing sun.

※   ※

When I was a senior in high school and all of my own efforts failed to find Lily, I went to the only person who held the secret I wanted to know.

"Dad, tell me where Lily is."

My father stared at me from his chair near the TV.

"Where is she, Dad? She's my cousin, and I have a right to know."

"She may be your cousin, but she belongs to me."

"Nobody *belongs* to anyone."

"I am her guardian, Josey. I own her."

"You think you can lock her away like some ship in a bottle? She's not a collectible, Dad. She's a woman who's scared of the light, hates hospitals, and has probably been living in fear for years now."

"The hospital will do her good."

"The only thing good about her being gone from here is that she's away from *you*. At least she doesn't have to worry anymore about you coming around and—"

Remembering my father's atrocities, my heart flamed with rage. I wanted to blast him to hell. "How could you hurt her like that?" I yelled. "What drove you to such cruelty?"

"She was a nut case, Josey boy, but a voluptuous one at that. And soft as chiffon pie—you should know."

To keep from slamming him, I began throwing clothes into a suitcase with my head pounding and wondering why I hadn't left sooner. When I ran away to Casey's years ago, what had ever possessed me to return home? This time, I was going for good. Our relationship was over.

I rented an apartment in town and took a job as a waiter in a fancy restaurant with white tablecloths, candles all around, fresh flowers on every table, and tiny white lights on the trees outside. I spent much time with Ralph and Tina, who, after graduating, both took jobs at another restaurant also in Willow Junction. Ralph was the cook, of course, and Tina was the worst waitress in history, frequently dumping entire trays of food on the customers. The three of us would sit at Ralph's apartment, eating caramel popcorn and laughing about how we all ended up in the restaurant business.

Sometimes Tina tried to set up dates for me with her girlfriends— seems Tina had a lot of girlfriends. Undaunted by my refusals, Tina stepped up her campaign by arranging chance meetings. She'd have one of her girlfriends coincidentally show up at places we planned to go. My lack of interest frustrated Tina. "Josey Rose," she'd say, "how can you turn down these opportunities? You would be the ideal boyfriend. You're an absolutely dazzling specimen with your dark hair and shining eyes. I know three women at this moment who have hopeless crushes on you. What's the matter with you, anyway?"

"I don't want to jump into anything too quickly," I'd say, knowing I had already leaped headlong into hopes and dreams for the only woman I would ever love.

Actually, in the end, it was Casey who convinced me to go on a double date with him and his girl. I hadn't seen Casey in a while, so when he begged me to go, I figured it'd be a chance to catch up with him and meet his new girlfriend.

The blind date Casey set me up with had teased blond hair, red lips, and rouged cheeks like a clown. Her perfume smelled of something toxic, and she wore green stockings. Her name was Zelda.

"That's Zelda with a Z," she said.

"Oh, is there another way to spell it?"

"Well," she said, chewing her gum, "it's just that Z is such an un-usual letter."

"Hey," said Casey, "didn't I tell you she was cool?"

We went to a movie. I welcomed the relief of not having to talk with Zelda. Then afterwards, despite my insistence on getting home early— "I have work tomorrow morning," I said—Casey drove us to a lonely lane, pulled the car halfway into the woods, and shut off the lights. I could have argued with him, but he had developed a hot temper lately that wasn't worth rousing.

While Casey and his girlfriend steamed up the front windows, Zelda accosted me in the backseat with her piercing voice and a fresh squirt of perfume.

"So, Josey Rose," she said, dragging her long fingernails through my hair, "you're kinda cute."

I rolled my eyes, pressed my shoulder against the car door, and looked out the window.

"Do you like sports—how about football?"

"It's okay."

"What really turns you on, Josey? I mean, tell me what you do to bring sparkle into them sweet lavender eyes?"

"Plants," I mumbled. "I spend a lot of time watering plants."

"Oh," she groaned. Zelda leaned forward, found Casey entwined and breathing heavily, tapped him on the shoulder, and said, "Hey, Bucko, your friend here is a real dud. Says he likes watering plants."

"I warned you he's a little weird."

"Well, ya didn't warn me enough."

Finally Casey drove back into town and dropped me off at my apart-ment. That's the last time I went anywhere with him. And the concept of "blind date" was added to my list of things never to do again.

❧   ❧

❧

After my falling out with Casey, I heard he took a job working the high iron with his father. In fact, Casey saw my dad more than I did since I had removed myself completely from my father's world.

That's why, only a few months later when I was nineteen years old, I did not know that the hospital had discharged Lily, and my father had returned her to the chapel. No doubt my dad figured my obsession for her had faded long ago. After all, I had been years without her. So when I left work that night to stop by the chapel, I had no idea she was there.

35

Like always, I parked the car in a secluded spot in the woods down the road. I had continued keeping my visits secret, more from habit than from fear. I was out of high school, but still stole my way through the meadow like a child sneaking cookies behind his mother's back.

Walking along Gypsy Lane that night, I mused on my visit earlier in the week. I had felt particularly low, not knowing where Lily was, having tried so hard to find her, wondering if she was well or even alive. As I watered the plants, I watched the September sun spill colored light through the stained-glass windows. The birds warbled nearby with the same sweet melody they had been singing for years now—*Hi-Lili, Hi-Lili, Hi-lo* . . . echoing through the window glass, filling me with sadness.

I lay on the couch that day and gazed upon the angels in the stained-glass, remembering when Leon and Norman helped assemble all the cut pieces years ago. The four of us had felt so good when we made the angels stop crying for Lily. Those days were gone. Norman was in college, and though I still searched for her, Lily was nowhere to be found.

That same day, I had let my eyes settle upon the cut-glass scene near the ceiling. It showed an angel ascending in the sky. Beside her, a male angel swirled angrily in the air, appearing to beat his wings in distress. His white robe was falling away, and a snake wound around his naked torso. On the ground below, one woman played a flute, another a harp, and yet another held a large golden key, trying to pass it to the two angels above her. But the snake was there with his mouth open, ready to snatch away the key. The images in the window pulsed in the afternoon sun. I suddenly felt Lily was in trouble.

I grew agitated, and all I wanted was to be near her. Over the years my memories of our time together had begun to fade. I tried to recall the sound of her voice, but the tones had fallen apart and trailed away like smoke. Her face, her skin, and the curves of her body, which I had held so often in dreams, seemed hopelessly out of reach. Her warmth hovered invisibly somewhere in the air, fluttering around the ceiling too high for me to touch. This drove me mad. As Lily had slipped away, now her memory was leaving me, too. Soon I'd have nothing left.

Over the years that I had waited for Lily, the world seemed to quake in pain. Our President had been assassinated along with his brother and Martin Luther King. There was unrest in the streets and on college campuses. And we were fighting a losing war. Little did I know that finally, not long before men reached the moon and walked upon its surface, my Lily would come home.

As I walked along the path to the chapel on the night Lily arrived, the darkness held magic as it had since I was eleven years old. Entering the pine grove sometime after midnight, I saw the stained-glass windows glowing faintly. I didn't think much of it as the light always played in strange ways upon the chapel. It must be the moon, I thought.

I was taller than my father and no longer needed the crate to reach the window. I pulled open the hatch and slipped inside. When my feet touched the floor and I turned around, I was astonished to see candles burning all over the room. Candles of ascending heights across the oak mantelpiece like organ pipes with flame. Candles pressed into the sand in the crystal garden, glimmering from the alcove there. And gigantic candles by the archway of the door set in huge holders with years of wax drippings still clinging to the base. The aroma of lilac and jasmine potpourri filled the room. My heart soared. The butterflies that had been sleeping for years began fluttering about, spinning circles inside the abandoned chambers of my heart.

"Lily!" I called. Then so as not to frighten her, I hailed to her more softly, though the joy in my heart was screaming to pour out. I called to her in almost a whisper, "Hi-Lili, Hi-Lili . . ." But all that answered back was the fire simmering softly, where the logs had been waiting since she left. "Hi-Lili, Hi-lo . . ." I sang as I peeked in every alcove, looking for the woman with whom I planned to spend the rest of my life. Then, roaming aimlessly through the middle of the room where Lily used to make her circles of stones, I looked up into the rafters as if she might be waiting for me there with the angels in stained glass reaching for the golden key.

Then, out of the corner of my eye, I saw her standing quietly at the top of the spiral stairway in her flowing fabrics, watching me with wonder. Her hair was still golden like a sunset, and her face mysterious, bewitching, and more beautiful than in all of my dreams. With hesitation, she came down the stairs, uneasy at first, moving through the moon shadows, wavering in the candlelight, unsteady from years of confinement, turning carefully around and around, stepping over vines that grew along the railing and crawled across the stairs. Frail like a fawn, she was coming to meet me.

I rushed to the stairs and caught her in my arms. My thoughts were all tangled, my heart filled with fireflies, and the air grew fragrant around us. She lay her head on my chest while every cell in my body began spinning in delight. How delicate she felt with her head beneath my chin—this woman who for years had towered above me. Now she was like a child folded in my arms, so ethereal as if any moment she would disappear—a whisper in the wind.

How unfamiliar I must have felt to her with this strange voice, trembling body, and large hands wrapped in her hair. Afraid of making her uneasy, I pulled away, only slightly, and looked in her face. Her cheeks were flushed from the rays of her enemy sun. And what sadness in her eyes. They were Lily's lavender eyes, but with tame light that barely flickered. "Lily," I breathed. Then I noticed her eyes were focused somewhere else. A timid glow said she knew me, but the empty gaze made me fear it would be impossible for her to even say my name.

Perhaps if we walked a bit, she would come out of her spell. Holding her hand, I guided her to the alcove with the plants. "Look," I said, "have you seen the ivy, how it's grown all down the walls? Careful not to step on the vines. And this one here found its way into the crystal garden. Sometimes it sneaks into the curls of your shells and gets caught there inside the dark, so I have to pull it out and send it on another path."

She watched my every move but didn't speak a word. I felt she was happy and that a silent bond remained between us.

"And over here—remember the plant that should have blossomed in ten years? Well, look at it now, only seven years and the flowers are so heavy the stems can barely hold them. It bloomed for your return!"

She followed me through the place, watching, listening, but unable to speak.

36

The first thing I did was move in with Lily. I kept my apartment in town but brought my clothes to the chapel. I parked my car at Leon's—no more hiding. And I tried to change my hours at the restaurant so I could work days while Lily slept and be with her when she was awake so I could watch over her. Hard as I tried, though, my boss would not agree.

Looking into Lily's eyes each day, I searched for a faint spark or any change that offered hope for drawing her out so she could speak again. As I talked to her, showed her things, and sat with her by the fire, she watched me intently. But there was no change in her response—only the same gazing wonder. Her eyes held the kind of tranquillity that comes not from a sense of peace but through years of terror.

Wanting to find out where she had been, I'd ask, "Lily, can you write down the name of the hospital where you were? Or tell me the state? Were you in Arizona? California? Nod your head when I say the state, then I'll call every place there until I find where you were. I need to talk with someone so I know what is best for you now."

But she gave me no signs. My father was the only one who knew where she had been. If I were to ask him—or even demand it from him—he would seek revenge. So I decided to return to my childhood house on my own when he was gone. I had an idea of where I might find some answers.

Waiting until my father had left for work, I walked down Gypsy Lane and along the road to the house. When I was a child, I had traveled secretly down this road in the darkness to the chapel—and now, years later, I was sneaking along the same road back to my father's house in broad daylight to uncover the mystery of Lily's last six years.

I found the house key under a rock, in the same place it had always been. Feeling like a burglar, I opened the door and entered the house for the first time in years. The marble box I was looking for was still on the mantelpiece. The key lay in the jar beside it. I opened the box and thumbed through papers, but I found no receipts, notes, or discharge papers from the hospital where Lily had been. All I saw were the same items that had been there years ago—various certificates and old letters. Although I had snooped through this box as a child, I did not feel right perusing it now—this was no longer my home. So I closed the lid on my father's secrets and turned to leave.

Looking around, I could see the place had descended into sheer chaos. At least before, my father's projects were separate from each other—his terrarium ingredients by the south wall, his shipbuilding materials on the buffet by the stairs, and his fishing equipment on tables by the window. But now it looked as though a tornado had swept through and shuffled everything together. The dining room table spilled over with moss, ferns, empty beer bottles, and bowls of marbles and gems. Pheasant feathers for his fly lures mingled with tiny sails and sinkers. Whiskey bottles, which he had probably emptied himself, lay throughout the living room ready to house his seafaring vessels. By the window hung the same birdcage, with only Jake within. When I said "Hello" he warbled meekly. I feared what might have happened to Lulu.

Sadly, I realized how my father and I had drifted impossibly far apart. After so many years together, I had nothing but memories of harsh words, gunshots, and things getting thrown at the walls. As for him, I don't know. I wondered if he thought of me at all.

So this was what had become of my father's life—confusion and despair. No doubt the same turmoil filled his mind. I wondered if he could ever again create beauty as he did years ago inside his glass bottles. Curious, I wandered to the heap of debris piled on the dining room table. There amid broken glass, tangled fishing line, and leftover pizza, I beheld a small bottle only six inches long. Inside lay a scene more intricate than ever—an enchanting vista of rolling hills, cotton-puff clouds, a shimmering rainbow arching above hillsides of trees in blossom, birds as small as little pearls, and stars of diamond chips twinkling along the horizon.

Here inside the bottle, amid his coarse world, raged wonder. As deeply as his spirit had fallen, his creativity had ascended to a place more delicate and refined than I'd ever seen—beauty as only angels could know, all under his command, safe within the walls of a tiny bottle.

I wondered where I fit into this world. I wanted to see my room—I wondered if he'd completely swept me from his heart or if something yet remained of the child he once had. I walked upstairs and peeked inside. Everything was exactly as I had left it on that afternoon when I suddenly departed in anger. My clothes from the day before were still lying on the chair. My desk was piled with schoolbooks and notes that I had abandoned in my haste. And the dresser top was filled with keepsakes of my childhood days with Lily—acorns that we had collected, pine cones, fossils, an opened robin's egg, and the perfectly curved fan of a tree fungus.

It looked as if I'd never left—as if my father had captured that moment in time and saved it in the capsule of my bedroom so he could peek in whenever he wanted and believe that nothing had changed between us. Maybe he could imagine his son romping through the doorway any minute, throwing his schoolbooks on the desk, and running outside for one last spin on his bike before sundown. But if all that were true—if he truly wanted things the way they were—I wondered why he hadn't tried to find me.

On the windowsill next to my bed was the long, clear crystal that Lily had given to me on my twelfth birthday. Leaning against the window, it glowed not of the sun but of the warm candlelight from the night she had shown me her garden of shells, amethyst, and quartz. I put the crystal in my pocket and left quickly. I locked the door and walked away from my father's house for the last time.

I had found no evidence of where Lily had been. My mind still flooded with unanswered questions. Should I encourage her to speak or let the words come at their own pace? Though she continued her daily life as she always had—sleeping during the day, taking long scented baths, and brewing her herbs—I wondered if there was danger in leaving her alone when I went to work. Something told me I should take her to a doctor who could explain the special aspects of Lily's condition. But the part of me that loved Lily was able to hear her fragile

spirit pleading that she wanted nothing to do with doctors ever again
and that, in time, she would come through the mist that had accumulated from being so long alone and away from home.

I returned from my father's house to find Lily still sleeping. When at
last she stirred, I went to her. Sitting on the edge of her bed, I laid her
hair across the pillow.

"Close your eyes," I whispered.

When she only looked at me with wonderment, I laid a piece of fabric across her face, veiling her sight. Then I took the crystal from my
pocket, wrapped her fingers around it, and slowly pulled away the fabric from her eyes. She sat up, gazing at the crystal in her hands. I wondered if, after so many years, she would remember it. Then she slid out
of bed, took my hand, and led me to the crystal garden in the alcove
where unlit candles still rose all around and pillows and fabrics covered
the floor. The long strips of chiffon that had always hung from the ceiling like clouds above me now swept across my face and shoulders as
we wandered through Lily's world of soft, muted colors.

Lily kneeled down and placed the crystal in the sand where she had
drawn it out years ago. Then in her first move of affection since her return, she came to me, put her palm on my cheek, and held it there for
a moment. I was lost.

I cared deeply for Lily and yet didn't know what to do to help her.
Sometimes, when she became very still, I knew she had fallen into the
dark place, probably even deeper than before. I let her wander there,
and like so many times years ago, she would come back gently, put her
hand on my cheek, and in a voiceless gaze, her eyes would say, "Hey,
Boo, where've you been?" Especially at these times, I knew she wanted
to penetrate the silence and to speak again.

One night, I returned to find her on the platform, bending over,
working on something. When I reached the top of the stairs, I found
her holding an ice pick, etching lines in the floor. Across the platform of
golden wood, she had carved lush images of meadow flowers with butterflies reaching inside the petals scooping nectar from their depths. Ladybugs crawled around the flower petals and praying mantises clung to
the stems. And carved in the space above the meadow were dragonflies
with veined wings and milkweed seeds with tails of silk. Off to the side,
Lily had assembled a palette of oil paints, tiny brushes, and small pans
of linseed oil and turpentine. She had painted a translucent coat over
the flowers and the insects, giving them a glaze of color with the wood
grain showing through.

When she looked up, the moonlight fell across her face, revealing something rapt and restless within. Over our weeks together, I had come to recognize her feelings in the slightest hints of her movements. In one shift of her eyes, she spoke paragraphs to me about the inner stirrings of her heart. And now she was clearly informing me that she wanted to emerge from her prison of silence. She was ready to be free.

The next evening I took her for a long walk. We gathered fungus from the trees for her to bring home and carve to her heart's delight. In one of her alcoves, I found her old etching tools, and the next day in town, I bought fresh oil paints, linseed oil, copal varnish, soft sable brushes of many sizes, and one brush with bristles in the shape of a fan.

"Now," I said, "you can create what you will without danger."

✿   ✿

For months, we continued like this. Me, babbling on about everything that had happened since she left. And she, silently absorbed in etching lines and painting pictures on the smooth white undersides of the fan-shaped pieces of fungus. Using her long silver probes, she created panoramas of outlandish life-forms as they might have existed eons ago.

She painted in dabs and swirls. I wondered if her fear of the light permitted her to see subtleties the way a bumblebee might, or the way Aunt Kitty saw vapor balls wandering through the air. Lily's skies emerged from her paintbrush lush and alive. Mist whirling around insects. Air drifting in back eddies. And the wind weaving itself through sprawling vines. If ever Lily broke through her silence, I would ask her if she really saw the world the way she painted it.

One night, she painted a rainbow that arched across the entire curve of her largest piece of fungus. At one end of the rainbow was the sun and many birds. At the other end hovered the deep-blue velvet of nighttime with stars of lime green and violet spilling out from the rainbow's end.

She rarely included people in her paintings, but one showed a woman crouched, then kneeling, then rising up and standing with her arms outstretched high above her. Each figure was of the same woman, like Lily, but becoming more translucent as if evolving from a carnal being to a spirit. When she showed me, I asked, "Is that you, Lily?" She said nothing but looked into my eyes for several moments as if she were crawling through my soul.

✿

When Lily came close to rising above her silence, she began writing things down. She never noted simple messages like "Let's have oyster soup tonight" or "I'm feeling a bit of a chill." Instead, her words seemed to come from her other world of which I was not a part. Sitting by the fire, she'd suddenly hop up, grab her pen, and write sentences that made no sense like, "The submarines are oddly familiar." One night, in the middle of a meal, she tore off the top of the raisin box and scribbled, "Soon we shall realize the apathy that comes when spit drifts upon the eye." I knew the time was approaching when she would speak.

One day, Lily painted upon a fungus a picture of a man leaning over and strangling a woman with long white hair. When Lily showed it to me, I asked, "Is that my father?" She nodded yes.

"I know how my father hurt you, Lily. But I'm grown now, and I'll never let him touch you again."

She looked at me blankly as if I'd completely missed the point.

"Why did you paint yourself with white hair?" I asked.

Again, an empty stare.

"That's you there, isn't it, like in the other pictures?"

She shook her head sadly, then turned over the fungus to show where she had painted the words "Our grandmother is dead."

That was the first time it crossed my mind that maybe what my father had told me about Grandma Ru might not be true.

※   ※

I suppose Lily and I could have continued like this for the rest of our lives, she living in her silence and me chattering on about stories at the restaurant, tales of how I missed her all those years, and tidbits of news I'd heard on the radio driving home from work. If this were our only choice, I would have been content to remain that way with Lily forever. But I felt she was close to breaking through her muted world, and even more so, I was certain she wanted the freedom. Furthermore, I wasn't keen on having to depend solely on fungus for Lily to express herself.

One night, when I gave Lily a piece of fungus, I explained that it was the last one in the house and, in fact, the last one anywhere around.

"My darling," I said, "it's autumn and all the pieces are gone. Look inside now, and find the words. You can paint pictures with your voice."

On her last piece of fungus, she painted an azure-blue sky with falling stars above a gravestone that said "Lily."

❦   ❦

As the days passed, Lily grew agitated with nothing to paint on. I wondered if she would revert to etching the floor or inscribing the walls. But no, nothing would suffice but fungus. With no way to channel her feelings, she paced across the stone floor, silently gesturing with emotion.

One night, she halted her incessant pacing and stared off into the upper regions of the chapel as if her guardian angel were sitting up there on one of the rafters. A feral light passed over her eyes, and she threw on her shawl and ran out into the darkness toward the forest— the ground was wet from earlier rains. I followed behind as she searched the trees, spinning circles around the trunks, finding only scars where we had once harvested fungus specimens.

She rushed into the river, me chasing behind her and hardly able to keep up. Lily ran like an angry angel. Suddenly she stopped, unaware of my presence, unaware even of the cold water running over her bare legs and drenching her skirt.

"Lily, I'm here."

But I had no meaning for her. She looked up through the trees and called out with such thunder that the vibrations of her long-lost voice could have rattled the stars from their orbits. She wailed on—her voice a siren hailing release, and her sorrow pouring into the river and floating away on the water.

Stunned, I let her cry out. When I approached her, she flew from the river and ran into the meadow in a wavering path, going nowhere and everywhere at the same time. I chased her, caught her, and we fell to the ground.

"Let me out," she cried, "let me out!"

"You *are* out, Lily, you are free."

Then at last sensing I was there, she laid her head against my chest and sobbed six years' worth of tears. When she had given every ounce of energy to breaking out of her prison, she fell limp in my arms, quivering from the cold and the strange sound of her own voice.

❦

37

I carried Lily home, laid her on the bed in a cloud of goose-down quilts, and helped her into dry clothes—her long white nightgown with tiny buttons down the front. As I held her, she said, "Josey, there is so much to tell."

It was wonderful to hear her soft voice after all this time.

"So much to tell . . ." She sighed again.

"And there is much time to tell it, my darling."

"Our grandmother," she murmured. "I can't even say."

"You're trembling . . ."

"The night you were here," she spoke deliriously, "you know, the night your father broke through the window and threw you out . . . then when you brought Grandma here . . . yes, Grandma babbled for a long time about Indians and butterflies, and on and on about thermostats and glue . . . then she spoke in perfect clarity—something about your mother and about your father's drunken rages and how she knows that he comes here sometimes in the night."

"So the heartless soul had her put in the nursing home," I said.

"Is that what he told you?"

"He did."

"That's not what happened, Josey. Your father went into a rage. He knocked Grandma on the floor on those pillows over there. When she lay screaming out a lifetime of bitter truths, he descended on her like a mad hawk and held his hands around her throat until she turned purple and stopped breathing. I still see her there lying limp, her eyes open wide, staring at the ceiling."

"No, Lily, it can't be. It's a bad dream."

"Grandma lay on the floor, so completely still. Then your father dragged me like a screaming child through the meadow in the blazing light of morning. So terrifying was the radiance that by the time we reached the road, I had fallen away somehow, fallen into the dark place inside me, so deep that once we arrived at the hospital, I couldn't bring myself out to explain to the doctors that my name was not Isabel Rose. The doctors, your father, the nurses, they were all so close beside me, touching me, calling me to talk to them. So close . . . I knew they were there, but their voices seemed far in the distance, echoing, and all I could see was Grandma, lying on the pillows with her green eyes staring at the ceiling."

My head had fallen into my hands. Who could say which of us was more caught in the chains of these terrible truths. I held Lily as she began murmuring incoherently, her words floating, fading, until suddenly something drew her back with a shudder.

"I'm so afraid," she said. "Will you stay with me here in the chapel for a little while, until this feeling passes? I don't want to fall into the dark place again. You are so good to look after me like this, for these past few days."

"Lily, do you know how long I've been staying with you?"

"Oh, days, I'm sure. Maybe even a week."

"It's been months." Describing the time in terms Lily could understand, I said, "When I came to stay with you, the milkweed pods had not yet opened, and now the leaves are gone from the trees."

She was quiet for a while, absorbing it all. Then pulling away as if to place my image in the context of her world, she said, "But what have you left behind to stay with me so long? Your life . . . your home . . . surely you—"

"Lily, you are my life. There is no one but you. I've loved you since the night you danced in the river on my twelfth birthday. Sometimes it feels like I have adored you forever, since before all your fossils were born. You are my only love."

She curled around me like a shining crescent moon embracing its cool dark side. I moved my hands across her hair. She trembled, then grew more calm as she drifted out on a thread of sleep, and her breathing fell into a rhythm of slumber. Oh, how I wanted to lie down beside her, to hold her through the night. But no, I would wait until this confused state passed so as not to startle her or cross lines between us that had always been there but never acknowledged.

I lifted Lily's tangled mane and laid it on the pillow, smoothing the golden tresses along her face and over her ears. Then I went to the place where I had been sleeping since I moved in. I made my nest of quilts and pillows and lay beside the burning embers of the fire and fell asleep.

❧   ❧

In the end, it was Lily who came to me. She came to me in the darkness, that same night she had found her voice. She came to me while I was sleeping, in the hushed hour before dawn. Beside the fire of sighing embers, she kneeled in the foothills of my pillows and quilts. She leaned forward and let her hair rain across my bare shoulders and chest, then cupped her hands around my face and kissed me. I awoke slowly to find her upon me, as illusive as the dreams that had haunted me for years.

Then she slipped a strip of chiffon behind my head and wrapped it around the back of my neck in a slow but ravenous gesture. Whether she had come to strangle me or love me, I surrendered to her mystery and let her do what she would. She pulled the fabric toward her, drawing me out of my nest, and we rose up and stood in front of the fire. Then she led me across the stone floor, moving beneath the stained-glass angels now with only moonlight to give them glow.

Across the chapel she led me, she in her long white nightgown and me with nothing but the veil she had put around my shoulders. She led me into the alcove with the candles, the crystal garden, and smoky mirrored walls. Strips of chiffon still hung from the ceiling like clouds, and they glided across my skin. She moved around the room, lighting the candles. As she crossed the floor near me, I reached to catch her in my arms, but she drifted aside like a leaf in the wind, sailing to the other side of the chamber to light another candle. We moved like this back and forth, in and out of the layers of chiffon, me pursuing, she dodging, all in slow motion. As she moved through the fabrics, shadows of colors painted her white gown in soft lavender, then blue, gray green, and rose—an eventide angel wandering through the aurora borealis, kindling the stars like a lamplighter. She played like a child, and when all the candles were lit she glided toward me, pushing aside the veiled layers like vines in the forest.

❧

When at last she reached me, I embraced her fiercely. She breathed softly, then raised her arms into the chiffon clouds above us and twined her hands around the streaming fabrics until they wound around her wrists so much they could not come undone.

As I reached up to unwrap her wrists, she whispered, "Leave me tangled."

"But Lily, your arms are bound. They're all caught in the clouds. What should I do?"

"Do the things you always wanted to do."

"But I want you to be with me willingly."

"I shall tell you if my will changes."

With some uncertainty, I held her gently as the light from the candles pulsed in colors I had never known. She looked at me with wonder— perhaps she had never felt gentle affection like this. Still in a soft embrace, I slid around her toward the back and held her honey hair off to the side as I kissed the nape of her neck, wound past her ear, and up to her forehead. Then I withdrew my embrace and stood before her, moving my hands down to the buttons of her gown, sliding the tiny pearl spheres through their loops, one by one. And when I came to the third button, any bit of remaining uncertainty flowed away into the valley between her breasts and drained down her skin, all silky and flushed. I had been caressing Lily in dreams for years—touching her now came easily.

In a whirl of pleasure, I tortured Lily with affection, her hands still bound in the streaming chiffon above, my hands exploring what until now had been forbidden terrain. My lips drank the trail forged by my hands, and I fell in love with each new curve until a pang of yearning rose in me so strong I could wait no longer. I pulled her from the fabric that bound her above to the soft pillows below while the streamers— still tied to her wrists—tore loose from the ceiling. She grabbed other streamers in her descent, which fell all around us. As I pulled her down, we tumbled into a world where gravity had disappeared and left us whirling.

As I took her there, pressing her arms against the floor, penetrating through all of our past, melting into the fury of the moment, I became lost in a place where, of all things, apples emerged in my mind. Not only green apples as I had smelled and imagined in younger years, but ripe plump red ones. All kinds of apples coming in colors, bobbing in the water, crashing slowly in and out of hot pools, submerging under, then rising above, sucking up liquid and casting it in all directions. Hot rivers of nectar pouring through the valley, rupturing dams, steaming across fields of snow. Jasmine filling the air, and—as I willingly surrendered my innocence to the angel in my arms—the distinct aroma of almonds.

We lay spent—amid flickering candles, crystals, and fallen fabric—knowing the sun would soon turn the gold light to blue. Then Lily came to me again with simply a kiss, but a kiss that broke my heart, changing me forever when she moved her lips across my hair, roving gently past my ear, barely touching, barely breathing. Then quiet like a distant storm, violent like a dove—she carried me to a land beyond all my dreams.

So began a time of splendor and inquiry for Lily and me. All my suppressed desires from childhood let go. And all her years of silence were made up for as she purred on endlessly during our most intimate moments.

As much as we talked, there were many subjects we avoided. There would be time for all that—time for unanswered questions. We both knew these subjects would not make easy conversations. Lily had just come out of a long silence, and I knew she needed space, lightness, and time to adjust to her own voice and all the memories that came with it. And perhaps we needed to adjust to each other as well. We would reveal ourselves to one another, slowly, one level at a time, like peeling an onion. So we began on the surface, spending weeks on end unwrapping the outer layer, which happened to be a fine place to linger, in this warm, perfumed, heaven-sent realm.

One night while walking in the meadow when the stars hung low in the sky, Lily said she wondered if orgasms are different for men than for women. "What does it feel like for you?" she asked.

"Well, it's kind of like a big explosion."

Unsatisfied with my simple answer, she said, "I mean really, how exactly does it feel?"

"Okay, Lily," I teased her, "why don't you tell me what it feels like for you. That way, you can give me an idea of the level of detail you require."

"Well," she said matter-of-factly, "first it feels like a feather tickling and then a sensation like yarn coming unraveled, rose petals unfolding and dripping with dew, an ebb and flow like a salty tide that thickens to honey with tadpoles crawling through, then trembling membranes, wet steam, and—"

"Oh, Lily," I gasped, as I had become aroused beyond what my heart could withstand. And I made love to her there in the meadow grass.

Sometimes we lay for hours by the fire while I dropped soft kisses along her pale neck, her shoulders, the foothills and valleys of her delicious terrain.

"Close your eyes, I am a cloud," she'd murmur in her smoky voice as she moved strips of fabric across my body and talked of silk ribbons and angora clouds. Then sipping from the wells of my neck, she'd whisper of angels sighing, butterflies breathing, galaxies falling, and the crackling hiss of dawn. And when her own visions made her cry, I drank away her tears and banished them with kisses, protecting her from a strange sadness that lay at the source.

Sometimes when she knew my arousal was a breath away from the point of no return, she'd touch me in a certain place, press her fingers there, and I'd reel back unspent, ready to begin again. And when she let my rush slide past that point, and I drove inside to claim the universe, she'd clench me deep within her as she became me, and I became her.

38

As autumn turned to winter, Lily emerged more and more from the depths of her fears that had kept her silent. As the days grew shorter, nearing the winter solstice, the threat of the ferocious sun lessened somewhat. I continued working at the restaurant. Wanting to spend all my free time with Lily, my visits with Ralph and Tina dropped off.

I'd come home directly after work, bringing along fancy desserts from the restaurant, which we often shared with Leon when he came to visit. Mostly, we passed the time around the fire or going on hikes in the snow, collecting fossils along the river, licking icicles, and watching the stars hiss and sputter along their course through the brittle December air.

Each day was wonderful, yet strangely illusive, as if another reality lay beneath the surface of our delight. Our glorious days turned to weeks, which were destined to become years, if not for one thing—my father.

Having not seen my dad for so long, my memories of him had retreated to the back of my mind. Fly fishing in the snow. A shiny new bike at the end of a long red ribbon. Tiny ships inside whiskey bottles. His wet eyeball sliding in the palm of my hand. And little sugar roses from my birthday cake soaring through the air when he blew out the last candle with the breath of his pistol. But I was about to have a new memory added to the gallery of our past.

The night he came, Lily and I were on the couch by the fire, in the same place as when he had come years ago. Perhaps my father had spotted us through the window, which had since been repaired with clear glass. But this time, instead of crashing through the pane, he knocked at the chapel entrance. Thinking it was Leon, I opened the door, and before I could even see who was there, my father burst past me in a drunken rage, pumped his shotgun, and aimed it on me.

"Well, Dad," I said, sarcasm being my only defense, "it's been years, hasn't it? By golly, you haven't changed a bit. Still got that beguiling charm."

"And isn't this a touching scene—my son Josey shacking up with his wench."

"Wench, eh? Gosh, I haven't heard that word in a long time."

"You don't even know the whole story," he said. "Why don't you ask your lovely cousin about her kid."

"I know about her son."

"Do you know she abandoned him? Yeah, left the bugger in a field to rot."

"No," cried Lily, "you said you went back for him. You said he would be given for adoption. You said that when you carried me off and locked me up again."

"Yes," taunted my father, "I remember it well—a sunny day in August, wasn't it? You left him there to be hounded by the heat. Who knows what really happened? The kid probably got fried in the sun, his little bones charred from the rays, and . . . yeah, do you know how much hotter the sun burns in the South? All the better to cook you, my dear."

Lily fell to the floor and covered her ears with her hands.

"Ah," said my father, "but enough of this reminiscing. My dear old dad taught me a lesson—what you own, you must possess. So come on, my sweet wench, let's have a friendly snuggle for old times' sake. I know you've been cravin' for your old Uncle Willie."

As he moved toward Lily, I lunged at him. The gun went off, and the pellets ricocheted off the floor near my feet, zinged against the wall, and rang a copper bucket like a bell.

"Oh, how gallant!" he snarled as he grabbed my shoulders, pinned me to the floor, pumped the gun again, and rammed it against my throat. "Listen here, you low down, rotten varmint. Let's talk bloodlines. What we have here is basic incest—my son, Josey, gully-rakin' my niece, Lily. I reckon that makes you kissin' cousins."

"Back off!" I yelled, but I was quickly silenced when the gun barrel pressed harder on my throat.

Then a sad veil fell across my father's face as he pulled away the gun, leaned down, and breathed into my ear, "The bloodline is too close for comfort Josey Rose—more than you know, believe me."

I pushed him back hard, and the gun crashed on the stone floor. I wrestled him down, but only for a moment. I may have been years younger than he, but he was still the stronger. Perhaps it had something to do with our vocations. At work, I carried trays of dainty cocktails and gourmet dinners while he climbed steel columns and set thirty-foot beams in place with eight-pound sledgehammers. With his overpowering strength, assisted by the barrel of a gun, he dragged me from the chapel, straight out the back door. As he pulled me along, he sang,

> *Waltzing Matilda, waltzing Matilda,*
> *You'll come a-waltzing, Matilda, with me.*

Once outdoors, he pulled me toward the well, lifted me, and threw me inside. I fell through the darkness and landed in the icy water, crunching through sticks and branches as I hit the bottom. And my father kept on singing,

> *And his ghost may be heard*
> *As you ride beside the billabong,*
> *"You'll come a-waltzing, Matilda, with me."*

I was terrified and raging mad—more angry than my father had ever been when he threw things at the birds and punched his fist through the wall.

"Leave her alone!" I cried. "You bastard, you'll destroy her. Just let her be."

"Hah, sounds like real love, Josey boy. Hey, let's talk man to man. Now what do you think of your cousin, Lily? When did you ever lay your hands on a body like that, huh? She's a real flesh-maggot's delight."

As he ranted, steam from his breath turned silver in the moonlight, piercing the stars behind him. I tried climbing up the sides of the stony walls but could only reach partway since the upper stones were covered with ice.

"All I got to say," I yelled with a ferocity that disgusted me, "is that if you touch her, you'll regret it to the end of your life."

My father leaned forward with the gun pointing at me. "Oh, such threats," he growled. "Maybe I should blow you away right here, you know, to be on the safe side. Or shall I save that pleasure for later?"

I tried to leap upward and grab the gun, but I only slid back into the water.

"Hey kiddo, it's a bit chilly down there, ain't it? Let me warm the water for you." He hopped up on the edge of the well, unzipped his pants, and took a long pee all over me. The warm urine landed on the back of my neck as I crouched in the water.

"Don't worry," he said, jumping off the well and turning to go. "I'll leave some of Lily for you, now that you've grown up to be a meathound like your old man."

I hoped Lily had escaped the chapel and run to Leon's house or deep into the woods down that part of the river where nobody goes. But the sudden sound of her screams told me otherwise. She had probably become so terrified by my father's grand entrance that she couldn't move from the floor, and now my father was upon her.

Lily was stronger than years before, and this time, she fought back hard. Through the opened back door, I heard her ranting, struggling, and—judging from my father's reprimands—clawing and biting him every chance she got.

"Shut up, bitch," he scolded, "or I'll tie you down and really have a go at you." She hollered above his threats until I heard him stomp into her room of fabrics and return. He bound her arms and legs, outstretched on all four bedposts, shouting out his every move so I could hear. Lily yowled like a wolf, calling my name. Then worse than the terror of her screams came the muffled cry of her voice when my father gagged her with something so binding that I could barely hear her. "Take this," he howled. "Maybe that'll shut you up!" Then I heard her long wailing cries, as if she were mourning the loss of everything she had regained since coming back home.

I felt like a caged animal, and with adrenaline raging, I scaled the walls halfway up, but slid on the ice-covered rocks and fell back down. My last resort was to knock away the ice. I reached into the water and grabbed at the sticks I had landed on. I yanked up a good-sized branch, braced each foot on the protruding rocks, and stretched up to chop at the ice. I thrashed away, but the ice seemed harder than stone. Then with one good wallop, ice chunks sailed through the air and crashed down all around me. That's when I suddenly realized I was holding a human leg bone.

Shocked, I fell back into the well. Chills ran clear to my heart. I dropped the bone in disbelief. Then I reached down into the water again. As my hands moved along the bottom of the well, I felt arm bones, ribs, and the smooth sphere of a skull. Quaking in the worst terror of all my days, I leaned my head against the wall and grasped the cold stones.

I heard a rustling above. "Oh, poor baby," sneered my father, "are you a little upset?"

Shaking the leg bone at him, I yelled, "How could you do this, you are mad, you are—"

"Oh, yeah, you found some company down there?"

"How could you—"

"Hey, kid, how do you like the concept of a common grave?" he said as he pumped the gun, staggered, and aimed it down the well. A swell of anger surged through every part of my body. Armed with the bone, I climbed up onto the rocks along the sides and sprung through the air, dropping the bone and grabbing his gun. As we struggled, the gun went off, and pellets twanged against the walls of the well. "You killed my grandmother!" I cried.

"You and your stories." He recoiled now that he had lost the upper hand. Then he broke loose, pushed me against the well, and turned to run. By the time my feet hit the ground, my father had run halfway around the building, gun still in hand. When I made it past the corner, he was through the pine grove and in the meadow. Still in flight, he turned around and shouted his good-bye message, shaking the gun above his head. "I'll get you, kid!"

I wanted to run after him and tangle with him there, in the dead grass and snow, but I turned instead and ran into the chapel. Lily lay curled and trembling on the bed, her hands wrapped around her knees and her voice whimpering.

"I'm going for the police," I said, tossing off my wet clothes and throwing on dry ones. "This has to end."

"No." She shot up like a bolt. "Absolutely no police, not now, not ever."

"But Lily, the man is stark raving mad. He'll be back. And Lily, he killed our grandmother. She's in the well, for goodness' sakes."

Lily slipped away and just kept muttering over and over, "No police, not here, not ever . . ."

"It's okay, my darling, they don't have to come here. I'll go to them at the police station."

"No," she cried, "they will come here. You know they will."

"Wouldn't that be okay? Just one visit?"

"They will separate us somehow. I'm sure of it."

"Then what can we possibly do? This must end. You cannot be hurt like this again. You see, even this time, I couldn't protect you."

"I don't know what to do. I only know what we cannot do."

"All right then. If you will not let me set this straight and get him arrested, then there is only one thing left to do."

"Yes."

"Go away together."

She slid from the bed and walked toward me with her blanket wrapped around her and trailing behind. She led me to the couch, curled beside me, and nestled there quietly without even a whimper.

39

After a little while, I left Lily resting on the couch and began tossing things into boxes, preparing for a hasty departure. Then in my frenzy, I felt Lily beside me. She was calm, frighteningly tranquil.

"There is still much to tell," she said in barely a whisper.

"Yes, after we pack and are gone from this wretched place, you can tell me everything. We'll go so far away that my father will never find us, ever again."

"Josey, I don't know if I can go out there into the open. I can't explain how terrifying it feels."

"My darling, we will travel in the dark and only for a while. Then we'll be somewhere safe, at last."

"I would be afraid."

"I'll take care of you. We shall marry."

"Oh, Josey, it's like your father said. It's incestuous and unspeakable."

"Lily, that means nothing compared to our love. Cousins have married."

"Perhaps."

"Yes," I continued, still packing boxes like a maniac, "we can leave here and live a normal life together far away."

"I want to tell you some things."

"When we are driving, Lily, we'll have all night to talk. But now we need to get some things together, whatever we need to take with us."

"The last time I went in an automobile, I couldn't speak for years."

"That was in the light, Lily, and under my father's bullying force."

"Well, there is something I want to explain—"

"Lily—"

"It won't take long to tell," she said softly. Looking in her eyes, I could see that we would not be going anywhere until she did.

So Lily talked. She dove headlong into the next layer of the onion that we were peeling together. Without my asking, she answered the questions that had been brewing in my mind for years. She told me about the torments she had gone through that made her fear the light and drove her inside the chapel to her hermetic life. And she told me about her son.

"Who was the father?" I asked.

"Your father," she said.

She had grown up in Tallahassee, Florida. When her parents were killed in a fire, Lily had come to stay with her Uncle Willie and Aunt Isabel, who lived on the outskirts of Savannah, Georgia. Grandma Ru lived there, too. (Although my father had talked about growing up in the South, I had never understood exactly where our home was.) Since Lily was thirteen, my father—her dear Uncle Willie—had been roving his fingers along her budding body whenever he pleased. Sometimes in the night, he'd crawl in her bed, clamp his hand over her mouth, lie on top of her, and drive into her. Though he didn't make a sound during the whole ordeal, his hot breath howled like a tornado in her ear. And when she climaxed from the sheer mechanics of it all, she despised herself, thinking that meant she liked what was happening when she knew in her deepest soul that she couldn't imagine hating or fearing anything more. My father had made her promise not to tell. If she did, he said he would send her to an orphanage in North Dakota. Seems he got a lot of mileage out of that one.

Even though Lily never told anyone about my father, she felt Grandma Ru may have known because she often heard Grandma and my father arguing in hushed voices. Soon after that, Grandma sought refuge in her world of visions.

When Lily became pregnant, my father kept her locked in the basement of an abandoned building in the middle of a field, way behind the house. He told Isabel that his sister—also a sister to Lily's mother—had wanted Lily to live with them and that she would take over raising her. But in fact, Lily was locked in the basement for seven months. She measured the time by the size of her stomach. Often, it was cold down there, but she got used to it. In the night when my mother slept, my father brought Lily food, water, and a clean bucket to use as a toilet.

The only light Lily had was a slender ray of sun that came in from the corner of the room during a certain part of the day—she never knew exactly what time of day that was, but she imagined it was morning. Among the things my father brought to her was one of the glass bottles he had done—the one with the castle inside, the one I had often gazed into as a child. Lily would hold the bottle up to the rare beam of sun to watch it illuminate the castle and enflame the jewels. Then moments later, or so it seemed, the ray flickered out as the sun moved behind whatever it was that cast the shadow across her only source of light.

Sometimes Lily thought of breaking the glass bottle so she could slice her veins and be free of the horror, but she couldn't bring herself to destroy the castle or the child growing within her. Then one day, feeling around the basement floor with her hands, she found another bottle, which she did break to use as a shovel trying to dig her way out. When that failed, she made a crystal garden with the shards of glass imbedded in the dirt. She tried to imagine what it would look like in the light of day.

Lily's baby was born in the basement, in the pitch of darkness where she couldn't see the color of his hair, although she felt it all thick upon his head. Two weeks after the baby was born, when at last my father opened the door to let Lily out, she ran past him, escaping into the field, where the sun blazed and the overexposed trees looked like thin wisps on a vast white plain, and the openness scalded her mind and tortured her eyes. She had no sense of balance, but something in her drove her to flight. She flew across the field with the baby in her arms, running for her life.

But my father caught up with her and threw the baby in the grass. The frail child rolled out of his small checkered quilt and lay naked and crying under the furious light. My father carried Lily back to the abandoned building. She, screaming for her baby. He, stuffing a scarf deep in her mouth to muffle her cries.

He locked her in the basement again, and that was Lily's life for three more years. My father continued to come to her with his sick appetites, but only when he was drunk. He would unlock the door and stagger down the steps with a lantern. Even though she knew of the horrors to come, she had a chance to look around the basement in the soft glow to see what was there. Those were the only images she had during those years, except for what was revealed in the one thin ray.

Sometimes in the darkness before he came, Lily rearranged various objects. She laid old planks, hunks of metal, and tiny brass findings against the dirt wall where they would be in view when he came with the lantern. But once he was upon her, she had to shut her eyes to keep from throwing up. She fought him in the beginning, but soon grew docile realizing how futile was her struggle. So she let him do what he would while she left her body and sought refuge in her mind, in a dark place, where she summoned visions to get her through—gardens alive with quivering petals, ladybugs in the sunlight upon velvet leaves, and clouds changing shape in the sky. All the things that years later she would paint upon the smooth surfaces of fungus and etch into the floor.

During those long dark years, she thought mostly about her baby. My father assured her that he had gone back to the child in the field and then had given him up for adoption. But she was forever haunted with the image of the child dying there in the sun with hungry ants crawling over his tiny body and vultures pecking at his eyes.

"Then," continued Lily, "after three years, your father took me from the basement into the open light of daytime and into a car. He drove me to this place so far away and cold—here in New Hampshire. He must have brought you here separately, Josey, because I never saw you or your mother. The way Grandma Ru spoke of how your mother adored you, I can only imagine he stole you from her—she having no idea where you had gone.

"All I remember is riding in the car, hiding under a blanket, absolutely terrified of the light, which I hadn't seen in years. Then he put me in this chapel here. He didn't lock me in because he realized I was so frightened I would never leave. He gave me money and bought me food. He hired Leon to fix up the place. Then Leon became my friend and helped with so many things. That trip up to New Hampshire was the last time I was in the light of day, except when your father took me to the hospital."

Long before Lily reached this part of her story, I had buried my face in my hands. For the first time I understood how Lily must have felt when she couldn't speak. The words froze in my throat, and I was lost in silence.

"And one more thing, Josey. Your mother is still living somewhere in Georgia."

40

Lily and I faced a major disagreement about what to do next. I wanted to have my father arrested, take Lily to Georgia to see my mother, then find somewhere far away to live, maybe California or maybe even Georgia near my mom if I could find her. Lily, on the other hand, would have preferred to stay where she was—choosing my father's fury over the wrath of the sun and of wide-open places.

We compromised on leaving the police out of our plans and moving somewhere far away. First I would visit my mother, if indeed she still lived on the outskirts of Savannah. There I would see about living in that area. I begged Lily to come, but she insisted on avoiding that part of the journey. "When a place is set up," she said, "I'll come there with you in the night." Since Lily refused to leave the chapel for now, I arranged for Leon to look after her closely while I made my brief trip to Georgia.

As I departed the chapel that evening, I stopped by Leon's house. I told him about Grandma Ru. That way, if the police ever got wind of my father's crimes after we left, then at least Leon would know where the evidence could be found.

"Where did he take her?" asked Leon.

"He put her in Lily's well. She was there for six years."

"Oh, Josey," he said, gazing out the window with that look he wore only for my father's crimes.

"I buried her in the meadow, Leon, next to the willow tree. There's a white cross in the ground. If anyone comes asking about such things, you know where she is."

"She was in that well all those years," murmured Leon. "That's what made them plants grow so wild. I knew there was something strange in that water."

That's the first time it occurred to me that I had been watering Lily's plants with the nutrients of Grandma Ru's remains.

※   ※

After all those years, I couldn't believe how easily I found my mother. I looked up Isabel Rose in the phone book, and there was her name and address. I guess I just needed to know where to start looking.

Driving along the winding road on the outskirts of Savannah, I opened the windows to the luscious southern air—so warm for December. Pale-green fields were dotted with knotted trees—their curling branches covered with weeping moss. Marshy plains in the distance oozed like primordial seas. Boiling mist, seemingly alive, carried scents of saltwater and emerging life.

Arriving at my mother's place, I found the natural wood house that Lily had described. Scanning the desolate field behind, I saw the abandoned building where my father had kept Lily for more than three years.

I had lived my first few years in this house of my mother's and, although I couldn't remember anything specific, the place stirred a familiar feeling, as if I had once dreamed it. Walking up the stone pathway, the place felt cozy with its natural gray wood, steep roof, lace curtains in the windows, and an old porch swing. Blue ageratums and lobelia bordered the pathway. Red geraniums flourished in window boxes and in pots hanging from the porch. And cats peered out of every window.

But the strangest thing of all was that the car in her driveway was the same model as mine. Now with my arrival, there sat two Chevy Impalas, side by side, hers light yellow and mine pale blue.

I knocked on the door. The butterflies that had been flying in high-winding erotic circles for the past weeks with Lily suddenly gathered together in the pit of my stomach, fluttering their wings like they always did when I faced something unknown. I was afraid and had no idea of what to expect. If my mother had really abandoned me, she might not want anything to do with her long-lost son. Maybe I would remind her of the violent husband she once had.

※

After several long moments, I was about to leave when a woman opened the door. She was holding a large gray cat in her sturdy arms. She had a courageous look, with soft eyes, thick hair pulled back in a loose bun, high cheekbones, and lush eyebrows. Except for her hair, which was dark with a wisp of white passing through, I didn't see myself in her. But then I hadn't thought I looked like my father either, although others said I was a spitting image of him.

"Yes?" she said with southern charm dripping in her voice.

Not knowing where to begin, I said, "I've come to inquire on the whereabouts of your son, Josey Rose."

Light sparkled in her eyes as if two tiny stars had suddenly soared down from the sky and landed on her velvet irises. "What *about* my son? Do you know where he is?" She flung open the door to let me in.

Three cats made circles around her feet, and I couldn't speak. We looked at each other for a moment.

"Who are you?" she whispered.

"Josey," I said.

She dropped the cat and drew her hands to her face. Her eyes grew moist, but the stars remained, twinkling through her tears. I grasped her hands, then embraced her while the cats paced around us, nuzzling my ankles as if they had known me all their lives. I was there with my mother, holding her, this total stranger, in my arms.

Then taking my hand, she led me across the room to a couch where several more cats were lounging. She removed two of them, and I sat down. She nestled into an old stuffed chair. Three cats descended on her lap while others took their spots on the chair arms and upper back edge, where one pawed gently at her hair.

Neither of us spoke for several moments. My eyes wandered. I had remembered my father talking about all her pets. There were cats on the buffet, cats on the dining room table, one in the fruit bowl, and another perched on top of a large birdcage that contained no birds.

"So," I said feeling strange, "how many cats do you have?"

"Twenty-three," she drawled. "Let me introduce you. This is Bones because he was skinny in his younger years. This is Guppy because he likes to reach into the aquarium and grab the fish. This little darling is Stargazer—her name used to be Goosedown until I saw how she loves sittin' on the windowsill, gazing at the stars. And this is—"

"Oh, so many."

"Yes, I shall acquaint you with the others gradually. Can't meet too many cats at once, you know." She drifted into a kind of reverie. Then,

"Josey, tell me everything. Where do you live? What have you been doing? It's been so long since your father stole you away. You can't imagine what I've been through trying to find you . . ."

Yes, I could certainly imagine—I thought of my search for Lily.

". . . so many failed attempts. Posting your picture in towns across Georgia. Putting ads in the paper. Hounding the police. Visiting schools all through the South."

"Well, I've been living in Willow Junction, New Hampshire—"

"New Hampshire. I never dreamed he'd go that far. All he knew was the South. Are you living with anyone?"

"Yes . . . a woman named Lily."

"Oh, such a lovely name. Did you know you have a cousin Lily? She lived with us for a while before you were born, when her parents were killed in a fire. But she went back to Tallahassee to live with her other relatives—your father's sister and her husband. And you know, I never heard from them, not even once. But then they never were much for staying in touch."

I was nowhere near ready to tell my mother about Lily. Instead I shifted the conversation. "Mom, what happened? How did my father and I end up in New Hampshire and you down here?"

"Is he still alive? I figured he'd have drunk himself to a certain death by now."

"Did he leave you?" I asked tentatively as a huge Angora cat crawled into my lap, reclaiming her place on the couch.

"Oh, Josey, it's all in the past. I'm trying to forget everything that happened. Why would you want to add such misery and woe to your memories?"

"I truly want to know."

She stroked the cat in her lap for several moments. "Yes," she said reluctantly, "he left me. But I left him first. When you were three, I couldn't bear your father's wild rampages anymore. So crazed were his fits that I feared he would hurt you. One night while he tossed his shoes around the bedroom, I packed up two suitcases and took you away with me to my sister Charlotte's. I hated leaving your grandmother with him, but it was all I could do."

"Where was this sister? How come I don't know of her?"

"In Savannah. She still lives there. Hasn't your father talked about her?"

"He hasn't talked about anyone, Mom. As for you, he told me you died of malignant melanoma."

"Oh, land sakes alive."

"Okay, so you and I were living in Savannah with Aunt Charlotte. Then what happened?"

"During the next year, your father took you for short visits from time to time, although quite against my wishes. One day on such a visit, the hour came for your father to bring you back, but he never arrived. I called on the phone, but no answer. I drove to the house and found his car gone. I searched for you everywhere. The police searched. And we never found you. When the police investigated your father's house—this house—they found he had left the place in disarray. He had withdrawn all the money from his accounts, and he left some things on the dresser for me."

"What things?"

"A note, three thousand dollars, and the deed to this house. The note was odd." She walked over to the buffet, scratched a cat behind the ear, and opened the top drawer. She shuffled through a pile of papers and near the bottom pulled out a folded sheet of yellow tablet paper and handed it to me. In my father's rambling scrawl, it said,

Isabel,
My love is yours forever,
but Josey is mine.
    Always, Willie

"So you moved back in this house?"

"Yes, I took a job in a pet store, and for years I searched for you. I never gave up. Knowing you had grown, I've been calling colleges asking if you are enrolled. I can't believe your father drove you all the way to New Hampshire."

"The man is a maniac, Mom. He's absolutely mad."

"Oh, yes, and he must have taken your grandmother with him, because she disappeared as well. Is your Grandma Ru living in New Hampshire, too?"

"She lived with us, yes, for a while."

Suddenly a coal-black cat darted across the room, leaped through the air, and landed on the buffet. Then he pawed through the papers in the drawer that my mom had left open, and he made a cozy nest there.

"That's my baby, Midnight," she said. "Isn't she a sweetie?"

"Mom, I want to tell you something, about Lily. You see . . . she's—"

My mom stood up and wandered in the kitchen. She returned with a glass of grape juice.

"You adored grape juice as a child," she said.

"Mom," I tried again, "Lily is my—" This time it was me who stopped. I wasn't ready to confess yet that I was in love with my cousin.

"What about Lily?"

"Well, it's about bloodlines," I stammered.

"Bloodlines . . ." She helped me along.

Then, hesitating, I shifted to another subject. "Yes, bloodlines. Well, sometimes this feeling wells up within me—something akin to anger—and I'm worried that I'll become crazy like my father."

"Yes," she said in a soothing voice.

"I don't want to be like him, you see."

"Josey, do you throw things around the house?"

"No."

"Do you slam people against walls?"

"No."

"Do you like cats?"

"Well, sure. They're all right."

"Then you will be quite fine. Anyone who likes cats has good blood."

"Mom, it may not be that simple."

"Let me tell you something, Josey." She stood up and paced across the floor, back and forth like a tiger with her retinue of cats surrounding her. "Now sugah doll," she purred, "it's no wonder you are concerned. Probably the slightest hint of anger you think is a seed for one of your father's frenzies. Well, I'll tell you this—you need never worry about inheriting his traits . . ." She sat beside me on the couch and tenderly held my face. "For you are the child of another."

"Whatever do you mean?"

"Well, I always wanted a child, Josey. For a while, your cousin Lily was like our own, but her aunt and uncle wanted her back so your father took her to Tallahassee. After she left I begged him to give us a child. Then several months after Lily left, your father explained that once Lily was situated in Florida, she had—well, as your father said, 'She got herself knocked up.'"

"Mom, what does this have to do with me being the child of another?"

"Well, since Lily couldn't keep the child—after all, she was only thirteen—your father offered to take him. You see, at times your daddy truly had a good heart. How odd it was. He had a protective feeling for that baby, as if it were his own, probably because he so adored his niece Lily."

"Oh, indeed," I said through my teeth.

"So we took the baby, and your father doted over him so. He insisted we change his birthday, make it a month later so there would be no connection with the birth of Lily's child. He said we had to do this because we hadn't gotten any legal papers, and there was no birth certificate. He further insisted that Lily never know that her child had come to us—something about her pining over him and that it would be easier for all involved if she didn't know. Since we heard nothing from her family, I never had the chance to tell her."

Blood raced cold through my veins, and my head spun dizzy. Please let this not be true.

"Oh, my," she continued rapidly, "but it was good we took the poor child, after all. Obviously Lily couldn't care for him. When your father brought the baby to the house, he was wrapped in an old checkered quilt and covered with field grass like a little lost Moses."

Her words rang like a death-knell, and I buried my head in the pillows of my mother's couch.

"That child was you, Josey. So you see, my lamb, you are free. You are not your father's child after all. You are Lily's son, your dear cousin Lily, whom you never met. But I can tell you, she was lovely as any angel in all the heavens."

My mother sighed in relief, having shared her secret at last. I cringed while so many memories flooded my head: My grandmother's words, *Your mother is alive, and she lives close by.* My father telling me, *The bloodline is closer than you think.* The note my mother had received from my father . . . *Josey is mine,* for I was his child, too. And of all the signs that should have made me realize—the eyes, our lavender eyes.

For several long moments, I lay back on the couch, letting my newfound bloodlines carry me to a place more deep and tangled than I'd ever known.

41

Once I calmed down, my mom and I talked for a long while. At first I wondered whether I should even call Isabel my "mom" after what I'd learned. But she had raised me through my first several years, and she was the only mom I'd ever known as a child. Even so, I was still confused. I was in shock, really, and my mind wandered, but I remember some of what we spoke. She told me stories about all her cats—which ones are friends with each other, which ones won't go outside, and which ones purr the deepest. I told her about Ralph and Casey, Aunt Kitty's winning the trifecta after she died, the boa constrictor that almost strangled Grandma Ru, and my job at the restaurant. I told her as much as I could about Lily without giving away her identity. And I explained that Lily and I wanted to move somewhere far away.

"Where will you go?" she asked. "Do you know people in another town—somewhere you can stay while you get your feet on the ground?"

"Not really, Mom. I haven't gotten around all that much."

"Well, where is Lily from? Perhaps you could start there."

"Actually she lived in Savannah for a spell."

"Whereabouts? Maybe I know her family. People from all over come into the pet shop."

"Well, east, I believe. Quite a ways east of Savannah."

"Josey, honey. East of Savannah is the ocean."

"Well, maybe north. I'm not sure actually."

"Ah, so much to discover about your new lady. When did you and Lily meet?"

"Mom, I really can't talk about all that right now. Too overwhelming, you see. I just know I have to get back to Lily very soon."

"Oh, Josey, you just got here."

"And what joy to find you, Mom, but I'm afraid I have to leave tomorrow. You know I'll be back very soon."

"Sugah, I know how you feel. Tell you what, I'll come with you to retrieve your Lily. I want to see the town where you have been living, and—"

"Mom, this might not be the best time for a visit. Let us get situated first."

"By that time the town of your childhood will be mere history. It's only right that I see where you've been living and, well, there are things I need to take care of."

"Like what?"

"I'm not quite sure yet."

"Mom, you can't see my father. He cannot know where I've gone. Please—"

"Sugah babe, come with me to feed the cats. If I'm late with their dinner, I'll have the whole pack after me."

※   ※

The next day, we prepared to go. My mom called the pet shop and told them she had a peculiar strain of flu—one that originated in the cold rivers of New Hampshire. As I carried her suitcases to the car, I noticed her tossing several cats into the backseat.

"Ah, Mom, what are you doing here?"

"Packing the cats, dear. Not all of them, of course. But there are a few who cannot bear to be left alone overnight. Take Twiddles, for example—she's deathly afraid of the dark. If she can't sleep on my feet, she will die."

"How many cats will be coming, then?"

"Only twelve."

Hmmm, bloodlines or no bloodlines, I wondered about my ancestry. My grandmother cavorted with the Indians, my father found madness inside whiskey bottles, and my mother couldn't live a day without these twelve cats.

The last thing packed into the car was a litter box that my mother placed carefully on the backseat. Then she put on a wide-brimmed dark-blue hat adorned with plastic fruit, and we were off.

The drive back to New Hampshire was fine, considering the circumstances. Driving north was like moving through time, from the warm weather of Georgia to the snowy winter of New England. The twelve cats made their home in the car, draping themselves wherever they pleased—on the dashboard, in the open glove compartment, and on my mother's lap. After the first day, the black cat called Midnight passed the miles on my lap as well. Once, when I pressed on the brake, a loud screech arose from an indignant feline. The one who liked sleeping on feet had curled herself around the accelerator and nestled her head on my shoe. I had become so used to cats crawling all over me, I hadn't noticed her there. When I put on the brakes, I flattened her tail.

The old Impala drove smooth as silk. But every time I looked in the rearview mirror, all I saw were cats sunning themselves on the backseat ledge. I took special care not to stop suddenly, so the litter box, which was becoming richer by the mile, would not fall forward all over the floor. My mother and I traded off driving and stayed in motels along the way. We had to ask for rooms out of sight of the motel office so we could sneak the cats in.

On the road, I had many thoughts, random ponderings. I considered, for example, how I would never become one of those folks who takes up chronicling family history. The more I had uncovered, the more I didn't like. I hoped I knew all there was to know. I spent many miles thinking about how to explain to my mom about Lily, and how to tell Lily that she was my mother, and, well, by the time we reached Pennsylvania, I still had no idea what to say to either one.

My own dilemma was beyond comprehension. Hard as I tried, I could not still the struggle between my head and heart. I knew erotic pleasures could no longer be indulged with the woman who begot me. Yet my heart yearned for her tenderness, her touch, the splendor we had found together.

Trying to resolve this turmoil was like blending oil and water. Never would the two mix—neither substance willing to sacrifice its essence to the other. The new knowledge gained about Lily could not be denied, nor could my long-held desire for her be suppressed.

Somewhere in Pennsylvania, my mother asked, "By the way, how ever did you find me?"

I recalled, "It was something my father said."

"To you?"

"No, to Lily."

"Really, and how do Lily and your father get along?"

"Not well, Mom. That's why we have to leave."

❦   ❦

Around midnight we arrived in Willow Junction. My mother insisted we stop at the 7-Eleven to pick up a newspaper. When at last we pulled off the road by the meadow, my mother asked, "What is this place?"

"It's a chapel, Mom. See the dwelling way back in those trees? The cats will love it."

"Who lives here?"

"Lily. Now it will be the three of us, but for only one night. Then unfortunately, we have to depart tomorrow, rent a U-Haul, and drive back to Savannah. I'm not sure what we'll do after that."

"Why must we leave here so quickly?"

"It's a long story, Mom." Lifting a cat from my lap, I turned to her. "Before you meet Lily, I want to tell you something," I stammered, my voice betraying emotion. How could I possibly explain? "Well, Lily is . . . she is . . ." I couldn't bring myself to say the words.

"She is what, son?"

"She is . . . waiting for me. I need to go to her before she wonders if I'll ever return." My mom would have to see for herself who Lily was. I asked my mother to stay with the cats for a moment to give me time to explain to Lily about her unexpected visitor.

"Sugah . . . ," my mother said softly, "take as long as you like. I'll need some time to get the kitties ready for what looks like a mighty long walk."

42

I ran through the meadow all the way to the chapel. I decided to tell Lily everything. When I arrived, she was in bed, half sleeping.

"Is it you?" she whispered.

When I saw her there in the chapel, I was stilled in my tracks, stunned to silence, bewitched by her radiance—this goddess in her long white nightgown, perched on the edge of the bed as if she had alighted there for one brief moment and soon would fly away forever. So taken was I that all my fears melted in the warmth of her beauty. My time away from her had heightened her luster. She carried magic with her like a dove carries gold light across the lake at sunset.

She drew me slowly to her and kissed me on the cheek, the neck, and the tips of my fingers. She moved gently upon me with darting lips, like a feather caught in a spiraling wind. "Sweet darling," she said with barely a sound, "hello."

"That is the last time," I said, "that we will ever be apart."

"How is your mother? Did you find her?"

"Oh, yes, I found her all right."

"What joy she must have felt to find her son after all these years."

"Lily—"

"What was the first thing she said to you?"

"Let's see," I recalled, "it was something about cats. Yes, she said she has twenty-three of them."

"Goodness, that's more cats than I remember."

"Lily, she told me other things, too—about you and me."

"Oh, really."

Lily waited patiently while I gathered my words. Then I managed to utter, "She said that I was your—I mean that you are—" I couldn't find the way to tell her the truth that would at last give her peace, knowing her son was alive. Or would it? I was afraid. How could I consider disturbing the world she had so carefully constructed for herself—Lily's fantasy existence in this enchanting fortress that protected her from people, light, and all the world. I had willingly joined her retreat—this bewitching realm—for I so much wanted to be with her, to be near her. But now reality was quickly breaking down the fortress.

"What was it your mother said?" Lily asked so gently.

"She said . . . ," I continued reluctantly, "she said so many things."

"What did she say when you told her we are together?"

"I didn't. She knows I am with a woman named Lily. But she doesn't know it's you."

"Well, that shall make for quite a surprise when we show up on her doorstep someday."

"Actually, Lily, she is . . . in the car, out on Gypsy Lane. She came here with me—she and twelve cats. I have to go help her bring in her things. Then we'll stay the night and leave tomorrow after dusk when we have a full night of darkness to travel in."

Lily sat up taller. "How dare you bring a stranger here."

"She's not a stranger, Lily. You lived with her for all those years."

"But I never expected this."

"Neither did I. Maybe it's best this way. If you had known days ago, you would have been anxious the whole time awaiting her arrival."

"Josey," she said, "come sit with me here." Expecting further pleas of protest, I was totally taken off guard when she spoke no words, but gently pressed me back on the bed amid the sheets and pillows where her scent lingered. The feather of her kiss returned to carry me wherever she willed. I looked into her lavender eyes as she moved above me, along me, as if it were the very first time.

I wavered in the strangeness of it all. This must stop. "Lily," I pleaded, "let me tell you—"

Her fingers roving, her lips sweet, her breath so warm.

"Stop for one moment," I begged. "Wait, please, no—"

Lost in the swoon of her touch, I wanted to pull her down with me and press her against the pillows. "Lily, about your son—"

That's when my mother pushed open the door and walked into the chapel, three cats following her. "Josey," she called, "I got tired of waiting so—" When Isabel's eyes found Lily tangled in my arms, she stared as if a ghost had descended upon her.

"Hello, Aunt Isabel," said Lily.

"Land sakes alive, Lily Milan. What are you doing here?"

Then she paused long enough to absorb everything before her. "Lord have mercy," she said as the cats came to attend to her distress. "I presume this is *not* the Lily you mentioned when we spoke earlier."

"Well, yes," I said, "before we knew the circumstances, of course."

"Lord have double mercy," she sighed.

After some restless moments, Isabel turned to me and asked, "Does she know about her son?"

"What about my son?" asked Lily.

"It's what I've been trying to tell you. You see, your son, well, he is not lost."

"Josey, how can you make jokes about this?"

"Lily, your son is alive and well—although recently he has found himself in quite a dilemma."

"Oh, Mother of God," said Isabel, turning aside.

Lily perched forward like a leopard ready to pounce, but not for prey, rather for joy. She held my shoulders, and her eyes stirred with light. "Have you actually seen my son?"

"Yes."

"Where? I beg you to tell me how to find him." She held my face in her hands.

"He is here with you, Lily."

Her fingers trembled upon my skin.

"I am your son."

Our lavender eyes locked, and the mystery that had always hung between us drained like honey all around.

❧   ❧

It took five trips through the meadow to carry the cats and all their supplies. Then my mom, Lily, and I sat around the kitchen table, trying to settle into the shape of our new ties. Lily stroked the long white fur of the Angora cat that had taken up residence in her lap. My mother perused the classified section for pets, circling the ads for cats that interested her most. And I sat, dazed. As the hours waned to dawn, we waltzed delicately through the tangled strains of our relationships.

❧

When Lily wandered to the other side of the chapel to light some candles, my mother turned to me and whispered, "Josey, how could she not have known that you are her son?"

"She was never told."

"But what does she think happened to her child?"

"Until tonight she had no idea. It's a long story."

When Lily came back, my mom boldly turned to her and said, "If y'all don't mind me asking, I've always wondered about something."

"What's that, Aunt Isabel?"

"When you left us to return to Tallahassee and you came to be with child, who was the father?"

In a voice clear as morning dew, Lily said, "Uncle Willie."

In her southern way, my mother simply raised one lush eyebrow, showing a vague hint of interest. But southern charm wasn't strong enough to maintain her composure, as she suddenly leapt from her chair. "Why, that bloomin' scoundrel," she ranted, pacing the floor. "If you could have heard him years ago, carrying on about how his sweet niece had lost all her senses, whoopin' it up with the boys in Tallahassee, getting pregnant and all. Looks like he was the one doing the whoopin'."

Lily sought refuge in her chamomile tea.

"Oh, yes," my mother continued, "what I wouldn't give to lay my hands on that swindling weasel right now."

"No, Mom," I begged, "please don't even think of it."

Then in the midst of her raving, she looked at her watch and asked, "I'm curious, when do you people sleep?"

"Now would be good," I said.

"Then perhaps," suggested my mom, "we can catch a few winks, rise at noon, and be off soon after."

"Actually," I explained, "we were thinking dusk would be best."

"And drive in the dark?"

"Well, that's another thing, Mom. Lily is not fond of the light."

"Yes, my dear, your skin has always been fair as an angel's. But we'll be inside the car, and the ultraviolet rays can never penetrate glass."

"Actually," I said, "the concern is more broad."

"Aunt Isabel," said Lily, "I am deathly afraid to be in the light of day."

"Since when, sugah?"

"Since—"

"Yes," I said, "since Tallahassee."

43

When Lily and I awoke in midafternoon that Saturday, my mother was gone. She had taken the keys to my car and the section of the paper where she had circled the cats.

"She's off looking for critters," said Lily. But I was tormented by the thought of her possibly finding my father's house and getting into trouble with him. Nevertheless, I refused to leave Lily alone, so we kept occupied by packing up as much as could fit into the car. It was odd what Lily considered important to bring along. She packed no kitchen utensils or furniture and only a few clothes. Instead, she gathered shells, crystals, fossils, and foliage of all kinds. As she had always said, these were the important things in life.

Then Lily set about preparing steaming bowls of lilac potpourri and placing them around the chapel. As dusk settled in, my frustration rose. I was at a loss for what to do. "Take some chamomile, Josey," said Lily, handing me a steaming cup. "It always put you at rest before."

"Lily," I exploded, "the man is deranged. He'll kill her if he discovers she is taking us away from here."

My comment was suddenly punctuated by a large rock crashing through the clear glass window. Following the rock came my father wielding a pistol. This time he wasn't drunk—he was just naturally crazed, which I feared all the more.

"What is this," he jeered, "homecoming week for the Rose family? I've had a charming visit from my darling Isabel. The woman was in the same frenzy as when she left me sixteen years ago. I figured she'd had enough time to settle down, but looks like she still ain't satisfied. The old babe just—"

I didn't hear the rest because I was soaring across the room to fling myself upon my father. But as I lunged for his shoulders, it was he who, as before, easily spun me around, swept me off my feet, and anchored me to the floor. With his sobriety, he was stronger than ever.

"Where is my mother, Dad?" I demanded. "If you dare hurt her—"

"I told her all about how you was lovers with your own blood mother. When she gasped in horror, I gave her a shotgun and said she could come here and take care of you both. But she's the same jelly-bellied weakling she always was, so reckon I'll have to do the job myself."

My father dragged me across the floor to where Lily had made a pile of her fabrics when deciding what to take. He pulled out several long strips, riling up five cats who had made their nest in the mountain of chiffon.

"Friggin' cats," he growled.

I lunged at my father again, but with the pistol jammed into my ribs, I ended up submerged in the cloud of chiffon. Then he flipped me face-down, tied my legs with strips of the fabric, grabbed me by the armpits, and pressed me against a marble pillar. He pulled my hands back around the column and tied them together so I was bound to the pillar facing outward. Annoyed by my shouting, he jammed a wad of cloth in my mouth and tied it there so I couldn't call out.

"Hey, before you check out of this world, kid, you might as well take a gander at Miss Lily havin' herself a grand old time. What do you think, my little wench," he said, turning to Lily, "one last kiss for old times' sake. A final hurrah to send you off to the blazin' hell you deserve. Think of it, the devil's domain—fire and explosions of light all day and night. No escape for the sun-fearing souls."

"Nooo—" wailed Lily.

"Why, of course, my sweet," he said, flinging her on the bed, "you didn't think you'd really go to heaven, did you? After leaving your infant child in the field grass to die?"

"He lived," sobbed Lily.

"He died," said my father. "I went back and found him there—his tiny bones gleaming like driftwood in the noonday sun."

I tried to call out, but my words did not make it through the gag in my mouth. Only muffled cries emerged as I called over and over again.

Lost on the bed, Lily slowly folded into a ball and wrapped her arms around her legs, still sitting, her golden hair falling down all around her. I knew she was drifting toward the dark place, and it was taking her away, far from the walls of this chapel.

I struggled to get free, but he had bound me so tightly I couldn't move to loosen the ties.

"Ho-hum, ho-hum," chanted my father as he scavenged through the pile for more fabric. He pulled out one of Lily's dresses, shredded it into strips, and carried them over to the bed. Lily's arms were still draped around her legs, and her forehead rested on her knees. When my father pushed her back, she fell like a feather, and she began to hum. He rolled her onto her stomach and crouched beside her like he was about to sit down to a great game of poker. Biding his time, he lifted her arm, then let it fall limply.

"Oh, so cooperative, my meager wench. And you're even singing. See that?" he said, turning to me. "Lily loves it. Listen to that humming, just like a dizzy cat. When I get through with her, she'll be howling opera."

My father lifted Lily's ankles, one at a time, tied chiffon around them, and let them fall like putty on the bed. "Oh, yes, I know I don't need to tie you down, with your being so willing and all. But I wouldn't want to deny you the fun."

"Stop, for the love of God!" My calls of fury rolled out as muffled groans. I was blind with horror, so much that I thought I would pass out. My vision had become blurred, and the only thing I could see now was the madness in my father's eyes above the listless heap that was Lily.

He rolled Lily on her back, pulled the pistol from his belt, and slid it gently—almost lovingly—into her mouth. "I hope you like the feel of that cool metal against your tongue because after I'm done with you, you'll get it again with an added treat—a big fat bullet. Yeah, a sweet cherry for your sundae. Lily's last meal—one final shot from Uncle Willie."

Looking around for more fabric, he complained, "Damn, I've run out of ties." He got up and went to the pile of fabrics again, carrying the gun with him. Finding nothing to his liking he staggered into the alcove with the crystal garden. Then he set down his gun and yanked several strips from the ceiling.

"This should be dandy, now, don't you think?" he said as he swaggered back in, twirling the strips in the air. He crawled back on the bed, straddled Lily, and began tying strips of chiffon to her wrists. Close to blacking out, I was terrified by what my father would do. Everything blended into a wavering light as if I were underwater.

Then suddenly from the side, I saw the doorway open and moonlight flood upon the floor. A shrieking black shape soared into the light. I blinked tears from my eyes to see my mother's black cat, Midnight, bounding across the room with her fur raised like she'd been hit by lightning. Then a shadow fell upon the moonlit floor. I turned and saw my mother in the doorway, wearing her dark-blue hat with plastic fruit. She had a brand new calico cat in one hand and a shotgun in the other.

"Well isn't this a cozy family reunion," she said, dropping the cat and raising the shotgun.

"See, Josey," yelled my father, "I told you she'd come and blow you away. Give it to him, Isabel. Knock the wacko kid out of his bloomin' misery."

My mother moved toward Willie, slowly, unmoved by his words.

"Oh, Isabel, my precious little fruitcake," he babbled desperately, "you shouldn't have left me, pet. Everything would have turned out grand. I never stopped loving you, babe. Even up here in New Hampshire, everything I did, I did for you—the birds, the plants, the pictures on the wall. All the while, I asked myself things like, Do you think Izzy would like a clipper ship in this bottle? How about a green hull? And we're having Spanish rice just the way you used to cook it . . . as if any moment you'd walk in and join us there. It was all for you, Izzy, all for you . . ."

"And I suppose kidnapping my son was all for me. What in livin' heaven possessed you to do such a thing?"

"Hey," said my father, "I didn't want the boy growing up in a feline jungle. Those friggin' cats crawling all over the place. I gave him a life of goodness, a stable home, didn't I, Josey? Didn't I treat you good?"

I moaned fiercely, but to no avail.

My father was still straddled over Lily. Rage flared in my mother's eyes as the truth about my father welled up within her.

"How long have you been doing that to her, Willie?"

"Doing what?"

"When did you steal her innocence?"

"Hey, Izzy, she was always a nympho. It was she who first took me. Even as a child, she couldn't keep her hands off me."

"Sure, Willie, look at her now," my mother said in a voice that could still the moon. "Looks like she's just dying to crawl all over your irresistible bones." Then, steady and cool, my mother moved in on him with the gun beamed straight between his eyes.

"Well," he said in a rising nervous frenzy, "she's kinda tired now. Musta gotten herself all tuckered out boppin' her own son all these months. Yeah, ever since she got out of the loony bin, she—"

"So long, Willie Rose."

My father ducked low and sprinted off the bed. Then, faster than my mother's black cat, he darted into the alcove where he had left his gun. He slid across the floor, grabbed the pistol, and rose to take his aim.

Both guns exploded simultaneously. The bullet from my father's pistol soared past my mother and thunked into the statue of the woman holding the apple. Meanwhile, the pellets from my mother's shotgun sank into my father and threw him backward. He crashed against the smoky mirrored wall and sent the crystals spinning and tinkling above. He slid slowly down the wall, leaving a trail of blood on the shattered mirror. Then he reached out his hand toward my mother, as if begging for her to come to him. "Isabel, Isabel . . . ," he called in a strained whisper that came gurgling from his lungs, "why'd you have to leave me?" Then he fell headfirst into Lily's crystal garden, where his glass eye plopped out and rolled across the sand.

My mother ran to the kitchen and pulled a knife from the drawer— the same long blade Lily had used to cut puzzle pieces the first night we met. As she sliced away the fabric that my father had tied on my hands and legs, I yelled through my gag, "Make sure he's dead, Mom. Make sure he doesn't get the gun again." Before she could ungag me, I flew into the alcove and pressed my fingers to his neck, searching for a pulse. My mother trotted along behind me, slicing at the remaining fabric bound around my head to hold the gag. By the time it fell loose, I had not found a pulse anywhere in the folds of my father's neck.

I ran to the bed calling, "Lily, darling, talk to me." When I sat beside her, she rose up and gazed at me with unnatural tranquillity. I knew we had to get out of that place. Certainly we had done nothing wrong— we had only defended ourselves. But I thought only of Lily and all that she would go through. Surely the police would be involved. She was so frail now, they'd swallow her up with all their questions, their investigations. We had to leave.

I said, "We need to go quickly, Lily."

"Okay," she sighed as if I had offered her a bowl of raspberry sherbet. She wandered around the chapel, blowing out the candles under the bowls of potpourri while my mother began gathering all the cat supplies.

"Mom," I commanded, "let the cats be."

"Never," she said as she marched out the door with two felines under each arm and another following her. Surrendering, I grabbed several suitcases, including one filled with cat food, and followed her through the moonlit meadow. I stashed the suitcases in the trunk and rushed back for the next load. My mom remained behind, setting up the litter box in precisely the right place.

"Don't dawdle!" I yelled back to her. "We have to get out of here fast."

Then I saw Leon sweeping through the snow, the moonlight reflecting off his dark skin.

"Josey," he called, "there was this crazy woman with a shotgun running toward the chapel." When he saw my mother coming toward us, he hollered, "That's her Josey, that's the one with the gun."

"Leon," I said, "I'd like you to meet my mom."

"Pleased to make your acquaintance," said my mother.

"Josey, what's going on?" he asked.

"It's okay, Leon, it's all over. Let it pass for now."

"I called the police," said Leon. "I thought you were long gone by now. I didn't see your car."

"How could you call the police when you don't have a phone?"

"Norman bought me one for my birthday. You know he's in college now. Yessiree, he's going to be a—"

"Call them back, Leon, would you?" I pleaded, turning to run back to the chapel. "Tell them it's okay now. Please don't let them come."

When we walked in, Lily was wandering around lighting candles again, still quietly humming. How far had my father sent her back into the darkness, I wondered.

"Here, Lily," I said as gently as possible, "wrap up in your shawl, put on your boots, and walk with us to the car. Come quickly now." My mother grabbed more cats, while the remaining ones followed behind. This would be our last trek through the meadow. When we came out of the pine grove, Lily ran to me suddenly and buried her head in my coat. "Josey," she whispered, "the moon burns hot. The blazing light—"

"It's okay, Lily. It's the same moon as before."

"But it's in a different place—it's all much too vast."

"Then look down at the snow, but keep coming. We'll be in the car very soon."

She wobbled along next to me with her hands over her eyes and clutching my scarf, feeling her way through the path in the snow. Never before had she shied away from the light of the moon, and I feared for her.

When at last we made it to the car, we piled in. With all the stuff that we already had in the car and what we had just added, the cats had to scrunch themselves in whatever nooks and crannies they could find amid the plants, boxes, and suitcases. Lily, my mom, and I crammed into the front. My mother insisted on keeping the new calico on her lap. As she prepared to close the front door, the black cat got spooked and shot out into the road. "Midnight," called my mother as she threw the calico into Lily's arms and lunged out after the cat.

As she chased Midnight along the road, I heard the distant whine of sirens.

"Mom, for Chrissake, get back here. The cops are coming."

"Midnight . . . ," she sang like a lark.

I sprang out of the car, grabbed my mother, and flung her into the car. I dashed around the other side and slid behind the wheel. Just before slamming the door, I spotted Midnight tearing around the front of the car. I held the door opened while she leaped into the air, glazed my nose, and landed on my mother's lap.

"Dizzy cats," I grumbled.

"Hush, sugah babe," my mother scolded, "that's what your daddy always said."

As we made a spinning U-turn on Gypsy Lane and wheeled away from there, we saw an eerie radiance gleaming behind the rise in the road where we were headed. Then two cop cars screamed over the hill with their lights twirling and their sirens wailing. Lily gasped and sank her head into the folds of my coat.

"Blazing torches," said my mother.

"Oh," gasped Lily, "the moon has finally fallen."

"No Lily," I assured her, "these lights are red. They're—"

"The moon bleeds, Josey. Surely you must know that."

As the cars sped by us, a frenzy of light and sound flooded our car, and Lily began to quiver.

"It's okay," I kept saying, "it's okay, it's okay . . ."

The lights softened behind us as they slowed to a stop by the path to the chapel. I kept going, keeping steady, wanting to drive fast, but not so fast as to attract attention.

We turned off Gypsy Lane onto the country road. Then my mother, with her southern resilience, asked, "Well, now, what do y'all reckon we should name this darling little pussy cat? We could simply call her 'Calico,' but that's too obvious. How about 'Sirens in the Night'?"

"Call her 'Lucky', Mom. That's what we all are this very moment— lucky to make it out of there. But quiet now, we have to concentrate. They'll be looking for us."

"How about 'Harvest Moon'?" she continued. "Yes, that's it. To-night is the full moon, and this cat is a spittin' image of the harvest moon with all her orange colors. And the charcoal patches are like dark clouds hanging low in the sky in front of a big harvest moon."

"Hush one moment," I insisted. "Let's see, should we take the main road, or a more secluded back route?"

"Absolutely the main road," said my mom, "especially with it being night and all. We don't want to break down in the middle of nowhere."

"Mom," I explained, "right now, I'm more interested in not getting caught than on breaking down. When they find Dad's body, they'll have every car in the county after us."

"Yes," sighed my mother, "Harvest Moon . . ."

44

I decided to take the main road, hoping to get out of town before they sent out more cars. The way things worked in this small town, they'd have every unit on the case—pronto. We turned down the country road and sped past my father's house.

"Look, Lily," announced my mother, "there's the house where Josey grew up. Charming place, isn't it? I stopped by this morning."

Lily was too horrified to look up for anything, much less the house where my father had lived. She huddled there with her head pressed into my coat, clutching my scarf.

We sped toward Route 11, the main highway out of town. That's when I realized we were practically out of gas. If not for that minor detail, we might have been okay. But knowing there were no stations for a long way, I had to detour for miles down a side road and find some gas.

After returning to the road that would lead us out of town, we continued several miles more, passing my school and, farther along, the old stone bridge where Casey, Ralph, and I had made our excursions years ago. I thought about the railyard and the day we found Maggie in the grass. A few miles farther, we rounded the bend to discover the road-block. Two cars were just coming together to form a V-shaped barricade in the highway with their lights whirling, while another sat off to the side.

A cop stepped out of the car to talk with us. Lily wouldn't be able to handle any part of this. I slowed as if to approach him, then turned around and drove away at a normal speed so he might think we had simply changed our minds. But something must have roused his suspicion. When I saw the cop run back to his car and suddenly peel after us, I crushed the accelerator to the floor, disrupting the cat who was curled there.

The car was on our tail in an instant, sirens wailing and lights spinning.

"Mom," I commanded, "pull the top box forward, and get ready to dump it out the door."

"What's in it?"

"I have no idea."

She pulled the box to the front, unlatched the door, and waited. As the road began a curve to the right, I yelled "Now!" and my mom shoved the box straight out. I reached across and grabbed her arm so she wouldn't fall. A pile of Lily's chiffon dresses and fabrics exploded all over the road behind us, flying up onto the hood and windshield of our pursuer. The cop swerved to the right to avoid the box. Then, blinded by all the fabrics, he veered to the left and crashed into the stone bridge. His car erupted into smoke and flames. Flaring pieces of metal spun through the air like whirligigs on the Fourth of July and fell sizzling into the snow-covered river below.

"We have to abandon this car," said my mother. "The whole police force will be after us." I was glad she had shifted her focus from naming cats to the logistics of our escape. I slammed on the brakes and rammed it into reverse. We screeched backwards to the bridge.

"We'll leave the car and take the river," I said. "There are trains upstream, not far."

"The cops will follow our tracks," said my mother.

I barreled forward again for about three hundred yards and fishtailed the car into a break in the woods. I jumped out and ran back to the road, smoothing over the tracks where we had entered the woods.

"We can cut over to the river from here," I said.

As my mom began sorting out which cats she would carry, I insisted, "Mom, we are absolutely not lugging thirteen cats on this trek. This is life or death. This is jail or freedom. Forget the cats, we'll get new ones. You've got eleven more at home."

"Sorry, Josey," she said firmly, "if the cats don't come, then neither do I. I'd rather be in jail with my kitties than in Savannah with-out them."

"Mom, they don't let cats in jail."

"Then they'll have to put me somewhere else."

"Listen," I cried, totally exasperated, "we have no time for this." I had been with my long-lost mother for less than a week and already we were arguing like we had been together all our lives.

"Aunt Isabel," called Lily softly, "you can put your kitties in here." On the far side of the car, Lily had opened a suitcase filled with chiffon, candles, and plant containers. She pulled out the containers and left in the fabric to make a soft nest. My mother tossed in three cats.

Realizing there was only one way this scene was headed, I opened another suitcase and dumped out my clothes as well. In went two more cats, a small bag of cat litter, twenty cans of cat food, a pile of bowls, some forks, and a can opener. Knowing which ones would naturally follow her, my mother pulled some cats from the car and plunked them in the snow. One screeched, and she picked it up. "Poor baby," she lamented, "never had her tootsies in the snow." My mother and Lily carried several cats under their arms while the others followed along on their own.

Wearing her high furry boots, Lily was well equipped for the snow. After all, whenever she left the chapel in the past, her trail was only through meadows, woods, and rivers. My mother, on the other hand, had never seen this much snow in her life, and her footwear showed it. She wore cute leather shoes that swooped down to her bare ankles in a graceful fashion statement. Lily gave her an extra pair of boots she had packed, and we headed for the river.

Hovering near Lily, I said, "Hang on just a little longer. We have only to walk down the river, and there'll be a train for us. You'll be all right." Then I realized how futile my words were. Lily was far more comfortable trekking through the woods than riding in a strange car along a road she had never seen. The high canopy of trees sheltered her from the glaring, merciless moon. So she simply meandered along like she was in search of fungus. Her composure frightened me.

When at last we reached the river, I could see that the bag Lily had slung over her shoulder was too heavy with all the cats she had in her arms. I suggested we empty some of it. When I set it down beside the river, I found not a bag of clothes and essentials, but a collection of more crystals, fossils, river stones, candles, and shells. Although I loathed removing any of these items, knowing we were carrying twenty cans of cat food, I dropped out some of the heavier shells and laid them on the ice above the river. In the spring, they would sink to the bottom, perhaps to be found centuries later by archaeologists who would make some very odd assumptions about the local fauna.

"Honey," said my mom to Lily, "you sure have some weird notions about what is essential." I thought how Lily and my mom had something in common.

As we followed the course of the river, I took a gander at our ragtag trio. Lily and I followed along the frozen river, a curving trail of ice and snow. My mother, however, walked in the woods along the riverbank. "I never learned to swim," she said.

"Even in the spring," I explained, "the water is only inches deep."

"You never know," she said, "water can rise. How do you think the Atlantic Ocean got started?"

As we trudged along, our footsteps fell silently in the snow. Only the cats' meows crooning from our suitcases gave us away to the squirrels and winter birds. When at last we reached the railyard, two lines of train cars were roosting on the tracks. I knew trains left in the evening, but I didn't know which ones. I was certain, however, which direction the trains went—assuming they hadn't changed since the days Casey, Ralph, and I romped these grounds.

"There's an open boxcar," observed my mother. "Let's get on that one."

"No," I said, "that train goes west. We need the one on the next track over—the southbound line."

"How do you know this, sugah?" asked my mom. "Do you hop freight trains often?"

"Something I picked up in my childhood," I said.

There were no open boxcars on this line, so we found a car that was not in sight of the people working on a building at the edge of the railyard. With some maneuvering, I unbolted the boxcar and hopped in to check it out. I found myself in a pile of straw, head to head with one large cow. "This will do," I said as I reached down to pull Lily and my mother aboard. Once inside, my mother and I struggled to get the door closed, but couldn't lock it from the inside. We only hoped no one would notice.

Our first task was to search the straw for cow pies. We found none, and the straw smelled clean. They must have freshened up the old girl right here in Willow Junction. I wondered why there was only one cow, and what she was doing in this boxcar. Didn't they usually jam cows together in cattle cars? Must be some kind of special cow, I figured. As we were getting nestled in, we suddenly heard voices approaching.

"Get under the straw," my mother whispered, "and bring the cats, too."

I hid the suitcases, and we huddled together in the corner, camouflaged in the straw, grasping onto whatever cats we could find. We awaited our fate as the men's voices came closer.

"Oh, yeah," said one, "they'll slaughter 'em this weekend, just you wait."

"Better not," said the other. "I've got fifty bucks on the game."

"Gotta admit, Jack, they're deep in the bench, and Plunkett is threadin' needles with that ball."

"Yeah, but can Little Randy catch it? The way people talk you'd think just because they both went to the same college, they're bleedin' soul mates, for Chrissakes."

"Hah, you watch. Plunkett is hot."

"Hot, my ass. He's jittery back in the pocket. I think the new stadium has him all shook up. You can't expect—"

"Holy dog crap, will ya look at this? That blasted Sam—he cleans the cow car and forgets to lock it up."

"Dumb coon, can't even deal with a cow."

"Hey, that's 'cause the cow is smarter than him. Old Agnes probably sweet-talked him into leaving the door open so she can leap out somewhere in the hills of Virginia."

Suddenly, the door slid opened, and I suppressed a sneeze.

"Still there, old girl?" said the man.

"Hey, Agnes," said the other, "maybe I'll see ya later—in between the buns of my Big Mac."

Then the cat under my arm let out a long meow.

"Get the cat," said the man.

"Aw, come on. It's the cow's last ride. Let her have some company."

"Well, ain't that a sweet thought."

The door slid along its metal rails and crunched shut. We stayed under the straw until the men's voices were gone. "Well," I sighed, "at least we'll get as far as Virginia, maybe farther."

"Lord have mercy," said my mother while Lily lay trembling in the straw.

"It's okay now," I said to Lily, trying to sound calm. "The men are gone. It's just us and ol' Agnes."

As my mother set about opening the suitcases, the cats sprung out one by one only to find themselves trapped inside a bigger box, this one shared by three people and a large creature with four legs. My mother talked gently to them while I pressed my ear against the boxcar, listening for more voices.

At last the train jerked into motion. As we accelerated along the tracks, I peeked through an opening in the wall. In several miles, I saw the blackness of the tunnel and then, crossing Route 11 with a long whistle blow, I beheld the welcome sight of lights from three cop cars barricading the south side of town. As we gained speed, the spinning lights receded into the distance. We were free.

Despite my glee, I was distressed about Lily, but not because she was lying in the straw trembling. Who wouldn't be a wreck under the circumstances? My concern was more for the way Lily wavered between fear and complacency. There was a distance growing, a lost link. Whenever I looked in her eyes, she seemed to drift farther away, her gaze more tenuous as if the very essence of her being were dangling from a slender thread.

"Lily," I said, "are you okay?"

"Yes," she answered, "except for one thing."

"What's that, my love?"

"All the dust from the moon makes it so hard to see."

Overwhelmed, I lay back in the boxcar and held her to my chest. Without a word, we thundered out of the county, then out of the state. Isabel opened six cans of cat food for her flock. My mind drifted. Remembering my days with Casey and Ralph, I thought about how I had grown up yearning for the mother I never had. And now I was in a boxcar with two mothers, a cow, and thirteen cats.

I thought about Lily having not seen television or the movies for a long time. That meant she had not observed a murder acted out in any way for years, and when she saw my father kill Grandma Ru, she had escaped into her mind. Even though she had no love for my father as she had for her grandmother, I worried that the trauma would upset her terribly. And Isabel, my lost mother—what had happened to her to make her able to walk coolly toward my father, unwavering with a shotgun against her cheek, and blast him against the mirrored wall?

Suddenly, I was pulled from my thoughts by a flash of light that

threw shadows dancing across the walls of the boxcar. Lily had taken
out candles from her bag, set them around the place, and had just
struck a large wooden match.

"Land sakes alive!" yelled my mom as Lily glided over to light the
first candle.

"Lily, honey," I said, "actually this isn't the safest place to light candles, with the straw being so dry and all."

"Agnes told me she needed some light," Lily said.

"She'll be all right. In fact, maybe the light would frighten her, you
know, with the cats and all."

"That's just it," said Lily, "she wants to see the other animals here.
She's absolutely dying to find out what they're eating. She knows it's
some kind of sea creature, but she's confused because she never saw a
fish before, let alone the ocean."

"Lily, Lily, come sit with me here."

"But I'm not afraid," she said, her eyes like veils.

"Oh, but I am," I said.

❦   ❦

As the miles rumbled on, we nestled into the boxcar. This would be our
home for thirty hours. The first night was extraordinarily cold. We
were glad when Agnes decided to lie down so we could cozy up to her
for warmth. There's nothing like the hot breath of a bovine on the back
of your neck to take away the chill. When we awoke the next morning,
we discovered that Agnes had risen before us and had chomped off the
silk leaves around the plastic fruit on my mother's hat. Furthermore,
she had consumed the entire brim. Although Lily was more reticent
than the day before, she showed a strong interest in Agnes's chewing.
"It's her cud," she said. "It's been down to her stomach and back up
three times."

"Well," said my mom, "I'll have you know that's the brim of my hat
she's heaving about."

"Maybe she'll make a blue cow pie," said Lily.

Indeed, Agnes made a cow pie, but it wasn't blue. When it came, it
was dramatic. Agnes raised her tail, and we all scrambled to the opposite side of the boxcar to remain clear out of range. We stared into
Agnes's deep chocolate eyes as they revealed the strains of her efforts. We tensed right along with her—holding our breath, grimacing

❦

our faces, as if Agnes were in the throes of birthing a calf.

"Look," observed Lily, "she stopped chewing her cud." Then, at last, with a final push, Agnes raised up her tail even higher and let loose. The cow pie burst out and plunged to the floor, and Agnes looked content. The stench was so bad we probably would have accepted the risk of fire if Lily had brought along potpourri to steam away the smell. Instead, Lily pulled a thread from her skirt and hung a crystal above the cow pie. "This will absorb the essence," she said.

As afternoon approached, a bad feeling welled up in my stomach, probably from the odor of Agnes's huge pie.

"No, Josey," said my mother, "you're hungry, that's all."

She was right. None of us had eaten except my mom, who shared a can of cat food with Midnight. Earlier in the trip when she offered one to us, Lily and I had graciously declined.

"There are more nutrients in this can of cat food," declared my mother, "than your average bowl of breakfast cereal."

"That's okay, Mom," I had said. "We'll save it for the cats."

But now, several uneaten meals later, we succumbed to her offer and ate heartily, straight from the can with Lily's chopsticks. It tasted better than any tuna I'd ever had.

In our journey, the train had stopped three times, once for more than an hour. Although we hid under the straw each time, no one came for Agnes. But on the fourth stop, somewhere south enough to be comfortably warm, a man unlocked the door, put up a ramp, and pulled out the cow. "Vamoose, old girl," he said, "this is the end of the line. Time to mosey on over to the hamburger factory."

Agnes put up a fight, and Lily lurched forward to go to her rescue. I pulled Lily back and held my hand over her mouth, gently. When the man departed with Agnes, he left the door wide opened. After several moments, we packed up the cats, sneaked out into the darkness, and scurried through the railyard. We had been on the train for more than thirty hours. Carrying cats and suitcases and all covered with straw, we hobbled to the road and followed the direction where a faint light loomed in the sky, indicating a town.

Lily pulled off her long furry boots and left them on the side of the road. She was quiet as we walked, frighteningly silent. I dropped one of the bags I was carrying, the one with my only remaining possessions, so that I could hold my arm around Lily's shoulders to keep her from wobbling. Every time a car whizzed by, her knees gave out somewhat, and she trembled. We walked on like this for miles.

Finally, as we neared the edge of town, we found a motel. I had almost a hundred dollars in my pocket left from the trip to Savannah. I brushed off the straw and went into the office to rent a room while my mother and Lily hid off to the side. We snuck in the cats, tore off our coats, and flopped on the twin beds in the small tangerine room with pictures of sailboats on one wall and a flock of wading flamingos on the other.

45

Lily's spirit grew more languid. I couldn't take my eyes off her, and I was afraid.

"I'll call Aunt Charlotte," announced my mother. "She'll pick us up."

My mother's words barely registered as I watched Lily sitting on the bed, staring at the pictures on the walls.

"Where should I tell her to come, Josey?" asked my mom. "I mean, what town is this? Do you think we're in Georgia?"

"Mom, I need to be with Lily for a moment. Perhaps . . . you could look in the phone book."

Then I heard the phone dialing. "Yes," said my mother, "is this the motel office? I'm wondering if y'all could tell me where we are . . . yes, I know the name of the road, we've been hiking on it for two hours. I mean, the state. What state are we in? . . . Really? Well I'll be a ring-tailed polecat, we overshot by an entire state. And what town? Okay, thank you kindly."

"Where are we, Mom?" I asked indifferently.

"Jacksonville, Florida."

"Hey, Lily," I said, "we're in your birth state. Yes, Tallahassee is quite a ways west of here, but it's your state all the same."

She stared into my eyes sadly.

"Hi, Charlotte," said my mother, "it's your dear sister here, calling from Jacksonville, Florida, of all places. Can you come pick us up? . . . Yes, I'm here with my son and my niece. The car, well, we had a minor mishap . . . yes, and bring the cats, will you? They must be so lonely for me."

"No more cats, please, Mom."

"Mm-hmm," continued my mother, "and make sure you bring Mindy's blanket. You know she can't even have a nap without her mohair blanket . . . Sure, I'll give you the address . . . and bring a case of cat food and a cooler full of milk. My babies haven't had a decent meal since we left New Hampshire." When my mother hung up, she gathered together some clean clothes and strolled off to take a bath.

I turned back to Lily.

"What a shame," she said.

"What's that, darlin'?"

Struggling to speak, her lips quivering, she gazed sleepily toward the window. "They've gone and shot the moon," she murmured.

"Lily," I pleaded, "please hang on. We're almost there. Aunt Charlotte is coming to pick us up, and then we're going home to Savannah."

She turned back toward me, with eyes soft as clouds. She put her hand on my cheek, aching and trembling. "The bullet went straight into the side of the moon, and it's wounded. It hurts, Josey, it hurts real bad."

"I know, darling, it hurts me, too. We'll get through it together. Okay?"

"All the moonlight," she said, her fingers sliding along my cheek, "all the silver moonlight is oozing through the wound and draining from the sky."

"No, Lily—"

"It's raining down, Josey. The moon is coming down in rivers of silver and white. It's like milk and dew and starlight all draining together into one pool—an opal pool, and I am sinking. Help me, Josey."

"Lily, you have to hang on."

"I can't."

"Don't leave me now, please don't go. I beg you, darling, you are my only love."

"Josey, it's falling . . . to darkness. It's draining . . ." Her eyes let go of me, but she gathered energy from somewhere, enough to hold my face with both her hands and kiss me like rain on my lips, my eyes . . .

"Lily," I whispered.

Then without voice, without sound, her lips moved to say, "The light is gone, and the darkness is here." I folded my arms around her and held her there as she seeped away slowly, on a tide of shadows, into a place deeper than the last time she was taken by silence, a place I could never share with her, the only haven she knew that was safe—a world without light, without sound—a moonless night, the sable sea, where her ships could travel to the other side of the world and back in the blink of an eye, and where the black velvet sky was her meadow, and the stars her lovers, and she could embrace all the quiet places that she held so dear.

Epilogue

Aunt Charlotte picked us up in her Pontiac Bonneville station wagon. We drove back to Savannah with twenty-four cats, all the cat supplies, and what few belongings we had left.

Now Lily and I live with my mother, Isabel. We live in her country house with the porch swing out front and dozens of geraniums in the window boxes. My first endeavor when we moved in was to hire someone to tear down the abandoned building out back so no one would have to face the bitter reminder of the pain my father had bestowed on Lily. I was certain that once we were safe in Savannah, Lily would come out of the strange mist that enveloped her. But that didn't happen. By the time we took her to the hospital, the doctors said there was nothing they could do and that perhaps time would bring her out of her silence.

Lily and I have lived with my mother for more than twenty-five years now. Over that time, I've actually grown fond of cats. I bring them home exotic fish dishes from the restaurant where I work in downtown Savannah. We have thirty-two cats now. I'll admit that's a few too many, but there isn't one of them we could possibly part with. Furthermore, when someone comes to the door with an abandoned tabby or an unwanted kitten, and we look into their sublime faces and rapt eyes, how can we possibly turn them away, knowing the little darlings could end up at the pound?

My mother and I have adjusted to each other's ways, and most of the time, we truly like being together. When we are not tending our feline flock, we spend hours doing jigsaw puzzles with thousands of pieces. The cats lie in the valleys between our piles of carefully sorted puzzle pieces. Sometimes when they purr, the whole table vibrates.

Before we left New Hampshire, we hadn't told anyone where we were going because we didn't want my father coming after us. Leon was the only one who asked, and we had told him we weren't sure where we would end up. No one knew of the whereabouts of Isabel or even that she was alive. So in the aftermath of what occurred on that dreadful day when we made our escape, we were never found out. When the police queried Leon as to who lived in the chapel, no doubt they had searched for Lily and me to discuss the crime, but their quest was in vain. Now Lily, my mother, and I live together in the haven of our own witness protection program. I don't even worry about being found out.

Sometimes I think about the people back home. I wonder how Casey is. I imagine him working the high iron with his father, or perhaps as a zookeeper in the snake house down at the Franklin Park Zoo. But for all I know, he could be an accountant.

All the people we knew will remain forever as they were when we left, unaffected by time. Even more than two decades later, in my mind, Eddie Lark is still pissed off over not being able to collect the winnings on Aunt Kitty's trifecta. Abigail is the svelte woman she always was with her understanding ways and her soothing voice. Benny still drapes his silken body in the chandelier above the dinner table and basks in the steam that rises from Abigail's long hot baths. "The steam is rising . . . ," calls Abigail. Ralph forever floats about his apartment, eating caramel popcorn with Tina. Norman babbles on about livers, gall bladders, and spleens. And every spring, Leon looks out over the freshly turned soil of his garden and sees on the horizon everything he needs to know.

Years from now, when I am hobbling along with my cane, frail and alone, all these people in my life will be alive and well, still with their youth, their strength, and all their idiosyncrasies.

These memories have been my shelter, protecting me from my own regrets. And oh, how regrets filled my heart from the moment Lily drifted into the darkness that night in the roadside motel. More than anything, I regret that Lily did not have more time to absorb my being her son. Perhaps some deep intuition had told her it was so all along. But looking back, if she'd had more time with the truth, maybe she could have stayed above the darkness. What I wouldn't give to be twelve years old again, knowing what I do now. I would hold her shoulders gently, look in her lavender eyes, and tell her that her son is not lost and that I am he.

If the truth had been known earlier, to this day I don't know how I would have handled my feelings for Lily.

I miss New Hampshire. After all, I was always a creature of home, despite how unsettling it had been. My roots had grown deep into the land where I grew up. Like the trees around Lily's chapel, I enjoyed the feeling of being there with her and letting my own roots crawl through the ground, wrapping around every rock in their path, which I clung to like a promise rendered. I would have been content to spend the rest of time wallowing in the shelter of Lily's chapel, roaming the rivers and meadows of southern New Hampshire.

As a child I measured life in snowfalls, in harvest times, and in fresh collections of autumn leaves. Now without the seasons, the days can no longer be counted. Sometimes I think time has not passed at all until I look into the mirror and see the lines around my eyes spreading through the skin like my lost roots that once penetrated a ground farther north. But even with all this nostalgia for the land of my youth, I am, we are, where we want to be. Though New Hampshire holds our roots, Georgia is our home now.

I think about my growing up surrounded by idealized families like Casey's, Ralph's, and even Beaver Cleaver's. I wanted so much to have a family like those—open and free and predictable—instead of the unsettled air in my own home where moods swung daily and where secrets were kept locked inside my father's memory and hidden behind my grandmother's illusions.

Of course, I think about my father—how he showed me the stars when they fell into our valley, his fishing expeditions, how he loved climbing things, his descriptions of the planets—especially Venus—and all his endless projects. This man who delicately installed tiny sails upon ships inside glass bottles was able with the same precision to tear out the souls of human beings and leave them lying naked in the darkness. And so he had done this to Lily.

In our house in Savannah, Lily stays in the room I had when I was a child because it's not as bright as the guest room, and I know she prefers the softer light. I take her downstairs sometimes because I think it might help draw her out. But I can tell by her restless breathing that she prefers the safe harbor of her own room.

I don't sleep with her, of course, but in the late afternoon when she's awake, I come in and lie beside her while she sits in silence and gazes out the window. Sometimes, on rare occasions, her hand falls randomly upon my hair or my shoulders—a mother's touch, a lover's touch—and I feel as if the angels in heaven have come down in a flock and lifted me into the sky to a place of tenderness and ecstasy.

I read to Lily, sing to her (when my mother is not in the house), and comb her hair. Yes, for hours, I comb her hair. I talk to her soul sometimes, using incoherent phrases like one might mutter alone in the shower. With Lily and me, everything has become more rarefied, ethereal, and resonant. If Lily tilts her head in a certain way, I reel with a delight that lasts for weeks. If her empty gaze settles upon my eyes and lingers for even a moment, my heart soars into the sky and waltzes with the stars.

Lily never seems to age, and her skin has grown luminescent. Her eyes have paled to a soft glow over the years, as if she is becoming the very radiance she had feared. Sometimes when I look at her, still overwhelmed by her beauty, I wonder, How could this angel with no physical scars have been through so much? Then I remember that her scar is her silence. She is the Venus I longed for even before we met. Lily, my Venus—silent and alone in the darkness, shrouded in mist. And me standing here, unable to reach her, but so content to be near her.

Sometimes when I'm combing Lily's hair and watching the light weave into her river of gold, a hope flutters in my heart, and a little daydream runs in my mind that goes like this: We're looking out the window for a long time—all afternoon. And just as the sun sinks below the horizon of the Savannah marshlands, Lily turns to me, puts her hand on my cheek, gazes into my eyes, and says, "Hey, Boo, where've you been?"

Lily's room is filled with the keepsakes she packed when we left the chapel. She had carried them in her bag on our trek, and upon arriving in Savannah, I unpacked all her things and set them around her room as I imagined she would have done.

Now her bedside table is covered with rocks and shells. A bowl on her dresser holds the fossils we collected in the river when she set candles on the shale ledges and danced in the water, when I was twelve years old. That was the night I fell in love with her. Also on the dresser are some pearls from her crystal garden and acorns that we gathered the night we made love in the meadow. And hanging from the curtain rod is the crystal she had given me for my birthday. I hung it in her window, hoping it would absorb anything that might make her sad. Since her plants never made it any farther than my light-blue Chevy Impala secluded in the woods off Route 11, my mother and I bought new ferns, ivy, and flowers, which are thriving in Lily's room.

Lily's jar of polished stones sits on the windowsill. When the light comes in, the amethyst sparkles, and the clear stones burn like stars. Sometimes I think about the two missing stones—the ones we had dropped in her well when I wished for Maggie to go to heaven, and she wished for me to "forever see things as they are."

The other item I had found at the bottom of Lily's bag was a letter she wrote and saved for me when I went to Savannah to find my mother. I keep it in a drawer and read it from time to time. She had written,

Dear Josey,

Days ago when you left for Savannah, I wondered if I could ever go anywhere again without the darkness settling upon me and stealing away my voice. But now my fears have settled down, and I know things will work out for us.

When we finally find a way out, maybe you could teach me to love the light again. I long to see the fields all filled with colors, and feel the warm sun on my cheeks. I often think of the first time you came to me, scared of the lightning, and I realize you've always understood fear. I suppose we all have something that haunts us, but you have made the haunting easier to bear. You have changed my life.

On this night, knowing that we'll be together soon, the world feels a little safer. The dark crows that once flocked in my head are high in the trees and ready to fly away. Come back to me soon, Josey, and we'll go someplace far where we can walk together and follow streams like we did when you were young—lighting candles to see ahead of us and finding fossils to see behind.

With love,
Lily

Most of my days are quiet now, and sometimes my mother comes in the room while I'm watering the plants. She looks at all the stuff lying around the place and says things like, "Josey, maybe you should get out more. It's not good to dwell so much on the past. Look at this room, filled with memories."

But I know that for Lily, these are simply the important things in life. And for me, they are life itself.

About the Author

Jane Wood's varied pursuits have included making jewelry from electronic parts, working in a gas station, digging artifacts in England, oil painting, and designing a card-counting system that got her thrown out of every casino in Lake Tahoe. She lived on the road for a while, purchasing monthly Greyhound passes and sleeping on buses. She has a daughter, Sarah.

Jane now designs computer applications for an insurance company and lives with her husband, Michael Kowalski, in Philadelphia. This is her first novel, and she is working on her second.